Please Let Me Destroy You

Rupert Taylor

NFB
Buffalo, New York

Printed in the United States of America

Please Let Me Destroy You/ Taylor 1st Edition

ISBN: 978-1-953610-64-5

Fiction> Literature>Contemporary
Fiction> Humor
Fiction> Thriller> Heist
Fiction> International

Cover art: Imogen Taylor
Cover design: John-Henry Pajak.

NFB Publishing
119 Dorchester Road
Buffalo, New York 14213
For more information visit Nfbpublishing.com

For Biljana and Milica.

Episode One.

The first time I saw Nhu, I was squatting on a toilet seat. She burst into the stall in the unisex bathroom at the bar, and found me perched on the wobbly plastic seat like some frightened forest creature. I may have squealed, or made a noise that came from deep in my humiliated soul. I definitely asked her to please get out, and she definitely did not. She stared at me, transfixed, a confused crease in her brow. I felt the breeze on my exposed buttocks. If I moved, I risked slipping off the seat and falling into one of the fetid puddles on the floor. So I froze, a lanky young man folded over on a toilet seat.

Not ten minutes before this mortifying encounter, I was sitting at the bar, which was on a rooftop in the heart of Saigon. Like a forest of metal and glass, tall towers sprouted up all around, with pink and purple lights strobing up and down their sides. The DJ played reggae, swaying from side to side behind her decks, and the heat was reasonably oppressive. The air wafting up from the street smelled of jasmine and woodsmoke and engine grease. Every few minutes a woman in a billowy dress floated in the door, and the up and coming corporate titans at the bar flexed their biceps, stretching shirtsleeves to breaking point. In the middle of all this,

I sat alone, sipping fresh lime and soda after fresh lime and soda, watching couples clink glasses, nuzzle into the napes of each other's necks, and show each other funny memes on their phones.

Sadly, I was celebrating.

I had only been in Saigon for five days, and had come to direct a series of branded social media films for a multinational insurance company. I spent pretty much all of the five days and nights in my hotel room, coming up with ideas for the series, but on this night, I had cracked a major idea, and so, blinking in the neon glare of the city, I slithered out of my hole in search of human connection.

What I got was an angry colon. This may have been from all the fizzy water and lime cordial, but it was likely the result of the five days I spent tearing my hair out trying to crack an idea that would blow the branded content space apart. Whatever it was, it felt like a wild animal in search of an exit. But the bar only had one toilet, and the seat was splashed with clear liquid. It may have been soda, or vodka, but it was more than likely urine. Why do some men refuse to lift the toilet seat in public places, like bars or libraries, and pee all over the seat? Do they do it at home? Do their Mummies clean up their pee-pee splashes? It enraged my heart, but more inflamed than my heart was my colon, which was now churning and bubbling and roiling and gurgling. I needed to sit on that seat, like, ASAP, but I wasn't about to lower my delicate cheeks onto the litres of piss that had sprung from the bladders of currency traders, marketing boobs and telco execs. Hell to the no. I scrunched up some toilet paper, wiped off the excess drops, climbed onto the seat and lowered my hips into a squat.

CLANK!

The door flew open. She stood before me, gawping.

"This is occupied!"

"What are you doing?"

"What does it look like?"

"I don't know. It looks weird."

"You think I don't know that!"

Stepping down from the seat, I left the stall and went to the mirror. Under my stubble, the skin was red and blotchy. I had been exposed as a seat squatter. Also, the stress toxins in my gut were rising to the surface to say hello we're here to make you look and feel like a lobster in the pot. Also, it was damn hot, and I was wearing an army green bomber jacket, which was like walking round with a furnace strapped to my chest. The problem was it looked excellent. Well maybe not excellent, but not far off. Actually maybe quite far off. At this time I had stupidly long and skinny arms, so the cuffs landed halfway down the forearm, accentuating the skinniness of the arm. I know I sound like one of those jerks that complains about being skinny, but I was super skinny, and super skinny as a man is no party. People saw me as weak. Piss weak, they said. Long streak of piss. Lanky noodle arms piss boy. But there were benefits, like my hands and fingers. Rare beauties they were. The digits were long and slender, the nailbeds deep, the skin blemish free, with just the right amount of vein action on the backs of the hands. I flaunted the hell out of them. When I spoke, I fluttered my fingers in front of my face. I was like a person with luscious hair – forever drawing eyes to my prime feature. It sounds silly, but in person it was quite mesmeric. The funny thing is, I don't know if I did it naturally or as a sales technique.

Back in the bar, the DJ played a reggae-house mix, and the corporates did a willowy dance where they gyrated their waists and waved their hands above their heads. The woman who invaded my stall sat at a high table near the edge of the roof, blue and green lights flashing up and down the skyscraper looming behind her. She sipped a drink, and read what must have been important messages on her phone. As I walked to her table, I saw that she came from money, but she was subtle about flashing it. Maybe her mother was the CEO of a milk company, or her father was high up in the party, and had scored himself a coal-fired powerplant to skim. She wore designer shoes, and her bag was designer, but none of the big name stuff. No brash Gucci logos on our girl.

"Listen," I said, standing at her table, "the toilet was filthy. Piss all over the seat."

"It's okay."

"I'm not a seat squatter."

"I get it."

"But now you've seen me squatting."

"You want to see me squatting?"

"I just feel like you've seen me in a vulnerable state, and now we have a connection."

"I don't feel it."

"Maybe if you bought me a drink."

She looked at the long arms poking out the sleeves of my puffy jacket.

"Aren't you hot?"

"Very."

"What's your name?"

"Apollo. And you?"

"Nhu. Where are you from?"

"Sydney."

"I hate Sydney."

"Why?"

"What do you do?"

"I'm a filmmaker."

"Really?"

Her eyes lit up, and she offered me a seat. This happened all the time. I told people I was a filmmaker, and they got all excited. But then they asked the inevitable: what films have you made? I told them the truth, and watched the light fade from their eyes.

"I'm here making a series of social media films for an insurance company."

"Oh. Not a real filmmaker then."

"Well, no, but I'm working on a TV series."

"Like Game of Thrones?"

"Bigger."

"What's it called?"

"Not sure yet. It's an Untitled Original Series Set On Multiple Continents, and it'll run on a bunch of platforms – on TV and social media, and in cinemas as–"

"What's it about. This original content show for all the continents."

"Untitled Original Series Set On Multiple Continents. Dunno yet. I kinda need to find the uhh, the stories."

She raised her hand, and a waiter scurried to her side. She ordered a scotch for her and a Red Bull for me. She spoke to the waiter like a servant. Or a dog.

"But you must get paid a lot, to make those... what did you call them? Social content videos?"

"Oh yeah, loads."

"Nice."

"Nah, it's not that much."

"Hmm."

"And what do you do?"

"Guess."

"Well," I said, looking her up and down, "judging by your purse, I'd say you work in fashion, but your boots are too subtle for a fashion person. They like lots of buckles. So I'd say you're some sort of curator."

"You motherfucker."

"Good right?"

"I own a gallery."

"When can I see it?"

At the end of a boiled-cabbage-smelling alleyway sat her shiny black Mercedes. This was some car. Getting in was like stepping into a whole new world. Outside was hot and loud and grimy, inside was cool and plush and quiet. We glided through the city streets, and it started to rain, pink and yellow neon lights reflecting in the drops sliding down the windows. But when we stopped, a proper tropical storm came down. I'm talking drops the size of a kitten's head, hammering the road with a deafening hiss. We jumped out and darted through the downpour, into a curved old colonial building on the corner of Dong Khoi and Ly Tu Trong. The foyer was dark, but a shaft of light illuminated the beads of sweat rolling over the taut belly of an old man asleep in a foldout chair. We stepped into an ancient iron cage elevator, and it rattled as it lurched us up the middle of a grand old wooden staircase. Nhu was talking. Something about how the building was built in the 1920s, and the architect or maybe his mother killed herself or ate too many snails or wolves tails or I don't know. Looking at her in her long wet dress and fancy boots, I found it hard to focus. I jumped ahead to a time in the future, the two of us driving down the coast in a vintage car. I won't lie to you, I've always had a thing for rich girls. I liked to rummage through their drawers. They always had nice serums and potions, and I suffered from dry skin, so it was the only time I got to slather the good shit on my face.

"Are you listening?"

"Of course."

"What did I say?"

"The architect liked wolves?"

"Are you smoking crack? I said my gallery space was the office of the CIA station chief in the Sixties, that's why I called it Station."

She yanked open the iron elevator cage, led me down a dark hall and through a door. When she flipped on the lights, an onslaught of colour flooded the room, my retinas, and every single synapse in my brain. "Take a look," she said. The room was a white cube, the walls were hung with giant tapestries, and they were stitched with green and yellow and violet strips, and shards that seemed to dance and shimmer under the light like living things. Some were sewn with stars made from gold and silver bullets – long and mean machine gun bullets, plus short, snub-nosed revolver bullets. Most were stitched with military medals, plus strips of material and pockets from uniforms that looked stained with blood. On all hung ribbons and insignia, plus random bling and junk, like the mass-produced Zippos that tourists bought at Ben Thanh market, the ones that came carved with inscriptions from American soldiers that said things like: *A sucking chest wound is nature's way of telling you that you've been ambushed.*

"This artist is from an old military family," said Nhu. "Her father fought the Americans, her uncle fought the Chinese, and her grandfather fought the French. The stuff she sews in the tapestries, it's real. All from her family."

I walked closer to a mustard and magenta tapestry, and stared at a blood-stained epaulet.

"Is that your favourite?"

"Maybe."

"You can have this for twenty thousand."

"Dong?"

"You're still smoking crack. US dollars."

"In a few months maybe."

"Not now?"

"Not now."

"But what will you take now?"

"I could take you to dinner."

"Where?"

"I don't know yet."

"What's that place, 'I don't know yet.' I never heard of it. Any good?"

"What about that place, ummm…"

"Ummm."

"L'usine."

"You can do better."

"You need a fancy place?"

"Why not?"

"You got a number I need to hit?"

"Five hundred."

"Are you serious?"

"Are *you* serious?"

Episode Two.

In the boardroom, I rested my forehead on the glass wall, and stared out at the fluffy clouds floating by, then down at the brown river snaking through the city far below. I was on the thirtieth floor of the Bitexco Tower. It gave me some serious vertigo.

"Let's get started," said Khanh. "We're very excited." Khanh was the Chief Marketing Officer of the insurance company. He sat at the boardroom table, watching me stare at the clouds. Next to him sat Mai-Mai, the Senior Marketing Executive. "Come on, Apollo Jones, we can't wait any longer," said Mai-Mai. For some reason she always called me by my full name. I peeled my forehead off the glass and turned to face them. A soccer ball-sized bubble popped in my stomach, and noxious gas sailed up my throat, but I forced it back down, where it bumped into a second bubble sliding up the escape hatch. This did not feel good. The night before, as I sucked down those celebratory lime and sodas, I was sure I had a winning idea for the branded social media series, but now, in the harsh light of the presentation, I was falling to pieces. Was it the pressure? Or was a Tasmanian Devil trying to claw its way through my intestinal wall? Could Khanh and Mai-Mai hear the violent growling? My knees were wobbly, my vision jittery. Hoping to steady myself, to bewitch my clients with my beautiful hands, I lay my palms flat on the table, but they left a clammy smear on the expensive oak. Did Khanh and Mai-Mai see it? No, they were looking at my face, which must have looked gaunt and green and not at all cool under fire. Fuck it. If they sacked me they sacked me. Opening my computer, I connected to the screen at the head of the table, and ploughed through my first four ideas. I didn't undersell them, but I made it clear they were undercards on the way to the main event. Khanh stared at me: emotionless. Everything about him was engineered to perfection – hair, suit, speech. He was the kind of man who lined his remotes up on the coffee table, and lost his shit if he found one out of place. And maybe the kind of man who whistled while drowning kittens in a sack. A sadist, for sure. Which was probably what drew him to insurance marketing. Mai-Mai was not like Khanh. Mai-Mai was anxious, but warm. She must have sensed my inner turmoil, for as I spoke, she smiled, urging me on.

After twenty minutes, I hit them with the big dog. The fifth idea. For this I had saved my prime reference imagery. Stone cold emotional shots. As I spoke, hands fluttering, the images flashed on the screen in full cinematic colour. "This series of films will form one big story that stretches right across Asia-Pacific – your entire market. Our first film takes place in Thailand, where a family set out on holiday. Their car crashes, and Mum breaks her hip. The next film tells the story of a family who were in a car crash in Singapore. Mum's in hospital, her kids holding her hands. The next film is set in Melbourne. Mum is home from hospital, and she's getting back on her feet. We go right through the region like this, each film set in a different country, with people from all walks of life, getting on with their lives, thanks to you. And we call it, The Story of Us..."

"Wow," said Khanh, "Just. Wow."

"Apollo Jones," said Mai-Mai, "this feels special."

I sat down. My stomach settled. No more putrid bubbles floating into the purified air of the boardroom.

"We need to get it in front of Jerry, our CEO," said Khanh. "But that's just a formality."

My heart sank. My stomach whined. It's never just a formality, especially when you're dealing with a CEO like Jerry.

I had heard stories about Jerry. Jerry was from Shanghai, but in casinos all over Asia, he was a known and respected whale. He spent three days a month at the casinos in Macau, where a hotel put him up in the presidential suite free of charge. During his stay he dropped a few mill on the tables. But his Feng Shui master went with him, and told him that peeing in the toilet would drain away his good luck. So Jerry peed on the carpet of his suite. The bedroom, the living room, wherever there wasn't a drain. That's about eighteen wees in three days. When he left, the staff changed the carpet in the entire suite. Every month. Brand new carpet. Hearing stories like this made me desperate to meet Jerry. But CEO whales don't attend piddly little branded content presentations, and rightly so.

Later that night, I sat on the back of a motorbike taxi, my arms wrapped tight around the driver's waist as he pushed the engine so hard it screamed in pain. We raced along at the heart of a swarm of scooters, red and pink and blue lights flashing by, warm air molecules crashing into the pores on my cheeks. The drivers in the swarm peered out from Hello Kitty helmets and knock-off Gucci helmets. We were like a shoal of shimmering metal fish, darting left, banking right, moving as one with the anarchic current of the night. And Lunar New Year was coming up, so lotus flowers made from white and yellow and lilac neon hung from wires that ran above our heads, and dangled down from the branches of centuries-old trees. As we zoomed under the flowers, I leaned so far back the world become a blurry tunnel made from neon sparks. When we popped out the other end, the air sizzled with the smells of pork smoke, jasmine, exhaust fumes, sage, cigarette smoke and fish sauce. And as we turned into Dong Khoi, a mass of slowly moving scooters swallowed us up. I watched the shoppers and the chatters and the eaters and the drinkers, zipping up and down both sidewalks. My phone buzzed in my pocket. I paid the driver and got off the bike, and as I waded through the crowds, fresh beads of sweat rolled down my spine. My phone stopped ringing, then rang again a second later, so I picked up.

"Bad news," said Khanh.

"Oh god."

"Jerry hated it. He was disgusted. You know what congee is?"

"It's like porridge? But with fish?"

"When I showed him your ideas, he spat his congee all over the room. The man nearly choked! Jerry is a legend in the insurance business. To lose him would be a tragedy."

"Okay, so what's the plan?"

"We need new ideas by morning."

"It's nearly midnight."

"I don't care. My career is on the line here."

"I mean that's–"

"If Jerry says he wants new ideas in the morning, Jerry gets new ideas in the morning!"

I was right: it's never just a formality.

In front of a Circle K, a man roasted a pig on a spit. Oh piggy, I thought, your smoky flesh smells so delicious. I wish I could stop and eat you, but alas, I must go into this global convenience store, purchase a six-pack of Red Bull, take it back to my hotel room, sit on the bed and work until dawn. And that was exactly what I did. And when the sun rose, golden light shimmering through the perma-haze above the city, I had five new ideas for the social media series, so I drained the last drops of Red Bull, showered, and rode the elevator down to the lobby. Early morning is the only time Saigon is still. From seven until nightfall, eight million scooters fill the air with beeping fumy chaos. But dawn is peaceful. I walked the deserted streets with an iced coffee in hand, and when I reached the river, I sat on the grass to watch silent boats slide up and down the brown surface. By the time I walked the three blocks to Bitexco Tower, the scooters were doing their thing. The elevator whooshed me up to the stratosphere, my ears popped, and a receptionist led me to the boardroom in the clouds. Khanh and Mai-Mai sat at the long oak table. I read the vibe and the vibe was not good – Jerry must have dressed them down over my ideas. Mai-

Mai looked as though she had just remembered she left the stove on, and she picked at her left cheek. Khanh looked the way Khanh always looked: perfect. But his right eye twitched, so I knew his insides were bubbling with murderous rage. I stood across the table, and synced my computer to the big screen. "I have new ideas, but I haven't slept, so maybe go easy on me?"

Khanh's eye twitched at me. Mai-Mai picked at her cheek. When I opened my mouth to speak, my tongue felt like a bloated slug carcass. Was it the taurine? The lack of sleep? Had the Tasmanian Devil died in my gut while reaching a paw up to the light? Whatever it was, my words were trapped behind it, and the ones that made it past sounded garbled and warped. I felt my career slipping away. The ideas weren't bad. The kind of stuff you crack at 4am, but not so bad. Mai-Mai's cheek began to bleed. Khanh held up a hand, glaring at me like I had gunned down his number one son. "This is all very disappointing," he said.

For the next two weeks, every day was the same as the last. All night I sat on my bed, swilling Red Bull, coming up with what I hoped were fresh and original ideas that met the brief. At dawn, I rode the elevator up to the boardroom in the clouds, where I presented to Khanh and Mai-Mai. Some days, their feedback was positive: "I like how you put our brand at the heart of this story." But most days it was not. "Your ideas are too Anglo. This is Asia." Or: "This will never work in Korea, it's too emotional." Or: "This won't work in the Philippines, it's not emotional enough." I slept in twenty minute bursts. Shaved my head, lived on Red Bull and iced coffee by the bucket. My hotel room was a dump. Chicken grease-smeared plates under the bedsheets, socks dangling from lamps, soggy French fries in the shower for some reason. In my head, soul-assaulting feedback played on an endless loop: "We need snackable content, Apollo, snackable! You've written a ten course meal!" My life became a single continuous presentation where Khanh and Mai-Mai beat my brain with mallets, and feasted on the scattered remains. One morning, I cried. Mai-Mai handed me a tissue from the box she kept for dabbing at the ever-growing hole in her cheek. Khanh stared at me like an apex predator looks at a mortally wounded beast.

"We need an omnichannel strategy! Mobile optimisation! Disrupt the culture!"

The final meeting. Mai-Mai picked at her right cheek. Both of Khanh's eyes spasmed. I spun in my chair. The lining of my skull felt like it had been scraped out with one of those spoons people use to dig balls of flesh from watermelons. I saw myself stand up, walk across the floor, and heave my carcass through the glass and into the clouds. When I emerged from my delirium, I wasn't sure if I had imagined leaping through the glass, or if I had actually done it, and was now a ghost looking out the hole through which I had ejected myself into eternity.

Episode Three.

I hadn't intended to study my arms in the mirror. I was in my hotel bathroom, brushing my teeth, when I caught sight of their reflection. I knew they were skinny, but they looked atrophied, like I suffered from some sort of flesh-eating disease. But skinny arms were the least of my worries. As I lay on the bed and thought about going out for a steaming bowl of pho, or the pork and rice dish the woman down the road cooked on a curb-side fire, my phone rang. It was Khanh.

"I have good news. We're putting three ideas into research."

"That's great."

"You don't sound happy."

"I'm very happy."

"You sound depressed."

"I'm not depre–"

"We will conduct one research group here in Saigon, one in Kuala Lumpur, and one in Auckland. Let us hope Jerry is happy with the results."

They were so scared of making a decision, they were farming the decision making out to strangers, who might also be farmers. Oh well. At least that made me a free – if partially broken – man. I did ten push ups. Went back to the bathroom mirror, flexed, phoned Nhu and asked her out to dinner.

"No."

That was her answer. Not an 'I'm busy.' Not a 'maybe another time.' Not even an 'I don't see you that way.' A fend to the face. It was brutal, but you had to hand it to her, the girl was concise. I hung up and cursed my lanky arms, telling them it was all their fault. Ten minutes later she called back. "I have a function actually. You can be my wingman."

The function was in a bar on the roof of a fancy hotel. We met in the lobby. She wore a dress made from light green silk, cut into a sort of box shape. That sounds odd, but trust me when I say she made it work. And then some. We stepped into the elevator, she stabbed the button for the roof, the shiny golden doors slid shut, and she studied her face in the reflection. I noticed her amazing ears. The tips folded over, like little wings. They made me think of a hummingbird, fluttering its wings like mad as it ripped a flower to shreds with its beak.

"The people you will meet tonight," she said. "I have known them a long time. They all have money, but most don't work."

"What do you need from your wingman?"

"I need you to be a successful filmmaker."

"I am a successful filmmaker."

"Your films are not real films."

Of course I knew this, but hearing it from her hurt. Plus she kind of spat the words at me. It felt like the elevator dropped five floors. I wanted to force the doors open, and toss my carcass down the dark shaft. But I rallied. If I showed weakness in front of her she would cast me aside like a piece of stale meat.

The bar was packed with the kinds of people that go to bars on tops of hotels. They danced and talked and looked around for better looking people to dance with or talk to. Some of them had pink hair with those huge Balenciaga sneakers, and looked like they worked for social media start-ups. But most of them were more conservative, with heels and dresses and suits, and haircuts straight off the Gap website. "I need to speak to donors for the gallery," said Nhu, "you will be okay on your own." She dumped me with a group of people standing at a high table, and vanished into the crowd. I looked around the table. The men sipped whiskey and spoke to each other in hushed tones, and the women sipped champagne through straws, checked their phones and said cheers to no one.

"Hi," said the woman to my left. "I'm Chi."

"Hi Chi, I'm Apollo."

"Cool name. What do you do?"

"I'm a filmmaker."

"Me too!"

"No shit."

"I just finished one, it's called Kings and Queens. It's about my cats, they're sphynxes. You wanna see?"

"What's the story?"

"Uh, they fall in love, like Antony and Cleopatra."

"Yes, I do want to see that."

As she searched her bag for her phone, the man to my right tapped me on the shoulder. He was handsome in a khaki-pant-wearing-knows-how-to-drive-a-speedboat-while-trading-stocks type of way.

"You're Nhu's friend right? Apollo?"

"Yeah."

"I'm Danh."

"Hi Danh."

"You play golf, Apollo?"

"No, but I hear people do."

"I'm developing a golf resort, up near Da Nang. It'll be a luxury sport and wellness retreat."

Chi leaned across me. "Will it have a pool?"

"Maybe the biggest in the country, with a waterfall and everything."

"Can I do a photoshoot in the waterfall?"

"You have a label?"

"It's for my cats, they're sphynxes."

"Oh my god, I love those cats."

Chi and Danh continued their conversation across me, nutting out the finer details of the sphynx photo shoot, so I went to look for Nhu. She wasn't at the bar, or near the giant speakers pumping out greasy house beats, or in the crowd of people dancing next to the pool. I went back to the table, and sat in silence as Nhu's rich friends ignored me. Right as I was about to leave, a high-pitched scream cut through the bass. I followed the sound, and found Nhu at a second bar I hadn't seen, tearing strips from the barman. She spoke in Vietnamese, so I didn't understand her words, but her rage was a magnificent roman candle. The barman looked ashen. Like he wanted to crawl back into his mother's womb and swim peacefully in the amniotic fluid.

"What's going on?"

"This dummy overcharged me."

The barman shook his head, his eyes pleading for me to call her off. Behind us, the speakers blasted the bodily-fluid-oozing dancefloor.

"Are you sure?"

"What the fuck! You're on his side?"

"Maybe."

She shoved the bill under my nose. "Twenty million dong! I didn't spend that!"

"Your table," said the barman, his voice quivering.

"Fuck the table. I didn't order this shit."

A door opened behind the bar, and a manager appeared. She wore a black dress. Her hair in a bun so tight I worried about facial stretch marks.

"What is the problem here."

"Your barman charged me for drinks I didn't order."

"Her table had Veuve… bottles of… bottle service…."

The manager raised a hand, silenced the stammering barman. She looked at the bill, then at Nhu, her nostrils flaring like a bull about to charge. "Refund it."

On our way down, the golden elevator doors lost their glimmer. Nhu stared at her feet. The doors dinged open, she stomped through the lobby, and walked in circles on the sidewalk, muttering to herself. Had she lost her mind? Maybe she had been losing her mind for years, and I had shown up for the final chapter. But I had a third theory. And when I have theories, I like to test those theories.

"You're not rich are you."

She stopped muttering and stared at me.

"What did you say?"

"I said you're not rich, you just pretend to be."

Fuming, she walked at me. "Why do you say that?"

"Doesn't matter."

"Why!"

"If you were rich, you wouldn't care about that guy overcharging you."

"I don't like to be cheated."

"And you wouldn't need donors for your gallery, you could just fund it yourself."

"What do you know about art? You're just a marketer."

"You're not rich. It's fine. I won't tell any–"

CRACK.

Her palm struck my cheek, then she spun, green silk dress flowing, to hail a taxi with her slapping hand. She climbed in the back, but she didn't close the door. I jumped in next to her. For what felt like miles, we drove in silence, gazing out at flickering lights, and torsos whizzing by on motorbikes.

"Do you think they know?"

"Who? Your friends?"

"Yes."

"No."

"How can you be sure."

"It's my job." She looked at me. "I make fake stories, and I'm good at selling them."

Episode Four.

The boardroom in the clouds. Mai-Mai sat across from me, picking a hole in her cheek. Khanh sat next to her, reading out the negative comments from the research groups, which he had printed into a ceremonial stack of paper. Peeling a sheet off the top, he read:

"These films make me think the company wants me to die in a fiery crash, just so they can take my money."

He let the sheet float to the floor, handed a fresh one to Mai-Mai. She shook her head, so he pressed on. "This made me think of my dead grandmother, and when I think of my dead grandmother I cry. This made me cry a lot."

"You made your point," I said, "but research is inherently–"

"I'm not finished."

He snatched a sheet from the stack.

"Where are the cookies?" he read. "They said there would be cookies."

"You see? You can't expect these people to tell you if an idea is any good."

Through the cracks in his perfect demeanour, rage spluttered out like hot lava. "You promised us greatness! But you don't know greatness! All you know is lies and gutter filth and shit!"

Mai-Mai placed a calming hand on his shoulder. He took three deep breaths, counting out the exhales. "If it wasn't for Mai-Mai, I would fire you. You have one more shot. One more chance to get this right."

They left the room, a trail of disappointment in their wake. I sat in my chair, watching the smog from the city turn the white clouds sepia.

THE elevator whooshed me down to the ground, and I walked to Tao Dan Park, with its tall trees, winding paths and wide blades of grass. And an outdoor café where birds chirped in cages hanging above the coffee-sipping heads of the diners. The park was an oasis in the chaos, with free exercise equipment. I did pull ups, and dips, and used a machine that made my arms go round and round, and more dips. Sweat soaked my shirt. I looked like a drowned sewer rat. And felt worse. I lay back on the grass and stared at the swaying tops of the trees. Khanh was itching to fire me, I could see it in his twitching eyes. The branded social media series was my shot. My chance to make people sit up and say, 'Damn that was for an insurance company? That's some serious auteur shit.' If I pulled off a coup like that – HBO, Netflix – all the streaming giants would come knocking. And I'd open the door and say: "If you liked that, take a look at my Untitled Original Series Set On Multiple Continents." But if I got fired, my name would be trash, and I'd spend my days shooting behind the scenes videos for human resources conferences.

"Cool shoes."

A young man stood over me. I could see up his shirt, into the dark recesses of his bellybutton. His hair was cut into a bowl-cut, and he wore a thin gold chain on his neck.

"Huh?"

"Your shoes, I like them. Where did you buy them?"

I looked down at the tattered white Vans on my feet.

"Online somewhere?"

"I must have them. Will they have my size?"

"What size are you?"

"Sixteen."

I looked at his feet, which were so small they were basically hooves.

"Joking! That is what I tell my waifu."

"Your wife?"

"Waifu, from anime. The object of my most passionate desires."

I liked this dude. I sat up and he sat next to me. I asked his name.

"Anhtheman."

"Antman?"

"No, Anh-the-man. Anhtheman. You like it?"

"It's probably the best name I've ever heard."

"Yes! I agree!"

"I'm Apollo."

"Apollo is also a great name. I can see you are a warrior."

"I've gone stale."

"No, no, no, you are very potent."

"I'm cooked."

"Is that why you lie on the ground to cry? I will help. Come to my house, I will cook you steak."

"Do you have any fruit platters."

"White men love steak."

"It's all we eat."

"I know it. What hotel do you stay in? I will pick you up tonight."

As the sun slid down the mauve sky, a lime green taxi van skidded to a stop in front of my hotel. The back door screeched as Anhtheman slid it open. "Apollo! Let's go for steak!" I jumped in next to him. An old woman sat facing us, staring at my throat like she wanted to rip it out and feed it to a stray dog. "This is Auntie," said Anhtheman, "she is very happy."

The green van swerved across lanes as we sped over a bridge. Out the window, the last light of day bounced off the shimmering brown surface of the river. Deeper into dense suburbs we drove. I lost what little bearings I had. Auntie glared at me, and Anhtheman chatted away about his job as a tourism operator in Pham Ngu Lao, and his love for the dynamic sector.

"Did you know that Thailand has the fastest growing tourism industry in the world? It is now more popular than Paris."

He also told me of his pathological fear of germs.

"Do you know where you find the most germs?"

"Where?"

"The headrests on seats on planes." He shuddered, squirting sanitizer on his hands. "My skin crawls right now. This is why I left the cabin crew of Vietnam Airlines. Headrest germs."

After a lot more talk of germs, the tourism industry, and more germs, the van turned down a narrow alley – "these little streets we call hems," said Anhtheman – and stopped near a tall and narrow powder blue house. Screams filled the air. We hopped out of the van, and I saw the source of the screams. In the front room of the house, next to a grease-stained couch, two young men had a red scooter up on blocks. They had stripped it down to a skeleton and were torturing the engine. "Duc and Binh," Anhtheman yelled over the noise, "the best motorbike mechanics in a city with ten million motorbikes."

He led me through the front room, past the screaming red scooter, to a windowless dining room with a long table and a door that opened onto the kitchen. Auntie went into the kitchen, and came back with dishes that she placed up and down the table – braised beef, bowls of rice, greens, dipping sauces, bottles of Coke and Fanta. Wiping scooter grease from their cheeks, Duc and Binh walked in from the front room, filled bowls with steaming beef and rice, and sat down to eat. "I'm sorry we have no steak," said Anhtheman. I said I liked this spread better. He said that was impossible, me being white. I sat down. Wearing a beef and sauce stained apron, and burping a baby the size of a small bear, a young woman rushed in from the kitchen, and sat at the far end of the table. "This is Thuy and Bo," said Anhtheman, pronouncing Thuy *twee*. "Bo is the fattest baby in all Saigon. He is also the smartest." The table erupted in chattering and clattering. Auntie yelled at Thuy who scolded Bo, whose eyes sparkled as he poured coke into his giant baby body. Duc and Binh buried their faces in their bowls.

Anhtheman sanitized his hands five or six or seven times. Then he walked in. Tall and rail thin, somewhere in his mid-fifties, he wore an open white shirt, and a gold chain on his chest, with the pointed toes of burgundy cowboy boots peeking out from under a pair of pressed powder blue pants. He ran a comb through his hair, then he shook my hand. I saw no less than four ruby rings on his fingers. "Uncle Frank!" said Anhtheman. "This is Apollo."

Uncle Frank sat across from me. He filled his bowl with beef and rice, and looked at me like I had come to him for a job interview. Then he asked me questions. Lots of questions.

"Where are you from? Are you married? You have children?"

"What kind of work do you do? Why are you here in Saigon?"

"Ever been in jail?"

"The army?"

"Were you a good student?"

"What does your father do?"

"Do you like fishing?"

"What about badminton?"

"Do you suffer from paranoia? Anxiety? Depression? Cancer of the blood? Any allergies?"

Were they intrusive? You bet. But I was a guest in their home, and they gave me fizzy drinks and pieces of beef to dip in delicious sauces, so I was more than happy to answer. I also liked Uncle Frank. He was an odd character. A true eccentric, with more than a hint of menace. What's more, I could smell a story in that house. Stuffed down the back of the couch or wedged behind a pipe under the kitchen sink. And if Uncle Frank took me into his heart, I was sure to draw the story out.

DINNER was done. I tried to help clear the table, but Auntie frowned me out of the kitchen. "Come," said Uncle Frank. "I have something to show you." I followed him up the stairs to his room, with Anhtheman following me. Once inside, he led me to a chestnut closet that looked wet from a recent polish. He opened it up, and pulled out a beautifully tailored royal blue suit. "What do you think?" he asked, turning the suit under the light. "Amazing." He beamed. Anhtheman sat on the bed and stared at his phone. But Uncle Frank pulled out a white suit, and a lemon suit, and a light pink suit. All were crafted by master tailors, and they came in silk and cotton and seersucker. He slid each jacket from its hanger, and showed me the cut with fastidious pride. He mulled over stitching, and satin lining, and he gave sermons on cuffs and seams and collars. I knew he was showing me the things in the world most precious to him, and I paid attention. When I asked about trouser legs and pocket squares, his face lit up like a boy on his birthday. Anhtheman fell asleep. I got the feeling Uncle Frank's family had long ago stopped caring about his fancy suit obsession.

At midnight, he stood at his ironing board.

His lilac socks reached his knees, and were held in place by little black garters. His underpants were white. He had the toned and sleek legs of a long distance runner. As he ironed a lime green shirt, he told me of his life working in casinos. Over the last thirty years, he had been a blackjack dealer, a craps dealer, a pit boss and a floor boss. "But I never rise to casino manager." He had worked in China and Macau, on cruise ships, and now in Cambodia. He told me stories about famed high rollers, and one about a casino in Macau in the 80s, where they kept a tiger in a cage on the casino floor. The tiger's name was Bambi. And once, when they caught a man trying to fleece the casino for a hundred grand, they stuck his hand in Bambi's cage. "I thought she would take the hand off easy, but she chews for minutes. Bambi was a lazy tiger. I never hear screams like what come from this man."

For the treatise on fine tailoring, and for the Bambi story, I traded my own stock stories:

I had told the first one many times, and had shaped it into a perfect arc over the years. In this tale, I fell from the roof of a house and got impaled on an iron fence. A fleur de lys to be precise. I gave Uncle Frank all the gory details. How I came home from the beach with a girl named Cate, and realised I'd lost my keys at the beach. I told him how I tried to pull myself onto the roof, intent on sliding in the skylight. I told him how I fell. How I lay in a pool of my own blood. How Cate ran screaming in circles on the road in her bikini bottoms and red lace bra. Uncle Frank's eyes shone. The story hit its mark. He asked to see my scars. I lifted my shirt to show him the fat pink centipede crawling across my lower back. "I tell people my kidney got stolen." He laughed at that. "Now tell me a funny story," he said.

"I once tried to get in bed with my friend's mother."

"Oh no."

"My friends name was Rex. We were friends as kids. His Mum looked like a Nineties Playboy bunny."

"What was her name, the Mummy bunny?"

"Let's call her Mummy Bunny."

"Oh, I like Mummy Bunny."

"I went to a different high school than Rex, but when we were eighteen, I saw him at a party. He still lived with Mummy Bunny, and he claimed to have a bottle of whiskey back in his room. We went back there, and I was hoping to see Mummy Bunny – I think that was why I went back to their house actually, to see her. But she was asleep. He found the bottle of whiskey under his bed and we drank it. And then he fell asleep, and I thought, *it's time.*"

"Oh boy."

"I remember opening her bedroom door, and it was completely dark."

"Where was Mummy Bunny?"

"She was asleep in her bed, but she woke up. She thought I was Rex. I told her it was me. She asked what I wanted, and I told her I knew. I had always known we would be together. I told her I loved her, and I had come to give her my love."

"What did Mummy Bunny do?

"She laughed."

"Oh no."

"And then I left."

He sank to his knees, his eyes filling with tears. His laugh sounded like a balloon deflating.

In the hour before dawn, I passed out on the scooter grease-stained couch in the front room. I woke up with smoke in my eyes. Uncle Frank sat on the edge of the couch, sucking nicotine into his lungs. He looked at me for a long second, and then he said: "Apollo, you are a young man, but soon I will retire. You know what the casino bosses will give me? Nothing. After thirty years. Nothing. I have a family. Many mouths. I love beautiful clothes, and to have beautiful clothes, you must have the money. But soon my bosses will open a new casino in Cambodia. I will heist this casino. I think you will help me."

There it was. The story I could sense in that house. It had shown itself to me, like a shy yet flirty ghost.

Episode Five.

Where shall I sit?"

"Uhh, one second."

Nhu picked up a pile of clothes, and searched for somewhere to dump them.

Her building was a bougie affair named *Saigon Pearl,* and it sat on a prime bend of river that ran through District Two. This was the real deal. Many residents woke up to sweeping views of the city. But not Nhu. Her apartment was an underground shoebox with no windows. Right off the car park. She had a messy mattress on the floor, and four racks stuffed with designer clothes and shoes and bags. The bathroom was a phone booth, and her kitchen consisted of a bar fridge with a hot plate on top. But while she lived in an underground bunker, her address matched her rich girl façade.

She kicked belts and jeans and bras off the bed, and stuffed skirts into thigh-high Chanel boots. I sat on the space on the bed she had cleared, and she sat next to me. In front of our faces, on a red plastic crate, sat a large TV and PlayStation.

"Do you play?"

"No it's for show."

"Looks great."

"What a dumb-dumb question. Of course I play."

"What's your favourite game?"

"Euro Truck Simulator."

"Euro what now?"

She reached into an Alexander Wang bag, and pulled out a slender joint.

"Smoke?"

"No thanks."

"Are you scared?"

"Is it strong?"

"Are you?"

She held a flame to the tip of the joint, drew smoke into her lungs, held it down for what seemed like minutes, then blew out a pungent yellow cloud. She was a pro. When she passed me the joint, I took a baby puff. This made her laugh. So I took a long draw, held it down, then coughed my lungs onto a yellow leather jacket. She patted my back and picked up a PlayStation controller. "Let's go for a drive." We passed the joint back and forth, and she drove a truck across Europe. East and West. North and South. Making deliveries. That was the game. She delivered washing machines to Dusseldorf, toasters to Athens, a load of socks to Kyiv. She was an excellent driver. She always made her deliveries on time, and she made good money. She was building a fleet. "I have twenty trucks now," she said, sucking the last gasp from the joint. "The most one person in the game has is fifty. In two years I can overtake them. I will have the biggest fleet in Europe."

Her bed became our island.

If we needed noodles or water or ice cream, we left the island.

But we always returned to the island.

I didn't tell her this, but I wanted to stay with her on the island forever.

On the second day on the island – it may have been the morning or it might have been the evening (with no windows it was hard to tell) – I lay back on the bed smoking a joint. Nhu lay next to me, driving her truck down a snowy highway in Serbia. She had a load of pigs in the back. Like two hundred pigs. As I watched, and puffed, I felt like a passenger in the truck. I could hear the snow falling softly on the trees lining the highway, the birds chirping as they fed worms to their babies.

"Your turn."

"I don't know how to–"

She handed me the controller, and I tried to drive the truck. I went okay on the straight. But when I tried to take a sharp turn, the truck veered off road, rolled down a bank and into a ravine, where it exploded in a ball of flame, cooking the poor piggies.

"I killed the pigs!"

"They're not real."

She got up and poured a glass of water. I was stressed out about the pigs. Really I felt bad. I was sweating a lot, and the beads of sweat running down my arms were acting weird. Some inched over the skin like warm glaciers, some climbed the short hairs, some popped like bubbles, some split into hundreds of tiny beads, some morphed into abstract shapes, and some raced around the freckles, seemingly driven by deep anxiety, like junkies chasing down smack in the midday sun. Nhu watched me drink the water, then she pushed me back on the bed and kissed me. This was our first kiss. I wanted to stay in it, but I was still in shock about the pigs, and the weird shit the beads of sweat were doing on my arms.

"What was in that joint?"

"Weed. And maybe some MDMA."

"Why didn't you tell me."

"I did."

"No you didn't."

"I did."

"I shouldn't do that shit."

"Will you go crazy?"

"Maybe."

"Cool."

She kissed me again. Her lips tasted like lemongrass and salt and icing sugar. She rolled me onto my back, and guided my hand up her skirt and into her underwear. I did as she instructed. But she yanked my hand out, got up and walked to the bathroom. Late that night, or maybe early the next morning, I told her about the casino heist. I won't lie, I wanted to impress her, so I dressed it up as a stylish and glamorous and lucrative project. Which it very well might have been.

"You should do it."

"You think?"

"Why not. Lots of money. You can stop making the shitty marketing films."

"They're not that shitty."

"They are quite shitty."

"The heist story could be the first season of Untitled Original Series Set On Multiple Continents."

"The what?"

"Untitled Original Series Set On Multiple Continents. I told you about it. You don't remember?"

"I don't remember."

"It's a TV show, so it will run on HBO or Amazon, but some episodes will run on social media, and YouTube, and in movie theatres too. And all the episodes will be different lengths, like some might be thirty seconds and others might be two hours, shit like that. What do you think?"

"You might die."

"Making the show?"

"Making the heist."

"How?"

"They might stab you and bury you in the jungle."

"Why would you say that?"

"It's true."

WE woke in the afternoon, our skin slick with sweat. The air con had crashed. She took my hand and steered it into her underwear. I did as I had the day before. This time she didn't yank my hand out. She closed her eyes. I tried to kiss her, but when she felt my lips on hers, she turned her face away. I thought she wanted me to stop, but she held my hand in place, so I willed my beautiful fingers to work some magic. They helped me out. She bit her lip when she came. I thought maybe then she would kiss me, as a reward for services rendered. But she rolled off the island and locked herself in the bathroom. "Go to the car park," she said through the door. "But come back in one hour."

Dawn. Or maybe an hour before dawn. I stared at the concrete ceiling. Nhu slept next to me, curled up like a caterpillar. It was time to leave the island. Time to roll off the bed, make my way into the city, and ride the elevator up to the boardroom in the clouds. Khanh and Mai-Mai were on the scent for fresh ideas. But I did not have fresh ideas. I had nothing. I tried to locate the exact moment I hit the self-destruct button, but I got distracted by the sweet expression on Nhu's sleeping face. I leaned over to smell the soft bursts of air leaving her slightly parted lips. Weed and pineapple juice. I loved that smell, but alas, I could not stay with that smell. I pulled on my pants and shoes, and silently shut the door behind me. A set of concrete stairs took me into the lobby by way of the fire exit. Outside it was dark. Misty. A path of shimmering lights led me down to the river. I walked along the sloping bank, hoping the lights and the mist might spark an idea in my cloudy brain. I couldn't tell you what was going on in my head. Nonsense mainly. Hundreds of images flew into my frontal lobe, but when I tried to grab one, they flew out, and in flew a hundred more. After an hour or two of this, the sun creaked over the horizon, and I stood ankle-deep in mud that smelled like an oil spill mixed with rotten canned tuna.

In the boardroom, I saw the people first. There must have been seventeen suits – men and women, old and young, sipping coffee, eating pastries, staring at phone screens and computer screens. My fingers vibrated, my eyeballs felt like they had been pulled from their sockets, rolled in hot sand, and popped back in my head. My sweat smelled sour, like fennel, which most of the time is a pleasant smell, but not when it smells like it's leaking directly from your lymph nodes. Khanh and Mai-Mai stood at the back of the room. Mai-Mai looked at me like she might a dog about to be led away at a kill shelter. The corner of Khanh's right eye twitched.

"How's everyday feeling today?" I said. "I mean everyone. Ha. Ready for a big day today?"

The corner of Khanh's eye spasmed erratically.

"Are you okay, Apollo Jones?" asked Mai-Mai. "You don't look well."

"I'm great! Never better."

"I hope you have some gold," Khanh sneered. "I asked the entire marketing department to join. I know you like an audience."

"Of course!" I held up my computer. "The more the merriment."

I sat at the end of the boardroom table, and flipped open my computer. More suits flowed in. Seats were scarce, so they leaned against the wood-panelled walls, and the windows with the clouds floating by. I had to focus. There were hundreds, nay, thousands of social media content scripts on my computer. I needed to find one that *might* work, and repurpose that fucker on the fly. Head down, I plumbed the depths of my hard drive. Then I heard it. A collective gasp rippled around the room. Murmurs of adulation. Before I looked up, I knew what had happened. Jerry had entered the room. He was north of seventy, and he wore a dark grey double-breasted suit with gold buttons. You'd think he'd be flanked by an entourage of minions, but of course the man rolled solo. He smoked a long thin cigarette, wore a massive jade ring, and slightly tinted glasses, so you could make out the outlines of his eyes, but never the emotional content of the irises. He was a profound boss. Maybe the coolest person I had even seen.

"Jerry!" cried the suits. "Jerry is here! Hi Jerry!"

They leapt from their seats, dropping coffees and pastries in their desperate rush to shake the boss' hand. But none were faster than Khanh. I have no idea how he got from one end of the room to the other. I'm sure I saw him knock a man to the ground and stomp on his stomach. "Thank you for coming, sir," said Khanh, pumping Jerry's hand, the suits at his back. "It is an honour." Jerry looked straight through Khanh, and sat at the head of the table. From the opposite end, I watched the lines in his top lip as he sucked on his long cigarette. The suits dropped back. Khanh produced a crystal ash tray, and held it in front of his master, but Jerry ashed on Khanh's perfectly pressed suit jacket. In Khanh's eyes, I saw white hot fury. He wanted to take that ash tray and turn the old man's head to pulp. But he swallowed his rage, and sat in the chair to Jerry's right.

"Good morning," I said, standing up. The room went quiet. No murmuring. No coffee sipping. No muffin munching. "My name is Apollo Jones, and I'm going to present…" I trailed off. I had no choice. Jerry stared at me, and I stared right back at Jerry. I saw through his tinted lenses, deep into his soul. The man was a gambler. A whale. The roll of the dice his one true love. It was faint at first, but I felt a flicker of electricity at the core of my being. It rolled and roiled, flashing and sparking as it surged up my throat, shooting shards of light into my veins, the synapses of my brain, the nerves at the ends of my long fingers. Script you say? Scripts are for mugs. Preparation? You must be joking. I could extract gold nuggets directly from my sub-conscious.

My mouth fell open and the words spewed out. I was five sentences in before my brain caught up to my tongue, and got a grasp on what I was saying. "We're going to get a truck. A real beauty of a truck – huge, majestic – and paint it the colours of your brand – gold, black and white. We'll put leather seats inside, and a big steering wheel made of gold. We're going to drive this truck all over Asia, from town to town, city to city, from mountain villages to futuristic shopping malls. In this truck we will use the latest in narrative technology to collect people's stories, real stories from real people from all walks of life – bankers, farmers, dentists, mothers who've lost brothers, sisters obsessed with chickens. This will be an ongoing tapestry, a beautiful and vivid odyssey…it will never stop. The truck will keep driving, collecting stories, beaming them out to the world, a perpetual content vehicle… The Truth of Life, that's what our truck will be called, our forever project… The Truth of Life…"

Jerry lit a fresh cigarette. He blew a jet of smoke at the window to his left, so it merged with the clouds outside the glass. Then he got up and walked out, his cigarette trailing ash on the plush white carpet. Khanh smiled at me, and mouthed the words, "You're fired."

Episode Six.

The elevator spat me out in the foyer. I don't remember leaving the boardroom in the clouds. And when I hit Nguyen Hue, the walking street with fountains and a massive bronze statue of a benevolent Ho Chi Minh, sweat poured from every pore in my body. Noise assaulted my eardrums. Engines mainly, yelling too. Some kind of jangly guitar tune. Dust clung to the walls of my tear ducts, and scooters jumped the curb, the front wheels biting the backs of my ankles. I wanted to lie down and die the death of a stray dog. I needed refuge. I needed the island. I phoned Nhu and told her I got fired.

"This is good."

"How?"

"No more toilet films."

"Those toilet films are how I make money."

"Now you will make money from the casino film."

"Casino series."

"Whatever."

Never ever had I been happier to see a bed. I buried my face in her pistachio green linen sheets, and inhaled deep into my lungs. The island smelled of jasmine, and sea salt, and the freckle on her throat, which is to say it smelled like a bird flying down from a tall tree, and gifting you a leaf from a plant with medicinal properties. I stayed like that, my face in her sheets, for what seemed like hours. From far away, I heard her deliver a load of couches to a shop in Copenhagen. The smell of skunk made its way to my nostrils. I was feeling raw. Very scared. It had taken me years to get my career to this point. Years of grovelling and selling and staying up all night to perfect pitch decks. And now, poof, it had gone up in smoke. Getting sacked was okay, but I had been sacked in the most degrading way. Word would spread. Never again would I tell a story on a screen. My stomach twisted itself into a painful knot, then a hand touched the back of my neck. The hand must have had an in-depth knowledge of the nervous system, for the touch fired a shot into the back of my brain, which is the part that tells you to stop being a whiny little bitch. "You want to eat?" asked Nhu.

She took me out for banh xeo and cold cans of lemonade, which if you don't know is maybe the best food and drink combo on the planet.

"Jerk off for me."

This was later in the evening. I was sitting on the island. She was standing near the bathroom door, flossing her teeth. I leaned back on the wall and went to work. She watched my hand going up and down, and pulled the floss from side to side in the cracks between her teeth. "Spit on your hand." I felt the warm slimy liquid on my skin, smelled the inner workings of my body. And from across the room I smelled the peppermint flavour of her floss.

In the morning, I lifted my head from her pillow. She sat on the edge of the bed, cleaning the pink sleeve of a leather Gucci jacket.

"I commissioned a new show, and the artist I love very much. She will make my gallery into a sweat shop, like H&M or Zara. The visitors to the show will sew garments, like real factory workers. This artist worked in a factory for six years also."

"What's her name?"

"Doan Q Le. The show will be called Reap What You Sew."

"Clever."

"I will be very busy for some weeks, so I can't see you. Okay?"

"Okay."

"This means no messaging, no calling. Nothing. Okay?"

"I get it. You don't want to see me."

"You're going to Cambodia anyway, for your original series set in all the world."

"Untitled Original Series Set On Multiple Continents."

"Yes, that."

"What if I get stabbed and dumped in the jungle."

"Then your death will be hot. And I will fuck your hot dead body."

Episode Seven.

Uncle Frank was not happy with my sweat glands. In fact, he was downright enraged. We were playing cards at a table in his room, near the closet where he kept his glorious suits. This was my boot camp, and he was my drill sergeant. He sat across from me, running a comb through his hair, his fury growing with each stroke.

"You sweat too much, you stinky tulip. Look at the pits. The pits are like puddles."

"I told you I was bad."

"When you say this?! You never say it."

"I–"

"The pits! They smell like onions. Nothing smells so bad as the white man's sweat. Oh boy. You think they won't see? This is a big tell. They will see in one second. Or they will smell. Then we are fucked."

The day I signed on for the heist, he asked if I could play cards, and I told him the truth, that my skills were abysmal. But the success of the heist relied on me not turning into a toddler with gastro the second I sat at the blackjack table, so the poor man made it his personal mission to raise my skills to an acceptable level. This was no easy task. I stuffed up subtle move after subtle move. After each stuff up, he ran his comb through his hair with such intense fury, I worried the teeth were doing permanent damage to his scalp. When my pits sprung leaks like a busted paddling pool, we had been playing for nineteen hours straight. My fingertips were numb and the vision in my right eye was blurry. And if I closed my eyes I saw the Queen of Spades strangling the King of Hearts. Anhtheman stood behind me, massaging my shoulders, lifting me up like a supportive soccer Mum. While Uncle Frank sat across from me, tearing me down like a disappointed Dad.

When I asked about the plan, he told me not to worry about the plan. "We will talk about the plan when you play cards better than my uncle in the leper colony. Ok stinky tulip?"

Once I had a fair to middling understanding of the big three – blackjack, craps and poker – we moved onto my tells. Aside from the sweating (in an attempt to train my pits to chill the fuck out under fire, he shut off the air con and force fed me pots of green tea) Uncle Frank said I had several clear giveaways. When I had a good hand, my right pupil dilated, when I had a not so good hand, my earlobes quivered, and when I was bluffing, I plucked at the short black hairs that grew from my nostrils. Beating the tells out of me took four whole days. By the end, we were either sworn enemies or best friends forever. But he didn't sack me, or cut me, so I went with the latter. Where did I sleep during boot camp? If I slept at all, it was on the grease-stained couch in the front room. This was actually a pretty peaceful spot. Late at night, when the house was deep in sleep, the air con unit whispered over my head, scooters puttered past the door, and old men selling rice cakes and pork dumplings rode past on bikes, with speakers that said: 'banh chung, banh gio.'

Before we move on, let me give you a rundown of every resident in the house real quick:

Uncle Frank, who you know, patriarch and chief breadwinner, loved clothes more than life itself

Anhtheman, his nephew, worked at a Pham Ngu Lao tour operator, paid the rent and bought food when Uncle Frank spent his pay on fancy clothes

Auntie, Uncle Frank's mother, bigtime grump

Thuy, Uncle Frank's current wife, told not to speak by Auntie, listened to Auntie

Bo, Thuy and Uncle Frank's one-year-old son, very round, very smart, spoke in full sentences

Doan, Uncle Frank's daughter from his second marriage, worked at a make-up counter in the Vincom Centre, had her own make-up tutorial channel on YouTube

Van, Uncle Frank's son from his first marriage, genius level motorbike mechanic.

Duc, Uncle Frank's son from his second marriage, genius level motor-bike mechanic, believed by Uncle Frank to be autistic, despite showing no signs of autism

Binh, Uncle Frank's daughter from his second marriage, excelled in school despite Auntie telling her to lose weight daily.

My primary mission in the house was to level up my gambling skills, but I was keen to connect with the family members too. This proved a tall order. Obviously there was a language barrier, and a cultural one too. Also they saw me as some sort of interloper, which was right on the money. They were kind, warm even, but not willing to form deep and immediate bonds with me. Also, Auntie. She hated me from day one. It didn't matter what I did – washing the dishes, sweeping the floors – she iced me out. And if she shuffled into the front room and saw me lying on the grease-stained couch, she cursed me out (I had been watching Vietnamese lessons on YouTube, and had picked up some swears, so I got the gist).

Her frostiness was made worse by an incident that went down one morning. I woke up at dawn, and, like most young men, I woke to a penis engorged with blood. On this morning, my erection was so intense it felt as though the skin might split, like a sausage left in boiling water too long. I had been dreaming of Nhu. Not of her riding my bloody corpse on the soggy jungle floor, but not far off. Anyway, I got off the couch, wrapped a towel around my waist and tip-toped up the stairs. Once inside, I closed the door, but I must have forgotten to slide the lock shut. The same moment I opened the towel, and my erect penis sprang out, the door swung open, and Auntie stood before me. Her back was stooped, which put her eyes perfectly level with my shining purple head. She stared for an unfortunate amount of time, her tired eyes bulging from their sockets. I tried to hide my shame but it was too late. She screamed. And then ran down the stairs screaming, and out into the street, still screaming.

Anhtheman found it funny. Thuy did too. Uncle Frank did not. As I sat on the couch like a naughty schoolboy, he stood over me, with Auntie tucked in behind him, vexing me in Vietnamese, her crooked finger casting who knew what spells.

"She says you are a pervert."

"Please, for the hundredth time, can you tell her I'm sorry."

"Are you sexually aroused by old women?"

"It was an accident!"

"She says you waited for her, so you can expose your genitals to her on purpose."

"Do you really believe I did that?"

"She is my mother!"

THAT night I got a call from Mai-Mai. "How are you, Apollo Jones? I worry for you." Good old Mai-Mai, she really cared. She said that Khanh felt bad for sacking me, but I knew Khanh dined on people's failures the way the French dine on defenceless littles birds drowned in brandy. But she did have good news – thanks to my contract, I would be paid for fifty percent of the insurance job, plus my hotel room was covered for three months, and was mine to use if I wished. This was a serious blessing. I needed refuge from the blackjack boot camp, and from a house where three generations of residents believed I had intentionally exposed myself to a helpless old woman. Once back in my room, I wrote ideas for the casino heist story on scene cards, and stuck them to the walls. Uncle Frank, Anhtheman – they were great characters. The boot camp made for good material, and Auntie added some comedic (if traumatic) relief. Man oh man, The Untitled Original Series Set On Multiple Continents was underway. And with the casino heist as the first season storyline, it was sure to be a banger. I saw an intense bidding war between Amazon, Apple and Netflix, with HBO swooping in at the final hour. Also, I tried to resist, but I couldn't help myself – I messaged Nhu.

The plan was to limit my messages to one per day, but I tried to game the system, sending one text message, one meme on Instagram, and an article on WhatsApp. Most of the time she didn't respond, but the evil 'seen' feature on Instagram, plus the two blue ticks on WhatsApp told me she had read my messages. I knew sending more made me look like a desperate and feeble worm, but I could not stop. Some days I got lucky, and she responded with a monosyllable:

Ha

Or:

Cool

Or just a thumbs up.

In many ways this was worse than no response. At least with no response I could lie to myself: 'she must be busy' or 'she's delivering a load of lamps to Moscow.' The monosyllables were a knee to the kidney. But if we're being honest here (and I hope we are) if you wanted me to love you, you had to treat me like shit. If you ignored me, kept me at arm's length, treated me like a dog with fleas, I would shower you with affection. If you showed me you loved me, that you cared for me, and you needed me to do that in return, I would run to a faraway place, like a cave or a forest or a mountain. Or a cave in a forest on a mountain.

ONE extra muggy evening, back in the house, I sat at the small table near the polished wardrobe. Uncle Frank and Anhtheman sat with me. Uncle Frank picked up the deck of cards, smiled, and tossed them in the trash. At last, boot camp was over. My skills had ascended to, well, maybe not those of a pro, but not a withered old man who eats prunes and wets the bed.

Uncle Frank rubbed his ruby rings. He stood up, pulled a lemon yellow suit from the wardrobe, lay it flat on the ironing board, and pressed the hot metal base of iron into the fabric. Just looking at the steam made beads of sweat run down my face, but at least Uncle Frank was back in his happy place.

"You have learned much, my sweet tulip, and now we will tell you the plan."

"You will be the gambler," said Anhtheman. "And you will–"

Shooting a jet of steam at a yellow lapel, Uncle Frank shot his nephew a look. "The casino is new. It's in the jungle. Very beautiful style. Roman style. Made for the emperors of gambling. And the staffs are all new. The dealers, the waiters, all fresh meat. I help to hire them, so I keep them all here in my pocket."

"We paid them with my savings," said Anhtheman, sanitizing his hands.

"The friendly dealers will know your face, and you will have their faces in your head. You will gamble at their tables only, and they will make it so you win."

"How will they do that?"

"Many ways," said Anhtheman.

Uncle Frank inspected his jacket, hung it up, then went to work on the yellow pants. "One way is like this: you win a small hand at blackjack, the dealer should give you ten dollar chips, but he gives you one thousand dollar chips. Oops. Your small hand is now twenty thousand dollars in your hand."

"Nice."

"You see?"

"It's good. But what about the chips? Do I change them? Or do I push them around in a wheelbarrow."

"A wheel what?"

"Don't worry."

"Listen," said Uncle Frank. "When you get to three hundred thousand, you change it, and then you–"

"I will dig a pit," said Anhtheman.

"A pit?"

"A pit. In a hut. In the jungle." At the thought of dirt he sanitized his hands again. "This is very close to the casino. You take the money into the hut in the jungle, you put the money into the pit, then you go back to the casino, you win more money, take this money to the pit."

"What if I get seen going to the pit?"

"Don't worry about the pit," said Uncle Frank, finishing up the pants. "We will talk later about the pit. Now, you have one final test."

He put the yellow suit back in the wardrobe, and pulled out a leather document case. From the case he slid thirty passport-style photos – the faces of the dealers, pit bosses, floor managers, slot managers, table games managers, money changers and waiters.

"You must remember these faces, and keep them in your memory."

Boot camp round two was now in session. They showed me the faces, and I had to tell them the person's name and role in the casino hierarchy. Sometimes it went okay, but mostly I did an appalling job. I got pit bosses mixed up with dealers, and floor managers mixed up with slot managers. I once mistook a general manager for a money changer. Anhtheman tried to keep the vibe calm and supportive, but the stakes, and the heat, and my incompetence, plus the incident with Auntie, pushed Uncle Frank far into the red. When I failed the test for the two hundredth time, he lost it. With a hand that felt like iron bound in leather, he grabbed my throat, lifted me out of my chair and slammed me into a wall. Now I'm not sure how familiar you are with the anatomy of the testicles, but inside the sack you have what feels like two hard-boiled eggs – these are the testicles them-selves – and they are very delicate. If you squeeze them hard enough, they feel like they might pop. Like a large tadpole. I got the feeling Uncle Frank knew what he was doing, because he thrust his free hand down the front of my underpants, latched onto my naked testis and squeezed. He squeezed extremely hard, until they were on the verge of popping. Also, he wore most of his ruby and emerald-encrusted rings on this hand. He must have turned the rings around, for he rolled the stones over the surface of the testis. The rolling technique, combined with the squeeze, produced a pain so severe it paralysed me. The only part of my body that seemed to function were my tear ducts, and they sent great salty drops rolling past my nose.

Episode Eight.

The old iron cage elevator was broken, so I took the stairs up to STA-TION. But Uncle Frank had done serious damage to my testicles. For two days they were the colour of an overripe grape. Then they shift-ed to a rather pleasing blue-meets-autumnal yellow. They were swollen too, and I worried the left one was filled with fluid. And so, bow-legged, I walked up the curved staircase like some deranged cowboy. At the top, I heard a noise like machinegun fire: RATATATATATATATATATATA... RA-TATATA... RATATATATATATATATATATATA...

I looked up and saw a line of people running down the hall. Most of them were cool young fashion type people, local and international, with blue and silver hair, nose rings, and tattoos of hamburgers, things like that. They waited to get into STATION. Stomping down the queue came Nhu. She clutched an iPad to her chest, and wore a white lab coat with *FACTORY MANAGER* stitched on the breast-pocket. She barked at a young man with a shaved head:

"How long is your shift?"

"Ten hours?"

"You want overtime?"

"Can I work underwear?"

"You work what I tell you to work, maggot."

She tapped a nail on her screen and moved down the line. Then she spotted me. "Get up here now!"

She grabbed hold of my shirt, dragged me to the front of the line and pushed me into the gallery, which had been transformed into a sewing factory. A sweat shop. Four long tables ran across the space, with five sewing machines on each table, so twenty machines in total. Young men and women sat under harsh fluorescent lights, with no air con, rivulets of sweat trickling down the limbs that tried to sew shirts and socks and shorts and underpants. The combined noise of twenty sewing machines made it hard to hear your own thoughts.

RATATATATAT... RATATATA... RATATATATATATA... RATATATATATAT...

On the front wall, a yellow neon sign said REAP WHAT YOU SEW. Dozens of bolts of fabric leaned against the back wall – blue and gold and white and pink rolls of cotton and silk and rayon and taffeta. The people working the machines were not professionals, and they made mistakes. A tall woman wearing bright red lipstick and a lab coat that said *PRODUCTION MANAGER* screamed at a blonde girl with Chanel logo earrings.

"This is bad work! You should be ashamed!"

"I am ashamed."

"Be more ashamed!!"

A young man jammed his machine. Rather than face the wrath of the Production Manager, he abandoned his post, and ran out the door. Nhu sat me in his seat.

"I like your new show."

"Shut up. Are you ready to work?"

"Yes, factory manager."

"You're on socks. Give me ten pair in one hour, or I will burn your feet, just like at H&M!"

I went to work on a navy pair of socks. But asking me to sew was like asking one of those tall skinny dogs (salukis I think they're called) to play the violin. Also, I was distracted. Watching Nhu stomping around the sweat shop, yelling in people's faces, rapping them over the knuckles with her iPad, it really got me going. I was so aroused by her power moves, I didn't see the sewing machine foot punch a hole in the little finger on my right hand, right at the base of the nail bed. My beautiful hand! I was distraught, but also happy. I knew Nhu would have to tend to my wound. I raised my hand, she saw the blood running down my little finger, and whisked me out the back to her office. She sat me at her desk and pulled out a first aid kit, which mostly contained Hello Kitty bandages.

"Lick it."

I licked the blood from my little finger. She took a glass jar from a drawer. "Spit into this." I spat a mix of bright red blood and bubbly saliva into the jar, and watched it slide down the glass wall. "I own this," she said, placing the jar on her desk. She then disinfected my wound, and wrapped it in a Hello Kitty bandage.

"I want you to come to Cambodia with me. To do the casino heist."

"Why?"

"I don't want to do it alone. I just. I'd feel better if you–"

"You see the line of people outside? This show is huge. I will take it to Basel Hong Kong."

"I'll give you half."

"Half of what?"

"Half of a hundred thousand."

She looked at me. Then she finished bandaging my finger. And then she said: "No."

Episode Nine.

I saw her robes first. Long and yellow, they floated behind her as she walked in the door. I was sitting on the blue-tiled floor in the front room, polishing the metal exhaust of a scooter, while Van and Duc ripped the guts from said scooter. It all happened in slow motion. The billowing robes, the breeze in her hair, the way she lifted each sandaled foot off the ground. I swear I saw a golden glow emanating out from her head. She knelt on the floor and prayed.

"Thao is home," said Van.

Thao was Uncle Frank's long lost daughter from his first marriage, and Auntie's favourite grandchild. At the age of nine, she started speaking with spirits. They were her friends. She let them play with her dolls, and took them for walks along the river. But when word of her powers spread, people banged on the door, begging Thao to reach out to the lost souls of their loved ones. Uncle Frank was more than happy to charge a fee for his daughter's gift, and that fee went directly into his tailor's pocket. By the time Thao was sixteen, she was done watching his wardrobe grow. Her powers had grown too strong for him to control anyway, and she struck out on her own. Up and down the country she trekked, performing seances pro bono. People killed in motorbike accidents, that was her specialty. Especially the sorry souls hit by trucks and buses far from home. For Thao, the spirits were always down to talk, and she figured the crushing weight of the ways they died was what made them chatterboxes in the afterlife. For a few years she was a member of the Cao Dai church in Tay Ninh, south of Saigon. But the bishops had not been down with seances for decades. Thao knew they had lost their touch, that her powers intimidated them, so she bailed. She took her gift and her robes to Thailand, where she got a job at an upmarket wellness retreat, reaching out to the lost loved ones of lost Westerners, charging fifty bucks per word.

The night Thao came home, Auntie made a magnificent feast. We're talking caramelised pork belly, braised beef with egg, pickled mustard greens, stir-fried morning glory, crunchy rice, and beer and whisky and soft drink for all. I sat at the laden table with Anhtheman and Uncle Frank, and Thuy and Bo and Duc and Binh and Van and Doan. It was meant to be a happy time, but the vibe was off. For one, Auntie was smiling. But Uncle Frank and Anhtheman looked like they were about to be led away to the gallows. Wearing her bright yellow robes, Thao marched in and stood at the head of the table. "Let us pray." All the eyes closed and all the heads at the table bowed. I tried to close mine, but a mysterious force pulled my chin up, turned my head, and I locked eyes with Thao. She had the poise of a cult leader, and while she was convinced of her connection to the divine, she was not the kind to lead her followers in a mass suicide, more the benevolent shepherd kind. I felt a curious shiver. As if she had attached a set of electrodes to my pituitary gland, and was hitting it with hundreds of microscopic shockwaves. She spoke her prayer out loud, but in my head I heard different words: "Why have you come? Are you a salesmen? A foreign invader? I am watching you."

From her first night back, Thao was a destabilising force in the house. When she walked into a room in her yellow robes, the air took on a frenetic energy. The family centre of gravity shifted from Uncle Frank to her, and this threw his moods out of whack. He took it out on me, and Anhtheman, and the casino heist plans. Going back on his satisfaction, he claimed my card skills were not up to scratch after all. Nor was my memory. Out came a fresh deck. Out came the photos of the dealers' faces. Again and again, he tested me every night. He blasted Anhtheman about the pit. And he made us wargame every possible situation he could think of, as well as every ridiculously impossible situation he could think of:

"What do we do if a dealer gets caught?"

"What do we do if the power goes out and the casino goes dark?"

"What do we do if Anhtheman turns on us?"

"What do we do if a snake bites Apollo on his way to the pit, and the venom makes his blood turn around in his veins so that his heart is drained of blood and he dies?"

Thao did not try to hide her plans to join the heist. Hell, she may have planned to usurp her father as the heist boss (the way she usurped him in the house) and turn the whole scenario into a quasi-spiritual operation. Late one sticky night, as we sat at the table near the polished wardrobe, going over the faces of the dealers for the seven hundred and ninety-ninth million time, she burst in the door in her yellow robes, a burning sage sprig held aloft, and proceeded to splash some kind of holy water on the cards, telling us the spirits had told her in no uncertain terms that we would perish in the jungle if we did not enlist her powers post haste. Uncle Frank believed in his daughter's powers with all the fear in his heart, and her proclamation rattled him to the core. He spluttered and he shook, falling to the floor. To me it looked like a seizure, but Thao placed a calming palm on her father's red hot forehead, and dragged him back to the world of the living. When he came around, and lit a rejuvenating cigarette, I was sure I saw a glint of satisfaction in her eye. After that, Anhtheman installed a lock on his uncle's door. But Uncle Frank was not quite right. His focus went all fuzzy, and he lost some of his love for ruthless precision. Most nights he locked me in his room with him. I sat on the bed and watched him iron his suits, listening to the disconnected narratives he spewed about exquisite needlework. In between these rants he spoke of Thao. He told me of the guilt he felt for not protecting her, for exploiting her gifts for his financial gain. "All these years I feel this like a pain I have in the cave behind my heart." I told him she seemed pretty together, but he just shook his head. "She looks strong to you, but I am her father. I see this is an act." I knew he was sincere, but it also seemed to me like he knew he owed his daughter a debt, and paying that debt meant cutting her a share of the casino cash, and that was a tough pill for him to swallow. So he kept on ironing and sermonizing.

Anhtheman too seemed psychically adrift since the return of Thao. One morning, he woke me up on the couch, his face mere inches from mine. His breath smelled of basil and hand sanitizer, and I wondered if he had tried sanitizing his insides, the way he constantly sanitized his outsides. "I want to show you something." From that range, I could see the desperation clawing at the back of his eyeballs, so I got up and got on the back of his bike, the hot leather seat sizzling my inner thighs. He drove us to a vacant shopfront in a Pham Ngu Lao backstreet. The air inside was thick with dust particles. He doused my hands in sanitizer.

"Do you wish to forget the heist?"

"What?"

"Apollo, I have a big dream, to build a tourism business, here in this shop. I will call it Organic Tours. We will take international visitors to the country. They will stay with families, work in the fields, like real peasants!"

"Uh, what do you mean we?"

"You and me. I run the business, but you are the master of content. We will share in the profits, and there will be so many profits, Apollo. This is the best idea. Westerners crave authentic experience. For this they will pay any price."

"What about Uncle Frank?"

"Do you like it? If you like the idea you should say yes."

"Is this because of Thao?"

"Thao is a snake with five heads. Let's make the deal. Do you want to make the deal?"

Goddamnit. If I said yes to Organic Tours, that meant losing the heist.

And losing the heist meant losing the first season of the Untitled Original Series Set On Multiple Continents. But if I said no to Organic Tours (which in truth was a pretty great idea – he was right about Western tourists paying top dollar to live as peasants) Anhtheman might cut me out of the heist out of spite. I told him I would think about it.

At about ten o'clock that night, a massive raincloud parked itself above the house and pelted the roof with softball-sized raindrops. Uncle Frank and Anhtheman and Auntie and Thuy and Bo and the others went to bed early. I sat in the dark at the long table, listening to the ferocious downpour, typing notes about the heist on my phone. I sensed a presence. And when I looked up, I saw Thao standing in the doorway in her yellow robes. How long had she been watching me? Could she see my notes? Read my mind? "Come with me." I didn't one hundred percent want to go, but her cult leader charisma was magnetic. It was like being pulled in a net. I followed her out the door and into the wet night, and got on the back of her bike. She drove us out of the rain and into the city, and over the Thu Thiem bridge. On the other side she took us down a dark road and parked under a tree. She led me down a scrubby bank. The air was hot and damp, and mosquitoes buzzed all the way into my ear canals. We trudged through marshland, and passed what I swore were three water buffalo, but were more than likely shadows, or my mind playing tricks on me. We popped out from the trees to find the river floating by, its surface flat and black and shiny, reflecting the orange and white lights in the buildings sprouting up on the opposite side. "Here the current is optimal."

I asked her what we were doing, and she said it was a test. When I asked what kind of test, she lifted her robes and led me into the mud. Slurping and sucking at our feet, it sent up pockets of air that smelled of tinned cat food. As we waded into the black water, I kept my eyes on the yellow beacon that was her back. The water lapped at her hips and she dropped her robes, letting them spill over the surface. She turned and took my hands in hers, sending sparks of energy from her fingertips and into mine. They felt like tiny lightning bolts. I knew then that her power was for real, and for real powerful. She closed her eyes and squeezed my hands, and muttered an ancient prayer as she spun us round and round, delivering ripples out to both riverbanks. Beams of light ran up my arms and entered my chest cavity, and I swore the water swirled up past my bellybutton, churning and frothing, turning ice cold then boiling hot as baby eels came to join the fun, curling in between my toes and round my ankles, their young fangs sending sparks up my legs to join the ones that came from Thao, then fanning out to flicker in my capillaries, to make the marrow in my bones sing, my eyes catch the warm violet glow radiating out from the back of Thao's head and into the black sky. My mind was clear, then it clouded over, and took me back to times when I was four and five and six, to times spent with Oscar, my father.

Oscar pushing me on a swing.

Oscar taking me to get sushi, and painting my nails pink.

Climbing onto his lap, fresh from my bath, for a bedtime story he made up.

Sitting in the sunlight, Oscar teaching me how to write the letter A.

The two of us fishing for tadpoles with my net.

Riding home on his broad shoulders.

Thao sped us back over the bridge, our legs caked in pungent mud. The rain came straight down, the road was awash with pitch black puddles, and they reflected the pink and green raincoats of the riders whizzing by. My fingers and toes were numb. My brain a fog. All I felt were the raindrops hammering the top of my helmet. I rested my cheek on her back, felt her heart beat into the pulse in my temple. "Now I trust you," she said. "I see your pain, and I will protect you. In Cambodia. But you must want my help." Did she speak these words or did they come directly from a chamber in the organ in her chest? I nodded into her robes, and she drove us home to wake up Uncle Frank and Anhtheman.

The four of us sat at the table near the polished wardrobe. Uncle Frank lit a cigarette, Anhtheman sanitized his hands. I told them I needed Thao on the heist. That I could not would not cross the border into Cambodia without her. That I would cut her in on my cut. Anhtheman muttered under his breath, slathering his forearms in sanitizer. Uncle Frank was silent. Tears rolled down his gaunt cheeks. Thao was crying too. Father and daughter stared at each other, communicating wordlessly. The air crackled with the same tiny lightning bolts from the river. Then Uncle Frank stood up to unlock the wardrobe. He pulled out a black box and gave it to Thao. She flipped it open, pulled back the tissue paper, and held up a long and elegant gown made from electric blue sequins.

"For the heist," said Uncle Frank. "I had my tailor make it special for you."

Episode Ten.

I lay on the scooter grease-smelling couch, but sleep would not come. The séance at the river had traumatised me. Or should I say what I saw in the séance at the river – images of an idyllic childhood – had traumatised me. As I stared at the dark, I felt like a tiny person in an oversized world. The shadows of the furniture loomed over me. Breath was hard to come by, my heart beat fast then slow then fast. I know what you're thinking. Silly Apollo. It was a panic attack. Poor thing. Poor little Apollo. Poor boy. Get up and walk that shit off. Silly goose. Baby boy. But this was no panic attack. I've had panic attacks, and I've been the one shouting, 'I'm having a panic attack!' when I wasn't having a panic attack. So I know.

I left the house and walked the streets alone. The odd scooter puttered past, incense smoke drifted down from an open window. After an hour on my feet, I felt no change in my emotional state. She might have been giving me monosyllables, but I needed her, so I called Nhu. It went to voicemail. Fuck it, I thought. She already saw me as a desperado, might as well go deeper in the hole. I found a motorbike taxi and raced over to Saigon Pearl, where I got lucky. I snuck into the lobby behind a drunk couple, then I took the fire stairs down to the car park, and knocked on her door. She opened it a crack. Heavy bags hung from her eyes, her nostrils were red and chaffed and her hair resembled an abandoned bird's nest. I could smell the skunk, and see her truck on the screen behind her.

"What do you want?"

"Can you come for a walk?"

"No."

"Please. I just found out some fucked up shit."

"What."

"Can you just come out."

"Come inside."

"I can't. I need to keep moving. If I go in there I'll sink into the floor and lose my mind."

She looked at me like a bug she wanted to squish. "Give me a minute," she said, and shut the door.

Forty minutes later she opened the door, looking like she was on her way to front row seats at Paris Fashion Week. The heavens opened back up. We huddled close and headed down to the river, rain lashing her black Chanel umbrella. She told me that her show – *REAP WHAT YOU SEW* – got shut down. One day a man in a suit turned up at the gallery, flanked by four armed policemen, to inform her of her government's special relationship with companies like Uniqlo and H&M. As she was so flagrantly insulting these companies, she was also insulting her government, and could shut the show down voluntarily or face the consequences.

"My career is over."

"It's never over."

"I don't know what to do now."

"Come to Cambodia with me. Do the heist."

"That's your dumb boy thing. You want to die over there?"

"I'll be fine if you come with me."

"Are you so dumb?"

"I'm pretty dumb."

"You can just run away. Back home to Sydney. What about me?"

"Come with me."

She looked at me like she wanted to slap me. I kind of hoped she would. Her hands were wet from the rain, and it was sure to sting.

"You are the dumbest man I ever met. I can't go with you, stupid. I have a gallery. I just need a new show, that's all."

We walked along the river. The rain bombarded the water, churning up weeds and mud, but the air was warm and smelled of jasmine. But that might have been Nhu's hair. I told her about the séance, and the tender moments I saw in my childhood – the reading, the caring, the playing and the holding close. "Why did you say it was fucked up? That sounds nice." I told her the story of the real Oscar. The man I knew as the father of the boy Apollo.

Oscar was a top restaurant man. A man who made heavenly dishes from rabbit and salmon and sprouts, even jellyfish. The man was gifted. The man was a broad-shouldered man, with a round, tight-skinned stomach, and wild black curls that sat on his head like some all-knowing insouciant creature. In the kitchen, when the mercury was high, he stripped down to his white underwear and a pair of yellow leather sandals that were made for him by a German cobbler named Hans. Hans was a minor detail, the stomach was not.

He wore no apron, letting the oil and the red hot stove-tops burn him, letting blades pierce and slash the skin, so that after years of working shirtless in the heat, his massive gut was cross-hatched with scars and nicks and burns and sizzles. He was famous for his pavlova, a cake he spent years crafting to perfection. He spent five years on the meringue, another three searching for the perfect kiwifruit to slice and place on top. The man was obsessed.

I loved to help him the kitchen. To wash dishes, watch him work, and once, watch him hold a knife to the throat of a half-blind kitchen hand. One day he catered a party – the fiftieth birthday of a local politician. At the age of seven, I was handed the important task of carrying the pavlovas from the kitchen, through the restaurant, and out to his red van to be driven to the party. So, with the first dreamy smelling pavlova in my arms, I sauntered through the restaurant, but found the front door shut. If I moved a hand from the bottom of the pav, it would fall, so I placed the cake on the ground and pulled open the door. The second the base touched the ground, Oscar came steaming round the corner with a bowl of tamarillo sauce in his hands, stepped in the pav, skidded, and sent the bowl of sticky pink sauce onto his face and neck. His rage was incandescent. He yanked off his belt and lashed my arms and legs and back and tummy. But I knew I had done wrong, that I needed to be punished. And so as the frenzy of leather on skin reached fever pitch, I screamed:

"I deserve it! I deserve it! I'm sorry I deserve it!"

That time his rage was volcanic, but other times it took on a quietly sadistic tone. In these more hushed moments, when I had done wrong, he took me to the bathroom and pointed to the three hooks on the wall where hung his three razor strops. A razor strop is a leather belt used for sharpening ye olde cut throat razors. The ones on our bathroom wall were ranked by their level of thickness – one being the thickest, three in the middle, and five the thinnest. My role in this fun game was to choose which one I wanted him to whip me with.

These stories of violence and rage, of cowering in corners and screaming that I deserved to be whipped – they formed my central narrative. They shaped me at my core. I told these tales of abusive woe over and over and over, to any set of ears that would listen. They were who I was. Before the séance, I could not name a single time Oscar had been kind to me. Had taken me in his arms or played a game with me or made me feel loved. But if Thao had dredged them up from the murky depths of my subconscious, then maybe they happened. Maybe I had repressed the tender moments in order to turn Oscar into a monster that suited the story I thought I wanted my life to be. Maybe he was a loving father, and the cruel and violent man I knew was but a work of fiction.

Episode Eleven.

The day of the heist. I woke up on the island, Nhu's arms and legs entwined in mine. Soft jets of air shot in and out of her left nostril. A flutter under her eyelids. She had never done this. Hugged me like this. Most nights she perched on the edge of the bed, her face in the wall. Maybe she didn't want to fuck my corpse in the jungle after all. Maybe she wanted me to stay on the island with her. I lay deathly still, listening to the gentle patter of a bug crawling up the wall, committing the feeling of her skin on mine to memory, the look of her sleeping black lashes. Then I got a text from Thao:

> Hello Apollo, I am sorry but I must return to my job in Thailand today. I have made peace with my father. I think this will be the reason I come home after all? I do not think the heist is the reason. Please be safe okay. My spirit flies with you.

This messed me up. Big time. She had destabilised my central narrative and sent all kinds of shock waves reverberating through my psyche. She had peered into the shady ravines of my soul, and had seen what made me tick. And that was precisely why I needed her. If I walked into the casino and my mind started to unspool, she was the only one who knew how to respool that shit. There was also her magnetism. Her undeniable power. I mean, if you were heisting a casino in the heart of the jungle, you'd want a supernatural being at your side too. But what could I do. I was way past the point of pulling out. I rolled off the island and into the shower. When I was done, I found Nhu laying out an outfit for me on the bed. Navy chinos, a short-sleeved green shirt with flowers printed on it, and loafers made from aubergine-hued suede. "Do you like it?" she asked. "No," I said. "I bloody love it." She told me to put it on. The pants and the shirt felt fine, but the second I slid my feet into the expensive-smelling leather of the loafers, I felt a rush of confidence. I no longer had Thao's other worldly powers, but at least I was taking Nhu's aesthetic excellence. Once I was fully clothed, she kissed me. The entire time our lips were touching, I felt as though space and time did not exist. I was no longer a person in an underground apartment, but a blissful amoeba swimming about in the life-giving fluid in the molten womb of the world.

Nhu drove me through the roaring morning traffic, and gave me one last kiss as she let me off outside Uncle Frank's house. Inside, with Uncle Frank and Anhtheman, I sat for one final meeting at the table near the polished wardrobe. They were both on edge. Anhtheman sanitized his hands like his life depended on it. Uncle Frank got up five or six times to iron and re-iron a crisp white shirt. Then he slapped a photo on the table: a man with high cheekbones and a top knot.

"That's Sam," I said. "One of the blackjack dealers."

"What happens when you bluff?"

"My earlobes quiver."

"When you have a good hand?"

"I tell the person next to me."

"Don't joke, tulip!!"

"Sorry. I make jokes when I get nervous."

"Nervous is good. Nerves make you sharp."

I climbed on the back of Anhtheman's motorbike, taking care not to scuff my purple suede loafers. We drove out of the city, through an endless grid of green rice fields. Ninety minutes later, our wheels rolled over the border into Cambodia. A long straight road shot us into the damp bowels of the jungle. Sinister life sounds leapt from dense trees, steam rose up from coiled vines. I knew an ancient Khmer civilisation had been found by shooting lasers into the ground. If I had a laser, and I shot it into the earth beneath our wheels, would I find a mystical city? I should have been an archaeologist. I would have been a top brush man. I would have worn great hats. I was distracted, that much was clear. Like a pre-pubescent rat with ADHD. Focus, Apollo! You've waited forever for this day – the day you get the story for the first season of the Untitled Original Series Set On Multiple Continents. I slapped my face. Punched my jaw. Anhtheman saw nothing. In my head I ran through the plan. My first table was Sam's – he of the top knot and high cheekbones. I felt like the hardest part would be getting in the door and to his table. Also taking the money to the pit. And going back in and winning more and taking that to the pit as well. Fuck. It was all hard. But hard was not impossible. I channelled the powers of Thao and Nhu combined. Then the jungle spat us out, and I saw the casino. It looked like a palace a Roman emperor married to a stripper might build – gold domes, pink marble columns, and a purple neon sign on the front that said HA TIEN VEGAS! But also men scampering up scaffolding, sheets of plastic flapping in the wind.

"Oh my gosh," said Anhtheman. "She is not finished."

We cruised up the dirt road, past some sort of shantytown, with makeshift buildings, fires burning in barrels and dogs sniffing in the mud for scraps of food. Through the open doors of huts I glimpsed pot-bellied men slap cards down hard on plastic tables. We stopped in the mud out front of the casino, not far from a crowd of shirtless men. Cigarettes hanging from their mouths, they stared at a golden crown the size of a house as it dangled from a crane in the darkening sky. A nervous-looking man sat in the booth of the crane pulling levers. The engine made a grinding sound, and the crown lurched and shook. He wanted to place the crown on the roof of the casino, but he sent it swinging out over the jungle, which made the crowd of shirtless men shout and run towards it, which spooked the crane man. And when he got spooked, he pulled on levers, which sent the crown hurtling back towards the wall of the casino, missing it by an inch. I got off the bike and Anhtheman hugged me, then he doused my hands in sanitizer. "This is my lucky germ killer," he said. "I will wait for you in the hut with the pit. Don't be scared. You are a warrior, Apollo Jones." He popped the sanitizer in my pocket, then raced back up the dirt road. In front of me I saw a path made from sheets of plywood. It took me over the mud, right to the mouth of the casino. Not a soul around. Maybe a dog sniffing around the trees. I made a mental note of an opening in the jungle – the path to the pit. Above my head the neon sign buzzed, beckoning me, so I walked up the steps and into the foyer. The walls and floor were made from white marble – high grade stuff. My footsteps echoed, and I smelled the dust of freshly cut tiles. "You're a whale," I whispered to myself. "The casino is in your belly." But that didn't stop my nerves from getting up in my face and making it sweat.

"Good evening, sir, do you like to win a new car."

A young woman in a red dress stood next to a white SUV wearing a massive red bow. Besides me, she was the only person in the foyer. She gestured to the car like a presenter on a game show, showing the contestants the prizes. I smiled at her and stepped into the main gambling hall, and was smacked in the face by the colour purple. Purple carpet, purple walls, purple felt on the card tables, purple leather on chairs and stools. There was no music, save for the clacking of chips and the dull thud of dice on felt. No crowds. Just a few gamblers scattered across the tables, and a startling number of them with comb-overs. Funny what you notice when your nerves are running a fever. Speaking of nerves, I could not see Uncle Frank, but I felt his eyes burning holes in me. At the bar, I ordered a ginger ale. As I walked between the tables, I sipped, savouring the spicy beads as they popped on my tongue. The gamblers held their cards at the ends of their noses, squinting at the smoke swirling up from the ends of cigarettes. A few looked up at me, but they paid me no mind. I tried to project an aura of calm. Like I was a whale gliding through the clear waters of my world. At a blackjack table out to my right, I saw a top knot and a set of high cheekbones.

Sam. My guy. Now was the time. I took a step in his direction and saw them: two guards, leaning on the wall, cradling AK-47s like sleeping babies. One of them turned to scan the room, and I got a look down the barrel of a gun that fired skull-shattering bullets. This was no story, this was real. In that moment the juice drained out of me. I saw the stupidity of my mission. The dumbass danger. If Thao and her powers had been with me, maybe, but alone I was a dead man walking. My sweat glands exploded. Air stopped entering my lungs. A swarm of bees flew in my ear. As I feared, the centre did not hold. I was too destabilised. Like an old video tape that had been recorded over one too many times, the threads of my mind unravelled, rolled across the floor and down the drain to the sewer, which might have been where they belonged.

Now this was a panic attack.

I kicked open the bathroom door. An oldish man came at me. The muscles in his face looked to be sliding around under the skin. He yelled at me. I did not understand his words, but there was worry in his tone. But I was in no mood for human warmth, so I stuck my face under the cold tap. My goal was to stay under the running water for all eternity. But I forced myself to pull my face out. When I looked in the mirror, I did not see a person looking back at me, but a blurry pixelated mess. Was this a person or a thing? Why was their shirt soaked with sweat? What was that sound coming from the hole in the place where their face was meant to be? What were they doing in a casino in the jungle? I needed a hug. So I crawled to the nearest cubicle, and wrapped my arms around the base of the toilet bowl. My heart beat so hard it nearly cracked the porcelain. I heard him. Uncle Frank. Was he in my ear for real? Or deep in my tormented head. "Get up, you weak tulip! Get up or I will take your limbs!"

I walked back out to the casino floor. All the colours ran together, like an oil painting left out in the rain. The purple of the tables bled into the red chips, the blacks of men's hair mixed with green eyeshadow. I ran for the nearest door, which took me into the kitchen. Pots boiling. Flames leaping. Chefs yelling. Hell, in other words. I ran down a dark hallway, burst through a door, and saw the steaming buzzing jungle coming for my face.

Episode Twelve.

My feet could barely walk, but they had to walk. They had to run. I had to reach the steamy safety of the jungle. Uncle Frank was coming for me. He would hurt me. Cook my testicle flesh on the base of his iron. I could smell it. At least he kept it clean.

I staggered up the road. Past the dogs and the huts with men playing rowdy games inside. Small children came at me from all angles, selling loose cigarettes and hotel-sized bottles of shampoo and conditioner. My brain was in a fog. Was I in Oscar's kitchen? In the river with Thao? On the island? Back in the boardroom in the clouds? I will say this – in the past I had felt alone. After the razor strop whippings I felt alone. But out there on that dirt road, with nothing but dense jungle stretching further than the eye could see, and men wanting me dead coming after me, I came to know the true meaning of the word alone.

"Apollo!"

I ran.

Well, I thought I was running, but it was more of a shuffle. A mud shuffle. My right kneecap felt like it was hanging on by a string of bone marrow.

"Apollo wait!"

Anhtheman. I could tell by the tone of his voice he was not mad, but maybe he was only pretending not to be mad so I would stop.

"Are you okay? What happened?"

"I fucked up. I'm sorry. I'm a bad tulip."

"Don't be sorry. Are you okay? You're hurt."

"Let me go back in. I'm ready. Put me back in the game."

He lay me down in a ditch on the side of the road and ran back to the casino, which was now a haze of purple neon rising up from the jungle. Lying in the ditch, I pictured the ancient cities that lay buried beneath me. From my aching body, I fired lasers into the earth, in the hopes that I could make contact with a civilisation more sophisticated than my dumb-arse. A single white headlight wobbled up the road. Anhtheman lifted me onto his bike and drove us into the night. There were flashing lights, and horns, and voices. But the drive back to Saigon is a piece that is missing from my mind. I came to in Uncle Frank's room, sitting at the table near his wardrobe. Anhtheman stood in a shadow by the door, Uncle Frank sat across from me. He looked calm. But the whites of his eyes had turned sepia, and that meant a deep and profound rage was surging through his veins.

"I want to kill you, tulip," said Uncle Frank. "You are lucky my nephew likes you so much."

I looked at Anhtheman. I had never been the biggest fan of his chirpy approach to life, but in that moment it would have been a welcome ray of light. He frowned at the floor. "You took much from me," Uncle Frank went on, "so I must take from you. Then we are okay. Okay?"

"Not really okay."

"It's okay."

"Is it okay?"

"It's okay."

"Okay. But what will you take?"

He walked to the wardrobe, and took out the silver jewellery box where he kept his rings. Opening the box, he placed it on the table in front of me.

Ruby rings, gold bands, emeralds and sapphires sat in the red felt lining. I hadn't noticed, but my right hand lay flat on the clean white tablecloth. Uncle Frank placed a hand on my wrist, pinning it with superhuman strength. I did not see the knife, but I felt the blade slice through my pinkie finger. Right above the bottom knuckle. In truth it was more of a crunch. And my brain blocked most of it out. It happened so fast, was so shocking, so surreal, that I was unable to register the extent of the visceral damage. Uncle Frank picked up the severed and blood-dripping pinkie, and held it in front of my eyes. "If you talk about the heist, if I hear of it in any place, I will take more from you. Okay, tulip?" He placed the finger in his jewellery box, so it sat among the emeralds and rubies and sapphires. I hated to admit it, but the finger looked happy. Like it belonged. A jewel among jewels. That's when I noticed the blood, pumping from my stump in a long arch, soaking the white tablecloth. I felt outside of myself. Anhtheman pounced. Ripping the cloth from the table, he wrapped my hand up tight and held it over my head. "Are you okay?" asked Uncle Frank. "Do you feel much pain?" He looked at me with what I can only describe as immense empathy, and this, combined with the shockwaves radiating through my system, left me more than a little confused.

The pain hit me in the taxi on the way to the clinic. My hand felt like it had been held in a blast furnace. Lava bubbled under the skin. Tentacles of molten fire slithered up my arms. My stomach felt hollowed out, like I was peering over the edge of a mile-high cliff. I was constantly on the verge of screaming and shitting and vomiting, but all I got out was a whimper. Then I was in the clinic, looking into the eyes of a doctor with a perfect bob haircut. She understood the whimper, and she shot me up. The morphine did what morphine does so damn well. I had to hand it to Anhtheman and Uncle Frank, they took me to the fanciest clinic in all Saigon. Very plush. With nice plants and subtle piano tunes tinkling from hidden speakers. They really made me feel special.

"What happened here?" asked the doctor.

"I like your hair."

"Thank you. They said you fell off your bike."

"Not many people can pull off a bob, but you sure can."

"Where is the finger?"

"I will never have a haircut like yours."

She smiled at me like she might a sweet old dog, then she lay me down, ushered Uncle Frank and Anhtheman from the room, injected me with more numbing needles, and did what she could for my stump.

In a taxi, Uncle Frank and Anhtheman took me back to their house in the dead of night. Or the middle of the day. I had no idea. My brain was buried in the silt at the bottom of a great body of water. My arm was bandaged, pinned to my chest in a sling. When we got back to the house, Auntie had laid the table with an impressive spread. I was sure she smiled at me, but that might have been the morphine talking. Seeing all that food made me miss Thao. Had she been at the heist with her powers, it would have been a different beast. I might still have all my fingers. We sat down. Anhtheman poured me a glass of Coke, and Uncle Frank winked at me, as if to say: 'No hard feelings, tulip. You took my retirement fund but I took your finger. We may never see each other again after tonight, so enjoy this meal, and know we are even.'

Episode Thirteen.

My hotel room was black. But all rooms are black in the dead of night aren't they. Nothing new there. I stood at the window, staring at the city curled in its slumber. Straining my eyes, I tried to see all the way to Uncle Frank's house, where my finger lay in his jewellery box. Then I tried to see across the border, into the jungle, where I lost my baby, the casino heist story, the first season of the Untitled Original Series Set On Multiple Continents. I saw nothing, so I packed my bag (not easy when you're down a digit, with one arm bandaged fat) and rode the elevator down to the street, where I got on the back of a motorbike taxi and sped through ghostly pools of streetlamp light. Occasionally we passed an old man with a speaker attached to his pushbike that said: 'banh chung, banh gio.' Otherwise the city was silent.

As we closed in on the airport, the stump of my severed finger went cold and numb. It felt like it was shrivelling up. Turning black. Was it trying to tell me something? Was it sad about leaving a part of itself behind? I asked the driver to turn back, and the second he swung the front wheel around, my stump tingled, as if magical healing water was trickling into it. That's when I knew. My stump was like a water diviner, but it sensed the whereabouts of stories. The casino story was dead and buried, but the city teemed with a million potent stories, and the stump was pointing me in their direction. We drove back into the city, my stump singing and buzzing with delight. At the hotel, the front desk staff let me have my old room back. I sat on the bed, watching the apricot sun rise over the city. I felt at home. In the sense that feeling like I had no home felt like home to me. I also knew I had nothing to fear from Uncle Frank. He had taken my finger, and would leave the rest of me alone.

Also, Nhu.

I wanted to go back to the island. I wanted to kiss for hours, tangled up in her sheets. I wanted to feel her tongue on my crooked teeth, to smell her freshly washed socks. I wanted her to tell me to go into the bathroom and not come out until she told me to. And while sitting on the toilet and waiting to be told to come out, I wanted to listen to her driving her trucks across Europe. Making deliveries. Building the grandest fleet the world had ever seen. But she didn't answer my calls. Or my text messages. Or my messages to WhatsApp or Facebook or Instagram or Myspace. Jokes. She didn't have Myspace. But if she did I would have messaged her there. I went to STATION, but it was closed. The message was clear. She had asked me to stay. Not with words, but by wrapping her legs around me and trying to keep me close as we slept. With her body, she asked me to stay with her on the island and not go to Cambodia, and I, an idiot, had gone. But why had she closed the gallery? Was she on holiday? Maybe she ran off with a real filmmaker. What I needed was my own island. If I was to find a new story for the first season of the Untitled Original Series Set On Multiple Continents, I needed a permanent base of operations. A quick Google search turned up a real estate agency called VN Rent. They had some fine listings. Furnished two bedroom numbers in District 1, a stone's throw from the river. And the prices weren't bad. I sent a message, and a man named Hung arranged to meet me at a place called Idol Bar in Japantown.

I had never been to Japantown, but right away I loved it. I walked down

Le Thanh Ton street, and turned into an alleyway that took me into a maze of alleyways that took up a sizeable city block. It was like finding a forgotten part of Tokyo. Lanterns hung on wires above my head, giving the night a warm orange glow. Scooters slipped past me. I walked past sushi restaurants, ramen joints, bathhouses, a darts bar, a bar that was also a driving range, and a female ninja themed restaurant, all with blue and pink and yellow neon signs buzzing out front. As I ventured further into the maze, the alleyways grew narrower, and I passed more hostess bars. It was still early, so the girls sat on crates out the front, scrolling on their phones, wearing nurses' uniforms and flight attendant uniforms. A girl with dyed yellow hair applied red lipstick in the wing mirror of a parked motorbike. Deep in the intestinal system of the maze, I found Idol Bar. Purple neon tubes ran along the wall behind the bar, so it was like stepping onto the set of a film about robots that learn how to love. Seven or eight hostesses sat in a line at the bar, and they turned as one to look me up and down.

"Apollo."

A very tall and thin man stood up from the table. He wore a billowy white shirt and suit pants that flapped about his ankles. As he extended a hand, I noticed his arms were skinnier than mine, but his hands were not of the same quality. Then I saw that he had all his fingers.

"You must be Hung."

He pointed at my bandage. "What happened to your hand?"

"Motorbike."

"Oh yes. You must be careful. Saigon roads is very dangerous. Many people die."

I sat next to Hung. A hostess placed a large fruit platter on the table – mango, pineapple, lychee, dragonfruit, oranges and grapes.

"Are you hungry? Eat some fruit."

As Hung showed me apartments on his iPad, I devoured the fruit platter. I ate every last sweet and juicy piece. When it was done, the hostess took away the empty tray, and replaced it with a fresh platter. I went to work on that one too.

"You love the fruit!" said Hung.

"These apartments are expensive."

"You are a modern professional. You must have the best. What if you meet a beautiful lady?"

The hostesses smiled at me. The penny dropped. Oh well. At least I was getting free fruit.

"Do you have anything cheaper?"

Hung looked dejected. "If that is what you want."

He showed me twenty more apartments, and I ploughed through the second fruit platter. As I popped the last lychee in my mouth, my phone buzzed. A message from Nhu. *I left Saigon now. I don't know when I will return. I don't want to see you. Don't contact me. I don't want you.* My stomach rumbled. Then it churned. It roared and squeaked so loud the line of hostesses turned to stare at me. I dashed out the door, ran to the far side of the alleyway, ducked my head behind a parked scooter, and vomited a technicolour waterfall of half-digested fruit. It was like a dam breaking. A truly biblical amount came gushing out of me. I sounded like a grizzly bear possessed by demons. It was as if all the trauma from the last month or so – losing my job, losing my central narrative, losing the heist story, losing my finger, losing Nhu – got ejected out of me in an epic purge. The hostesses poked their heads out the door. Most laughed, some covered their mouths, one handed me a napkin. I wiped my mouth, my bile tasting of apricot. It was not unpleasant. As I staggered up the alley, Hung called after me: "Apollo! Look here! Two bedrooms and a pool, by the river!"

I turned into a second alley, then a third alley, which led me to a dead-end alley. At the end of this alley I found a pitch black bar. No lights, the odd candle maybe. Using my hands, I found the bar, then a stool, where I sat my arse down. "Whisky dry, thanks." The barman lit a candle, placing it on the bar in front of me, next to my drink. The golden liquid glowed. Bubbles rose to the surface, where they popped, sending sweet aromas into the air. Momentarily this masked the smell of the bar, which was one of sex and stale sweat, and pills that stop your arteries from hardening. I hadn't had a drink in seven years, and the last one did not go well. I had vomited into a puddle, then fell face first into the puddle, where I drowned in the puddle water and the contents of my own stomach. A stranger walking past pulled me out and gave me CPR, but I was legally dead for about a minute. The barman lit more candles, and I lifted the glass to my quivering lips. That's when I saw the beasts. Old white men with ruddy faces and purple turnip noses. They belched and leered, shooting reptilian tongues in and out of arid lips. Those tongues! Pink and wet and covered in that chalky coating that Chinese doctors say means you're sick. Not sick as in cool sick as in terminally ill. They groped at girls wearing scraps of red and black lace as dresses. And the girls bounced from lap to lap, giggling, milking retirement funds for every last cent.

A purple-haired young woman with round glasses sat next to me. "You want to go upstairs?" Without taking a sip, I put the drink down. Then I walked out into the maze. But I went back. Oh boy did I go back. I strolled into the maze every night, orange lanterns bobbing above my head, judging me. I pretended to be in the market for sushi, maybe some seafood pancakes. But I went deeper. Past the bar with the girls in the nurses' uniforms, the bar with girls in flight attendants' uniforms, the bar with girls on roller skates. This bar was harder to walk past. The girls skated in circles around me, going faster and faster, until all I saw was a blur of pink and white fabric and long flowing black hair. "Hello handsome!" "Buy me a drink!" "Try our delicious fruit platter!"

The first two nights I did not set foot in a single bar. Mr. self-control. On the third night I walked into a bar and stood in the corner, sipping Coke like some brooding loner. I watched the women take the chalky-tongued men upstairs. I was not like them. No sir. I was no sex tourist. I did not wear sandals and socks, or a money belt, or cargo shorts or a Bintang singlet over biceps gone to bags of cottage cheese. I did not slaver over flesh that hated me in its bones. And yet there I was, in the bar, needing the seediness and the shame. It called to me like some twisted siren. Her name was Lan, the first woman who took me upstairs. The room had a single bed, a sink, a bedside table and a lamp with a lampshade smeared with forty years of finger grease. We sat on the bed, sipping Cokes. She wanted it to be over and it soon was. I paid her, lay back on the bed, watched her swirl water in her mouth and spit. Back in the maze, the guilt was immense. It sprouted on the back of my neck, then spread all over like a million hot prickles on my skin. I wanted to run but my feet said no. I needed to fill the empty pit in my stomach. Even though I knew that filling the pit made me feel emptier, and I'd have to go back and fill it with more emptiness. At the next bar, a woman named Vy took my body upstairs. Same deal: single bed. Lamp. Lampshade grease.

"What do you want?"

"Do you have any video games?"

She laughed. "You like games?"

"Have you played Euro Truck simulator?"

"What's that?"

"You drive a truck around Europe, delivering things."

"What things?"

"Like shoes, and washing machines, cars."

"This is a bad game."

The next night, I walked into a bar called Moon Bar, which had nothing to do with the moon. A woman named Joy took me by the hand and led me up to a room with a tiny bathroom off to the side.

"Can you tell me to go in the bathroom and not come out?"

"You need the toilet?"

"I want you to shut me in the bathroom."

"Why?"

"It's just... what I want."

She shut me in the bathroom. I sat on the toilet, waiting to be told I was allowed to come out. But telling someone to tell you what to do is not the same as that person taking pleasure in telling you what to do.

Most nights I roamed the maze, skittering up and down the alleyways, bouncing off the walls like a pinball. One night I bumped into Hung, the real estate agent.

"If you like it so much here in Japantown, you can live here."

"Show me an apartment worth renting and I'll rent it."

He took me to a building in a back corner of the maze. We walked up three flights of sweaty stairs, to a room with a double bed, an air con unit, a desk, a tiny bathroom and a bar fridge with a gas stove on top. The rent was wonderfully cheap.

"I'll take it."

Episode Fourteen.

Sweating through my socks and my shirts and my underwear, I spent my days walking the city streets. I walked miles down Tran Hung Dao, way past Cho Lon. I walked along canals, under bridges, into new developments where Teslas sat on the curbs, their engines idling. My brain was like a pack of rodents fighting over food pellets. I was plagued by images of Thao in her robes, Oscar's scarred belly, my finger lying with Uncle Frank's ruby rings, the purple felt on the card tables, the mole on the left side of Nhu's ribcage, the scenes I wrote on cards, and what I imagined (and would probably never know) the inside of an HBO boardroom looked like as I was handed a deal for the Untitled Original Series Set On Multiple Continents. To fight my way out of this loop, I focused on the details of the city that I saw on my walks: The mess of powerlines tangled on every pole, the smell of oil, and ginger, and dried squid, the navel-high piles of socks for sale on the street in Cho Lon, the air con units busting out a million windows, and the patterned tiles on the sidewalks. Also, I downloaded a Vietnamese language app to my phone. And as I plodded the broad boulevards and the narrow hems, I murdered words with my barbaric take on tonal complexity:

Bạn làm nghề gì?

What do you do?

Bạn đã làm một công việc tuyệt vời!

You did a great job!

Tôi nên đi ngủ sớm vì ngày mai tôi có việc

I should go to sleep early because I have work tomorrow

On my fifth day on my feet I saw him. The Hey Man Guy. He was in Ben Thanh Market, walking past a woman as she sliced open the belly of a pig that hung by a chain from the ceiling. "Hey man," he said, as blood and guts gushed from the pig and swirled down the drain. He only said these two words, but I heard his Kiwi accent, and I've always had a thing for long flat vowels. The next night the air was mushy, and the city seemed to be wading through sludge. As I walked through Tao Dan Park, slowly, he road past on a bike with a wicker basket on the handlebars. "Hey man," he said. The light may have been scarce, my senses dulled by the heat, but I saw that he was tall and that he used his limbs in elegant ways. His eyes were kind. The kind of eyes that had seen bad things done to innocent people. Also, he wore his black hair slicked back on his head, with black jeans and a white tee with extra short sleeves. The whole look gave off a 50s vibe that I was into.

On a white hot day, I saw him sitting on a bench outside The Rex Hotel. "Hey man." A rainy afternoon, as I stomped up the stairs of a communist apartment block that had been transformed into a mecca for tiny cafes and clothing stores, he came walking down. "Hey man." Was he working with Anhtheman and Uncle Frank? Was he friends with Nhu? I once saw him on the balcony at L'usine, reading a book as scooters beeped on the road below. I ordered an éclair and took a table inside, from where I studied the fine dark hairs on his forearms, the way he scratched the patch of skin behind his right ear before he turned a page. His hands were even more beautiful than mine (pre amputation) but rather than envy him, I wanted to know him. He looked up from his book, saw me staring, and through the glass, he silently said, "Hey man."

Night time. I was an hour or two into my stray dog routine, roaming the streets of District Three. I passed a tall building with a pink and yellow neon sign above the door that said KARAOKE KINGDOM. And when I peered in the glass doors, I saw him sitting behind the front desk. The Hey Man Guy. My heart made a noise like a dog getting kicked in the guts. He hadn't seen me, so I walked around the block strategizing an entry point into his life. In the end I went with the first thing that popped into my head. And so, heart juddering, dry scalp itching, I walked in the door and up to the counter.

"Hey man."

"Hey. I need a room to sing karaoke."

"Just for you?"

"No, no, no…. No, my friends will be here soon. A whole bunch of them. Maybe twelve."

"Cool man, I can give you the Versailles room, or the Olympus room. The Louis Vuitton room is free as well."

He slid a laminated menu over the counter. I looked at the photos of the rooms. Never before had I seen such baroque décor.

"I'll take the Versailles room."

"Cool, what name should I put the booking under?"

"Apollo."

"Hey Apollo, I'm Anaru."

"Hey man."

He led me into a gold-plated elevator. The doors closed. And the air seemed to get sucked from my lungs and down the shaft. When you meet a momentous person, mundane details take on profound meaning. Did the way he glanced at his watch say he was bored and wanted to escape? Or did it say he wished his shift were over so he could sit and chat with me until the sun rose over the river and said: 'Look who's getting on famously, you boys might be soulmates.' Why was I so nervous? Was I attracted to him? Probably. He was super handsome, with his black jeans and his white tee and his army boots scuffed to perfection. But it was more than that. I wanted him to be my friend. Lord knows I needed one. And with friendship there's often more at stake than with a romantic relationship.

"You're Aussie right?"

"Yeah, from Sydney."

"My Mum was from Sydney."

"Whereabouts?"

"Paddington."

"Nice."

"She said it's a shit-hole."

"It is."

"You just said it was nice."

"It's a nice shit-hole.

"Hm."

"You're a Kiwi?"

"Yeah bro, from the Far North. A nice little shit-hole called Kororareka."

The Versailles room was modelled on the palace, but with gold walls, gold floor tiles, gold lions crouched on gold plinths, and gold couches with white satin pillows. Oil paintings of old kings and queens were framed with gilt, and the ceiling was circled with white and gold neon tubes. It was an all-out assault. I shielded my eyes from the glare.

"Pretty crazy right? My boss designed it."

"I kind of love it."

He looked at my bandaged hand. "You come off your bike?"

I hadn't noticed until then, but my stump was throbbing. Maybe it was doing its water diviner thing. 'What is it boy?' I wanted to ask my stump. 'You smell a story nearby? Or are you just infected.'

"I tried to open a coconut with an axe."

"Smart."

Handing me several remote controls, he showed me how to work the TV and the karaoke machine and the air con. In the pocket of his black jeans his phone buzzed.

"I gotta run," he said, checking the screen. "I'll bring your friends up when they get here. Just shout if you need anything."

On the couch, the white satin pillows slipped around under my bum. A massive gilt-framed TV took up the wall in front of me. I pointed the remote at the screen, and scrolled through songs in Vietnamese, songs in Chinese and songs in English. What was my plan? Sit on the golden couch and sing by myself? I had no friends. No cavalry coming over the hill. I was stuck in the Versailles Room, alone with my loneliness. Anaru was probably in his office, watching me on CCTV, laughing with his staff, who loved him for being such a cool and kind boss who was really more of a friend and mentor. To avoid turning into a frothing pile of pure anxiety, I watched a music video. The song was DOI KHI, by NODEY. The video was a contemporary meets traditional dance art piece. It reminded me of Nhu, so I skipped to the next one. WAN FANG, said the title, NEW EV-ERLASTING LOVE. Was this a sign? The lyrics and piano melody of the song were syrupy, designed to make you long for a love you'd never have, or regret cheating on your ex with a person that made you feel like you were bad in bed. Or maybe that was just me. The video was about a couple on the rocks. They argued in the kitchen, slammed doors and wept on buses (heads resting on rain-speckled windows, obvs). She was a nurse, and he was the kind of man who wore a waistcoat over a shirt with no collar. He wasn't happy with the long hours she worked at the cancer ward. He want-ed more, so she gave him more. They swung on swings in the rain. Things were looking up. But I guess more wasn't enough, because he packed his saxophone into its special case, and got on a train that left in the dead of night, which is the only way those waistcoat dudes know how to leave. The pain got so bad she let one of her patients die, which was bad because you knew she was a truly great nurse.

After two more videos, Anaru opened the door. His outfit was different. He still wore his white tee, but with black running shorts and white socks, and a pair of dove grey Adidas. He didn't mention my zero friends, my pathetic attempt to appear un-alone. "I'm going for a run in the park," he said. "Then I might grab some noodles from this place that makes them by hand. You keen to join?"

Episode Fifteen.

Located deep in the bowels of the maze, Smile Bar was not popular with the crusty old white men. The Japanese businessmen, however, were big fans. Wearing creaseless khaki slacks, golf caps, mafia style polo shirts and shiny white sneakers (all items I coveted) they lined the bar, happily sipping watered down whisky.

SMILE! Said the sign on the wall behind the bar. Whoever made the letters of the sign did so by winding fairy lights around green and gold tinsel. It was not without its charms. Beneath the sign was a shelf, and on this shelf was a pink stereo and a stack of CDs. Smile Bar was owned and operated by a woman named Blossom, who spent most of her time perched on a stool behind the bar, filing her (sometimes blue and sometimes green) nails into daggers. Once upon a time she had been the singer of a mildly successful karaoke band, and the CDs were strictly 80s and 90s classics. She was deep into Pat Benatar and Bon Jovi, but Whitesnake was her favourite. *Here I go again* got played about seventy-nine times a day, the Japanese businessmen nodding their flushed faces along to the riff.

Since moving into my shoebox in the maze, I went to Smile bar several afternoons a week. But I never went upstairs. I sat at the bar and sipped

Coke, and shot pool, and chatted to Blossom about her favourite bands and her favourite TV family, The Kardashians.

"Kris needs to treat Kylie better," she would say.

"I think she should kick her out."

"No! How can you say this? Kylie is the number one sister."

"Chloe is the clear winner. Look what she's been through. And she has more personality. Kylie is a robot."

"I should kick *you* out! I *hate* Chloe. Kylie is the best."

One afternoon I was sitting at the bar swirling ice in my glass, when I saw a long fake eyelash lying in the grit on the tiled floor. I picked it up, and when I stood up, a young woman pointed a DSLR camera at my face. She wore white sneakers, cut-off denim shorts, and a Hawaiian shirt with lobsters printed on it. A solid outfit. 10/10. I had seen her in the bar before, but she never asked me to play pool, or to go upstairs. Most days she sat alone at the bar, sipping orange juice and watching what looked to be You-Tube tutorials on her phone. Click. Click click click. She shot me holding the eyelash in front of my right eye. "Hang!" yelled Blossom, pointing her nail file like a sword. "No photos down here! I told you!"

Hang took her camera up the stairs. I hung back for a second, then trotted up after her. Smile Bar was situated in a tall narrow building, with a wooden staircase zig-zagging up the middle. On the first floor landing, a young woman lay sleeping, her jet black hair spilling over the steps like a pool of ink. I stepped over her and Hang glared back at me.

"Why do you follow me?"

"I want to see the photos you took of me."

"You have to pay."

I shrugged.

Then she shrugged.

Then she walked up to the third floor and slipped through an open door. When I poked my badger face into her room (I don't have a badger face but snooping like that made me feel like some sort of badger so let's go with it) I saw a queen bed with red sheets, a sink, and an oval mirror hanging over the sink. Scooters beeped on the other side of sheer red curtains. Hang sat on the end of the bed, scrolling through the shots of me and the eyelash on the screen on the back of her camera.

"You should use some purple light."

"You should not tell me what to do."

"I like purple light."

"I don't care what you like."

"But I'm really good."

"Then why are you here?"

"I'm hiding."

"Hiding from what?'

"Everything."

She looked up at me.

"Go under the bed."

I crawled under the bed, where I stared up at the brown stains on the bottom of the mattress, and thought about the millions of DNA strands coiled in its fibres forever. "Now put your feet out," she said. I did as she said. Then I peered down the gap between my body and the bed, and saw her sneakered feet standing on either side of mine. Her camera clicked. She told me to come out and wash my face in the sink, and she watched me do it. She told me to do it again, but this time take off all my clothes except my socks. The nakedness didn't bother me, but my odd socks did. One was yellow and one was purple, and the purple one had a hole in the big toe and the nail peeking out needing cutting. She took a photo of this nail. It made me squirm. But I wanted to please her. To be a supple and obedient muse.

"Wash the hair on your chest."

"Place your toe to your stomach."

"Look out the window, with your eyeball touching the glass."

"Lie on the floor with the sock in your mouth. No, the yellow one."

Three hours, twenty seven poses, four hundred and ninety two clicks later, we sat on the bed, scrolling through the shots. It was like seeing myself as a newborn baby, or a very old and vulnerable man. Like looking at a version of myself I knew but was also a total stranger.

"Do you shoot photos of all your customers?"

"You are not customer."

"I know, but, I mean, all the men who come here."

"Not all."

"How many have you shot?"

"I don't know."

"Ball park."

"What?"

"Two hundred? One hundred?"

"Maybe one thousand."

"Do they like it?"

"Some like it, yes. Some no."

"Can I see?"

"Hm."

She pulled a MacBook out of a blue backpack and flipped it open. We looked at photos of young men, old men, obese men, skinny men, American men, Chinese men, Icelandic men and Syrian men. Men with disabilities, men missing toes, one missing an eye. I saw men with tattoos of their children on the backs, muscled men looking wounded, old and frail men with eyes that beamed out eternal life. They lay on the red sheets, on the tiled floor, wearing looks of post-coital bliss, looks of despair and warmth and fear and longing. In every shot she had captured a brutal truth the man had spent years trying to hide. I'm not afraid to say it, her photos made me weep. Looking at them was like peering through the bars of a cage that held a withered and scarred but still powerfully beating heart. The contents of my stomach (an iced coffee, a chicken banh mi and a choco pie) swirled around then dropped down a foot or so to the left. How had she done it? Did she have any training? Where had she come from? Armed with a lens, she had taken the power these men had over her and she had flipped it. I was in the presence of genius, that much I knew. "You ever show these in a gallery?" I asked.

"I don't think they will like it."

An idea formed in the slimy stem of my brain. She was my new main character. Her story – the sex worker who shoots photos of her customers and rockets to international art stardom – would be the arc of the first season of the Untitled Original Series Set On Multiple Continents. What an excellent show. A real watercooler type series. We're talking serious buzz. People would watch the shit out of a show like that. I saw it all so clearly, streaming into homes all over the world on HBO or Netflix. Created by Apollo Jones.

Episode Sixteen.

Anaru had a scooter, and her name was Gloria. Gloria was matte black, with dents and nicks and dings, and scratches and scrapes and cracked wing mirrors. But she was an exceptional machine. A bike with heart. I loved to sit on her cracked leather seat, behind Anaru, so I did just that for one week straight. He drove us out of the city – on a highway we shared with neon buses and thundering trucks – to the sand dunes at Mui Ne. The dunes were fine (lots of tourists on quad bikes) but I liked the drive there and back better. The hot wind. The way it dried out my eyeballs, turned my lips into cured ham skins. And the dust. How it coated my nostrils and made me sneeze black snot for a week.

He also showed me the hidden pockets of the city he loved – spots I would never find on my daily walks. He took me to his number one noodle shop, his favourite coffee shop, a dearly beloved vintage store, and an antique shop where the stock looked like it came from families who lost vast fortunes via poor investments. Here I bought a framed black and white photo of an elegant family sitting at the bottom of a grand old staircase, and even though Anaru called me a creep, I put the photo next to my bed, and gave Mum and Dad and the kids names and back stories, which I don't have time to go into right now but maybe later if you stick around and are good.

One night he called in sick to the Karaoke Kingdom, and took me to the President hotel, which was an abandoned apartment complex at 727 Tran Hung Dao. We parked Gloria in front of the blackened building, and Anaru paid a white-haired old man (who spoke to me in French) to let us in. We walked up thirteen flights of stairs, every one of them riddled with holes big and small. If your foot went through one of the holes, down you went to a black pit. And if the fall didn't kill you, the rats would sort you out. When we reached the roof, my shirt was so soaked with sweat it felt like I was wearing a backpack. But it was worth it. In the centre of the roof sat an old oval pool with a jungle growing around the stagnant rainwater collecting in the deep end. From up there you could see the entire city – rivers, glass towers, miles and miles of houses built on top of each other. On the edge, we sat with our feet dangling into oblivion, and Anaru told me all about The President Hotel. How construction commenced in the early 1960s, and the owner was warned about the bad juju associated with thirteen floors, but went ahead and made his baby thirteen floors. Bad shit went down right away – labourers falling into pits of wet cement, that sort of thing. To appease the angry spirits, the owner visited a local hospital, where he purchased the bodies of four dead virgins, and buried them at the four corners of the construction site. This got a big thumbs up from the ghosts. But in 1964 the US army rented out the entire complex to house their officer corps, who were their own special type of ghoul, and while partial to dead virgins, were much harder to appease. The complex was decommissioned in the early 2000s, but the locals claimed to still see the ghosts of a US officer and a young woman walking hand in hand down the dark corridors.

I don't know if you've ever experienced a romantic friendship, but all my friendships with men have resembled my romantic relationships with women. About an hour after meeting them I get obsessed with them, can't stop thinking about them and need to see them every second of every day. I have conversations with them in my head and spend hours picturing our future lives together. With Anaru it was no different. If I wasn't with him I wanted to be near him, and when I was with him I never wanted to leave his side. I was smitten. I admit it. Lying on my bed in my room in the maze, when my phone buzzed, I felt a mule kick the underside of my sternum. And when I saw his name on the screen, I grinned like a schoolgirl. Plus his message game was on point. And so you know I'm not making it up, here's some examples:

1. Haere mai ki te kai is Maori for come eat some food you skinny bitch (I made the skinny bitch part up)
2. I just saw a man eating a puke smelling durian in the street and thought of you.
3. Can I pull off a paisley silk scarf? Of course I can.

On the last day of our long week on Gloria, he took me to a record store in District Seven, where he dug through dusty crates for 35 inch reggae tunes. It was obvious he had a crush on the owner, a man named Jun. Jun was in his fifties, and so effortlessly stylish and handsome it hurt my eyes to look at him. He wore faded jeans with work boots, a white singlet, and his salt and pepper hair formed a perfectly ruffled wave on top of his finely shaped head. As we browsed the vinyl, I watched Anaru sneak looks at Jun over the tops of crates. I won't lie, I was jealous. Why didn't he have a crush on me? Was it due to my deformed hand? Because I wasn't a successful filmmaker? Maybe I needed people to love me more than I deserved to be loved. Oh well. Whatevs. Anaru paid for his records (cheeks flushing as he handed Jun the cash) we went for banh xeo, and to the roof of The President Hotel, where we sat on the edge and watched the blazing sun slide off the side of the earth.

"See that?"

He was pointing to a narrow road about a mile away. I squinted my eyes, but all I saw was a coffee stall and a computer repair shop.

"The coffee stall?"

"The dog chasing its bent tail."

"Have you got superhuman eyesight or what?"

"He reminds me of you. When I used to see you walking around the city all lost and shit."

"Sad."

"The saddest. Like me when I first got here."

He lit a cigarette, made a face like the cigarette said something offensive only he could hear, then he tossed it over the side. We watched it float down to the street, the wind lurching it left to right, and he told me the story of when he first came to Saigon.

Before he even stepped on the plane, in Auckland, a rock of dread was forming in his stomach. A rock the size of a marble. This was his first time on a plane, and the experience was not exactly pleasant. The cabin shook. People puked. The toilet doors banged, the overhead compartments flapped like the vessel was possessed, and the old woman next to him muttered feverish prayers while white-knuckling a string of rosary beads. Good times. By the time the wheels touched the tarmac, the rock of dread had grown to the size of a golf ball. He presented his passport to the customs official, who glared at him like he might be a master criminal, and the rock grew into a baseball. Sitting in the back of a taxi, speeding past scooters and buses and neon, and smelling smells he had never smelled before, the rock ballooned to a volleyball. A basketball. That's how big the rock was when he checked into the hotel. He was pregnant with dread. He made it to his room and locked the door and lay on the bed, stroking his dread baby. The hotel was called The Spring Hotel, on Le Thanh Ton. Anaru was in room 304. He did not leave his room.

The contents of the minibar – beer and nuts and chips and chocolate – he lived on them for three days. When they ran out, he moved onto room service. Ordering soups and pasta and salads and cakes. Through the peephole, he watched the staff knock on his door. "Hello. Your burger is here. Hello?" He told them to leave it on the floor, and when he was certain they had gone back down in the elevator, he opened the door and dragged his food inside. The room itself was not a bad room in which to become a shut-in. It had a small sunny window, and he sat by this window most days, tracking the movements of the family who lived in an apartment in the next-door building. In this family there was a father, a mother, twin girls, a boy and a grandfather. Anaru monitored the mundane details of their daily lives, taking notes on his phone. He knew the mother and father snuck into the kitchen to kiss like hungry teenagers. He knew that when a twin's shoe went missing, and the family spent hours searching, it was usually found in the other twin's backpack. And he knew how many times a day grandad told the boy to get off the computer (14). Most of all he liked the curmudgeonly closeness of the old man and the boy, but he felt connected to the family as a unit. They were his only human contact (if you could call it that) and he felt they anchored him to earth. Without them he felt he would drift off into the stratosphere. Plus he was pretty sure they were helping him to shrink the dread baby.

But the dread baby was an elusive baby.

A woman named Cam owned The Spring Hotel. She was a smart operator with numerous interests across several sectors (entertainment, optometry, a bakery that sold anime character cupcakes) but The Spring Hotel was her favourite. So when the manager told her some tourist had been locked in his room for over a month, that he took all his meals in there, dumped his dirty sheets in a ball in the hall and used the fresh ones the cleaners left folded by his door, she took a personal interest. "Hello? Are you there?" said Cam, banging on Anaru's door, which was actually her door. "I am the owner. Please come out? Are you sick? You need a doctor? Hello? Want me to call the police?" Anaru didn't answer. He lay on the bed, whispering to the dread baby, trying to convince it not to grow to the size of a beach ball, which it seemed hellbent on doing. He was low on cash. Gone were the orders for pasta and salad and cake and ice cream. He now limited his intake to a bowl of chips and three bread rolls per day. Placing the order in the morning, he ate a chip roll for breakfast, a chip roll for lunch and a chip roll for dinner. All washed down with water he boiled in the kettle. The dread baby thrived on this stodgy diet. It grew to the size of a swiss ball, which made it considerably harder for Anaru to go to the bathroom, or even get off the bed. Forget about sitting in the window and watching the Moon Unit Family (that was the name he gave them). All the while, Cam banged on the door. "Come try our new cocktail menu! Want us to break the door? We will get you a doctor. Or maybe you go to jail."

The room service orders dried up completely. The balls of dirty sheets and towels stopped getting dumped in the hall as if by a ghost in the night. The staff were spooked for real. What if the man in 304 had hanged himself? Who would clean it up? What if he had cursed them? What if he haunted the halls forever? They took turns sniffing at the crack under the door, checking for the unmistakable odour of a decomposing corpse. Cam had had enough. One day she walked in with an axe, handed it to the head chef and ordered him to break down the door. As he smashed the wood to splinters, she yelled at him to watch the frame, and to hurry up. She was eager to give this guy hell. As soon as the hole was big enough, she shouldered her way in the door. The room smelled of stale sweat and mouldy sheets, and some unnamed hormone. The kind that floods the brain during a psychotic break. Anaru lay naked on the sheets, his eyes cloudy, skin like paper, sharp bones fighting their way through weak layers of flesh. Cam came in furious, but the sight of him broke her heart. She was not a mother (her businesses were her babies) but looking at this poor man felt like looking at a child of her own.

On the roof of The President Hotel, Anaru lay back. I lay alongside him, and we watched the city lights turn the sky from peach to purple.

"What happened then? She took you to the hospital?"

"She moved me into her massive apartment. And gave me a job in the kitchen at the hotel. A year later she moved me to the front desk, then to the Karaoke Kingdom."

"She owns it?"

"Mmhmm."

"Damn."

I pulled out a cigarette.

"Don't light it."

"Why?"

"It's gross."

"So am I."

"True."

I put the cigarette back in the pack. "Who gave you the dread baby?"

"Uh, that's a super long story."

Episode Seventeen.

The rain hit the roof of the café hard. I looked out the window and into a wall of water. It was like sitting in one of those tunnels that take you through an aquarium – I half expected a stingray to fly past my face. Hang sat across from me, sipping iced coffee, looking at me like she wanted to see me face down in the lake-sized puddle outside. Her lips moved, but I heard nothing over the buffeting rain.

"Sorry, what?"

She rolled her eyes. As if on cue, the rain stopped.

"Why did you bring me here?"

"For your work."

"Bar work?"

"Your photos."

"What about."

"Why aren't they in a gallery?"

"I told you. They don't like it."

"So you tried?"

"No."

"Then how do you know?"

"Are you stupid?"

"Very."

The corners of her mouth turned up a millimetre, but before they could form the beginnings of a smile, she turned them back down.

"The people in a gallery, they see me as a bar girl."

"What if I help you."

"I don't want your help."

I put a GoPro camera on the table. She picked it up and looked at it, then she put on a big fake smile.

"For me?"

"It's great for weird angles. You can shoot your customers with it. Put it under the bed or on the ceiling fan or something."

She dropped it on the table. "I don't like it."

"I can get you meetings with galleries. I can help sell your work. I can–"

"I doubt."

"Why do you doubt?"

She rattled the ice at the bottom of her cup.

"That's what I do. That's my job. I sell–"

"What do you want?"

"I want your story."

"What story?"

"The story of your life. Where you come from. How you started working at the bar. How you started taking those amazing photos of your customers! I want to turn your story into a TV show."

"Like Game of Thrones."

"Bigger."

"I doubt."

"Listen this show won't just be on TV, it'll be on social media, in cinemas, it'll go all over the world. Shanghai, New York. I want your story to be the first season. I'll pay you, *and* I'll get you a show in a gallery."

"I don't care."

"You don't believe me?"

"No."

"You know Station, the gallery on Dong Khoi and Ly Tu Trong?"

"Yes."

"I know the owner, Nhu Nguyen."

"She's your girlfriend?"

"Not really."

"You have sex with her."

"No. Sort of."

"Tell me."

"We never had sex, but… she made me get her off."

"With your hand? Is this how you break it?"

"No. Listen. That's not important. Do you want a show with her or not?"

The rain started up again. She stared at the caramel liquid in the bottom of her cup. "I think you want something from me, so you say many things. Just like men at the bar. Please can I do this, let me do that. I buy you this ring, take you to the island. Too many lies."

Episode Eighteen.

Days. Two or three twenty-four hour periods. That's how long it took me to work up the courage to message Nhu. I thrashed about in bed, composing the kind of pithy texts I hoped would lure her onto her bike and into my arms. Then I deleted the texts. I went on my walks, composing and deleting and composing and deleting. Finally, I sat in a café across the street from September 23 Park, sipping coffee so nutty and strong it may have contained crack, and sent this bad boy: *Hey, I know you don't want me, and that's fine, but I need to borrow your art brain for one second. I met this genius photographer and I need to get her a show. Can you give me a gallery contact? I will be grateful to you until the end of time and will never ask you for anything ever.*

It should come as no surprise that she left me on 'read'. She knew how to make a mess in my head, and she got off on making that mess. She also knew that I would hear the buzz and jump out of bed in the dark and bang my shins on something hard, so she sent her reply at 4am the next morning: *Send me her photos. I will decide who is genius.*

That afternoon it rained. Then it stopped. Then it rained some more. Clutching two extra-large coffees, I walked into Smile Bar dripping wet.

Blossom sat behind the bar, filing her yellow nails into points. I said hi and she said hi, and then something about the Kardashians I didn't catch. I was already halfway up the stairs to Hang's room, where I found her washing her face in the sink. She looked in the mirror, saw me standing in the doorway smiling, and frowned. For the next three hours we sat on her red bed, scrolling through thousands of photos, while she ummed and ahhed and at times quietly raged over what shots to send to Nhu as a sample.

"What about these three?"

"I don't need your help."

"Okay I'll tell Nhu to forget about it."

"Don't be a fuck!"

Eventually, the bar downstairs filled up with horny, sunburned men. Blossom yelled up the stairs for Hang to start work, and this forced Hang to choose her top three shots: a man who claimed to be a Saudi prince, an obese Danish man covered in smudged prison tats, and a Japanese man sucking his toe through white stockings. I emailed the photos to Nhu. She wrote back ten minutes later: *Go see Ren at Bunker in D5. Tomorrow at 12.* I showed Hang the message.

"I can't go."

"Of course you can–"

"I have work."

"You work nights."

"Tomorrow I work day too."

"Then talk to Bloss–"

"She will hate me this Ren. It's better for you to go okay?"

I watched her paint her lips red, then I followed her down to the bar. She grabbed the hand of a bald man with sunscreen smeared on his scalp, and led him up the stairs. I sat at the bar. Blossom poured me a Coke. When Hang came back down she looked right through me. She took a young man with narrow shoulders and no chin up to her room, so I went home. I messaged her later that night, trying one last time to change her mind, but she simply said: *You say you sell so now you sell.* And so at twelve the next day, with a fresh bandage on my hand and a clean blue shirt on my back, I rode a motorbike taxi to Bunker, Ren's gallery in D5. I sat in her office. She sat across from me, staring at her phone and never once looking up at my face. Ren had a tattoo of Pikachu that took up the top of her left arm, and she wore clothes that could have come from a sci-fi themed fashion show. She was one of those hyper cool people that find looking at less cool people to be mildly offensive, or sapping of their infinitely cool powers. In some situations I can be cool. Like I can be the coolest damn cat in a boardroom of insurance marketers, but compared to Ren I was a retired real estate agent sliding into the DMs of Instagram models.

"These make me feel a little vomit," she said, flipping through Hang's photos on her laptop.

"That's what's so great about them," I said. "They're disgusting but they're also tragic and beautiful."

"Disgusting, yes. Beautiful, no."

"They're like looking into a cave of fragile human truths."

"I hate caves."

"A well then."

"Where is the artist?"

"She's sick."

"Fine."

She closed her computer and picked up her phone.

"Listen, Hang is a genius. All she–"

"Everyone is a genius."

"She came from nothing. She's completely self-taught."

"She won't sell."

"Come on. Are you kidding? A sex worker who takes photos of her clients? Who flips the power dynamic? That's a great story. Collectors will eat that shit up."

She scrolled on her phone. "I need to meet her."

On the end of the red bed in the red room, Hang sat wearing a light blue dress. While I had been in the meeting, she had scoured Ren's Instagram, where she found photos of her wearing two thousand dollar sneakers. She had seen the gaping class divide open up between them, and she let it swallow her up. Her commitment to not attending a meeting with Ren had now doubled. I had no choice but to lie.

"She loves your work. She was in tears."

"Yes?"

"She thinks you're a genius."

She narrowed her eyes and folded her arms across her chest. "Balenciaga."

"You think her parents bought her those? She comes from nothing. She worked for those shoes."

"Ha!"

"Fine. You want to stay in this room forever. That's fine with me."

The gallery was an oven. And I don't mean that as a weak metaphor for the heat (although it was brutally hot) I mean it was like walking into an actual oven where all sorts of savoury dishes were cooking. The floor was dotted with camping stoves, the gas-powered kind, with naked flames leaping up to lick the bottoms of pots of various size. There must have been three hundred pots on three hundred stoves. All of them cooking soup – bubbling, steaming, boiling – tomato soup, pumpkin soup, pho, borscht and minestrone. All at once my olfactory sensory neurons were flooded with aromas of beef and duck and lamb, and lemongrass, shallots, cabbage, beetroot, ginger, turmeric, chilli, coriander and congealed blood. My nostrils spasmed. Condensation ran down the walls. Sweat bubbled under our skin. Hang's shirt was white. She saw that it was sticking to her chest, and she turned to run, but I held her by the wrist. Ren was in the corner, wearing overalls made from a shiny silver fabric that looked like it was meant for the world's top astronauts, or cosmonauts, or whatever. Next to Ren stood a woman in a snakeskin minidress and purple heels that made her seven feet tall, and next to her was a pile of loaves of bread that nearly reached the roof. Ren and the tall woman took slices from this pile and pinned them to the walls, creating wallpaper out of bread essentially.

Ren saw us, and turned the corners of her mouth down, like she had seen a stray dog eating a soiled nappy.

"This is Hang," I said. "The genius I told you about."

I felt Hang tense up. But the tall woman turned, slice of bread in hand, saw Hang's see-through shirt, and smiled.

"Hello genius. I am Magda."

Hang knew how to handle predators. "Is this your work?" she asked.

"Do you like it?"

Hang nodded.

"Magda is an artist from the Ukraine," said Ren. "Her show opens to-night. We don't have much time but if you want, let's talk."

We sat in a circle on the floor, surrounded by boiling pots of soup. Hang opened her computer, and showed Ren and Magda her photos. Magda stopped on a shot of a man with a badly burned face.

"So powerful."

"You think?" said Ren.

"I know. Where did you shoot these my dear."

"At work."

"They're her customers," I said.

Magda shot me a look that said she did not care if I lived or died, and handed me a slice of bread.

"Take this. Dip in some soup. Let us talk."

Episode Nineteen.

Bun bo hue. That's what I ate with Anaru, at a little place on Tran Hung Dao. Damn that broth was good. I'm pretty sure they put serotonin in it. I don't know how you do that, maybe they had a guy out the back with an eye-dropper, and maybe he took one look at me and gave me a few extra drops. Whatever he did, I was grateful. And when I get grateful, I get chatty.

Noodles slurped down, we left Gloria out the front and walked along the busy street. Past a powder blue mosque, a Honda dealership, and government buildings with armed guards patrolling the gates. All the way to the President Hotel. Anaru paid the old man in the lawn chair at the entrance, he spoke a few words to me in French, and we headed up the first flights of stairs. Peering through the holes that gave you a grand view of the rat-infested basement, I told Anaru one of my stock Sydney stories: "I was living in this shit-hole share house in Surry Hills, and one Friday I got wine drunk at the beach with this Kelly person. We took the 380 bus back to mine, but I had lost my key back at the beach. The house was a terrace, so it had the fence on street level, with metal spikes on top, and a second floor balcony above that. I was like, fuck it. I hopped on the fence and tried to pull myself up to the balcony. I was nearly up when the balustrade snapped, and I fell onto the metal spikes. I got impaled basically. One spike went into my foot and the other stabbed me in the side."

We reached the fifth floor. My face and arms were streaked with specks of city grime. I looked like some sort of miner, Anaru looked perfect. On we walked. "My foot was split from toe to heel, I had this gaping wound above my hip, and I sat in a pool of my own blood on the ground. Kelly ran in circles on the road, wearing a red bra and footy shorts, and screaming. When we got to hospital, I went into surgery. While I was under, my house-mates got home. They had no idea about my fall – guess they missed the pool of blood by the front door. But they were wasted, and they proceeded to get more wasted, on blue and pink pills and whatever. And Renton, one of my mates, he loved to climb. That night he climbed right up to the top of the roof, then he fell onto the road. He broke both his legs, and his hips, and his arms, shattered his jaw, and smashed his skull like a hard-boiled egg."

The tenth floor. Anaru panted. My shirt was so weighted down with bodily fluid, I felt like a family of animals were hanging off me. I stopped talking. This was intentional. A dramatic pause if you like. With a look, Anaru urged me up the final flights of stairs, and to get onto the third act of the story. "The ambulance took Renton to the same hospital I was in, and right about the time I was waking up from my post-anaesthetic slumber, they were putting him into a coma. But his brain wouldn't stop swelling, and the doctors told his parents they might have to, you know, pull the plug. I got released three days later. I went home on crutches, with a cast on my leg and a hundred-odd stitches in my side, and found my friends still partying. When Renton got carted off, his head falling apart, they didn't know what to do, so they kept doing what they were doing, consuming drugs. The vibe was so grim I went upstairs to my room. I sat on the bed, thinking 'what the fuck is my life'. My mate Susie came up and asked if I was okay. I said I wasn't sure, and she asked if I wanted a bump of K."

On the roof of the haunted old hotel, our legs hung over the side. Smog lingered above the city like a fuzzy halo.

"You know My Mum," said Anaru, "her name was Carolina. And she was from Sydney, I think I told you that, eh."

"She grew up in Paddington you said."

"Yeah, but Sydney, she was not a fan. She called it the shit stain, and God's toilet, and the home of the lizard brains, and giant pus-oozing pimple town, and Hatesville."

"What made her love it so much?"

"Griffin."

Griffin was Carolina's younger brother. Like her, he had a full head of bouncy red curls. Also like her, he was pleased with what he saw in the mirror. But he was convinced he looked better than her in tight black jeans.

"I got an ass like an overripe apple," he told her.

"Sounds rotten," she replied.

Growing up, the siblings shared everything – bedroom, clothes, food, albums, shoes, and secrets. Lots and lots of secrets. The night Griffin turned twelve, they sat on his bed munching a mud cake called Queen of Sheba soul cake by the fistful. "You know I'm gay," he said. Stuffing her mouth, she punched him in the arm. "Yes, doofus, I know that." After high school, Carolina went to art school, and Griffin joined her a year later. It was here that Carolina met Rocky, who was not pugnacious in any way. Rocky had the look of a ferret crossed with an eel, in that he was long and tanned and slippery, with a rat's tail, and a fringe that hung past his chin. Rocky's income came from ecstasy, which he sold in insignificant amounts. And his turf was the Taylor Square area, where Surry Hills meets Darlinghurst. From Thursday to Sunday night, he roamed from club to club, offloading up to two hundred pills per evening. Kicking off in Kinselas, he slunk over to Arc, up to Gilligans, across Oxford Street to Stonewall, then back to Kinselas and maybe up to Middle Bar. He was small time, and that suited him just fine. He had no desire to move up the food chain. He was an artist, a fashion designer, with his own patented garment, an apron-cum-skirt for men, which he called The Lap-Lap. This was a ridiculous creation. Doomed to fail. Carolina knew this, but his absurd ways were a huge part of his charm. Rocky made her laugh. He made her thighs quiver, and he gave her free drugs. Lots of free drugs.

Carolina did not accompany Rocky on his rounds, but Griffin often saw him in the clubs. Slipping out of a bar manager's office or into a disabled toilet. One night at Stonewall, as the drag show was building up a head of steam on stage, Griffin waited at the bar to be served. He flipped open his wallet, and noticed a long greasy fringe get flicked in the crowd next to him.

"Wanna drink?" Griffin yelled over the noise.

Rocky leaned in close (he was a chronic close talker) and Griffin smelled lamb kebab on his breath. "Malibu and pineapple."

"That's a poof's drink."

Rocky shrugged. When Griffin handed him the coconut and sugar concoction, Rocky slipped four pink Mitsubishis into his hand.

Four days later, Rocky told Carolina that her brother owed him for the pills, so she phoned Griffin (this was in the days of landlines). But Griffin claimed the pills had been a gift. Carolina hung up the phone, and told Rocky what her brother had told her, to which Rocky said yes, the pills were given, but given on tick, meaning Griffin now needed to pay. For five days the boys went back and forth, with Carolina caught in the middle. Griffin coughed up the cash eventually, but the mix-up caused a sizeable rift between her brother and her boyfriend.

When it came to her connection to her little bro, Carolina could sense the slightest shift in atmospheric pressure. But she was dropping pills and snorting bumps six nights a week, and sleeping most days, so you could say her senses were dulled. One sunny morning she emerged from a ketamine haze, looked around, and found herself in an overgrown garden. She reached out, touched a dewdrop on the yellow petal of a rose, and realised she hadn't seen nor heard from her brother in weeks. Such silence was unheard of. Where had he been? The beats, and the bars, but mainly the beats. The public toilets, the bushes in the parks, the clifftops overlooking the Tasman Sea. He had always been a casual attendee in the scene, but since his sister slipped from his life, he had become obsessed. Sure it was dangerous. Rumours were everywhere. Young men were disappearing, gangs of youths were to blame. The cops didn't care. Shit, they probably endorsed it. Some of his mates claimed to have been bashed, but the bruises on their pretty faces weren't so bad. Besides, Griffin wasn't stupid. He was careful, and he was quick.

Hours after reaching out to the dewdrop, Carolina spotted her brother. She was on the back of the 380 bus to Bondi Beach. It stopped at the lights outside the Paddington Library, and she saw him skipping down Oxford Street in his favourite pair of short shorts. Banging on the window, she called out to him. He looked up. She was sure that he saw her, but then he turned away. The next morning the cops knocked on her door. Griffin had passed, they said. Jumped from a cliff near Tamarama Beach. His body had been found that morning. "We are not treating this as a homicide," they said.

Not a homicide.

Not a homicide

Not a homicide.

For weeks those words rang in her ears. She knew they were lies. No way he jumped. No fucking way. He was pushed. Thrown. Heaved. A gang of thugs found him with a lover, and tossed his sacred naked body with its beating heart to the jagged rocks below. Eight, nine, ten times she went to Tamarama Park. She searched the grass, the top of the cliff, the rocks. She hounded the police, but they weren't buying it. "No sign of a struggle," they said.

No sign of struggle.

Not a homicide.

Struggle. Struggle. Homicide.

Homicide.

Homicide.

Struggle.

The words drove her mad. Every day they detonated little bombs in her head. Constant throbbing. Perpetual pain. She couldn't escape it. The only way was to leave the city with the ocean cliffs. The city with kids who threw men like her brother to their deaths. It was the city's fault. What kind of city raised kids like that. What kind of a city paid police to turn a blind eye to that. Yes, it was all the city's fault.

Episode Twenty.

I woke up in the dark before dawn. From the green neon signs in the maze below my window, a soft glow rose up to greet me. On the wall the air con hummed softly. I reached for my phone, and found an email from a person I did not expect to get an email from:

> Dearest Apollo,
> My friend how are you? I miss you so much. The house is never the same when your warm smile is away. Uncle Frank speaks of you. He has no one to talk with when he irons his suits! Auntie wishes for your return also. Hahaha! But let me say that I am the one who misses you the greatest. Do you remember my business? The name is Organic Tours. The best tourism business in Asia also the world! I will build this one Apollo. Of course I welcome your help. If you wish to invest your skills please contact me without hesitation. Maybe we can also return to the casino. Ha-ha. I wink at you.
> Warmest regards, Anhtheman.

Interesting. But not as interesting as the story Anaru told me. Griffin would not vacate my head. I kept returning to the night he was thrown over the cliff. It was haunting, and hard to think about, but I looked at it from every angle. And as I walked the streets with ice melting in my coffee, I recreated the details.

Jules.

That was the name I gave to the man he met at the park. Griffin was sat on a bench, staring at the moon as it hovered over the ocean. Jules sat next to him. The first thing Griffin saw were his thighs. Huge and strong, the thighs of a front row rugby player. The thighs of a man who lifted great weight with his glutes and quads. Griffin had no idea why, but he loved big thighs on a man. Seconds later, they lay under a bush, tearing at each other's clothes. A sharp wind ripped over the surface of the sea, up the cliff, biting into their exposed skin. But that only made the hook up hotter. On top of desire, each man's body needed the other for warmth. Griffin pawed at Jules' back like he was trying to dig into his chest. Teeth chattered and clashed. Jules flipped him over, Griffin took a deep breath, but felt nothing. When he turned, Jules was gone. Straining his eyes in the dark, he saw Jules' bare arse and big thighs pumping as he ran across the park. Griffin reached for his jeans. Why did he do that? Was it the cold? Modesty was not his speed. Public nudity was not a problem. So why? There must have been twenty boys. Young boys. Boys with fists and boots and sticks and rocks, kicking and punching and screaming and spitting. They dragged Griffin, still naked, over the grass to the cliff. Sharp rocks tore at the skin on his stomach. Somehow he sprang to his feet and ran. He saw a house, a light, an open door. He cried out for help but the door closed. How? Why? What! The pack had him now, kicking him to the cliff edge, popping his nose. Way down below, the waves pounded the rocks. He fought back, but they were too many. A million little fists. As he went over, he reached out. A plant came loose from a rock face. Roots in his hand. In that moment he heard the girls. Girls who were just kids. Girls who probably slept with teddy bears in their arms. "Kill him!" screamed the girls. "Kill that fucking faggot!"

Damn.

I was in trouble.

I was smitten with Anaru. I mean I really loved the guy. He was special, that was for damn sure, and I wanted us to be best friends forever. But I was driven by an engine made from twisted metal, and I wanted his story. The story of Griffin and Carolina, and all the tales that made the beautiful man who sat with me on the roof of the President Hotel. I craved it, like a vampire craves the metallic aftertaste of human blood. But I couldn't just take it, no, that would make me a thief. A vicious, white mis-appropriator. A piece of shit. Also, that would destroy our blossoming friendship. I hadn't even told him about the Untitled Original Series Set On Multiple Continents. About Hang or the heist. Deep in my sordid subconscious, I must have known I wanted his story, and telling him about the series would have made him reluctant to tell me his story. The only solution was to make it together. The Untitled Original Series Set On Multiple Continents would be ours. We would take his story, and mash it with my story, and mash those stories with Hang's story, as well as some made up stories. Co-creators, that's what we'd be. Hang too if she wanted. Fine by me. All I cared about was making content that melted the minds of a generation, and maybe some generations after that generation. Pitching it to him was the problem. How did I make him fall in love with the series without making him fall out of love with me, his possible dear friend for life.

Episode Twenty-One.

Hang felt a hand on her thigh. This was not uncommon, so she did not flinch. She looked down, and saw the nails on the hand were bitten to bloody stumps. She lifted the hand and placed it back on the thigh of the owner. The owner was Magda. Magda smiled at Hang, and Hang saw that she had stumpy brown teeth to match her stumpy red nails. Ren sat across from them. She had not seen the hand on the thigh. The light in the bar they were in was nearly black, and the music was a monotonous hammering, like a broken machine.

"Magda is a big fan of your work," said Ren.

"Very big."

Hang felt the hand creep back onto her thigh. She did not remove it.

"I will give you a show," said Ren, "but you need to make some changes in your work."

"We need to shoot self-portraits," said Magda, "with your customers."

"No."

"No?"

"I don't think it's good."

The hand slid up to her inner thigh, fingers dancing up an inch or two further. "It's a big opportunity for you," said the owner of the hand.

Hang was not a fan of the hand with the stumpy red fingernails, but she was closer to a show than she ever hoped to be, and that made her a fan of me. She found me in Smile Bar, chatting to Blossom about the latest batch of evil acts from Kris Kardashian. "She's a witch!" Blossom hissed. "She put spells on her girls!" Hang yanked me off my stool, and shoved me so hard in the back I stumbled on the first step of the stairs. Once she had me in her room, she sat me on the bed and shut the door.

"You come here each day. You pay me for the hour, like a customer. For twenty millions I give you one story."

"Twenty?!"

"Don't haggle."

"But you got the show."

"Not yet."

"But I–"

"You are buying my life. You think it's not worth?"

"Ten million."

She gave my ear a light slap. "Are you deaf? I have customers. You don't want this, say no."

"I don't have any cash on me."

"ATM down the street."

The ATM had a two million dong limit. So did the next one and the next one and the next one. When I walked back to Smile Bar, rivulets of sweat ran over my ribs, and my brain nibbled at itself. How many episodes could I afford to buy from Hang? I wasn't exactly swimming in cash. I'd need to find more branded content work. Fine. That was fine. I walked into Smile Bar, up the stairs, and handed Hang the cash. She counted out each note on the red bed, I pressed record on the voice memos app on my phone, and she gave me the first instalment of her story.

Hang worked her first shift at Smile Bar on her sixteenth birthday. Right away she was a hit. All the men chose her, and she earned more money than any girl in the history of the bar. But she hated it. The men breathed hot mustard gas in her face, they suffocated her with excessive flesh, and pawed at her with hands that smelled like over-cooked pork. After every shift it took four showers to get the smell off her skin. And her colleagues were not nice. The other girls picked on her for being younger and prettier, and for always getting picked first. They said her crotch smelled like dried squid. One night a man rammed his fingers down her throat so hard his nails nicked her epiglottis, and when the girls found her crying in the toilet, they laughed. Hang trudged up to the office – where Blossom sat at her desk filing her nails – and quit.

"But you have a special talent!"

"For fucking old men?"

"I will pay you more."

"I want one million for every customer."

Blossom laughed so hard she nearly fell backwards in her chair, and had to grab hold of the desk to stop from toppling over. The most she'd ever paid a girl was three hundred thousand from the two million the customer paid per hour. "Are you crazy, girlie? No. One million, my god."

"Eight hundred thousand."

"Five hundred thousand."

Roy was an old man from the North of England. He had red hair that he wore in a Fifties style pompadour, but it was so thin it looked like a vaporous tube sitting on his head. Like it might blow away at any second. Roy went to Smile Bar every night. Every night he chose Hang, every night he asked her to marry him, every night she said no, and every night he threatened to shoot himself in the face, or drown himself in the river, or throw himself under a bus. It was too much. Hang found Blossom in her office, struggling to open a fresh bottle of lime green nail polish. She quit, but Blossom countered: "Eight hundred thousand."

Next time she quit for real. Blossom offered her an unprecedented one million per customer, and she still said no. But Blossom wasn't about to let her most profitable asset stroll out the door. She knew the exact location of Hang's heart. She had seen her sitting at the bar every night, scrolling through endless travel blogs. She gave Hang three nights grace, then she knocked on her door bearing tickets to Bangkok, and the promise of a week on the beach at Koh Samui. Exactly seventy-two hours later, the two women sat at a table in a restaurant on the roof of a skyscraper. The Bangkok lights stretched out like a glittering ocean. In the neighbouring buildings, Hang saw people working in offices, sitting in important looking meetings. For the first time in her life, she ate sashimi.

"You like it?"

"Yes."

"Tomorrow we will go shopping at Icon Mall. Buy you some dresses and maybe new shoes."

Hang looked at her.

"What?"

"Why are you being so nice?"

"You are my number one girl. I want to show you how special you are to me. Is that okay?"

Hang chewed her tuna sashimi. "Yes."

"After the mall we'll go to the beauty parlour, get our nails done, and maybe some fillers for your lips."

"I don't want fillers."

"Sure. Just a little. All the girls here do it."

"I don't know."

"Come on. You're not in the village anymore."

Swan of Siam, that was the name of the beauty clinic. Blossom led Hang through an automatic sliding door and into a waiting room. The walls were pink. The chairs were pink too and wrapped in clear plastic. Hang sat next to Blossom (who was busy filling out a form) and looked at the other girls in the waiting room. They had style, that was for sure. Sophistication. One had silver hair. Maybe she could be cool like them.

"Do you have any allergies," asked Blossom.

"No."

On the form, she put an X in the *No* box.

"Take any medication?"

"No."

"Diabetes?"

"No."

"Heart disease in your family?"

"I don't know."

"I'll put no. Sign here."

"What is it?"

"So they can do the lips."

"Not too much."

"Of course. We don't want you looking crazy."

Hang signed the form. From a door down the hall, a nurse rolled out on pink rollerblades. She wore clear-framed glasses and a white uniform. She rolled right up to Blossom, took the form, scanned it, and rolled back down the corridor. Blossom turned to face Hang.

"This is very expensive. I hope you know."

"I know."

"Don't tell the other girls, okay? They already think I spoil you. But I do. I think of you like–anyway, you deserve it."

Hang blushed. No one had ever spoiled her before. "Thank you."

The nurse rolled back into the waiting room. "Your room is ready," she said, then she rolled down the hall. Hang and Blossom followed her into a pink-walled room with a single bed, a vase of white roses on the bedside table and a window with a view of a concrete wall. "Please change and lie on the bed," said the nurse. "Dr. Charakorn will be here soon." Hang stepped out of her clothes, slipped the pink gown over her head, and climbed on the bed. Blossom sat in the chair under the window and stared at a chipped yellow nail on her right hand. A woman in a white coat walked in. The skin on her face was stretched tight over the bones, her eyes were bright violet, and she held a bedazzled iPad to her chest.

"Good morning, I am Dr. Charakorn," she looked at her tablet, "and you are…"

"Blossom," said Blossom, standing to attention. "This is Hang."

"Hello Hang," said Dr. Charakorn, walking to the side of the bed. "We're doing the lips, yes? Some filler in the lips."

"Not so big," said Hang.

"Don't worry dear, my work is elegant. Very subtle." She swiped at her screen. "We also do the breasts, yes?"

"No."

"Hang," said Blossom, "you signed the form. This is what you want. Trust me. Dr. Charakorn is an artist."

"You want the C cup?" said Dr. Charakorn. "We have a very beautiful shape. Like a teardrop. Perfect for your frame."

Hang tried to sit up, but Blossom pushed her shoulder down.

"You said just lips."

"You want to be beautiful or not? You're a big city girl now."

"I don't know."

"I already paid. We agreed. I told you it's expensive."

"It's natural to be nervous," said Dr. Charakorn, "But when you wake up, you will love it."

In the seconds before she opened her eyes, her body sent a message to her brain. This body is no longer yours, said the message. Her eyes opened. She touched her lips. They felt bigger than her face, like they had been struck with hundreds of tiny hammers. Her chest felt like it had been trampled by a herd of cows.

"You're awake," said Blossom. "Take some water."

Hang reached out for the glass. When she sipped, the water ran down her chin.

"What happened?"

"Oh my gosh, girlie. You are beautiful."

Hang touched the bandage on her chest. It felt huge, like touching another person.

"So big."

"When you went to sleep, we decided on the C cup."

"What?"

"C is the best."

"It's too big!"

"No, it's perfect."

Hang panicked. She was not in her own country, or her city, or her bed, or even her own body. She clawed at the bandages on her chest, tried to rip them off, but Blossom held her hands tight.

"Don't be stupid girlie! You want an infection?"

"I want them out!"

"Are you crazy?"

"GET THEM OUT!"

Blossom pushed her down and lay her full weight on her. Pain ripped through Hang's abdomen, settling in her throat, silencing her screams. "I paid for those! They belong to me, so don't touch. Don't damage my property!"

Episode Twenty-Two.

Romantic relationships have a song. You hear people in couples say: this is our song. It's gross. But only for those outside the relationship, AKA the entire world. In a friendship you don't have a song, you have a spot. A place where you go to trade stories and share secrets. Mine and Anaru's spot? The roof of The President Hotel of course. Night after night we went up there, to dangle our feet off the edge, watch scooters clog arterial roads, and say goodbye to the burnt orange sun as it ushered in a dark purple night.

I gave him my stock stuff.

Like the one about the time I stayed home sick from school, and saw Oscar nearly beat a man to death with an oar in our backyard. But I also told him stories I had never told a soul. Like the time I went home for Christmas after a huge fight with my ex, and got so drunk I got into bed with my grandmother, where, drunkenly thinking she was my ex, I tried to have sex with her. But maybe not. But also maybe? I was in a blackout so I couldn't be sure. And even though I probably hadn't done it, the not knowing for sure made me paranoid that I might have done it. And I couldn't exactly go up to grandma and say, 'Oh hey, Grandma, did I by any chance try to have sex with you last night?' Anaru didn't judge me. He looked out over the dark but still sizzling city, put an arm around me, and said: "It probably didn't happen. And even if it did she was probably flattered that her handsome grandson wanted a piece of her old ass." And then he gave me the rest of the Carolina story:

Carolina had a rock. Not a crystal. A rock she took from the top of the cliff where Griffin was pushed to his death. She bought a one-way ticket to Christchurch in New Zealand (the furthest she could afford to go) packed a bag and took a train to the airport. The rock was in her pocket, collecting sweat from her palm. But when she got to her gate, and they called her row, she dumped the rock in a rubbish bin and didn't look back.

At the bottom of the South Island, she swam in an icy fjord, ate oysters off the rocks, and saw a man kill a wild boar with a knife (he gifted her the tusks).

As she worked her way north, she saw whales and cheeky green native parrots.

She slept under the stars on the side of an active volcano.

She bathed in a pool of mud.

And as she walked on the side of the state highway, listening to her Walkman, she narrowly avoided a biker who sped past and tried to snatch her off her feet.

Kororareka. That was the name of the town in the Far North. In Maori it meant 'little blue penguin.' The cuteness of the name was why she stayed, that and she was broke. But summer was coming, the town was teeming with tourists, and she got the first job she went for, as a waitress in a waterfront restaurant called The Gables. This was a popular spot, run by a husband and wife team named Alan and Sue. He was the chef and she ran front of house. Their four children – three girls and a boy – lived above the restaurant, in rooms overlooking the water. And Sue had just sacked the nanny – a Swede who made too many calls to her boyfriend back in Malmo – so Carolina spent the first month looking after the kids. She took them to the beach, read to them, applied band-aids to skinned knees, fished off the wharf for sprats with them, and helped them collect the edible orange flowers that were used as garnishes on dishes in the restaurant.

"Carembert. Would you like some carembert."

A waitress was sacked for mispronouncing cheeses, so Carolina's tenure as nanny came to an end. She waited on German tourists and American tourists and Japanese tourists. And she missed the kids, but they treated the restaurant like a playground, always darting underfoot. Plus they had little jobs, like clearing ash trays or cleaning puke from toilets. After her shifts ended, she sat at the bar drinking rum and coke, and she went to parties on boats, or in paddocks, or in the bush. That summer she had four flings. The first was with Paul, the kitchenhand. When she broke it off, he necked a bottle of Coruba Rum, stole his father's yacht and smashed it into some rocks. There was a teacher from the local school, Mr Harris, who insisted on wearing knee-high brown socks during sex. And the artist who lived in a caravan in the bush. One day while he sat on the toilet, he yelled out for her to go to the shop to get him some smokes. She took his wallet, went to the store and never went back. The fourth was Rawiri, a Maori academic who taught contemporary literature at Auckland University. She liked him a lot, but he was passing through, killing time before he took up a post in America. By the time the tourists left town, she was pregnant. She chose to believe Rawiri was the father. With the others she had (mostly) used protection. And besides, she could sense the intelligence of the life growing in her belly. She chose not to tell him. They weren't really in touch anyway – the odd letter maybe. He was on another continent, his career taking off. The last thing he needed was a baby pulling him back down to a tiny town at the bottom of the world. That was what she told herself anyway. She rented a house, and Sue, her boss, gave her a cot, a stroller, a change table, and ten sacks of baby clothes.

Anaru was born on a clear night. He weighed 3.4kg, had none of his mother's red curls, but a shock of jet black hair like his father.

His childhood was an obsessive one. His first obsession being the way he looked. If his socks were not pulled up to the exact same height on his shins, or his cuffs were not rolled back to the exact same spot on his wrists, or his hair was not side-parted to perfection, he bawled. Big game fishing was another obsession. Carolina did not have the cash to send him out on a charter boat (one captain offered to take him out for payment in kind but she was not about that life) but she did buy him a pair of binoculars from the second-hand shop, and he sat at the kitchen window every morning, notebook at his side, staring out at the bay and writing down the names of boats chugging out to hunt the sea for prey. When a boat made a catch (a black marlin say) they radioed it in to Glen, the manager of the Kororareka Swordfish Club. At the club they had flags for all the big fish – striped marlin, blue marlin, mako shark, hammerhead shark, bluefin tuna, yellowfin tuna – and Glen took a flag (a black marlin flag say) down to the wharf to run up the flag pole. As soon as Anaru got home from school, he pointed his binoculars out the kitchen window, pulling focus on the flags fluttering against the sky. In his notebook he wrote down the day's catches. At six, with his homework halfway done, he ran down to the wharf, notebook in hand, to see the magnificent creatures hoisted up by their tails. He loved the smell of diesel fumes from the boat engines. The sounds of tourists snapping photos of the anglers, who posed with rods in hand and cigarettes dangling from sun drenched lips, as oily blood dripped from the swords and teeth of sharks and marlins hanging upside down next to them. Anaru jotted down the names of the anglers, the skippers, the weights of the fish and the weights of the tackle.

But his longest running obsession was local history. He spent entire days at the big old computer with patchy dial-up, reading about famous Maori chiefs like:

Hone Heke, who in 1844 chopped down the British flag that flew above Kororareka for the fourth time, inciting a bloody war.

Hongi Hika, who took a boat load of shrunken heads to England, traded them for muskets, met King George (who gifted him a suit of armour that he later wore in battle, properly spooking his enemies), and helped transcribe the first ever Maori dictionary at Oxford University. Hika spent the last year of his life with a bullet in his chest. Rumour had it his favourite party trick was to whistle through the hole.

And an escaped Australian convict named Jacky Marmon, who was one of the first Pakeha Maori. The European settlers believed he partook in cannibal feats. They hated him.

Carolina had her own obsessions going on. Exercise being her big one. She rose at dawn, pulled on her black and pink spandex, and made Anaru breakfast. On winter mornings, she made him porridge with cream and brown sugar, and a mug of hot milo. In summer: Weet-Bix with canned peaches and orange juice. She then put on a workout DVD and went hard. Anaru sat on the couch, bowl in lap, watching her do push-ups, sit-ups, star jumps, burpees, downward dog, upward dog, triangle pose and chair pose. When the DVD ended, she flexed her sweaty biceps in his face. "Feel it!" she said. He rolled his eyes, but he loved it.

While he was in school, she worked in the restaurant. If the restaurant was dead, she worked in the pub, filling jugs of frothy beer for thirsty fishermen. If the pub was quiet (unlikely) she rode the ten speed bike she found at the dump to Opua, the next town over. Or she swam up and down the beach. Or she rode over a hill to a beach called Long Beach (guess why) to run in the soft sand, pushing herself until she puked. The local pony club girls rode their horses on the hard sand near the water, and Carolina tried to race them. The horses laughed and galloped away, hooves kicking saltwater into her face. She pumped her human legs as fast as they would go, and she often felt like she could run forever, but she never once beat a horse in a beach race. The pony club girls called her crazy. "Oh god," they said, "here comes that crazy redhead, guess she wants a race." But she never stopped trying.

One rainy Sunday afternoon, Anaru lay on his bed, plucking lint from his bellybutton. Carolina called to him from the living room. He rolled off his bed and shuffled down the hall, and found her sitting at the computer, the massive plastic monitor stained sepia from the sun.

"What's this?" she asked.

He looked at the screen. From the search box, three words stared back at him: boys kissing boys. He turned and ran, and she ran after him, snatching his collar as he skidded over the cracked linoleum of the kitchen floor. He screamed and cried and tried to wriggle free, but she was fit and she was strong. She wrapped him up in a hug so tight he thought he would suffocate.

"It's okay," she said, "just tell me, do you like boys or girls."

"I can't breathe."

"Tell me, Anaru."

"Mum please!"

"Tell me!"

He honestly thought he would die in the crook of her elbow.

"Boys."

When she released him, he couldn't say how long he'd been in her embrace. His cheek felt like it'd been pressed against a radiator for hours. He almost felt reborn, but not in a rejuvenating way. And when he looked at her face, he knew he was not looking at the same person. He knew she was no longer the Mum that made him porridge and made him feel her biceps.

Episode Twenty-Three.

P lease don't do this."
"It's okay."
"It's not."
"You have money. Don't cry. Don't be a baby."

Hang pouted her painted red lips, and walked downstairs to the bar. That was my cue to go to the ATM. Like some sad sack old man customer. She had doubled the price of her stories, from twenty to forty million dong. And there wasn't a damn thing I could do about it, so I walked down the stairs and out the door. The heat right hooked me in the face. As I walked up the street, a scooter wheel swiped my right anklebone, leaving a rubber-smeared blister. Thanks. Thank you so much. At the ATM, I watched blue 500,000 dong notes flitter from the slot, and thought up ways to make more money. At the rate Hang was draining me, my well would run dry any day. Maybe Anaru could hook me up. Surely Karaoke Kingdom needed some flashy content to match the décor of their rooms. Back at the bar, I handed Hang the cash. She counted it twice, then she looked at me like she was about to count it a third time, then she put it in her purse. "Blossom tricked me," she said.

The flight from Bangkok to Saigon took an hour and ten minutes. When the wheels skidded on the tarmac, Blossom took Hang's hand in hers. Gave it a little pat. She told her to take three days off. To rest up. But to come back to the bar ready to work and to work hard. She had shelled out a small fortune for her breasts, and she expected a decent return on her investment. "And you know I have friends in the police, so don't try to quit, or I will make life hard for your family. Okay girlie? Now, give me your passport."

Hang worked seven nights a week. Some nights she took on ten customers, but she never complained. She sipped her juice at the bar, and when the men walked in the door, and pointed at her, she took their hands and led them upstairs. When their hands went up her skirt, or their tongues slithered in her ear, she didn't even blink. She stared dead-eyed at the ceiling. The men were not doing things to her, but to the body of a stranger. Since the surgery, her body had not stopped changing. Like the modifications were spreading to other parts of her body – arms, thighs, neck – and changing them too. Now when she washed her face in the sink, and looked up into the mirror, she did not recognise the face staring back at her. This person had puffy lips and breasts that jutted out like a shelf. Her eyes were smaller, set deeper in her skull, and her left eyebrow looked permanently cocked. Her nose was narrow too, her shoulders slumped, the tendons in her neck stood out like taut ropes.

"I sat at the bar," she told me. "This was morning. I was staring. Staring at nothing. I did this a lot. I worked many hours, twelve maybe. The cleaner came to me, she had a bag. She found this in my room. When I look in the bag, I find the camera. It was big and black, expensive. A customer had left it. I can sell it, I thought, so I go to the shop. The man says I need the charger, so I go to the electronic store, but there was none, so I go to the electronics market. The man he says they are all gone, so I go the café. I was sick of the camera. It starts to rain. I thought, I will throw this camera in the puddle. It's a stupid camera. Who cares. I go to the park, and I see the flower. It's a pink one. A lily maybe. I don't know the name. It sits on the water, looks so beautiful. The... what do you call it? The petals. They were so pink, with raindrops on them. I could hear the sound – sssss – I wanted to take a photo of this sound. I turn on the camera, point it at the raindrop, the rains on the petal. I push the button. Click. Then I see the photo on the back. So beautiful. I hate that photo. I want to scream at that photo. I put the camera over my shoulder, with the strap. Then I get on my bike, and go to Ben Thanh market in the rain. I say to myself, if the camera breaks, I will leave it in the street. But she did not break. I think she wants to stay with me. Care for me."

It was hot under the roof of the market. Hot and loud and steamy from the rain. The dense air smelled of leather and fish and lime and chilli, and coffee and meat and freshly pressed fake Gucci tees. Hang walked past men haggling over chickens, women haggling over greens, children snipping stems from flowers with scissors. At the far end, she found the butcher women, standing behind rows and rows of loins and legs and wings and heads. An older woman in a white plastic apron cut open a pig that hung from the rafters by a chain attached to its hind trotters. Hang watched her slash the guts and organs away from the ribs. As they tumbled onto the white tiles, she smelled the heart and the liver and the lungs, the shiny brown intestines, and the bubbling river of blood that ran down the drain. The woman walked away to wash her knife, so Hang poked the lens of her camera into the body of the pig. She took photos of the empty cavity, the remains of guts and organs, and some kind of yellow slime that smelled like burnt hair.

"When I take these photos, I feel warm in my stomach. I did not know this feeling. But I know I want it again."

The girls who worked at Smile Bar – Duc, Nga, Kim, Minnie and Phuong – were the first humans she turned her lens on. She shot them performing little tasks, like taking off make-up after their shifts, changing the sheets on their beds, or bickering at the bar. Kim was the girls' self-appointed leader. After Hang, she was the girl most chosen by the men, and for her second place rank she was resentful. At times cruel. She once spread a rumour that Hang made her customers shower so she could go through their pockets.

But she knew an opportunity when she saw one. On Instagram, Kim had 987 followers. She was desperate to crack a thousand. She got close once, all the way to 998, but then she got drunk and posted a selfie of her smudged make-up self sitting on the toilet, and woke up to an exodus of 17 followers. Many a tear flowed that morning. With Hang, Kim planned her approach well. She had seen her sitting at the bar watching photography tutorials on her phone (Hang no longer looked at travel blogs or stared dead-eyed into space, but at video lessons on ISO, shutter speed, lighting and aperture) and one night she climbed onto the stool next to her.

"You are such a good photographer now."

"What do you want."

"Nothing!"

"Just tell me."

"I want you to do a shoot for me."

Hang paused her framing tutorial. "What kind of shoot?"

"A shoot to get me more followers."

Hang took Kim's phone and scrolled through her Instagram. Most of her posts were selfies, with pounds of flesh pushed at the lens. About every third shot was her in a bikini at some pool party. The water in one of the pools was grey, and looked like a dead body had just been fished out of it. The story Kim told was one of desperation. Hang's idea for the shoot was to turn her into a boss. A woman with self-respect. For the location, she secured Blossom's office for two hours on a Sunday afternoon. She dressed Kim in a severe black skirt, white shirt and black-framed glasses. She told her to look strong. To embrace her power. But Kim insisted on undoing the top three buttons on her blouse, and lying prostrate on the desk. The collab was not a success.

Duc, the youngest member of staff at Smile Bar, had a one-year-old daughter named Minu. Her father was a one-time customer who lived in Seoul. He refused to visit, or call, or send money, or even acknowledge little Minu's existence. "Can you take some pictures of Minu?" Duc asked Hang. "I'll send them to her father. If she looks cute, maybe he will send money."

Hang loved the idea. For the shoot, her concept was to dress Minu up as a tiger, and have her crawl around a tiny jungle. Blossom let them use an empty room on the third floor, and Hang stayed up all night, crafting trees from coloured paper, setting up lights, shooting tests with a toy tiger. Baby Minu was a natural. She crawled around in her tiger suit, giggling and cooing and munching on paper leaves. The camera loved her. Hang selected five of the cutest shots, and Duc emailed them to Minu's Dad. He did not send money, but he did ask for more shots. Maybe this was a sign he felt something, however small. They wrote back, saying they would send more shots if he sent money for nappies and formula for a month. They also asked if he wanted to see her as some other type of animal. He sent $US50, and asked to see her as a wolf cub.

A week later, a girl from a bar down the road came looking for Hang. She had heard about the baby photography studio, and the sending of the shots to unresponsive fathers. Her baby's daddy lived in Sao Paulo. Hang dressed her son as a lion, and they sent the shots off to Brazil. The father blocked them, but this only made Hang more determined. Over the next few months, she shot babies as unicorns, and fairies, and snakes and monkeys. And she sent the photos to fathers in Finland and France and India and Kenya. Sometimes the fathers sent money, sometimes they sent out-of-office auto-replies, but mostly they sent silence.

Episode Twenty-Four.

I'm a little embarrassed to admit this. Actually I'm not. I mean I am. Sort of. The thing is, I bought a pair of black jeans to make me look like Anaru. I had begun to dress like him, which I guess meant I wanted to be like him, which made me feel pretty queasy. But he was dressing like me too (wearing more colour for example) and so in these subtle ways (which weren't always so subtle) we were fusing together as one. As best friends sometimes do.

Also, I need to own something I felt awful about, and that was the thieving of his life story. I was yet to pitch him on the Untitled Original Series Set On Multiple Continents. I didn't know how. And I wasn't worried he wouldn't like it, I was worried he would think I only wanted to be his friend so I could get my greasy hands on his story (not true) and that would make him end our friendship, which was a very dear thing to me as you know. But even though it made me feel like a steaming piece of human shit in the street, I did not stop stealing the stories he told me about his life. I wrote them down on scene cards and locked the cards in a drawer in my desk in my room in the maze. And don't look now but here come some of those cards:

Card 1:
In the seaside town of Kororareka, there was one clothing store, called Adobe Fashions. Anaru found a shirt he loved in Adobe Fashions, and the shirt was pink with a yellow dalmatian spot print. He saved his pocket money for fifteen weeks to buy that shirt.

"You can't wear that shirt," said Carolina.

It was Friday, and they were off to the Swordfish Club for dinner.

"Why not?"

"You want all those fishermen staring at you? What do you think they'll think?"

"Then what should I wear?"

"Wear the green one."

"I hate the green one."

"Then wear the white one!"

"It's dirty."

"I just washed it!"

"I spilled coke on it."

Card 2:
After the 'boys kissing boys' Google search incident, Carolina limited his internet access. She let him play games for one hour per day, and she sat in the room with him. She told him there were men online that searched for boys like him, and when the men found out where boys like him lived, they burned them in their beds.

Card 3:
She made a habit of telling him what not to do and what not to say. At night, before bed, she watched him brush his teeth with his Ninja Turtles toothbrush.

"Don't do that thing with your hand."

"What thing."

"Don't play dumb with me."

"What thing?"

She snapped her wrist in front of his face.

"That thing."

In the morning, as he poured milk over a steaming hot bowl of porridge, she peered at him over the top of her glasses.

"Don't hold the bottle in such a prissy way."

"Huh?"

"And don't sign up for soccer. And if you do sign up for soccer, don't act like a glory boy, scoring all the goals. And if you do have to score goals, for god's sake don't rip off your shirt and hug your mates like those dickheads on TV."

Most of the time he let it wash over him, like sets of small but slightly suffocating waves. "Never tell a soul what you told me. Not your friends and not your teacher. And for the love of god don't tell those gossiping girls I see smoking cigarettes under the wharf." But there were times he pushed back. He said his shoes or his shirt or the way he said thanks was fine thanks. He called her a controlling so-and-so, and he slammed doors. But she would not be swayed. She sat on the edge of his bed, or she stroked the hair on his head, and said she loved him too much to see him hurt. That the world was filled with men with evil in their hearts, and it was her job to protect him from those men.

Card 4:

She cut stories from the newspaper and left them on his bed. Stories of men who had been spat on, beaten and abused. Stabbed even. Stories about men with futures. Men who wanted to love their families and work jobs they loved or did not love. Men who wanted to eat in restaurants, and go grocery shopping, and watch movies.

Card 5:

They came to him in his dreams. Men with mashed faces and battered bodies. They warned him, and he took heed. He stopped dreaming of learning to play the guitar. He put away his binoculars, and he stopped running down to the wharf to see the swordfish and the sharks get weighed.

When he walked down the street, he did not hold his head high, for that showed too much pride. But if he stared at his feet, that gave off a sense of inner shame. And if he held his head to the side he looked cocky, and cocky was not good. When he spoke, it was never in a voice that was too high or too low, and he never spoke of the things he longed to speak of, like pre-European history, B-grade action films, or the novels that made him weep. If he looked at boys he did so for no longer than two seconds at a time, and that was only to see how they looked at each other, so that he might copy those looks. But the looks he saw were ones of love and affection, and if people saw those looks coming from his eyes, they would give them new and dangerous meanings.

He became an expert in the art of behaviour modification.
He moved about the town like a ghost.
But he preferred to think of himself as a ninja.

Card 6:
One summer night, he sat at the kitchen table, puzzling over his algebra homework. Carolina was behind him, mashing potatoes, one eye on the cheese-filled sausages sizzling on the stove.
"I think it's time we started testing you."
He looked up. "Testing me?"
"First question," she said, scooping mounds of mashed potato onto their plates. "What do you say if someone asks if you like boys?"
"I say I don't."
"Wrong, you say you have a girlfriend."
She put their meals on the table – three sausages each, mash, corn, broccoli, plus a stack of buttered white bread and a bottle of tomato sauce.
Anaru grabbed a slice of bread. "What if they ask what her name is?"
"Then you tell them!"
He wrapped the bread around a sausage, covered it in sauce, and bit into the end.

"So what is it?"

"Uhh, Dominica."

"Don't be so bloody ridiculous. You're a nice boy with a nice wholesome girl."

"Tracey."

"Much better. And what do you and Tracey do for fun?"

"Go to the movies?"

"And?"

"Walk on the beach."

"Do you hold her hand?"

"Yes."

"Do you kiss her?"

"Yes."

"Have you had sex with her?"

"No."

"Of course you have. Men are obsessed with sex, and you're a red-blood-ed, red-meat-eating man. Even if Tracey were real and you hadn't had sex with her, you'd lie and tell your mates you had."

She bit into a slice of buttered white bread. The sight of the gooey white balls that got stuck in her teeth made his stomach flip.

"I need to study."

"Eat your dinner, and tell me what you'll tell your mates about the sex you're having with Tracey. Think you can shock me? I've heard far worse believe me."

He felt as though he had a boot on his throat. The boot of a fisherman from the pub perhaps. Crushing his windpipe. His throat closed up. He felt dizzy. He forced mashed potato into his mouth but it stuck to the roof like cement.

"I feel sick."

"Tell me what you do."

He remembered the things he heard older boys saying at school.

"I touch her boobs."

"And?"

He was sweating now, oxygen hard to come by.

"I rub her vagina-hole."

"Well, I mean, I guess. What else?"

"Take her from behind and... please don't make me do this."

"This is how men talk! They're disgusting! And you want them to think you're one of them. Now tell me how you fuck Tracey!"

Card 7:

He developed what you might call issues with food. His chest went tight when he tried to eat, and his throat shut up shop. And if his mother was feeding him fish or steak, and lecturing him on how to be a man, he got the throat thing and the chest thing, his head spun, his vision blurred, and his general experience of life turned into a nightmare ride on a rollercoaster with rust on the tracks and some key parts of the engine missing. He ate less, which made her worry more, which made him eat even less. And because she saw her worry and her food as signs or her deep and everlasting love, she saw his refusal to eat as a rejection of that love.

"What the hell is wrong with you? Why won't you eat my food?"

"I can't."

"You can't or you won't?"

"I can't. I want to. I don't know why I can't."

They were in the kitchen. She opened the oven door, took a potato cube from the baking tray, and came towards him, potato cube poised.

"Open your mouth."

"No."

"Open your damn mouth."

She backed him up against the wall, pried open his jaw and stuffed the hot cube in his mouth. His throat closed up, his head spun, his chest went tight and he nearly passed out.

"EAT THE DAMN POTATO!"

"I can't!"

He was crying.

"Stop blubbering! What are you, a woman? Only women skip meals. Men have appetites! Eat! Eat or they will come for you!"

Episode Twenty-Five.

The tiny bronze Buddha statue flew at my head. It slowed down, and I watched in horror as it spun, end over end, directly for my right eye. I saw the hand that threw it, which was Hang's. I saw too the rage in her eyes, the clenched jaw, the red curtains fluttering at her back. DONK. By the time I hit the deck, blood was trickling into my right eye. When I wiped it away, I saw Hang standing over me, her eyes like hot coals. In a feeble attempt at surrender, I waved the forty million dong story fee in the air. She snatched it away.

"Where is my gallery?"

"What?"

"My show!"

"You got a show with Ren!"

"She cancelled me!"

Ren gave no reason for the brutal cull. But Magda had flown home to Kiev, and she was a big personal fan of Hang. With her gone, Ren had no need to give Hang a show, so she sharpened her axe and swung. This was bad for Hang and bad for me too. I had been plotting the story arc for her season, and what a season it was shaping up to be. But now, until I got her a new gallery, she was withholding episodes. I had no choice but to call Nhu. She didn't answer (duh) so I tried again. And again and again and again. After the fifth failed attempt, Hang drove me to a clinic. While I went in to get five stitches in my eyebrow, Hang sat cross-legged on her bike. I came out to find a message from Nhu:

What do you want.

I wrote back: *Sorry to bother you, but I need a new gallery for Hang. Ren cancelled her show for no reason.*

Stupid

Please?

This is the last time.

Hang drove me home to the maze in rush hour heat. As I peeled my thigh skins off the hot leather seat, Nhu wrote back:

My friend has a space in Can Tho. The name is 7/11. He can see you tomorrow at 2

7/11 like the store?

Yes. Can you make it?

Yes. Thank you!

Can Tho was a three hour drive south of Saigon, depending on the mental stability of the driver. For our trip, that would be Hang. The person who had just assaulted me with a bronze Buddha statue. She messaged a few minutes after sunrise, and I ran downstairs and found her waiting at the mouth of the maze. She handed me an iced coffee, and said she couldn't decide what to wear. "You look good," I said, and she did. Black jeans and a black singlet with semi beat up Chucks. A real deal artist's outfit.

Nine buses. That's how many I counted. Nine buses that nearly killed us in the two hours it took to reach the Mekong. Most were filled with tourists from Europe and China and America, and as they roared past, nearly crushing us under massive dusty wheels, the passengers took photos of us out the windows. After the tenth bus thundered past, mere inches from our bare arm flesh, Hang turned off the highway, and took a narrow road that cut through bright green rice fields.

"I need to do something."

"Will it take long?"

"We have time."

"Our meeting's in two hours."

We rolled through a small town, past men drinking beer at outdoor restaurants, women selling chickens in roadside cages, kids playing badminton in a park. Hang turned off the main strip, and took a road that ran along a calm brown river that ran into a thousand more calm brown rivers. I saw banana trees and jackfruit trees and trees that bloomed a million yellow flowers. On the road ahead a woman walked towards us. She wore turquoise pants with a matching turquoise top, and two boys at her side booted a soccer ball back and forth in the dust. Hang stopped the bike, slid off her helmet. Her face was calm, but I felt her heart beat against her spine. The woman saw Hang and ran to us. The boys looked up from their ball, confused as to why their Mum had run off. When they saw Hang they ran too. Weeping, the woman threw her arms around Hang. She looked at me over her shoulder, then squeezed her eyes shut tight and gripped Hang's back so hard her knuckles turned white. The boys crashed into Hang's legs, nearly knocking both women into the dust.

Hang introduced me to her mother, Nguyet, and her brothers, the twins, Hung and Hieu. She hadn't seen her family in a year, but the joyous reunion soon descended into conflict. Not two minutes after the hug-fest, Hang and Nguyet were screaming at each other on the side of the road. We're talking red-faced yelling with spittle flying, the works. I kicked the ball to the twins, and they kicked it back to me. When the storm passed, Hang said her Mum was insisting we go to their house for lunch, so Hang could see her father. But he sunk beers in front of the TV all day, and Hang had no desire to see where the money she sent home went. Plus we had our meeting. "Why don't we get a coffee," I said. Hang shook her head, but her mother smiled, and led us to a café in town.

Inside, the air con was turned up to freezing, AKA heavenly. A teenage boy in a pressed white polo served us coffee, with Cokes for the twins. The coffee was on the crack end of strong, and Nguyet dumped a barrage of information on Hang. Hang did her best to translate (as Nguyet moved onto the next topic) and I learned about the twins' grades, how her father's knee had swollen to the size of a soccer ball, which of Hang's friends had moved to the city, who was pregnant and who wanted to get pregnant but couldn't due to chemicals in the water.

"She tells me to tell you about my running."

"You were a runner?"

"I won many medals. And what's the other one? The big cup."

"Trophies too?"

"Yes. This is another reason she wants you to come to the house. She keeps the trophies. She cleans them always."

"Why did you stop?"

She shrugged. Nguyet asked her a question.

"She asks about your wife."

"I don't have a wife."

"She says why not."

I shrugged.

"She says a man like you needs a wife and children."

I blushed and sipped my crack-strength coffee.

"My mother asks what is your mother's name."

"Her name was Daisy. She died when I was three."

Nguyet looked at me in a way that made me look at the floor. Tears rolled off the tips of my eyelashes. Nguyet spoke. Her tone much softer now.

"She says she can see you missed her. That you needed her."

I nodded.

Nguyet reached out, placed her hand on mine. Her skin was warm from the sun, and hard but soft at the same time. This small gesture sliced me down the middle. My throat closed up. My chest heaved. Intestines contracted, twisting into complex knots. We sat like this for about eleven seconds. For the first time, Hang looked at me with eyes that held something akin to kindness.

Nguyet waved as we raced away from the café. Our wheels kicked up dust, the twins ran after us laughing. Forty-four minutes later, we darted down the narrow Can Tho streets. We were late, but I had GPS on my phone, and I fed directions into Hang's left ear. After a few wrong turns and being told to *proceed to the route,* the GPS said we had reached our destination. Only it didn't look like our destination. It looked like an actual 7/11, not an art gallery in a former 7/11. Maybe that was the point. That it was some post-post-modern space that sold snacks and cigarettes and water, and that was the art. Was that why the owner wanted to meet with Hang? The transactional nature of her work? I walked inside, took a bottle of water from the fridge, paid at the counter. But I wasn't taking part in some cool performance piece, I was buying a bottle of water. I walked outside and gave the water to Hang.

"What is it?"

"I think, um, I think that um…"

My phone pinged. It was Nhu.

Did you find it?

It's an actual 7/11

Yes

Is it a gallery?

Does it look like a gallery?

So there's no gallery called 7/11

No

Are you kidding me?

I told you don't message me. Now you learn.

Chunks of half-digested food and a thimble-full of bile lurched up my throat. I coughed and spluttered. Hang rubbed my back. "Are you okay?" I told her the truth. That Nhu had told me not to message her, so to punish me for messaging her, she had tricked us. There was no gallery called 7/11, this was an actual 7/11. Hang stopped rubbing my back. Her face went blank. She got on her bike, pulled her helmet on, and rode away. I watched her go without protest. Okay, I thought, that's okay. Take one of the killer buses back to Saigon. But my wallet was in the compartment under her seat, along with my sunglasses and sunscreen. With the maps app on my phone, I plotted a route to the highway. My plan was to hitchhike. Catch a ride with a local or some tourists in a taxi. But the GPS sucked the life out of the battery, and my phone died after five blocks in the yoke. I asked to charge it in a café, but they pretended not to understand me. In the next one they just said no. I did the only thing I could do. Trudge the streets, hoping to find my way north. But it was hot and dusty, and the sun turned my nose into a flaming red bulb. I was hungry and thirsty. My spirits crashed, but I plodded on. I saw a bottle of water sitting on the seat of a bike, so I stole it, and that kept me from total dehydration. Was I walking in circles? Was the 7/11 I passed the 7/11 that was meant to be a gallery called 7/11, or some other actual 7/11. On I walked, the canvas of my shoes rubbing skin from my heels. As the sun went down, a bridge took me over a wide brown river. Was I heading north? Hopefully not east or south or west. I sat in the grass on the far side and slipped off my shoes. As I peeled off a blood-soaked sock, a bike stopped in front of me. I looked up and into the face of Hang.

"Get on."

She drove us down the highway. A bug flew into my mouth. After about thirty minutes, she pulled into a roadside café. This was a roof on poles, with a bar and a kitchen. A bus had stopped, and tourists lounged in hammocks, tongues hanging out of their mouths in the heat. She found us a table. Food and drink appeared, and I stuffed it into my mouth without checking what it was.

"I feel a little bad," she said. "Not much, but a little, so I will give you one free story."

"My phone died. I can't record it."

"You have paper?"

I shook my head. Stuffed more food in my mouth.

"You can remember."

"Sure."

"This is from when I first shoot my customers. The first man, I don't remember his name. He was from Nigeria. He had big muscles, very tall. He was a beautiful man. And he ask me actually. He ask me to take his picture when he see the camera."

After the Nigerian man, she asked every customer the same question: 'Can I take your photo?' Many said no. Some said hell no. And some said yes. Most of the yes-men assumed the yes would lead to a discount. It never did, but they didn't mind. She shot bankers and builders, chefs and teachers and doctors. She liked shooting the good looking men the least. Nordic backpackers with bouncing curls, Koreans with flowing fringes, Canadians with gleaming white teeth. They gave so little to the lens. She liked men with obvious pain and secret shame. Men who had abandoned their families, only to find loneliness dressed up as freedom. She shot a man as he lay naked on the floor, weeping over a photo of a daughter who discarded his name. She shot them as they smirked, as they grimaced, as they stared at her lens enraged. She shot hands sliding notes from wallets, fists pulling hair, fingers tracing outlines of babies on her belly. She told them to get on their knees and pray, to eat soup, to slurp it, to look at her as they sucked their fingers. To spread their arse cheeks. And to tell her all the ways they had hurt all the people in their lives. She didn't see it coming, the way she felt for these men. Men who had been no more than wallets on legs. Now she thought of them as she ordered coffee, as she boiled water on her stove, as she waited at the lights on her bike. Through her lens, they crept into her life. Tiny dashes of joy crept in too. If she spent all night shooting her customers, the next day she liked doing little things a little more. Like washing clothes or sweeping the floor. Even tasks that once made her veins boil – like haggling with Blossom over tips – she now found strangely bearable.

When George walked into Smile Bar, Duc screamed. Kim and Nga scurried upstairs. Hang sat on her stool. She watched him walk to the bar, sit down, order a beer. Blossom's lip curled. Hang could see she feared contamination, but wanted the man's lovely money. Hang did not look away. She wanted him to know she was not afraid of him. He sipped his beer – once, twice – then he looked over at her. She could see he had been burned.

His lips were gone, so his teeth were permanently bared. There were two holes where a nose had once been, and his eyelids were melted to his brows.

"Hi."

"Hello."

"What's your name?"

"Hang. What's yours."

"George."

"You want to come upstairs with me, George?"

Episode Twenty-Six.

Bad news. Actually the worst news. Anaru went missing. He disappeared. And he didn't answer my calls or texts or emails. I wasn't sure what to do. I felt lost and alone, and more than a little heart-broken. And let me tell you one thing: I had never in my life had my heart broken. I don't know why. Maybe I had never let anyone near enough to my heart to break it, or maybe I was better suited to breaking hearts (two and counting). I'm not sure.

But one thing was for sure, and that was the physical pain in my chest, like the pectoral fibres were being ripped apart. There was also a dull emptiness in my stomach. To be honest, that had always been there, but now it felt bigger. Before it had been as big as a pudding bowl, but now it was the size of a cave where a family of wolves could live comfortably. What if Anaru was hurt? Or dead? I knew he had been looking for a new apartment, and was staying in a room above the Karaoke Kingdom, but when I asked at the front desk, they said he had moved out and had taken several weeks off. And I was not entitled to anymore information.

At least he was alive. But it might mean he hated me.

Luckily, I had a distraction from this dystopian prospect: I was broke. I mean I wasn't on my knees, but there was more going out than coming in. A lot more. What with Hang and her arbitrary rate hikes. I needed work, so I called Mai-Mai, and threw myself at her mercy. Luckily for me she had a side hustle – an online real estate agency that rented apartments to expats happy to pay well above market value – and she needed content. The pay was poor, and the opportunity for narrative expression was less than woeful, but so what. She had a DSLR camera and a tripod, and she picked me up on her bike in the mornings, and off we went. Most of the apartments were in the inner city districts – One and Three and Two, with lots in Thao Dien, the expat Mecca. Her needs for each listing were simple – a 60 to 90 second video with a jazzy soundtrack and a sprinkle of (but not too much) wow factor. Have you ever seen a real estate video? They're disgusting. If we're being honest, making them was well beneath my skill level, but I liked Mai-Mai, and I wanted her little business to succeed. Also, we were selling homes, places for humans to eat and sleep and raise families. So I gave the videos cinematic lighting, poetically paced edits, and well-considered colour palettes. All this I did to establish authentic emotional connections between people and properties. I shot all day and I edited well into the nights. I even spiced the pictures up with some amateur VFX. And let me tell you, the videos worked. In two weeks Mai-Mai rented more properties than she had in three months. That meant more work for me. Every day we sped around the city, shooting our sweaty socks off. Some nights I took my computer to the roof of The President Hotel, and hung my legs off the side as I cut together shots of empty homes, hoping Anaru might come home to me.

One afternoon, as I was shooting a marble bath in a bougie apartment, I got a text: *Hey man.* My heart jumped out of my throat and damn near disappeared down the drain. Anaru was alive! He didn't hate me! I can't tell you how happy this made me. He sent me his new address – 147 Vo Van Tan in D3 – right down the road from my old friend Tao Dan Park. "I have an emergency," I told Mai-Mai, then I ran down the stairs five steps at a time, and hopped on the back of a motorbike taxi.

His building was a bit of a dungeon, with moss creeping up the once pale blue walls. The stairs took me up a dark shaft, past musty hallways, and doors with chicken feet hanging off them. His door was on the third floor. When I knocked, no one answered. I knocked again. And again and again and again. I called his phone but got no answer. What the fuck. I stood there for a minute, staring at a bug poking its feelers out of a hole in the wall. Then he sent me a text: *It open.*

His apartment was no dungeon. Sleek and modern it was, with a kitchenette off the living room, shiny white tiles on the floors, and a wall of windows running down one side with sheer white curtains that billowed into the space like chilled out ghosts. Despite the pleasant minimal aesthetic, the air smelled off. Like stale sweat mixed with congealed bodily fluids, and subtle bouquets of decaying flesh. The kitchen bench was stacked with dirty plates and old instant noodle pots, and as I walked down the hallway, the smell came at me harder. When I opened his bedroom door, my stomach sank. But for a tiny pair of black shorts, he lay naked on the bed. He looked like he weighed less than a doll, with ribs that jutted right out. His cheeks had sunk, as had his eye sockets, and his skin was yellow and waxy. Did he have jaundice? Malaria? Scurvy? His eyes were the worst. The flicker of life that danced when he smiled was gone. They looked dead. That's what brought on the tears, looking into them. Was he about to check out? Had he got me over to say goodbye? I really thought I was losing him for good. As if hit by a sudden wind, my skin quivered as I sat on the bed.

"What happened?"

"I'm sick."

"Sick how? What sick?"

"I don't have cancer if that's what you think."

"That's not what I think." (It was totally what I thought)

"I get these, um, episodes. Depression. Migraines. I can't sleep. Or eat. I can't do… I dunno."

"What do you need? I'll go out and get whatever. You want soup? I'll feed you soup."

He asked for juice.

Artificially sweetened with god knew what orange juice. And who could blame him. I found a bottle in the fridge and cleaned a glass. As I poured the vivid liquid, my hands shivered on the bottle. I had never seen a person I loved so much in such bad shape. I thought he was about to ask me to euthanise him. Yes a big part of me was happy to be near him, despite his deathly sickly ways, but some rancid gassy feelings bubbled up under the happiness. Guilt. That's what it was. Maybe I was to blame here. I had pushed him to dredge up his most traumatic memories (for my own benefit) and now they were running amok in his body and mind. I took the glass of juice (hands still shaking) back to the bedroom, where I found him sleeping, so I went to work. I washed and dried the mountain of dishes. I dusted every surface. I picked up socks and towels and underwear, and washed them in the washing machine that was weirdly on the little balcony off his bedroom. I took an old toothbrush to the tiles and the grout in the shower. I scrubbed the sink and the taps and the dark green algae-looking mold in the plughole. And then I scrubbed the toilet. As I cleaned, I made the call to abandon his story. No more stealing. Not if it hurt him and made him as sick as he was. I had Hang's story for the first season of the Untitled Original Series Set On Multiple Continents, and that was bound to kill. I'd find a new one for the second season. I filled a bucket with bleach and boiling water, and then I–

He woke up. I poured him a fresh glass of juice and found a Choco Pie in the fridge. It contained a grand total of zero nutrients (maybe some protein in the marshmallow) but at least it was food. He nibbled at the edges, took teeny-weeny bites. Thirty minutes in and he was only halfway done. Watching made my stomach growl.

"You want some?"

"Nah that's all you. But listen, I might stay here for a few days if that's cool."

Nipping a tiny piece of marshmallow with his front teeth, he said, "If you want."

I walked out into the night, and found it buzzing with life. In Tao Dan Park, I performed four sets of badly formed pull ups. In my room in the maze, I slipped my computer and some clothes into a backpack. And at the VinMart on the top floor of the Vincom Centre, I bought fruit and meat and veggies, and juice and milk and eggs and nuts, plus a pack of Choco Pies and a dozen pots of probiotic yoghurt they had on sale. I figured both of us could do with a dose of live cultures. Back in his apartment, I helped him from the bed to the couch, then I changed the sheets and helped him back to bed, where we sat eating Choco Pies and sipping cups of tea. And he told me about a secret project he had been working on for some time. "One night about a year ago I was sweeping out the front of Karaoke Kingdom, and I saw these two lady's swap scooters. One lady's bike was shittier than the other lady's, so she gave her some money to make up the difference. I did some research and I found out there was no online market for scooters in Saigon. In a city of nine million scooters that's pretty crazy, so I started developing an app where you can trade scooters with people. I called it Swappy. And I put down some ideas and, like, the scraps of a business plan, but then I got busy with work and all sorts of bullshit. Plus there's Cam, my boss. If she knew I developed an app on her dime she'd be after a cut. And when I say a cut I mean a hundred percent cut."

I've never been a morning person, but I rose at dawn and made him scrambled eggs. He ate in bed. Slow going. Painful to watch. He chewed each bite a hundred times, and at times he stopped chewing, and stared at the air in front of his face while the half-chewed egg in his mouth begged him to please get on with this slow form of torture. Mai-Mai picked me up at nine. We shot a three bedder in District 7, then zipped back into the city to shoot a glass-walled pad in a building so tall and thin it seemed to sway in the wind. After that we hit up L'usine for coffee and eclairs.

"I want to offer you a trade," I said, biting into the chocolate shell and cream.

"What kind of trade?"

"I need an office space, but I don't have the money to pay for it."

"The office is for you?"

"It's for my friend, he needs a space to develop his app."

"What app?"

"I can't say, but if you give me the space for a couple months, I'll give you content."

"How much content?"

"The whole cake. A platform, social series, a brand campaign with scripts and everything."

"And social posts for one year."

"Uhhh."

"Two per week."

"How about one every two weeks."

"One a week. And you direct. Then I find you the space."

Episode Twenty-Seven.

Hang led George up the stairs. He held her hand tight, which she didn't like, but he smelled great, which she did like. But his was no ordinary scent. This was leather on the saddle of a stallion as it galloped under a mountain waterfall and winked at you. Also his smile. He smiled non-stop. A manic smile. Slightly deranged. She wasn't sure if the burns on his lips and face made him look deranged, or if he was actually deranged.

"How much?" he said when she shut the door to her room.

"Three million."

He pulled out his wallet and handed her the full amount. No haggling. This, on top of the superior scent and megawatt smile, was a green flag.

"Can I ask you one thing?" he said.

Here we go, she thought.

"Can you call me Mr. George?"

"Yes."

"Thanks. Can I ask you one more thing?"

Okay now here we go, she thought.

"Do you want to meet my sister?"

"What?"

"Take a seat."

She sat on the bed as he stripped naked. Then he faced the wall and took a breath. When he turned back to face her, his penis and testicles were tucked between his legs, so his pubic hair made it look like he had a vagina. He danced in front of her, smiling his deranged smile.

"Say hi to my sister!"

Hang stared. Wide-eyed. Then she burst out laughing. Another green flag.

Mr. George came to see her every night. She led him up the stairs, he handed her three million, and leapt naked on the bed. Most men liked to get their money's worth, to squeeze more than sixty minutes out of the hour. But Mr. George was different. His goal was to milk the maximum amount of feeling out of every touch. When her throat touched his earlobe, she felt him zero in on the moment. When their stomachs scraped or her lips grazed his left shoulder, he went into a sort of trance. But sometimes he snapped out of the trance to tell a bad joke mid-stroke:

"What's red and bad for your teeth?"

"What?"

"A brick."

Or:

"What kind of tea is hard to swallow?"

"What?"

"Reality."

Some nights he laughed so hard at his own jokes he went soft, and had to wait for the laughter to pass to return to full strength. Hang laughed pretty hard too. Not at the jokes, but at how hard he laughed at his own bad jokes. Still, she had never laughed until she cried with a customer, so that was a first.

Mr. George was her most willing model. He was so touched that she wanted to shoot one photo of him, let alone hundreds, he did whatever it took to get the shot. He strutted about the room butt naked. He rolled on the floor, imitated a male peacock's mating call, crouched under the sink, screamed out the window at the moon, and he knelt on the bed and peered back at her – a pose he called 'coquettish Bambi'. "I'm your muse," he said, and she didn't correct him. But she did delete the shots. His silliness frustrated her, but she persisted. It was as if he sensed her attempts to mine his truth, so each time she shot him, he fed her a new story about how his face got burned. One night he said he saved a kid from a burning car, another night he blew up a chemistry lab, another night he got grilled by a flamethrower while serving in Iraq.

"I want to take you to dinner."

"Not allowed."

"Who says? Blossom?"

"That's her rule."

"I'll speak to her."

"No."

"I already did."

They walked down Nguyen Hue. No breeze blew off the river, so the air sat on the city like a soggy pillow. All the families from all the family houses were out, plus all the tourists from all the tourist hotels. Pretty much all passers-by stared at Mr. George. Men covered their mouths, sisters pointed him out to brothers, women placed hands over babies' eyes. To Hang's amazement, Mr. George smiled at them. He nodded and waved. But when she took his hand in hers, she felt sweat pooling in his palm. She stood on her tippy-toes and kissed him. A proper kiss. A soldier going off to war kiss. Long enough for the gawkers to get a good hard look. Mr. George grew two feet. "You like that?" he said to the starers. "Nice pointer finger you got there." In the restaurant, the waitress refused to look at him. Chefs peered out the round window in the kitchen door. "I want to buy you a present," he said. They were back out in the night now. Hang looked around, pointed at a pair of sneakers in a shop window. Mr. George paid in cash. They got ice creams with the change, and sat on a marble ledge near the Vincom Centre. A group of maybe ten teenage girls walked past. Snickering. They walked past again, and again and again and again. Hang scolded them and they scattered. But five minutes later, they popped out from behind a parked car, snapping covert photos of Mr. George. "You girls want a selfie?" he asked, walking up to them. The girls froze. No snickering now. "Hand me your phone." Their leader gawped at him. "I won't steal it!" She held out her champagne gold iPhone, like she was feeding steak to a lion at the zoo. With her phone outstretched, Mr. George crouched at their feet. "Everyone in the shot." The girls formed a semi-circle at his back, but not too close, heaven forbid they touch him. "Closer!" he roared, and they inched closer. "Now everyone say burned cheese face!" One or two muttered, maybe three smiled. Most stared at the lens like they were facing a firing squad.

"My stomach doesn't feel so great," said Mr. George, watching the girls skulk down the street. "I need to use the bathroom, like, now."

Before she could answer, he was off and running. She caught him at the door to his hotel. The Rex. In the elevator, gripping his stomach, he shut his eyes tight. Muttered what sounded like a desperate prayer. He also held the back of his shorts. The doors dinged open, he dashed down the hall, into his room, and locked himself in the bathroom. He was groaning when she walked in. Crying maybe. "You need the doctor?" she asked through the door. She heard a moan and a splash, so she looked around the room, which was really more of a two-bedroom suite. Out the window, lights on dinner boats glowed as they slid along the river. A suitcase on the bed. She flipped it open, and found maybe forty bottles, all containing various shades of amber liquid. Different kinds of cologne all. Some of the brands she knew – Tom Ford, Louis Vuitton – but some had no label. Picking up an unbranded bottle, she sprayed a burst in the air. It smelled of petals, pepper, the ocean, and money.

By the time he was done with his bathroom groan-fest, she had smelled the contents of all forty bottles. She felt dizzy and disoriented. And more than a little high.

"You ready to go out?" he asked her.

"I'm going home now."

"What? No. Please? Just one hour. One dance. Please."

He tugged her down Dong Khoi street. He was giddy, manic. Opaque drops of sweat rolling over the folds on his scarred face. Hang was still groggy from the suitcase perfumery. They passed a family, and a small boy pointed at Mr. George, so Mr. George crouched down and screamed in the kid's face: "LOOK AT ME I'M A SCARY MONSTER WOOOO!" The boy let out a blood-curdling howl. His mother picked him up, the father yelling for the police. Mr. George and Hang ran. At the door to a club called Apocalypse Now, a bouncer frisked them for weapons. Inside it was a cauldron. Pink and blue and green flashing lights. A heaving mass of slick limbs on the dancefloor, the DJ up front, blasting a bassline that rattled Hang's ribs against her lungs. Mr. George dragged her to the bar, bought vodka Red Bulls, then dragged her to the dancefloor to grind his body on hers. His smell. What had once been sweet was now overpowering. An ocean of cologne. Strobe lights pierced her retinas, dripping flesh pressed into her. Mr. George shut his eyes and swirled under the technicolour lasers. A hairy hand slid up her skirt. A long pink nail scratched her neck. She tried to tell Mr. George she needed the bathroom, but he was too busy reaching for the giant disco ball that hung above his head, and reflected shards of light onto the wet faces of the revellers.

She locked herself in the stall, wiped the seat and sat down. The walls vibrated. Closing in. She smelled urine and blood and cheap perfume. Outside, at the mirror, girls chattered about boys they liked and girls they didn't. For five minutes she sat. Breathing. When she left she felt a little less pukish. She didn't go back to the dancefloor, but to the courtyard in the back of the club. Draped across the open space were strings of red lights, the stars above. Locals and tourists sat at tables. Drinking, smoking, eating hotdogs. And watching a commotion in the corner. "You freak! Goddamn crazy-ass freak!" Mr. George was surrounded, a gang of mainly blonde men taunting him. Some spoke English, and some a language that sounded like dogs barking. The ring leader was box-shaped, with red hair and a fiery red beard. "Don't ever touch my woman!" he hissed. "Freak of nature!" Mr. George's eyes were white and wide with terror. Blood dripped from his burned bottom lip. "I'll kill you! Cowardly dogs I'll kill you!" He spat and kicked and punched, but they were too many. They laughed and jeered, threw pints of beer. It was too much. Too heart-breaking to watch. Hang headed for the door, then she heard a smash. Holding the neck of a broken beer bottle, Mr. George lunged at his tormentors, desperate to slash human flesh. Hang darted through the men, grabbed the wrist of the hand that held the bottle. For a second she thought he might stab her, but he saw her face and let go. Smash. Hot chips hit her face, bourbon splashed the back of her neck, but she pulled him free.

Spitting and cursing and bleeding, he raged his way up the street. People stared, jumped out of his way. Hang's heart raced. All it took was one cop and they were cooked. But she got him to his hotel. Pushed him into the lobby, bundled him into the elevator. In his suite, she lay him on the bed. The sight of the bottles in the suitcase made her gag. She wanted to run, to be relieved of this burden. But he wept like a child. She knew what came next. Begging. So she sat with him, and stroked his hair as he blubbered himself into slumber.

An hour later, she was back in the street. Head swimming. Synapses misfiring. She smelled of bourbon, blood, and liquids that smelled of all the things men think they want to smell like.

"What are you doing here?" asked Blossom. She sat at the bar, polishing the purple spikes on her fingers. "It's your night off."

"I need to work."

"You look like shit."

A red-bearded man walked in the door. Her heart jumped. Was this the man throwing beer on Mr. George? No. This man was older. Much older. He chose her, and she took him upstairs. She pulled his pants down thick hairy legs. The light from the street hit him just so, and she didn't have time to ask permission. Maybe she didn't want to. Maybe she didn't care. Her mind was so foggy. He heard the click. But when he turned his head, the camera was back in her bag. The next man was slender, young, with light green eyes. When they walked into her room, the grey light of dawn was creeping under the curtains. He took off his shirt and jeans, folded them, stacking them in a neat pile on a chair. His back was a mess of tattoos, like a child had drawn them. Hang saw a wolf, a tortoise, stars, a nuke, and what looked like a box of McDonald's fries. She needed to capture the messy ink next to the neatly folded clothes. She reached in her bag for her camera.

Click.

"What are you doing?"

Click.

"Can you stop."

Click click click.

"Are you fucking deaf or something?"

Like an animal that had evolved into the perfect predator, he jumped over the bed, snatched the camera, and smashed it on the wall. She screamed. But the scream only made it to the end of her tongue before his fist forced it back down her throat. After that: darkness.

Episode Twenty-Eight.

Have you ever tried Queen of Sheba soul cake? It's a rich chocolate cake with rich chocolate sauce, and it's named after the Queen of Sheba (obviously) who was a queen in the bible and maybe also a queen in real life. But also maybe not.

Anaru made Queen of Sheba soul cake for my birthday, and he served it on plates painted with green chickens. We were in the office Mai-Mai found for him, which was a tiny white cube with a desk and a round table and a slender window that looked onto an alleyway with a pho cart down below. In exchange for this office I had given her the social media content that was sure to boost her business to the next level. And Anaru was happy. Recovering from his episode, putting on weight and working on his app.

As far as birthdays go, this one was right up there.

He bit into a slice of cake. Then told me how he went to see Jun, the handsome record store owner he had crushed on for months. He didn't want a year to pass without asking him out, so he swore to make this the trip to overcome his cowardice. When he walked into the shop, Jun offered a swift nod, like always. Anaru paid for the two rare dub releases Jun had set aside for him, and then he said:

"Listen, um, do you want to get a drink sometime?"

"Oh."

"You don't have to."

"Hm."

"Don't worry about it."

"Can I be honest?"

"Of course."

"You are young, and to me, there is nothing more annoying than a young man."

Anaru popped a big bite of cake into his mouth, and stared at a stain on the grey carpet. I asked him what he did about Jun's harsh burn, and he said he did the only thing he could do – laugh. But then I noticed a shadow pass over his face. I was pretty good at reading him. And after nursing him, I was hyper attuned to the slightest shifts in his mood and what they might mean.

"You thinking about your Mum?"

"What makes you say that?"

"You get this look sometimes."

Stacking my plate on top of his, he took our plates to the communal office kitchen down the hall. When he came back, he put his laptop on the table in front of me. "Check this out," he said, sitting in the chair next to mine. He opened Google Maps and typed in, 'Christ Church, Russell, Bay of Islands, New Zealand.' A map of a seaside town appeared. He clicked on street view, and zoomed us in until it felt like we were standing in the graveyard of an old white church. With the cursor, he moved us among the graves, stopping next to a tall narrow stone with a cross on top. "That's the grave of Tamati Waka Nene, the famous Ngapuhi chief. He was related to Hongi Hika. I told you how Hika took a bunch of shrunken heads to England, and got a suit of armour from King George, and how he brought it home and wore it in battle, which buzzed his enemies out apparently."

With the arrow on the screen, he clicked us around the back of the church, to a small stone grave. "This is Mum." I tried to read the epitaph, but he walked us to a seat under some trees, and swivelled us in a circle, making it seem like we were sitting on the seat, looking at her grave. "I come here sometimes, to talk to her." He slid the cursor to the top of the screen, and we looked up into the branches. The leaves glitched, as if blown by a digital wind. Another shadow, darker than the last, passed over his face. "I bailed on her, man. I bailed on my own Mum. I know she lied to me. For, like, years. But she was cool, and I was a dickhead. A real little shit-head. Or I dunno. I know what she did fucked me up, feeding me all that stuff about how I'd get killed like Griffin, but she was so messed up herself. I just. I couldn't be around her anymore, so I moved over to Paihia with my cousin, Justice. Man, Paihia was the big smoke to me. It's just another shit-hole town, across the water from Kororareka, but man, me and Justice had our own house and everything. Selling foils. You know what that is? You guys called them sticks in Oz. It's just a stick of weed, wrapped in tin-foil. Twenty five bucks for one foil. Me and Justice sat in the house all day, selling foils through a slot in our front door. I thought I was Tony Montana. Justice was even worse, bought a big hunting knife and everything. I felt safe with him at least. But after I left, Mum just went to pieces..."

Clicking on the arrows, he marched us down the street, through a small park, then along the waterfront. We passed a café, a souvenir shop, families on the pebble beach, their blurred faces frozen in time. He stopped outside a small cottage. "This was our house. My room was around the back. Every day after school, we sat on the front step eating gingernut biscuits. But after I..." He closed his eyes. I put my arm around him. "After I bailed on her, she filled the whole house with junk. And rubbish. She hoarded everything – old newspapers, jars of olives, broken umbrellas, dead plants, busted ra-dios, TVs and DVD players. She wouldn't throw anything away. Or she couldn't. I don't know. Crazy shit. It looked like she'd emptied rubbish bins on the carpet every day for three years. Just boots, old phones, tattered books, cracked vases, tools, belts, old socks, dirty pots, sacks of flour, rotten pasta. It stunk. Rats everywhere. Possums dying. The works."

He clicked us over the front lawn, right up to a dark and dusty window. "They told me she died in the kitchen. This was in the morning. Reckon she got a yoghurt from the fridge, looked out this window at the waves, and boom. Heart attack. She died on the floor with a spoon in one hand and a pot of yoghurt in the other. After they took her body away, and I went in to clean the place up, I couldn't stop staring at the spot on the floor where she died. It was filthy, man. Thick with black grime. Mold everywhere. She wasn't even washing her dishes, just dumping the plates in boxes with bits of cheese and god knows what stuck to them. Queen of Sheba soul cake maybe. And when she ran out of plates, she went to the second-hand shop to buy more. Then she ate off those and dumped them in a box. That was probably the last thing she saw before she died. A box of plates covered in rotting food. And not me. She didn't see me because I wasn't there. I wasn't there to hold her hand."

Episode Twenty-Nine.

I remember where I was when I got the message from Hang. At least I think I do. You can never be too sure with the old memory now can you. Anyway. I was sitting at my desk in my room in the maze, plotting her first season story arc. Lord was it shaping up to be a beauty.

In the first episode, she left her family in the Mekong, headed to Saigon and started work in Smile Bar. In episode two, Blossom flew her to Bangkok and forced her to get breast implants. In episode three, she came back to Saigon, suffered a major breakdown, found the camera and shot her first photos. In episode four she created the baby daddy photo studio, then in episode five she met and fell in love with Mr. George (here I took some major narrative liberties, as you do). In episode six, Mr. George lost the plot after she left him, and in episode seven they got back together and she nearly got bashed to death. That took us up to the climax for the first season. Now all we needed was the final episode – the resolution.

Come to apocalypse now.

That was all she said in her text. Oh shit, I thought. Oh hell yes. She's taking me to the location from the previous episode (where Mr. George was attacked) to give me the story for the final episode. I jumped up and down and punched the air five times, then I flew down the stairs. The streets were hot and humming, women in heels and men in designer sneakers. At the door to the club, the bouncer gave me a vigorous frisk, then let me enter the jungle-like heat. The pink and blue lasers were doing their thing, the dancefloor thrashed with all brands of limb, and the bass made my vital organs feel like their time was up. I pushed my way to the bar, but Hang wasn't there, and she wasn't at one of the high tables on the outskirts of the dancefloor either. She sat alone at a table in the courtyard, sipping orange juice. Red lights on wires above her, purple sky above the lights. I pulled up a chair and pointed to the corner of the courtyard.

"Is that where Mr. George got beaten up?"

She turned and looked at the corner, then turned back to me. "I had a meeting."

"Oh yeah? Who with?"

"A woman. She lives in Hanoi. She has one big gallery. She saw my photos, from Ren maybe. I don't know how. But she will now give me a show."

"That's great news!"

She stirred the juice with her straw. "Good for me, yes. But I cannot give you my story."

"What do you mean."

"The story for your TV show. My story. You cannot have."

"But I bought it. You sold it to me."

"I can give you the money ba–"

"I don't want the money, I want the story. I've already written it."

"Okay, but you cannot. The story is mine. I want to tell it in my own way."

"I get that, but–"

"You don't get."

"I do get, but we had a deal."

"What deal?'

"The deal we made!"

"I doubt this deal."

A stinging sensation crept out from my armpits and down my long arms. Like I was under attack from millions of microscopic jellyfish. Hang stared at me and chewed her straw.

"I make it up," she said.

"You made what up."

"The story."

"All of it?"

"Some. Much. I forget."

"What parts were real and what was made up."

"Doesn't matter now."

"Mr. George?"

"I doubt."

"You doubt he's real or you doubt he's made up."

She shrugged.

"What about Bangkok? The surgery?"

"I doubt."

"Just let me use it. If it's not real and it's not from your life then let me use it."

"I own it."

"Do you?"

"Of course. The ones I make up are still mine. Same for you right?"

She had me there. I buried my face in my hands. I wanted to scream, but the bouncers would toss me on my face in the street. So I screamed internally. I screamed so loud internally it felt like I ruptured some of the sacks inside my lungs. When I looked up, Hang was crying. I had never seen her cry before.

"I thought you believed in me," she said. "In my photos."

"I do."

"Then let me tell it. Let me tell my story."

Episode Thirty.

Three strikes:

The casino heist story – strike one.

Anaru's story – strike two.

Hang's story – strike three.

I was out. And it broke my heart. Really it did. I lost a finger, I was broke, I gave countless hours of my life, and I nearly killed the person most precious to me. And for what? The Untitled Original Series Set On Multiple Continents was a pile of ashes on the ground. Sometimes I poked at the pile with a stick, but I saw no embers. No glowing signs of life in the charred carcass of my dreams. When I thought about my fantasy meetings at HBO or Netflix, where I sat in the boardroom signing a three season deal for my bombastic series, I wanted to ram that stick into my stinking guts. Or my pitiful throat. Or better yet my cockroach-infested brain.

Saigon was telling me to stop too. To please just stop and go home. Remember the night I first tried to leave? And my stump tingled like a water diviner telling me to go back and find more stories? Yeah, no tingling this time around. My stump was silent. And if I didn't make some money soon, I might be forced to eat the nine fingers I had left. Mai-Mai had been sucked back into hundred-hour weeks at her insurance marketing job (thanks to Khanh, the sadist) so her real estate business was on a short or maybe long-term hiatus, which meant no content work for me. And I didn't care to get my money back from Hang. I wanted her to kill it. To reign supreme at Venice or Basel or one of those big deal international art festivals. But that meant I had to bail. To fly home to Sydney and find a job. To rot in the short-term, then go someplace else to find more stories for the Untitled Original Series Set On Multiple Continents. That's right. I wasn't abandoning my baby. I may have been a burnt-out husk. Knocked down. Seeing stars. Smooching the canvas. But I wasn't out cold. My brain wasn't damaged from repeated blows to the head. Not yet anyway.

The only problem was Anaru. The thought of leaving him made my bones weep marrow. But my flight home was booked, and he had to be told. To do that, I had to take him to our spot on the roof of The President Hotel. I asked him to meet me out the front on a Tuesday evening, and I walked all the way down Tran Hung Dao. Past the powder blue mosque, the Honda dealership, the mysterious government building with guards at the gate. My mouth was dry and my socks were oozing sweat when I got there. And he was leaning on Gloria.

"We can't go in," he said.

"Why not?"

"They're tearing it down."

"No way."

"Symbolic huh."

"Sure."

"Do you have something to tell me?"

"No?"

"You sure?"

"I think so. Why?"

"You look guilty. Like a little boy who's done something wrong."

"I'm just sweaty."

"You're always sweaty. This is different. Are you leaving?"

"Um."

"Just tell me. I knew you would at some point."

"I'm broke, Anaru. I need money."

"What about the real estate thing?"

"Dead."

"Come work at Karaoke Kingdom. I'll give you a job."

"I dunno."

"Unless you want to go."

Gloria took us down the road. To the spot with beef noodles that warmed your heart and brought your soul back from the dead. But no amount of comfort food could revive mine. Our chat had once been lively and exciting, but now it was cold and stilted. This hurt nearly as much as losing my finger. Never before had I wanted to get away from him, but in that moment, I wanted to be skittering around the maze. Or on the island with Nhu. I hate to admit it, but when he got a call from the Karaoke Kingdom, and they said they needed him right away, I was kind of relieved.

After that, I didn't hear from him. It was the same as last time. I called and messaged and emailed. I knocked on his door and went to his place of work, but they said he was sick. He had gone to ground, and I feared the worst. That he wasn't eating. Wasting away. Rotting. But maybe I flattered myself. Maybe he wasn't fussed about me leaving at all. Maybe he was lying on a beach, or cavorting in the Mui Ne sand dunes with Jun.

Dawn. The day of my flight. I woke up with a boulder on my chest. My room was dark, so I took a walk around the silent city, to say goodbye to all the spots I would dearly miss. I walked down to the river, and blew a kiss to the muddy bank on the other side, where Thao performed her séance. I walked up to Tao Dan Park, where old ladies exercised in the morning mist, and lay on the patch of grass where I first met Anhtheman. Was my finger still in Uncle Frank's jewellery box? Surely the flesh had rotted by now. On the corner of Dong Khoi and Ly Tu Trong, I sat on a crumbling marble ledge and stared up at the window that opened into STATION. Was Nhu up there? Working in her office? Did she still have the jar with my blood and saliva inside? As the minutes ticked by, the scooters at the lights swelled to the hundreds. Beeping and roaring, ready to go. I hoped Nhu might come down, and tell me to lick her boots or slither in the dirt like a worm. Instead, my phone buzzed. It was Anaru. "What time's your flight?" I told him it left at two. "I'll drop you at the airport."

He picked me up at eleven. My bag was heavy, but Gloria didn't even flinch under the weight. I loved that bike. And I loved the bad traffic, because it gave me an extra forty minutes on her back. Outside departures, I stepped off, but Anaru did not.

"I won't come in, I don't wanna get all teary."

"No."

"I'll miss you though."

"I'll miss you too."

"Yeah cool. I know. And look, whatever happens, you can always come back."

"Or you could come to Sydney."

"True. I do wanna see where Mum grew up. Her and Griffin."

"Do it."

"I might."

"You should."

"I'll try."

"You better."

"Alright dickhead."

He stepped off Gloria and wrapped his long arms around me.

"Go catch your flight."

I hugged him harder. Hot tears on my face. "In a minute."

Episode Thirty-One.

In Sydney, I went on walks. I went on walks under branches blooming purple jacaranda flowers. And I went on walks down the dusty highway that is Parramatta Road. I walked over the harbour bridge, along ocean cliffs, through the botanical gardens, along train lines and into Chinatown. On one of my city walks, I walked into a plush antique shop, where I saw an old Maori tool. The woman who owned the store had used an unfathomable amount of hairspray to set her blonde hair into a helmet as hard as plastic. And her blue eyeshadow was so thick the clumps caught on the ends of her lashes.

"A beautiful piece," she said. "It once belonged to a prominent Maori chieftain."

"Is that so?"

"Certainly. He came from New Zealand to trade in the 1880s."

"That's a good story."

"It's the truth."

"I bet."

"Do you want it or not?"

"Not."

"Hmph," she said, and a blue eyeshadow boulder rolled down her cheek.

As you might have guessed, the tool reminded me of Anaru. I walked back to the tiny apartment I had rented in Darlinghurst, sat on the balcony, and pictured him on Gloria, or the roof of The President Hotel. That night, I went on my fifth walk of the day. It was meant to be a short walk. Thirty minutes or so, to clear my head before bed. But as I crossed Oxford Street, and trundled down Crown Street into Surry Hills, I began to cry. The tears were silent. They slid down the skin on my cheeks in a covert manner. Little CIA tears. I walked like this for some time. Walking and weeping and walking and weeping. It sounds dumb, but I was in some sort of trance. The pain and the muck and the trash I had stashed in the pockets behind my vital organs – all that shit was gushing out of me. And maybe it was a whole new thing too. Maybe my ducts and my veins and my brain were teaming up with the earth beneath the city and telling me not to head back out into the world in search of the big fancy story, and to just stay at home for a little goddamn while.

The next morning, I was back on my balcony, watching storm clouds roll off the harbour to hug steel towers in the city. The tears must have flushed me out, because I felt reborn. Like a baby that gets squeezed down a narrow birth canal, and pushed into the world covered in blood and womb juice, with no sense of its own identity. I thought about calling Oscar, my father, but stopped short of picking up the phone. I had been home one week and had not contacted a single soul. No friends and no family. I was ashamed to tell them the truth. That I had failed to do the bright shiny thing (Untitled Original Series Set On Multiple Continents) and was once again the scummy old cum sock I had always been. My old clients. That's who I reached out to. I was back in town to earn was I not? My cinematic skills were ready to serve their branded content needs, and they needed to be informed. I sent out ten emails, then I mooched around, did some washing. At some point in the afternoon I was sitting on the couch, looking at my hand (the one with five fingers) when I thought: Holy shit this is my hand. Like I'm an actual person with a body and limbs and everything.

Such was life for a week. I rolled out of bed and sat on the balcony, emailing ex-clients to let them know I was back in town and ready to work my tail off. I got no replies, so I sent follow ups. And when I sunk to total desperado mode, I sent follow ups to the follow ups. Radio silence. Not good. Maybe they heard about my Saigon stint – how my arse got turfed from the boardroom for presenting a pitch in gibberish. Again, not good. And I know I already told you, but I really was perilously broke. Overdraft city. The bank sent emails daily, asking in a nice then not so nice tone when I might get my balance back in the black. Also the hand thing. I had an episode at least once a day where I stared at it for several minutes, freaking out that it belonged to me and that I was a living breathing body. Odd. Nearly as scary as looking at my bank account. Then I received an email from:

Mary Badger.

Chief Marketing Officer, True State Insurance Group, Australia

When I worked with her, Mary Badger was the Brand Manager at a small health insurance firm. But she had always been ambitious, and in the years since she had risen to become the CMO at True State, a large firm that specialised in business insurance. Mary was your classic only child from an old money family. She had bright red hair, wore floral dresses, and was superior to everyone in every way. If you played piano, she performed at the Opera House. Oh you write poetry? She won a prize at university. She was also an excellent cook, a talented painter, knew how to break in wild horses, and had the best form in her pilates class (her instructor *always* said so). Basically she was a chronic one-upper. Which as you know is a trait more detestable than loud chewing. But if she was happy to pay my full rate, I was happy to be summoned to bask in her omnipotent genius.

The True State office was on the twenty-ninth floor of a glass Martin Place tower. I popped out of the elevator, and was led down a plush carpeted hallway, to a meeting room where Mary sat alone. Her dress was printed with red roses. It was the kind of thing a young horse-loving girl who had never heard of the internet might wear to a birthday party. Over her shoulder, the green harbour and the Opera House sparkled in the afternoon sun. "Apollo, my darling!" she said, standing to plant kisses in the air an inch from both my cheeks. "I was soooo happy to hear from you. I have *such* an amazing job and you are the *only* filmmaker I want to shoot it!" I knew my role. I was a seal that performed for fishy treats. And boy did I perform. I jumped through hoops, balanced a ball on my nose, and when she told me about the waterfront home she bought at auction, I barked and clapped. As a reward for my performance, she dangled a bucket in front of my starving maw. My brief was to create a series about small businesses insured by True State. "You need to find real business owners," she said, "and tell their authentic and aspirational stories."

I already had an idea cooking.

"What if, instead of the founders, we tell the stories of their employees. The people further down the ladder."

"Oh. I'm not so sure about that."

"Think about it. How many times have we see–"

"What happened to your finger?!"

"I lost it."

"Where? Down the back of the couch?"

"In the jungle."

"How mysterious."

"But listen. The founder story. Person starts business, person struggles, person overcomes obstacles, person succeeds. It's been done to death. No one tells the stories of the people at the bottom, what goes on in their lives. If we do that, people will see what a positive impact True State has on *all* of society."

I saw the cogs in her brain turning. She could see herself on stage, giving a rousing TED talk about being a force for good in the marketing world.

"This is why I like you, Apollo. Out of the box thinking. The life blood of True State."

Now came the hard part. The degrading part. The part where we haggled over my rate. Mary loved nothing more than driving people's fees into the dirt. It might have been her favourite pastime. The lower she pushed you, the redder the flush in her cheeks. I was sure it turned her on, and she saved the debasement in her memory bank for later use. But I stood my ground. I transformed from the performing seal and into a stubborn and blind and possibly mentally defective mule. I dug in my hooves. I would not be moved. She had already hired me, and I knew she had the money, she just didn't want to part with it. But part with it she did. After a few rounds (and me adding fuel to the speaking tour image she had in her head by promising the most effective content series in the history of insurance marketing) she signed off my invoice. And I took it to the bank to wave in the teller's face like a white flag.

I was back in business. First thing I needed to do was find my old friend Ruth, the casting director with a talent for hunting down real people. Ruth worked out of an old terrace house in Paddington (similar to the one where I was impaled) where she also lived with her wife, Thompson, who at one time played rugby for Australia. In the 1980s, Ruth was a smash hit in the film business. But decades of daily cocaine use had eroded her fine motor skills. It also gave her a nervous tic where she bulged her eyes every few seconds. This, along with her insistence on wearing the latest fashion from her most successful year (1987) – like a shoulder-padded suit jacket with the sleeves rolled up to reveal worn silk lining, a flotilla of bracelets that jangled at the slightest movement, and a peroxide crew cut with a shock of pink in the fringe – meant people were not that keen to work with her. But I loved her.

"Don't worry, kid," she said, bloodshot eyes bulging, "give me a week and I'll find you the most charismatic damn bottom feeders the screen has ever seen."

Find them she did. She sent me a dishwasher from a Moroccan restaurant insured by True State, and a woman who worked on the production line of an Ugg boot factory. This woman overcame crippling shyness to rise to the role of packing room manager. And these people were great. Wonderful in fact. But I needed to unearth a rough diamond. Someone truly special. Three days later, Ruth sent me a man named Rudy and his daughter, Natasha. Rudy drove a forklift in a homewares company insured by True State, and Natasha was a gifted ballerina. Also, Rudy recently got a pay rise, and he used the money to buy Natasha the lessons she needed to take the next glittering leap. Gold. This story was pure gold. It had heart. Not to mention the contrast of the working class father (a bearded mountain of a man) and the artistically minded daughter. It was perfect.

"A forklift driver?" Mary sneered. "Seems a bit... No. I think we need to keep looking."

I did not keep looking. I remained the stubborn and mentally defective mule, and at times I transformed into a terrier with a rodent in its jaws. I pestered Mary day and night. Badgering the Badger. I sent an endless stream of texts and emails. I sent a video of ballerinas and forklift drivers cut to an operatic score. I called her early in the morning and late at night, hoping to seed my vision into her dreams. She told me to fuck off more than once. But I had used this tactic on clients before. As long as I kept talking, she'd get sick of the sound of my voice and give me what I wanted. Either that or fire me. But I'd sooner go back to being broke than not shoot Natasha and Rudy's story.

After four days of punishment, she caved. Here's what I shot:

The soundtrack was a simple pizzicato violin piece. The opening shot was tight on Natasha's pink ballet shoes as they pirouetted over the concrete warehouse floor. Cut to Rudy's calloused right hand, turning the ignition on his forklift. The forklift blades lowered to the floor, and Natasha jumped, dancing the length of the left blade en pointe. Rudy hit the lever, and the blades rose, lifting Natasha into the air as she danced. When she reached the height of her father's eyeline, she hopped to the right blade, kicking her legs out in mid-air. Rudy watched from the cabin, and a voice over told their story. How True State helped the business he worked for do well, and how this gave him the money to fund his daughter's passion. When the blades reached maximum height, Natasha leapt into the air, sailing over the cabin where her loving father sat looking up at her.

I shot the dishwasher and the shy woman from the Ugg boot factory too, but Rudy and Natasha were my special darling babies, and I treated them as such. Four days and nights I stayed awake crafting their edit. I nearly broke the woman who composed the music, as well as the sound designer. But it was worth it. On a wet Monday morning, I took the edits to the True State boardroom. Mary introduced me to the board, who were mainly grizzled old men with dandruff on the shoulders of their suits. I dimmed the lights and played the films. Played them again. A few sage nods. A half smile. That was fine. I knew I had made a special thing. "Why don't we come back to you with consolidated feedback," said Mary.

Later that night, as a storm battered my window, I lay in bed eating pork dumplings. My phone rang. Mary Badger on the screen. I answered.

"They love them!"

"Who do? The board?"

"The board, everyone. We showed the CEO and she cried. Oh my god, Apollo."

"Natasha and Rudy?"

"They *adore* Natasha and Rudy. I'm so pleased I pushed you in that direction."

"It was all you."

"Hush. Listen, I sent the films to our team in LA, and now they want their own versions. Exactly the same but American. And they want you to make them. So when can you fly to LA?"

Episode Thirty-Two.

My plane landed at LAX on a clear blue morning, and I was greeted by airport cops who saw all travellers as potential national treasure blower-uppers. "Move! Move! Move!" they yelled at us like a batch of recently incarcerated crims. "Form an orderly line!" I joined a queue that snaked around several corners, and by the looks of the haggard faces further up, went on for months. An old couple from Queensland stood in front of me. She had a blonde perm and nicotine-stained teeth, and he wore a white cowboy hat and had a face the colour of a lobster getting lowered into the pot. They pulled suitcases printed with blown up photos of their faces. In the massive images, I saw the scars where they'd had skin cancers removed. I counted five for him and three for her.

"This is bullshit!" said the man.

"Calm down," said his wife.

He turned to me.

"How bloody long we gotta wait here ya reckon? Bloody Yanks. So bloody up themselves."

An airport cop watched him. Her hand an inch from the holster of her gun.

"Sssssh," I said.

He blinked at me, and turned to his wife. "This young rooster just shushed me."

My Uber slid me down the darkening freeway. Out the window, I watched the blurry lights of cars flying past, oil derricks suspended above the rocky earth. The driver looked at me in the rear-view mirror.

"First time in LA?"

"Yeah."

"You in the biz?"

"The film biz?"

"Yeah."

"Yup."

"You a director? You kinda got that look."

"Huh."

"You making a film?"

"A series of films."

"No way. Marvel?"

"True State."

"What's that? Graphic novel? Sounds cool, man."

"It's an insurance company."

"Oh. Okay."

We were silent for a few minutes. I didn't care. What did I care what an Uber driver thought of my work.

"I'm working on a TV series too."

"Oh yeah? What's that?"

"It's an Untitled Original Series Set On Multiple Continents?"

"That on Netflix?"

"It hasn't been made yet."

"Gotcha."

The Ramada Hotel, West Hollywood. That's where they put me up. Not a suite at the Chateau Marmont, not a bungalow at the Beverly Hills Hotel, a small beige room with a view of a car park. Did I care? I did not. I was juiced. Like a little boy at a birthday party, ready to crack the head of the piñata, and swoop on the treats. My skin tingled. The family of hairs around my nipples stood on end. I needed to move. To run and to roam. I pulled on a pair of shorts, laced up my sneakers, and headed out the door. Google maps guided me to Sunset Boulevard, where the Saturday night crowd was out in full force. Drunk couples fighting, suburban men running in front of headlights, horns honking. I saw a woman's heel snap as her friends (one of them mid-vomit) dragged her into a bar where the main attraction was a mechanical bull. I ran past strip clubs and comedy clubs, past Apple billboards and Cadillac billboards, past a billboard for the new James Bond film, and one for Fast and Furious one hundred and nineteen. I watched bouncers rough up patrons and patrons spit on bouncers, only to get roughed up some more. When I reached the Chateau Marmont, perched on its hideaway hill, I jogged on the spot, watching models and fat producers emerge from limos like giant lizards of the land. As they slithered up the driveway, I smelled the sick and twisted power. The delicious vapour. An illusion that people came from all over the world to chase. And I tell you that I wanted it. I wanted it so bad my heart made a noise like a small dog getting crushed under the wheel of a bus. Down the strip I ran. Past a line of bone-thin women waiting at the door to a club, their heels high and their dresses no more than scraps of fabric hastily placed on sections of their torsos. Athletic men were ushered in a side door. Basketball players? Action heroes? Rappers? The women – who were there to hunt and be hunted – watched the men hungrily. I pictured them getting ready in their studio apartments. Burning their hair straight, waxing whatever, contouring their faces in mirrors smudged with years of make-up residue. Would tonight be the night they made it back to a mansion in The Hills? Or would they slink home in the cold hour before dawn to stare at a beef Hot Pocket rotating in their grimy microwave.

At daybreak, I woke to an email from Wyatt, the marketing director of True State, California. The email was a horror show, with maybe fifty bullet points. This did not bode well for our working relationship. I scanned the dense forest of text, barely taking in the blather about brand tone of voice. In the fiftieth point, he said an Uber would pick me up at 7:00am. It was 6:30. I took a shower, dressed, and headed downstairs, where I found a black Prius driven by a man named Jesus, who wore transition lenses and twirled the waxed tips of his long moustache. Jesus drove me down a jammed freeway. Nearly two hours later, he dropped me at a business park in Santa Monica. A path led me into the park (which dubbed itself an *innovation hub),* past lush green lawns, a build-your-own salad bar, a creche, a pilates studio, several entertainment law firms and one or two minor tech companies. True State was situated in a squat, four storey building. The foyer was four shades of grey. A headset-wearing receptionist told me to sit on a metal-grey couch, that Wyatt would be right down.

"Apollo Jones?"

I looked up to see a petite man wearing a tweed cap on a light bulb-shaped head. Pressed white shirt, polished black shoes. His eyes were large and moist, and they darted left to right, like a scared creature scanning the space for predators. I shook his hand. Cold, delicate and damp, with a slight quiver, it was the hand of an anxious child.

"How was your flight?"

"Long."

"Hotel okay?"

"It's not the Chateau."

"Ha. Well. Hm. Why don't you come with me. We have an office all set up. And we're ready to start the casting, like, now."

He led me down a corridor that led to another corridor, that led to another corridor that led to a small white office with a desk, a red couch and a camera on a tripod. On the red couch sat a second petite man. Like Wyatt, he had large and jittery eyes, and he radiated a powerful anxiety. Also, he was Black. "This is Wayne," said Wyatt, touching Wayne's shoulder. "He'll be producing the films." I sat on the couch. Wayne and Wyatt stood in from of me, filling the air with nervous vibrations. It was obvious they were more than colleagues. Fascinating. How did a couple contain so much anxiety and not implode? Maybe they cancelled each other out. Who knew. Not me. Twitching and fidgeting, they gave me the run down. How we could cast actors as real people. How they loved the ballerina girl, but she didn't fit the True State California values. Right there on that red couch, I vowed to give them smooth sailing. I would not be the stubborn mule or the terrier with a rodent in its jaws. I would be a fluffy kitten that curled up on their laps and soothed their worrisome souls. LA was a small town. Wayne was a producer. Once I had a new story for the Untitled Original Series Set On Multiple Continents, it was highly likely he could get me in a room with the top brass at HBO or Netflix.

"If you're ready," said Wayne, "I'll bring the first actors in."

I switched the video camera on, and got my head in the game.

Wayne brought in a man in his 50s, then he closed the door and left with Wyatt.

"Good day, sir, my name is Jerome."

Jerome wore a light blue suit, and his wrists were wrapped with worry beads. He had hair plugs, but they looked like he did them at home with an online tutorial, using dog hair. There was an X taped on the floor. I asked Jerome to stand on the X, then focused the lens on his face.

"Can you play a café owner for me please, Jerome."

"I sure can."

He paused to think. Then he made a pretend coffee in character as a low rent James bond.

After Jerome, Wayne ushered in a woman named Wanda, and Wanda was in her 60s. "Today is my anniversary," said Wanda. "I've been in LA for forty years. This is my ten thousandth audition." I asked her to play a yoga teacher. She said okay then she stepped into the hall to prepare. When I went out five minutes later she was gone.

"My name is Ray," said a Black man in a well-cut suit. "I have my own law practise. I'm a divorce attorney. But acting is my passion. My business side and my creative side. The yin and the yang."

Emma and Gemma were identical twins. "We were born in Korea," said

Emma. "Our Mom and Dad brought us here when we were three," said Gemma. "You can cast us in the same role," said Emma. "And we can work around the clock," said Gemma. "Twenty four hour acting," said Emma. After Emma and Gemma, I got five men in a row named Craig – a name they all pronounced *Creg*. All five Cregs could have been the same person. They wore jeans with tight white tees, curled their hair on top of their heads like waves, and crinkled their brows in a way that let you know it didn't come naturally, but from years of standing in front of a mirror, perfecting movie star looks. They were handsome in a way that was painfully plain. The kind of handsome that made them the most handsome men in their small towns, where people stopped them on the street and said: "Creg, you are one handsome fella. Get on out there to Hollywood and give them jokers a run for their money." So here they were. All the Cregs. Giving me a run for my money.

Finally, the last of the Cregs left, and I walked down a long white hall and into the sunlight. Wayne came out with two cans of Coke, and we sat on the grass, sipping the fizzy brown liquid. "I don't see anyone I like," he said. "Me either."

For ten minutes I sat on the toilet. Staring at the tiled floor. When I got back to the small office, she was sitting on the red couch. She wore paint-splattered jeans, white sneakers with holes in the toes, and a green flannel shirt. Skinny was not the word, malnourished was more like it. Her head was shaved, and her right front tooth had a large triangular chip out of it. But she had the bone structure of the genetically blessed. And her eyes were cobalt blue, like those frogs with poisonous skin. When she looked at you, you knew she meant business.

"You got a script?"

"Who are you?"

"Ari. Who are you?"

"Apollo."

"You got a script, Apollo?"

"You need a script?"

"Fuck no."

She leapt off the couch.

"You want characters? I got characters."

"Show me your characters," I said, sitting on the couch.

"Okay let's see. How about Moira. She works the checkout at Ralph's. Been on the job thirty years. Seen some shit."

"What's Ralph's?"

"A shitty supermarket where Hollywood burnouts go to buy their frozen dinners at three in the morning."

"Paradise."

"Damn straight. Okay, here she is. Here's my girl, Moira."

Episode Thirty-Three.

Wendy, the True State HR Manager, found me an apartment in Santa Monica, right down the road from the business park. But if I took this apartment, I would:

Live above a Starbucks

Live across the road from the DMV

Live so close to the office I would basically be tethered to my desk

This would not do.

"What part of LA do you hate most?" I asked Wyatt.

"Downtown. It's a cesspool. The buildings are crumbling and the streets smell like piss."

I knew I would love whatever he hated, so I took an Uber Downtown.

Unlike Wyatt, the place was on a charm offensive. I walked up Broadway, past baroque old theatres like The Los Angeles, The Palace, The Orpheum, and the United Artists Theatre, which had been turned into the Ace Hotel. Outside The Ace, two bearded barmen played a performative game of dice, while three women shot photos of each other's butts. From here I headed north, past the shops that sold quinceanera dresses, which are the pink and blue and yellow meringue-like creations Latina girls wear to their fifteenth birthdays, and sometimes come strung with fairy lights. I passed stores that stocked cowboy hats and boots and gloves, and blasted music for the rancheros, who stood outside smoking like the last legit Marlboro men. On my way into a diner from the 1950s, I watched a purple Lamborghini cruise past an old man emptying his bowels on the curb. Inside, I ordered black coffee and opened Craigslist, where I found a one bedder on the fifth floor of the Santa Fe Building, on the corner of 6th and Main. Forty-seven minutes later, a real estate agent named Seth (who smelled of weed and unwashed socks) showed me the apartment. It had a kitchen, a tiny bathroom, and a bed under a giant window. The building had once been a bank. Seth gave it to me on a month-to-month basis, then drove away in a beat up Prius that probably smelled of bong water.

The next day it rained. The hissing kind of rain that hammered your bones. Saigon rain, basically. At the height of the downpour, I moved my suitcase into my new Downtown digs. After that I needed a lie down. My stomach was all aswirl. As you know, when you meet someone special your insides turn into the deck of a ship on rough seas. I'm referring to Ari. In the casting, she knocked me out cold with her characters. There was Moira the midnight checkout lady, a blind bodybuilder named Gladys, and a sociopathic German CEO who liked to watch people drink pineapple juice until they puked. Her range was insane. With her shaved head and her broken tooth, I knew W&W would stomp on the idea of casting her in the True State films, but I was desperate to work with her. Also, she had touched me in ways that were deeper than character development. I needed to talk to her. To know her. To eat waffles with her and ride with her on a lake in one of those peddle boats shaped like a swan.

The rain slowed to a drizzle. To cure my sickness, I went in search of greasy food, but got sucked deeper into a vortex of images of a working life with Ari (shooting, travelling, long nights in the edit suite) then I got hit with one of my episodes and stood on a street corner staring at my hands for several minutes, and then, discombobulated, I wandered into Skid Row. Tents dominated the sidewalks – packed too tight to walk. Also, I would never stroll through a stranger's dining room, so why walk through the living spaces they created on the concrete. I walked in the middle of the road. No cars out there. Just the occasional lost soul loafing over the centre line. I kept going, and came to a block bubbling with life. Outside the tents, people sat on couches – chatting and swigging and laughing and hugging. Pushing shopping carts, cooking up, shooting up, passing bottles, bickering and coming to blows. The road smelled as if decades of piss had soaked into the concrete, and along with the human shit, had baked in the hot sun each day. Also, hints of dead rat under piles of rubbish, plus rotting human flesh and pulverised lives. It was like walking through a war zone – a war between vulnerable people with no safety net, and a society that told them it was all their fault. The deeper I went, the harder it got to make it out the other side, or to backtrack. People stared. I hunched my shoulders and stared at the ground, but that made it worse. "Yo, skinny motherfucker!" "The fuck you doing in here?" "Come over here one minute."

My feet wanted to run. My brain screamed at them to run. But run where? I heard a voice.

"Behind you."

As I turned, he pulled up on my right side. Walked lockstep with me. The cap on his head had once been red, but was now light pink. His beard had once been white, but was now sepia, with a noodle poking out of his moustache. His eyes however were clear.

"I think you might be lost, friend."

"Can you help me get out?"

"Sure man, follow me."

He turned us around, and we headed down a narrow side street. At first I thought it was a trap. But the tents were fewer, the taunts non-existent. I don't know why, but I felt safe with him.

"Name's Barry."

"Apollo."

"You like big naturals, Apollo?"

"As in big natural breasts?"

"For sure man, just as god intended."

"Sure. I like small ones too."

"No way, man. Big naturals all the way."

"You sound like an expert."

"Worked in porn for years, as a sound recordist. So yeah, I am something of an expert."

"I'm a director."

"Of porn?"

"No I make, um, branded content."

"I don't know what that is."

"They're like ads, but longer."

"Sounds like a bummer, man."

"Well–"

"Hey! You need a soundie?"

"Maybe."

"Man, that would be sweet. I haven't worked in, uhh, about four years now."

"You remember how to do it?"

"Sure man, that shit's like riding a bike."

"Let me talk to my clients. You got a phone number?"

"Sure I do."

I handed him my phone, and he added his number.

"Say, you mind if I look at some big natchies real quick?"

For forty minutes we stood on the corner of Los Angeles and 6th Streets, while Barry watched big naturals videos on my phone. He watched seventeen entire videos, which seemed excessive. The content was pretty soft. There wasn't any penetration or even any men, just women with large natural breasts covered in oil. They jiggled them, and pushed masses of smooth flesh at the camera, and actually some of the clips were very well lit. I guessed they had pretty good cinematographers in porn. Barry was all business. I could see by the way the big naturals reflected on his eyeballs that he was uploading the images directly to his brain.

The elevator took me to the fifth floor of my new building. The doors dinged, and my phone pinged. When it comes to phones I've always had a sixth sense. If my phone contains new messages, and I pick it up, I swear it feels heavier. I know that sounds like some tea leaves wizardry, but it's my truth. And when I stepped out of the elevator and slid my phone from my pocket, it felt weighted down with promise. (Yes it might have been the big naturals but I choose to believe it was fate).

Hi, said the message, *this is Ari, just want to ask if you like frogs or dolphins better.*

Frogs, I wrote back. *How did you get my number?*

I blew the casting director. Frogs huh. I'll allow it.

U serious about the casting director?

Yes. I mean no. I mean

You could have asked

That's worse

The high that hit me was like nothing I'd ever experienced. I'm talking a full body high, with tingling and throbbing and fluttering. The kind of high you get when you climb to the top of a mountain, and look out over the shimmering sea as a whale blows water in the air and you shoot pure MDMA in your veins. And this high did not fade. If anything it got more intense. We messaged back and forth for a good four hours, but it felt like time out of time. I was in a haze. Adrenalin receptors firing. I needed more than words on a screen. I needed to be close enough to count the freckles on her forearms, but I would settle for the sound of her voice.

"Can I call you?"

"I'd like that."

My brain turned into a canyon, with her words careening off the walls in an endless echo. The first hour of conversation was a blur. I was too buzzed to remember what we spoke about. But I do know that as we spoke, I paced the apartment. I walked across the bed five times, climbed onto the kitchen bench, and sat in the shower. I walked the halls of the building, into the laundry – where I pushed the coin-operated slots in and out – then up onto the roof. The night sky was what you'd call midnight blue, and the lights in the monolithic towers winked down at me as if to say hell yes look at you go.

"I want to go to Mexico and watch turtles lay eggs in the sand," I said.

"I hate Mexico."

"Nobody hates Mexico."

"I hate the whole damn country."

"Okay?"

"Me and my friend Daisy drove down there to see some dude she was in love with. Some poet or some shit. And when we drove through Tijuana city, the cops pulled us over. And you know Tijuana has a bunch of US army bases, or navy bases or whatever, so the bars were all filled up with sailors. Anyway the Federales, who are bitch-ass Mexican sleazebag cops, they said I was speeding, which was a bullshit lie, but the fine was two hundred. I didn't have the money, and Daisy had curled up into the foetal position on the backseat. The bitch was catatonic. So I had to go into a bar and go round asking sailors for a buck or two each."

"How long did that take?"

"Couple hours. And you know what happened next?"

"Oh god."

"As soon as they let me go, they radioed ahead to their buddies at the next traffic light. They stopped me, and made me go into another bar and ask more sailors for money.

"Holy shit."

"These motherfuckers did that six times!"

"Six?"

"Took all night. It was morning by the time we got out of there."

"That's some traumatic shit."

"That's why I hate Mexico."

Episode Thirty-Four.

I wanted so bad for our night to be special. Like the nights we hung our feet off the edge of The President Hotel, and gazed at the heat vapours swirling off the Saigon rooftops. I took an Uber to the Mulholland Drive lookout. From up there you could see all of LA – endless flickering girds cut through with sluggish rivers of headlights. I sat on the bench and held my phone at arm's length, so the city spread out in the frame behind me. Then I face-timed him.

"Anaru! Can you see me?"

"Yeah I–woah. Where are–"

"Guess where I am?"

"The Gold Coast."

"Ha-ha. Fuck the Goldy. I'm in LA."

"LA? They kick you out of Australia or something?"

He turned his phone around and I saw he was sitting on the roof of The President. The sun sat high in the smoggy sky, looking like a giant overripe peach. He had gone to our spot, I hoped to be closer to me. Tears banged into the backs of my eyeballs.

"The President! I thought they were tearing it down."

"Nah it's been postponed or something. Dunno. I came here today and the old fulla let me up. Guess he could see I needed it."

"Damn I miss being up there with you."

"I miss you too, mate."

The next forty minutes were a vocal fireworks display. With the lights of LA behind me, and the Saigon sunset behind him, we brought each other up to speed on our lives. I told him about Natasha the forklift ballerina, W&W, and Barry and his love of big naturals. And he told me he had sunk into a week of not eating. And in that week he had dreamed of his mother getting up in the night to go to the toilet, but her house was so filled with trash she couldn't make it. And the thought of any human, let alone his mother, sick and alone and stuck in a house so filled with rubbish they couldn't make it to the bathroom filled him with guilt and sorrow. I told him about my evening walking the streets of Sydney weeping. And he told me he had been dating a Russian named Viktor, who came with the shaved head and faraway stare and long-limbed emaciated look of all the top Eastern European models. After five dates Viktor wanted to get matching neck tattoos, and when Anaru said that kind of commitment wasn't his vibe, Viktor flipped out and made a melodramatic scene in the street, kicking cars and biting trees and ramming his beautiful head into brick walls. The entire episode had been so emotionally draining Anaru booked his first trip home in three years.

"How you feel about going home?"

"Dunno, man. Scared? I dunno."

"You want me to come with you?"

"Ha-ha nah man you slay your dragons in LA."

"Reckon the dragon will probably slay me."

"Maybe."

A long silence. The light behind him shifted from peach to blood orange. A shiver slid up my spine. I got scared. Was the pressure of the ocean between us cracking the foundations of our friendship?

"You never told me what happened after she died. Your Mum I mean. Sorry. I don't want to…"

(I may have stopped stealing his story for the Untitled Original Series Set On Multiple Continents, but I still wanted to hear the rest of it.)

"I'm sure I did."

"You don't have to."

"Nah you're good. Reckon it's good for me to talk about it. But uhh… where did we leave off? Oh yeah, after she died, I went to live in Paihia, across the bay from Russell."

"Right, with your cousin."

"Justice, yeah. We had our little weed operation. Small-time dealer shit. But Justice had bigger plans, so he moved us to this farm near Kerikeri."

The farm was less of a farm, and more of a lifestyle block. The old couple who owned it planted an orange orchard (Kerikeri being NZ's premier citrus district) and five rows of macadamia trees. A river cut across the bottom of the property, with eels lounging in clear pools, and red-winged dragonflies hovering over large round boulders. The house had been done in the style of a 70s Chilean ranch house, on account of the old couple spending that decade in South America. They installed a giant fireplace, cream shagpile carpet, gold filigree wallpaper, green velvet couches and wagon wheels on the bedroom walls. Not a lot of demand for a place like that. And the old folks were way past tending the orange orchard, the macadamia trees, the gooseberry bushes, the rambling garden and the huge lawn, so Justice talked the rent down to nearly half the asking price.

"Check this shit out," Justice said to Anaru, leading him into the large modern barn attached to the two car garage attached to the Chilean style ranch house. "You know what's going in here right?"

"A crafts market?"

"Hydro. Already ordered the lights. Get those set up, and we'll grow the stickiest, nastiest skunk in the Far North."

Anaru was silent. He walked to the ride-on mower in the corner of the barn. Forest green, it had two gears: tortoise and hare. Anaru smiled at that. Behind his back, he felt his cousin simmering. Justice hated it when Anaru wasn't on board with his ambitions.

"What? You wanna be broke forever, cuz?"

"Won't we step on some toes?"

"Fuck. The gangs? You think they care about a little hydro set up? Nah bro, all they care about is meth. Don't be such a fuckin' pussy."

But Justice had always been big on dreams, and short on execution. It fell to Anaru to spend months studying the proper methods for setting up a productive and safe hydroponic system. Add in some trial and error, and some more trial and error, and a prolonged period of basically just error, and they still hadn't produced a single sticky bud. There were days Justice got so mad Anaru sent him down to the river to cool off. But even on the days they fought, and fretted, and got so low on cash they lived on tins of baked beans, they sat by the roaring fire at night, and laughed at the stupid mistakes of the day. They didn't know it, but the set up was the hardest part. Once they were up and running, they were rolling. Under the hot white lights, the plants produced buds so dense and purple they were nearly navy blue. They looked as if they'd been sprinkled with sugar, and their sweet chemical scent was pungent enough to make your sinuses contract. And no cop would suspect a Mum and Dad orchard as being a criminal enterprise. Even the dealers, who made pick-ups once a week, were given citrus boxes packed with purplish-blue buds. Often the boxes had actual oranges and macadamia nuts in there too, to mask the smell.

Anaru hated the skunk, but he loved the fruit and the nuts. He was not a born green thumb, but he was blessed with a naturally inquisitive mind, and this made him a stellar researcher. He felt his way through the first harvest. By the second, his trees were dumping so many juicy oranges and creamy hard nuts he sold them to fruit shops as far away as Whangarei. The orchard was the perfect front, but he built the front into a legitimate business. He even gave it a name – *Carolina Farms* – and had a local signwriter paint a wooden sign at the gate in scripted font. On Sundays, the dealers drove past the sign, and down the gravel driveway, where they picked up orange boxes packed with buds. And on Wednesdays, the fruit shop owners picked up orange boxes filled with actual oranges.

Their life was peaceful. Swimming in the river, tending the buds, the orchard, the rambling garden, mowing the lawn on the ride-on mower, shifting gear from tortoise to hare. But for Justice, peace was a problem. He wasn't about the simple life. He craved action.

"Come in here," he called to Anaru one night.

Anaru put down his phone (he was reading about an organic fertilizer that made buds smell like coffee) and headed down the hall. He found Justice in his room, wearing knee-high leather boots, white jodhpurs, a tweed cap and jacket, and cradling a double-barrelled shotgun in his arms. The room smelled of leather polish and gun metal.

"What do you think?"

"I think you might need help."

"Fuck off. I'm the lord of this shit."

"Okay."

"It's cool right."

"If you say so."

"Whatever. You don't know shit about style. Bitch."

Anaru knew his cousin to be sensitive, so the insult came as no surprise. What he didn't know was that along with dressing up as a lord, the quiet life had driven him to the pipe. For weeks Justice had been smoking meth in secret. At night, in his nobleman get up, shotgun in hand, he roamed the property, stopping to perch on river boulders, hit his glass pipe, then move on to shoot at rabbits and hedgehogs, and the midnight wind whistling in the trees. One night, at around 2am, Anaru was woken by a shotgun blast. He peered out the window to see Justice, sitting on the ride-on mower, sucking on his pipe. Anaru was scared. Not scared enough to confront his cousin, but scared enough to keep a close eye on him. And what he saw didn't scare him more. Despite his nightly exploits – blasts from the barrel of his gun and the barrel of his pipe – Justice kept his shit together. He helped out with the hydro, and he dealt with the dealers and the fruit shop owners when they picked up their produce. In his tweed and his jodhpurs, the fruit shop owners thought he was manor born. And the dealers saw him as an eccentric weirdo, and therefore not to be fucked with.

THE fire roared. The night outside was black. Justice looked up from polishing his boots.

"We need a crew."

Anaru sipped his tea. "What do you mean?"

"Muscle. Protection."

"Protection from who?"

"From them."

Who was them? Justice didn't elaborate, but he did recruit a crew. His muscle. Local toughs from places like Kawakawa and Moerewa – towns with sky-high unemployment. From grimy couches the crack fumes summoned them, and they drifted past the *Carolina Farms* sign, the orange trees, and in the front door, to park their butts on the green velvet couch or warm them in front of the fire. There was Kerry, an obese redhead, Spit, a wannabe rapper and sometimes fisherman, Mushy, another rapper-slash-fisherman, and Darryl, who got sacked from the local meatworks for repeated acts of cruelty to animals (which, at an abattoir, was quite an achievement).

They trailed Justice like a pack of mangy dogs. He was their king. He controlled the weed, the meth, and the money. He was also funny, and usually kept a loaded gun on his person. Justice loved the company. The adoration of his following. A gang to laugh at his jokes or fetch him a Coke. And when he went on his nightly rounds, his crew stayed up until dawn. Playing GTA, passing the crack pipe, wrestling, rap battling, burning cigarette holes in the cream carpet. Yelling faggot this and homo that. Bash that bitch-arse faggot. For Anaru, this was not an easy adjustment. His peaceful farm life had fallen apart, and he stayed in his room with the door locked. When he tried to eat, his throat closed up. And when he worked in the barn, or the orchard, his skin broke out in hives. Maybe his Mum was right, he thought. Maybe the world did want him dead. All day his head swam with gruesome imagery – getting dragged from under an orange tree and tossed off a cliff, or taken down to the river to have his skull splattered on a boulder. Justice was no help. He upped his nightly stalking to include day-light hours too. Sleeping nil. He kept his princely clothes clean and pressed, but his eyes were ghoulish, his skin like paper, cheeks dotted with scabs he picked at. Some days, as he tended the oranges and the nuts, Anaru caught glimpses of his cousin. The flash of a gun barrel, a shadow slipping between trees. Like a ghost haunting him. On a crisp dawn he saw him sitting on a rock, sucking hard on his pipe. When Justice looked up, Anaru found him-self looking into the milky eyes of the nearly dead. Obviously, Justice had checked out of the business, leaving all the work to Anaru and his crew. When the dealers and the fruit shop owners came to make their pick-ups, Mushy and Spit spat on the ground, or called them bitches. Kerry slapped a dealer for looking at him. They lost valued clients. Only a matter of time before the cops busted the entire operation.

Then Blow-arse turned up.

He was called Blow-arse because he blew hot air out of his arse, meaning he lied constantly. He had blond dreads, high cheekbones, and his lies were performative. Most evenings, as Anaru hid in his room, Justice roamed the property, and the gang sat on the green velvet couch passing weed and crack pipes, Blow-arse stood in front of the roaring fire spinning yarns. He told them his father had been a tap dancer in a circus, that he was born in an elephant cage, and lost his virginity to a one legged candy floss maker. Also that he had been tarred and feathered at the age of ten, by an elderly lesbian couple who lived in a caravan in the bush. And that he once caught a black marlin so big it pulled him from the boat and tried to spear him. The crew loved the entertainment. On the fifth night, Justice himself came in from shooting ghosts to listen. And Anaru, while not bold enough to sit by the fire, unlocked his door and sat in the hallway, laughing along with the crackheads that stole his idyllic life.

A Sunday night. Kerry, Mushy, Darryl and Spit were at the movies. Anaru lit the fire, poured a jumbo glass of Coke, sat at the kitchen table and opened his computer. His plan was to go through their sales projections for the coming financial year. In the distance, a shotgun blast. Justice had taken to shooting eels in the pond on the edge of the property. Anaru ignored it, sipped his Coke. He felt a hand on his shoulder. It was Blow-arse. His dreads were tied up, elevating his already high cheekbones, and he wore a Hawaiian shirt open, showing off his smooth chest, his abs, the tattoo of the sperm whale breaching below his right nipple. Blow-arse bent his neck and kissed Anaru. Anaru froze. Terror spasmed up his spine, paralysing him from the eyeballs down. If Blow-arse sensed this, he didn't show it. Pushing his tongue into Anaru's mouth, he twirled the tip. Anaru's brain told him to run to the river and hide, but the tingle spreading over every inch of his body told him to shut the fuck up and enjoy the ride. He gave in. Let his tongue slip into Blow-arse's mouth and reach for his rear molars. He tasted the gums, the teeth, and walls of his cheeks, and they tasted like spice and weed and bubble-gum, with distant hints of bourbon.

Anaru woke at dawn, with Blow-arse lying next to him. In his bed. Naked. He panicked. His throat closed up, his chest went tight, and he ran to the bathroom to puke. He thought about running away. But where to? He walked back into his bedroom, and Blow-arse pulled him under the sheets.

Episode Thirty-Five.

All morning, Barry sent me messages:
Did I get the job?
And:
Ready to work boss.
And:
What time you want me on set?
Also:
I'm excited about this opportunity.
Plus:
I get the job?
And on and on and on. I was sitting on the red couch in my little windowless office, looking at locations. I wanted to shoot at a house in Los Feliz that looked like a concrete bunker (I realise now what a cliché director move this was) but W&W were insisting on a ten-room mansion on Santa Monica beach. This, they said, reflected the, "authentic American family values at the heart of the True State brand." I blinked at them. They went to the salad bar for matcha tea. So I took an Uber Downtown to meet Barry at the Nickel Diner. We ate sugary donuts, and sipped black coffee, and he

told me the free advice his friend gave him on the job front: "Clean your stank ass up." I didn't have the heart to tell him he didn't have the job yet (I had been waiting for the right time to pitch him to W&W, but given their position on middle class housing, working with a homeless man would be a tough sell) but his friend's advice gave me an idea, so I asked him to take us to the nearest barber.

"What can I do you gentlemen for?" asked the barber.

"A number one for me," I said, "and the works for my friend here. Hot shave, haircut, whatever he needs."

"Hallelujah," said Barry.

Our barbers sat us in soft leather barber chairs, tied strips of paper round our necks, and floated red capes around our shoulders. "God damn," said Barry, as the barber massaged smooth white cream into the whitish-yellow bristles that sprouted from his throat like wild bramble, and smelled like a woollen blanket left out in the rain.

"I got a funeral tomorrow," said Barry. "Four funerals actually."

We were facing the mirrors. My barber ran his clippers over my head, Barry's took a gleaming razor to the thickets of hair on his cheeks.

"Four funerals?" I asked. "How does that work?"

"In LA, if you die, and you got no family or friends to claim the body, or pay the four hundred bucks it costs to release your body, your stiff stays in the morgue for a few months. After that they burn you up, then they toss your ashes in with the ashes of all the other burned up unclaimed bodies. At the end of the year, they bury all the ash together in one grave."

"How many people they bury in the grave? How many people's ashes."

"About fifteen hundred."

"So it's a mass grave."

"LA is built on bodies, man."

"Jesus."

"He don't care. But they put a funeral on, over at the crematorium cemetery. A little service and everything. It's nice. I usually got a couple buddies getting buried so I go along every year. Got four going in the ground tomorrow, so this shave will do me up real nice."

"Who are the four?"

"My old friend Mary died in a crack house, Donnie went out like a light in his tent, bunch of thugs beat Lamp to death over in Hollywood, and Scooter choked on a chicken bone."

When we left the barber shop, Barry looked like one those silver fox GQ models. Seriously. By some miracle of nature, his skin had been preserved under all that coarse hair and street grime. At a menswear store, we bought some button up shirts. In Pershing Square, we found the perfect light, so I snapped a round of head shots on my phone.

INDIGO night. Headlights probing the corners of the winding canyon road. Coyotes howling, scrubby bush on both sides, the eyes of a mountain lion reflecting back at mine. Or maybe not. Maybe that was a trick of the night or the mind or both. I had hired a car, and it was meant to be a powerful car they called a hell cat, but this one only looked powerful, and was less of a hell cat and more of a neurotic house cat that constantly mewed for kibbies. Did I care? I did not. Ari sat next to me, sending her enchanting beams in all directions, and telling me about the hundreds of auditions where she had been humiliated or insulted or straight up assaulted. "At a party out in Calabasas – not far from here actually – I was starving. Like my body was eating its own muscle fibres for fuel type of starving. And the owner of the house, some sweaty agent, caught me stealing his fancy prosciutto. He threw me in the pool, so I broke a bottle over his shiny head. My auditions kinda dried up after that." She also told me about the goat farm she grew up on in Texas. The goats were Angora. Very fancy. The kind that provide the mohair for the sweaters of the Monaco royal family. Her father – a bottle of vodka and six oxys a day man – once had the bright idea to sheer his prize goats in the dead of winter. Two days later, a storm ripped across the land and stripped the life from the entire herd. Little Ari, bawling her eyes out, had to drag the bloated carcasses into a secluded gully so her father could set fire to the evidence of his cruelty. Anyway. I'm not saying who cares about goats because she clearly cared a great deal for those fancy fellows, but in that moment all I cared about was the magnetic pull between us. Boy was it strong. I'd go as far as to say hypnotic. I was desperate to reach out and touch her wrist or her knee or hold my hand an inch from her skin and feel the hot hot heat coming off her. I mean I knew she was one of the special ones, like Anaru, but hearing her enigmatic stories in such a confined space really put the zap on me. As we breached the peak of the canyon, she turned her cobalt blue eyes and her chipped tooth on me, and flashed a smile filled with such deeply charming insanity that I felt a tightness in my chest usually associated with acute heart failure. I nearly pulled over and puked in the dust while howling at the moon.

But I need to be honest and tell you that I lied. I lied to her about the True State job. Earlier that morning, right after my barber date with Barry, I spent hours locked in the little office with W&W, doing my best to get Ari the lead role and Barry the sound recordist gig. I tried all my tricks. Constant talking, passionate appeals, gas-lighting. I went as far as shedding tears on both of their head shots. But W&W were a double brick wall. Cold-blooded. They told me to stop. To give it up. To please stop talking for one second. But I made a solemn promise to Barry, and Ari was a whole other deal. I saw us as partners, in the personal and the professional sense. She had talent, she had bright shiny ideas that flew from her head like bees, and she had the power to turn my bones to jelly, which she could suck up with a straw and spit in the trash. But I did not have the raw animal attraction a person like her went for. I was a director of branded social media content, which meant I was not a real director. But if I cast her in the lead role of the branded social media series, I could then cast her in the lead role of a real show (Untitled Original Series Set On Multiple Continents) which would make me a real director, which would make her want to wake up every morning and plant kisses on my eyelids. Spoiler alert: I went too far. I turned that office into a psychological war zone. My endless pushing and shoving triggered some serious anxiety in W&W, and this kicked off a bout of shaking and sweating (in matching argyle sweaters) with much puffing on all sorts of asthma inhalers. An aortic aneurism was on the cards. Did I stop? I did not. Barry this and Ari so talented that. Gripping his hairless skull, Wyatt slumped to his knees and rocked back and forth like an insane and gibberish muttering baby. Wayne was aghast. The love of his life was checking out before his eyes, or so he thought. He cradled Wyatt in his arms, whispered sweet words in his ear, then shrieked at me like a banshee: "You get out! Go! And if you mention that bum or that bald toothless bitch one more time I will have you shipped back to Australia in a casket!" At that point, I called it a day. I mean come on. I'm stupid, but I'm not *that* stupid. I walked to the car rental place, picked up the gutless black housecat, and revved the engine outside Ari's building. And when she jumped in the front seat, blue eyes shining, I told her the role was hers.

ON the morning of the True State shoot, I took Barry to the Nickel Diner, and bought him a breakfast of bacon and eggs and waffles with a side of home fries plus coffee and juice and a slice of key lime pie.

"I didn't get the gig did I?"

"I'm sorry, man. I tried. I really fucking tried, but the client–"

"Brother, don't sweat it. You took a chance on me when everybody else saw me as trash, and I'm grateful. I truly am."

This choked me up. I tried to hide it by sipping my strong black coffee.

"Say," said Barry, "mind if I use your phone for a minute?"

"You need some big naturals?"

"They always cheer me up, man."

Like a roman candle, Ari exploded in the front seat of the gutless black car, shooting balls of fire from her eyes and her mouth. She blabbered all the way to Santa Monica: "So I know this is for an insurance firm and I'm playing this very conservative type of pretty lady but I had this idea that I'm actually these conjoined twins and we've recently been separated so me and my sister – who I also play – have this new lease on life and one of us is nice but the other is, like, not evil but maybe something of a sociopath." She spewed out such a torrent of words I could barely hear the GPS directions. We made it. But when we pulled up to the mansion W&W forced me to agree was a middle class home, production trucks blocked the entrance, and we had to walk down a side path to find the front gate, which opened right onto the white sand.

"Oh my god waves!" said Ari.

She ran down the beach, yanked off her shoes and skipped into the shallow water. Way out to our left, I saw the pier, and heard the first screams of the day drifting on the wind from the giant ferris wheel. Ari kicked at small waves. For a second I thought she was high, but then I remembered how long it had been since she had been on set (long before she bottled the sweaty agent) and put her erratic behaviour down to nerves.

"Listen," I said, dipping my fingers in the cold water, "full disclosure. The client doesn't know you're coming."

She stopped kicking the waves. "But they cast me."

"I know. Yeah. But they didn't. I tried so hard to make it happen, but, look, just come to set and–"

"Fuck this."

She grabbed her shoes and marched up the beach.

"Ari, just come to set. Show them your characters. Show them how good you are. If they see your talent in the flesh they'll–"

"Fuck you, Apollo. You tricked me. You lied."

"I know and I'm sorry, but just come to set and give it a shot. Don't you want to give it a shot? You're Moira. You work the midnight shift at Ralph's. You've seen it all. Moira don't give a fuck about this. This right here is nothing."

She stopped.

"You have to introduce me as Moira."

"I can do that, sure."

She closed her eyes and slipped into character. "Let's do it."

The gate opened onto a marble path that led to the house, which was all white arches and ocean-facing windows. We walked past palm trees, and a pool, and exotic plants with purple flowers that appeared to leer at us. Gaffers and runners and grips rushed back and forth, carrying lights and dresses and trays of specific coffee orders. I looked at Ari, and she glared back at me with fiery eyes. "Can we hurry this shit up? I've been on my feet all night. My corns are killing me!" On we marched. As we passed a row of white rose bushes, Wayne popped out on the path in front of us.

"What is *she* doing here?"

"Who?"

"Her!"

"Moira?"

"I thought her name was Ari."

"Have we met?" said Ari/Moira. "You come into Ralph's? I work the midnight shift over at the La Brea store."

"I don't shop at Ralph's."

"You strike me as more of an Erewhon man."

Wayne snorted through his nose. I had never seen him laugh before. This was my chance.

"I think we should cast Moira. Not as the lead but–"

"Why not as the lead?" asked Moira.

"Well, there's better–"

"Waste my time will you? Fine, I'll head on back to the store, but I'm taking some roses with me." Ari/Moira picked a rose from a bush and smelled the creamy petals. "We don't got roses like this at Ralph's."

"Those flowers are private property," said Wayne, watching her pick and sniff more roses.

"Let's cast her. She's an amazing character. Totally authentic. Just what your brand–"

"We've replaced you."

"What?"

"You've been replaced. I hired a new director. She's Korean, she's insanely talented, and she gets our brand essence. She's inside right now, framing up the first shot. She's in, and you're out."

"But I. You can't. I have a contract."

"We'll pay you out. Which is *extremely* generous, considering all the harm you've done. But I want you and your flower-stealing lunatic friend off this set, before I call the police."

Episode Thirty-Six

What we needed was an engine that roared. A car so loud it drowned out the voices in our heads. Voices that were (for me anyway) cursing and hissing and calling me a cruel and worthless person with a heart like a raisin kicked under the couch, only to be vacuumed up a month later all twisted and hard. But we didn't have that car, we had the gutless black neurotic housecat car. And its engine made a high-pitched whining sound. So up the Pacific Coast Highway we whined, the ocean out the window like a screen saver come to life.

"Look, the ocean."

Ari didn't look. I pushed my foot down hard on the pedal. I had no destination in mind. My goal was to outrun the vomit surging up the back of my throat. What the fuck. I had now been sacked on two continents. Was I gunning for dismissals on all seven? Maybe. Set some kind of record. I was an ambitious guy.

"I guess that went pretty bad, huh."

A silent tear rolled down her cheek.

How do you feel about crying? For me it's okay, but I prefer howling. Histrionics I can stand, because it fills the room and flattens you. Like a weather front. Silent weeping sucks the soul out of the room (or the car) and leaves too much space for contemplation. And when you're the one to blame for the tears, all you're left to contemplate is your own shittiness.

"Shall we go to Malibu? I hear the beach is top shelf. Or we could just keep dri–"

"F F F F F F F F F U U U U U U U U U U U U U U U U U U U U U U U U C-CCCCCCCCCCCKKKKKKKK!!!!!!!"

Her scream was guttural, like an animal with its head caught in a trap. It came from deep in her lower intestine. And it was so loud and shrill that it perforated my ear drum, and made me swerve over the centreline. I nearly collided with the grill of a white Mercedes jeep. Lots of shouting and swearing and shaking of fists. Horns galore. When I righted the housecat, my ears were ringing so bad I couldn't hear.

"That was pretty intense."

"Yeah well, my life is over."

"Sorry, what?"

"I said my life is over! I can't pay rent. I can't eat. I can't even afford tampons! I'm a failed actress. The most pathetic type of failed there is."

"I'll make it up to you."

"Ha. You're just as pathetic as I am. We're a couple of losers in a shitty car."

I let this sink in, like some toxic chemicals seeping into the soil. We whined past a row of beachside mansions. Their balconies jutted over the sand, boasting views of boats bobbing out on the Pacific.

"I mean look at this shit," said Ari, flicking a hand at the mansions. "What made us think we have what it takes? LA is a pile of bodies, and we're two carcasses rotting underneath them all. We're bottom feeders. Destined to spend our life crawling along in the sludge, scavenging for whatever the apex predators digest and shit out."

I hated hearing this. I tried to push it into a damp cave in the depths of my psyche, but it popped out and poked me in the eye. My palms were sweaty. My vision blurry. The gases in my gut were gathering an army of angry bubbles. I needed to right our ship, stat, so I said:

"I want to see the desert."

"You're going the wrong way."

I had heard about a hotel in Palm Springs called The Parker. That it was some mid-century oasis in the desert. That directors and artists and poets and models congregated on its lush grounds, eating beautiful food and getting their beautiful bodies rubbed by beautiful hands in the nautical-themed spa that played relaxing chime music and hopefully meditative sea shanties. I knew that a room was a bomb that would blow a hole in the hull of my already sinking finances, but I also knew we needed to escape our shitty selves. We needed to frolic in flower beds, float in a fancy pool, and pretend we were an up and coming power couple with a bright future.

If only for a few days.

A man in crisp white shorts and a crisp white polo shirt parked our gutless black car, and we walked through giant white doors and into the lobby. Seventies pop art graced the walls, and a mob of hot people waited to take selfies under a sign that said DRUGS in light bulbs. At reception, I handed over what I hoped was a sound investment, and a woman with a yellow orchid in her hair led us to our room. It had a four-poster bed and double doors that opened onto a lawn, and we ran out and rolled on the soft grass, gazing up at a desert sky and pink flowers on the bougainvillea vines that twisted up the trunks of palm trees. In the kidney-shaped pool, we swam among neck-tatted trustafarians, Saudi princes, Peruvian models, Japanese fashion moguls, cowboy hat-doffing conceptual artists and willowy white girls with cosmetically enlarged butts and lips. Craggy mountains peered down on us. I liked the desert air, hot and dry as it was. Lying in my sun-lounger, with perfectly weighted beads of Italian mineral water bursting on my tongue, and Ari floating in a purple bikini I bought her at the resort shop, I felt part of the most privileged enclave on planet earth. Sure I was pretending. But I figured we were all pretending, and those who weren't pretending had only been pretending for so long it felt real. Or maybe they were born into it. No matter. Adventure time was ours. We played tennis and croquet, then we walked into the desert and left an offering of chocolate-coated almonds for a scorpion we saw sitting on a rock. In the nautical-themed spa (no sea shanties, I asked) we charged white fluffy robes to our room, because by that point I was in fuck-it mode when it came to money. We got massages and cleanses and manicures. And we took a yoga class with a lithe-bodied old man named Russ who told me that in a past life he had been a pastry chef in the palace of Cleopatra. Our bodies and minds free from the trauma of the morning, we floated to the patio restaurant to eat stacks of blueberry pancakes under the stars. Followed by whisky for her and tea for me, and cigars as big as babies' legs for us both.

Giddy.

Hazy.

And wobbly.

We walked across the dark lawn and slipped in the side door to our room. Ari stripped naked, then she got down on the floor and cranked out twenty push ups. I did the same. Then we did sit ups, then planks, then side planks, then more push ups, star jumps, chair poses, push ups, planks, side planks, sit ups, star jumps, planks, chair poses, push ups, sit ups, planks, side planks. With the muscles in our arms and legs and back and core pumped with blood, and sweat running down our necks and ears and elbows and calves, we stood five inches from each other. She looked up at me – dilated pupils eclipsing her cobalt blue irises – and I looked back. Our lungs heaving, our hearts hammering, steam rising off our heads and shoulders, we kissed. For a long time we kissed. So long the interior of her mouth became my entire world. One I was free to explore. Running my tongue over the rough crevice of her broken tooth, along the rolling hills of her gums, and up the soft warm cliffs of her cheeks.

I woke up with an idea bashing against the inside of my skull. A fresh idea for the first season of the Untitled Original Series Set On Multiple Continents. Ari's side of the bed was empty, but I heard the shower running. I sat at the desk looking over the lawn and the desert dawn, and began to write. When I was halfway through, I felt an episode coming on stronger than usual. I stared at my hand and thought: this is my hand, and I'm a living person with limbs and organs and all that jazz. But the longer I stared at my hand, the more terrified I became of the realization I had a hand.

"Are you okay?"

Ari had walked into the room. She stood next to me, a white towel wrapped around her torso. I told her about my episodes.

"You're dissociating."

"What's that."

"You're, like, disassociating from your own body. You might be about to have a breakdown, or maybe you're already having one, I don't know. You should probably see a doctor."

"I can't right now."

"We can go into Palm Springs. Go see a desert doctor."

"I need to tell you about an idea I had. For the first season of the Untitled Original Series Set On Multiple Continents."

"What's that?"

"It's a show I've been working on for… doesn't matter how long. It'll run on TV and in cinemas, on social media, everywhere."

"Sounds cool."

"Thanks. I woke up with this idea in my head. For the lead character. She's called The Dream. And she's an influencer who lives the dream life in LA."

"The dream life? What the fuck is that? That's not real. You should show the reality."

"What's the reality?"

"Well, like, you know what you see on Instagram is all bullshit, right? Influencers post photos sipping twenty dollar cocktails at five-star hotel pools, then go home to roach-infested apartments, and eat, like, onion skins for dinner. So you should call her The Dream, but show her shitty real life."

"What if she's living the dream life in the beginning – cool parties, free clothes, fancy shit – then something goes wrong and her life unravels, and she ends up homeless."

"On one condition."

"What's that."

"I play The Dream."

"You are The Dream."

Episode Thirty-Seven

Ari picked up the axe. She wore a black latex catsuit, thigh-high black boots and a blonde bob wig. As she raised the axe above her head, sunlight flashed on the silver blade. Under a tree on the far side of the lawn, I squatted down, filming her on a brand new DSLR. She swung the axe – THWACK! – two pieces of wood toppled off the chopping block and onto the grass.

"Nice," I said, watching the shot back. "Looks good."

"I feel like I had a flaccid look in my eye."

"I didn't see it."

"When The Dream chops wood, The Dream means business. Let's go again."

We were in a house in the Hollywood Hills, shooting content for The Dream's forthcoming Instagram account. The house was a sprawling brutalist bunker, with a black-bottomed pool surrounded by rows of bamboo trees that sashayed in the soft wind. The house belonged to a friend of Ari's, named Rah-Rah. He was out of town but he let us use the pool for the shoot, on the condition we stayed clear of the house. Rah-Rah was a producer of revoltingly offensive reality TV shows.

"The kind that put people in prison with violent criminals to see if they can survive," said Ari. "His new one has something to do with incest. Did I tell you he used to be my sponsor?"

"I didn't know you were in AA."

"I wasn't. Jesus. Yick."

"Then why did you have a sponsor?"

"A sponsor is an LA cultural delicacy. It's a wealthy older man that pays your rent and co-signs the lease on your car."

"I see."

"I know what you're thinking."

"What am I thinking."

"If I fucked him, the cash would dry up pretty quick. Being a sponsee is all about the tease."

"Wait, so he's still your sponsor?"

"No, no, the cash did dry up. But that had nothing to do with my ass and his shrivelled old man dick."

In a frenzy of creation, that's how we spent the weeks leading up to the wood-chopping shoot. We built The Dream from the inside out, and she usurped all aspects of our lives. If I'm honest, in the first week, I wasn't sure she would work. Our ideas were so different. Ari wanted to make her a vacuous narcissist in activewear. "She should speak in that baby doll voice, and sound like she has two brain cells. Like she's so dumb she can't keep warm." While hilarious, her impressions of this version of The Dream were frightening. I didn't want people to mock her. Sure, her followers needed to envy her, but they had to connect with her on a human level too. That was the only way for them to sympathise with her downfall. I suggested we make her a hot writer of poems that mixed tenderness with caustic wit. Ari hated that. For three days we bounced ideas back and forth, inventing various personas for The Dream – politically savvy conceptual artist, knife-wielding environmental activist, dog-loving stay-at-home trad girlfriend. In the end we mashed elements from all of them into a complex and multi-dimensional character that Ari was happy to slip into. Next we created her content calendar. This was an arsenal of posts and stories and poems and confessions, and memes and clothing hauls and dating tips and yoga clips – all the content we planned to roll out three times a day for two months post launch. In the thick of a flash heatwave, wearing only our sticky underwear, we wrote these ideas on cards and stuck them to my bedroom wall, crafting the arc that would lead to her unravelling. But here, drenched and dehydrated, we fought over the *trigger* for her unravelling. Ari was a fierce advocate for public humiliation (a drunken brawl at The Chateau Marmont for example) where as I was after more of an internal coming to Jesus moment. "Are you some kind of eunuch?" hissed Ari, her blue eyes afire. "Did they castrate you at customs? I'm the one with skin in the game. Why are you crying for your Mommy?"

Yes, we fought.

Yes, we screamed.

But we formed a bright and scintillating creative partnership. Ideas flew from Ari's brain, which made them fly from my brain, which made them fly from hers. Clanging and sparking, they collided in mid-air, transforming into rare gems we could never create on our own. Once we had her character down, we moved onto wardrobe. Ari had friends working in all the boutiques on Melrose, and so, like a feather and sequin-trailing hurricane, we went from store to store, trading skirts and jeans and shoes and bags for future posts. "Babe, don't worry," Ari told the semi-bemused counter jockeys. "The Dream will hit five million followers in her first month. Our posts are worth their weight. Mwah." She was a born hustler, and I loved that about her. Now all we had to do was shoot the content.

I mentioned the wood-chopping catsuit shoot, but we also shot her shopping for gowns on Rodeo Drive, sweating up a storm in Soul Cycle, and hiking up Runyon Canyon. Standard influencer stuff. But we also took some risks. Like we shot her chasing coyotes in Topanga Canyon, dancing in traffic on the 405, giving an impromptu lecture on performance art at LACMA, and eating canapes like a ravenous animal at the cocktail party of a Hollywood heavyweight. My personal favourite shoot took place at an air strip on the outskirts of the city. Ari had a friend named Pete, and Pete had a private jet that he rented out to influencers by the hour. The jet did not take off. It sat on the runway as the influencers sat in its plush leather seats, sipping bubbles and posting selfies to fool their followers into believing they had the funds to fly private. For our shoot, Ari and three of her friends – Krissy and Maria and Jacky – dressed up in furs and bikinis and we filmed an all-girl royal rumble in the cabin. To say the girls were committed is a gross understatement. I filmed headlocks, and body slams, and suplexes, and even a double-legged dropkick to the face. Krissy cracked a rib, Maria nearly snapped her left femur, and Ari lost another tooth, but the content was golden.

The Dream also wrote poetry. And here is one of the poems she wrote:

Deep feelings
I saw you on the mountain
You wore your cape
I think I feel a burger coming on
Don't blame me if I kill you
I'm an axe, after all

"I need you to know something about me."
"What's that."
"I like men to take charge. To tell me what to do."
The night Ari told me this, we were in my bedroom Downtown. She was kneeling on the bed, and I was standing before her. The lights in the office buildings flickered out the window. In the distance, and then not in the distance, sirens. You may recall a scene from Saigon, in Nhu's bunker, when she told me to go to the bathroom and not come out until she told me to. And I really dug it. I was not so into being the dominant man in the bedroom, I was more into being dominated. And so when Ari told me that *she* liked to be dominated, I felt a chill creep up my spine, stopping at each vertebrae to say what's up. If I could not be the man she needed me

to be, I would lose her. And if I lost her, I would lose The Dream. And if I lost The Dream, I would lose what was shaping up to be my last shot at making the Untitled Original Series Set On Multiple Continents. So I pretended to be the dominant man. I tied her up and told her to call me daddy. I slipped off my belt and whipped her butt. Lightly at first, then not so lightly. Some days I told her what to wear and some nights I told her what to eat for dinner (three pieces of salmon sushi, one piece of nigiri, four slithers of tuna sashimi, one scoop of green tea ice cream). And of course, I closed my hands around her throat and squeezed until her cheeks turned red and tears filled her eyes. I found all of this hard, but she always wanted more. And even though I was pretending, I did like pleasing her. You could say that in pretending to be the dominant one, I was actually serving her, which made her the one dominating me.

The night we planned to launch The Dream on Instagram, the devil winds arrived. They whipped up the streets, blowing what felt like sand from the desert and salt from the ocean into my eyes. I bought a bottle of champagne, a bag of Cheetos, a box of Cheez-its and a pack of Reese's peanut-butter cups and drove to Ari's to celebrate. But when I walked past the fountain in front of her building (where two frogs named Max and Deirdre lived) and rang the bell, she did not appear. I called, but she didn't answer. And I messaged, but she did not write back. So I called and called and called some more. Still not picking up. Holy moly. I sat on the edge of the fountain. Max and Deirdre croaked, and my rectum got sucked up into my upper intestine. On wobbly knees I walked to the car, where I sat staring at the wind. I lay on the grass by the side of the road. And then I got hungry, so I sat in the backseat munching Cheetos and Cheez-its and peanut-butter cups. An hour passed. Two hours. I drove to the gas station, purchased more peanut-butter cups. Drove back. Parked in front of her building. Ate the peanut-butter cups. Vomited in the grass. Drove back to the gas station. Bought a fresh pack of peanut-butter cups. Drove back. Ate them. Vomited. I felt hollowed out. Unhinged. Adrift. What had I done wrong? Was she onto me? Did she know I was pretending to be the dominant man she needed? Was she pretending to be the person I thought she was? Was I about to lose her? Lose everything? Again?

Ding!

Never in my life had I ripped my phone from my pocket so fast. On the screen, a message from Ari:

Please come to me.

Where are you?

101 diner Hollywood

The neurotic black car got pushed to its limits. I skidded round corners, gunned yellow lights, and swerved into lanes with cars beeping and my heart beating on the base of my tongue. Café 101 was an old school diner on Franklin Ave in Hollywood. There were booths made from caramel pleather, caramel formica tabletops, caramel stools and caramel rocky road looking rocks on the walls. The staff looked like they'd been on the payroll since 1953. Ari sat in a corner booth, a plate of chocolate brownie waffles and ice cream in front of her. I slid in opposite.

"Sorry I disappeared."

"Are you okay?"

She shook her head. Then she took a bite of ice cream-soaked chocolate waffle. Then she hit me with a firehose of doubt and fear.

"I don't want to be The Dream. I don't want to be an influencer. I'm an actor. I wanna make films that move people, not post shit that makes them hate themselves. I mean what if she fails? Or worse, what if she succeeds? I'll be stuck in that bitch forever. It's fine for you. You're behind the scenes, pulling the strings. Mr. fake-ass puppet master over here. Don't smile! I'm the one they'll come for with pitchforks. They'll spit on me in the street. You don't have any skin in this bitch and don't shake your fat Australian head at me because it's true! You don't know. There's so much you don't know about me, Apollo. I'm not as tough as I look. I'm fragile. I break. I've done a lotta fucked up shit and a lotta fucked up shit has been done to me. Like, proper fucked up. And, like, what if I fuck this up? You'll hate me. And don't say you won't because you will and honestly sometimes I think you're using me to make your ultra-massive movie show thing and a part of me is flattered that you think you need me so bad but what happens when you don't? Need me I mean. You'll throw me away like a ripped condom wrapper. And don't. Just shut up. Shut the fuck up and let me eat my waffles and don't try to stop me from throwing them up in the toilet after, okay tough guy?"

Episode Thirty-Eight.

Four days and five nights. That's how long it took me to persuade Ari to play The Dream. It took all I had. All my resources. I became the stubborn mule, the soothing lap cat, the terrier with a rodent in its jaws, and I also became a snake hissing promises into her ears.

"You could be the first actor to win an Oscar for playing a social media character."

"When you're huge, you can rub it in the faces of all the people who fucked you over."

"You can buy ten goat farms."

In the end, all it took was the assurance that I wouldn't blame her if it all went belly up. Easy. And so we soft-launched The Dream. No fanfare. We didn't swing for instant and out of control social media celebrity. We posted a simple photo of her floating in the sea in a bright orange bikini. Of course, we bought a couple thousand followers. But who in this day and age doesn't need the help of a few bots.

When building a following, consistency is key, so we carried on shooting and posting and shooting and posting. On the beach, in the stores, at the markets, in front of roaring fires and under star-laden skies. After an all-night desert shoot (where The Dream went in search of magic herbs for an ancient waffle recipe) we drove back to the city so Ari could prep an audition (one condition of her playing The Dream was the freedom to pursue other acting roles). In the car out front of her building, with Max and Deirdre croaking in the distance, she fell asleep kissing me. After five minutes she woke up and went inside, and I drove the streets to stay awake. I felt jet-lagged. The sounds of horns and wheels and engines made their way to my ears as if through a series of long pipes. Sliding down Third Street, right outside The Grove, I saw myself smashing into the back of a midnight blue SUV. I then felt as though my hands would act independently from my brain, and do just that. It's terrifying, the feeling your body wants to take control of your brain and plough you into oblivion. I needed help, so I pulled over to message Anaru. Apologising for the hour (it was 3am in Saigon) I asked if he was free to chat. He said he was clocking off work and would facetime me in forty-five minutes from our spot.

Relief.

Guided by complex GPS algorithms, I drove to the Mulholland Drive lookout. There I climbed a fence, half-walked-half-skidded down a scrubby bank, and sat in a patch of dirt with a prime view of the city.

"What's going on? Are you okay?"

Seeing his face on the screen, a wave of well-being washed over my noxious body. Behind him I saw the beautiful sight of Saigon, humming softly in its slumber. I turned my phone around to show him the flat surface of LA going about its merciless burning business.

"Have you slept?"

"Not a wink."

I vented. I told him how I got fired. How I took Ari to a desert resort that cost more than I had any business spending. How I hoped to make the money back on a never-been-done social media content experiment. How I vomited a sea of peanut-butter cups. After ten minutes I was so sick of listening my own bullshit, I lay back and let grains of dirt roll down my shirt and stick to the damp bumps on my spine.

"I cancelled my trip home."

"Why?"

"Dunno man. Just couldn't face that place. And I've been seeing Viktor again."

"The Russian?"

"He's Belarussian actually."

"He lose his shit in the street again?"

"The melodrama depresses me. Don't talk about it."

In an attempt to hide my face from the burning sun, I shuffled under a bush.

"Hey, you never finished telling me about Blow-arse."

"Why you wanna hear about him?"

"I liked his vibe."

"Yeah, me too."

At the ranch / orchard / drug barn, Anaru had not been comfortable with Kerry, Spit, Darryl and Mushy knowing about his blossoming romance with Blow-arse. So they snuck around a lot. But there were times he felt a bliss he had no idea was possible. Most days they rose at dawn and walked across the crisp grass to the orchard, carrying sticks with cut-in-half Coke bottles attached to the ends, which they used to gather the oranges growing in the high-up branches. By ten o'clock the sun was hot, the air clicking with cicada songs, their shirts soaked with sweat, crates overflowing with fruit at their feet. Searching for Justice, Anaru scanned the tree-line. His cousin was still stalking the property in his princely outfit, shotgun in hand and crackpipe at the ready, and he sometimes popped up in the orchard. But Anaru had tracked his movements well. He knew Justice liked to spend his mornings near the river, that he usually only came to the orchard at night, to shoot the bunnies and the hedgehogs that hopped and shuffled down the lines of trees. But he could never be too careful. Once he was sure they were alone, he and Blow-arse lay under a tree, exploring the rolling hills, wide open plains and deep ravines of each other's bodies. Belts re-buckled and mischievous grins on their faces, they lugged the crates of fruit to the barn to tend the pungent crops of buds. Then it was time for lunch. Blow-arse made cheese and pickle sandwiches, while Anaru fried two rashes of bacon, dicing them into squares when done. This feast they took to the river, where they sat on a log that separated the rushing water from a large calm pond, eating the cheese and pickle sandwiches and feeding bacon to an eel they named Kevin. Kevin was long and fat and pale-eyed – the self-appointed king of the pond. Kevin loved bacon. And he loved attention. He grew quite tame, letting them stroke the silky brown skin on his back and scratch behind the cockle shell-shaped ears on the side of his head. When Kevin swallowed his last bacon square, Anaru and Blow-arse headed upriver, over hot boulders and smaller rocks coated in slippery green slime. They had a spot. A bed of pine needles under a giant tree. Here they lay down. Anaru waited eagerly for Blow-arse to smoke a joint, and outline his plans to set up what he called a "legit archaeological dig." He hoped to find Moa bones and maybe even shrunken heads, which, he reckoned, could be sold for top dollar. Blow-arse was full of get-rich-quick schemes. Anaru heard him out, and offered considered words of advice, and only then would Blow-arse yield to his impatient hands.

One afternoon, as they picked their way back downriver, past black and red dragonflies hovering over clear pools, Blow-arse stopped. He turned and pulled Anaru into him, kissing him hard. When he pulled back, his eyes were like two hot coals desperate to hang onto their heat. Downriver they heard a splash. It was Spit and Mushy, swinging from a rope they had tied to a tree, doing bombs in Kevin's pond. Anaru's throat closed up. His breath was ragged, but he managed four strangled words:

"Did they see us?"

"Who gives a fuck."

"I give a fuck!"

"Bro–"

(Anaru hated it when he called him bro)

"–any of those guys try to hurt you and I'll stab them like the worthless mutts they are."

Anaru's air passage shrunk to the size of a pinhole. A crushing weight on his chest. He sat down on a small boulder. He knew Blow-arse was enamoured with gangster shit. He wanted people to think he was tough, but was he the type to plunge a knife into another man's flesh? Sure he talked about it, but it was all for show. That was the problem. Blow-arse was nothing if not a committed showman.

Two days later, Justice got clean.

Anaru stood at the kitchen bench, braising a whole snapper with a sauce he made from butter and garlic and finely chopped dill. Blow-arse sat by the fire in the living room, smoking a joint with Spit, Kerry, Mushy and Darryl. They were debating the efficacy of elbowing an adversary in the head vs kneeing him in the head. Justice waltzed into the kitchen, raised his eyebrows at Anaru, and leaned his shotgun on the wall. He then silenced his crew by striding into the living room, stripping off his tweed jacket, his jodhpurs and his riding boots and tossing them into the flames. The leather hissed and popped. Naked, Justice walked to his room and shut the door. He slept for three days. Anaru took him all his meals – bowls of oats, snapper fillets, chicken wings, chip sandwiches (Justice's all-time favourite), pippies, mussels, sausages, spinach, steak, mashed potato, pork chops, lamb chops, ice cream and of course oranges. Not one dish woke him from his cold turkey slumber. As the meals went cold, Anaru sat by the bed, fretting over his beloved cousin. He checked his pulse every five minutes, held fingers under his nose in search of breath. And when he burned up, muttering feverishly in the dark, Anaru mopped his brow with a cold cloth.

On the fourth night, at 7pm, Anaru took a plate of chicken tenders into the room, and found his cousin sitting up in bed. Justice said nothing. He devoured the plate, the rest of the bird, plus an entire oven tray of roast carrots and kumara.

"I heard what you were saying," he said, sucking grease from his fingers.

"What do you mean?"

"You were plotting against me. The whole time I was asleep. You and Blow-arse and the other goons. Planning to kill me, eh?"

"I don't–"

"Don't fuckin' lie, cuz. I heard you. Reckon you can kick me out of my own business? I can understand the others, but you and me are meant to be family you fucking dog."

For days he ranted like this. Paranoid. Delusional. Accusing Anaru and his crew of sharpening their knives, plotting his demise, digging his grave down by the river. Anaru tried a million ways of soothing him, talking him down, but the more he spoke the angrier his cousin became. He flew into a marathon rage. Foaming at the mouth, he ransacked the house. Pulling pictures from the walls, smashing plates and cups and bowls. He body-slammed a coffee table and splintered chairs with a fire poker. He ripped cushions to shreds with his teeth, hurled his body at windows, punched and kicked and head-butted anyone who came near him. Anaru was sure he would kill himself, or do serious harm to one of them. He was like a hurricane picking up speed as he tore through the house. No one knew what to do and no one wanted to get in his path. Eventually Darryl threw a pink featherdown duvet over his head, and Blow-arse tackled him round the ankles, while Kerry and Spit pinned his arms and legs to the floor. From under the pink duvet came a torrent of abuse. He kicked and screamed and howled, letting out deep guttural growls that sounded like they came from an atavistic abyss. "Do something!!!" yelled Blow-arse. What they needed was a sedative. A needle to stick in his butt and knock him out. It wasn't like they could sit him down and make him smoke a joint. Anaru was dizzy with terror. His breath having long ago abandoned him. On rickety legs he walked to the kitchen, took a rolling pin from a drawer, and clobbered the wailing mound under the pink blanket. Donk. Donk. Donk. Silence. Out cold, they carried Justice to his bed, where they tied his ankles and wrists to the posts. When he woke up screaming, they stuffed a ball of socks in his mouth and taped it shut.

"He needs to fight."

Anaru was in his room, lying on his back, his eyes closed, focusing on the pressure in his chest, his throat, and the lining of his skull. He opened his eyes to see Blow-arse standing over him.

"What?"

"Justice needs to fight," said Blow-arse. "He's angry, and he needs to get that anger out. Me and the boys were talking. We'll build a ring on the lawn. We'll fight him. One fight each day."

"You'll kill him."

"We'll go easy."

"He'll kill you."

"Nah, we'll tire him out. It'll be good. It'll work. Trust me."

Through the wall, Justice roared. He thrashed against his constraints. Shook the walls.

"Fine," said Anaru.

To build the ring, four fence posts were hammered into the lawn, with three lengths of rope strung between them. To prevent serious injury, they needed a referee. Anaru put up his hand, and went to town to buy a whistle and two pairs of the softest boxing gloves he could find. Blow-arse called dibs on the first fight. He pulled off his shirt, pulled on the gloves, and stepped into the grassy ring. Spit and Kerry brought out Justice. He didn't scream or rage or foam at the mouth. Radiating steely calm, he locked eyes with Blow-arse. This worried Anaru. For good reason. The second Justice stepped into the ring, he battered Blow-arse mercilessly. Blow-arse was no pugilist. He tripped over his feet, walked into punches, threw haymakers with no hope of connecting. "Hook him, bro!" yelled Kerry and Spit. "Smash him!" shouted Darryl. "Ha-ha, Blow-arse, you're all shit, man" – that was Mushy. In less than a minute, Blow-arse was gasping for air. Blood poured from his nose, bloomed like a rose in his right eyeball. Anaru blew his whistle. But Blow-arse brushed him aside and ran at Justice, who knocked him out cold with a shot to the solar plexus.

The fights went down every day at dawn. The idea being to drain Justice of his destructive energy before the sun came up. He knocked out Kerry, punched Spit through the ropes, bit a hole in Darryl's cheek and nearly ruptured Mushy's kidney. On more than one occasion, he clipped Anaru. For this he always apologised. "Sorry ref," or, "sorry cuz." Anaru took this as a sign his cousin hadn't lost all human empathy. And he had to admit, the fights worked. By the third day, Justice was calming down. One night, as his crew nursed their wounds in front of the fire, he curled up on the couch and fell asleep like a cat.

Blow-arse was the worry.

Out of everyone, he fought the most. At least twice a day he stepped into the ring. Often, Anaru tried to stop him. "Step the fuck off," hissed Blow-arse. Justice knocked him down. Time and time again he knocked Blow-arse off his feet. Bone-crunching punches. The slap of leather on skin. Anaru could see what Blow-arse was up to. He was putting on a show, and Justice was his audience. No matter how black his eyes, how bloody his nose, how wobbly his teeth, he got up off the grass. And every time he touched gloves with Justice, he earned a little more of his respect.

Episode Thirty-Nine.

The light in the bathroom was perfect. And I stood under the perfect light and stared at my hands. The fingers, the lifelines, the stump, the fingernails, the veins under the skin. I still found it strange they were my hands. I still could not quite believe they belonged to me. So I stared and stared.

These episodes were hitting with serious regularity. But this bathroom one hit different. With this one, I watched my hands, but I watched myself watching my hands as well. Like I was watching a film, and I was the main character in this film, watching myself watch my hands. I was also the director of this film. I could move the camera, zoom and pan and whip, and watch the protagonist (myself) from any angle. So that's what I did. I moved down to a low angle shot, so I was looking up at my face looking down at my hands. I circled my head, taking in my eyes and my ears. Then I moved above the crown of my head, and looked down at the tip of my nose and the hands below that nose. From this angle, I watched myself leave the perfect bathroom light and walk down a dark and moody hallway. I needed to find Ari.

We were at Rah-Rah's brutalist bunker in The Hills, for his fifty-fifth birthday party. I watched myself walk into a room that opened onto a lush pool area. The room was packed with Hollywood regulars – producers and agents and showrunners – and I had a mind to hustle them all. I heard music. Screeching and pounding and distorted yelping. It sounded like an accident at an industrial worksite. I watched myself walk outside, skirt the edge of the pool, and stand at the back of a crowd of sweating, slamming bodies. Up front, Ari's friend Ramona prowled a small black stage. She wore a yellow leather catsuit with a yellow leather gimp mask, and her red lips poking out a zip-up mouth-hole, howling into a microphone. Behind her, on drums, sat her boyfriend Elwood. He wore nothing but a pair of sweat-soaked white underpants, and as he hammered his drums, he screamed into a microphone he had duct-taped to his cheek and run through some sort of distortion pedal. His body was covered in what were meant to look like authentic prison tats, but were in fact the work of a highly coveted tattoo artist who charged exorbitant fees. Elwood's father was a Beverly Hills real estate mogul. Their band was called *BITCH CRAFT*. From that close, they sounded like people killing cats by ramming them into walls with shopping trolleys.

Somewhere in that slamming pit of bodies was Ari's body. I watched my face scan the faces for her face, and when I did not see it, I watched my face crumple.

The last few weeks had not been great for us. Rather than sky-rocketing to social media stardom, The Dream stalled out on two thousand followers. This depressed Ari, and she called me all kinds of mean names. Svengali. Master manipulator. Liar and user and faker. Ninth rate filmmaker. Wombat-fucking Australian fucktard. The more depressed she got, the greater her need for me to take control in the bedroom. The greater her need for me to take control in the bedroom, the more I avoided the bedroom. Excuses. Excuses. Excuses. I invented all manner of reason why I couldn't choke her, or tie her up, or lean her out my apartment window and spank her bare butt as cars sped up and down Main Street. I said I had to read the data. The data held the answers to our failure. The Dream needed me.

She needed fresh content ideas. I had to feed her. An invisible wall went up between us. And neither of us were mature enough to climb the wall, poke our head over the top and ask how the other was doing. So we sat, alone, on either side of the wall. Sulking.

One night, to get to me, she told me how she once had sex with a director with five Oscars under his belt.

"You know what else he had under his belt?" she asked.

"A giant cock?"

"That thing was as fat as a Coke can. Boy was that a rough workout."

If that was meant to make me feel like less of a man, she was on the money. But what she didn't know was that feeling like less of a man turned me on. After that, when we fucked, I pretended to be the director with five Oscars and the girth of a Coke can. But I only pretended in my head, never out loud. This made me feel like a worthless and putrid worm. But feeling like a worthless and putrid worm really did it for me on a sexual level. For a few days, our sex life was restored. I may not have been choking her, but at least I was touching her.

At Rah-Rah's party, I watched myself sidle up to a young Black woman with green eyes and a lavender leather jacket.

"Hey, I'm Apollo."

"Hi Apollo! I'm Anna. What do you do?"

"I'm a director."

"Amazing! I'm an actress. What are you working on right now?"

"Uhh, this big social media film series project thing."

"Interesting. Do you have a deal?"

"Not yet."

"That's so interesting. I'm just popping to the bar. Great talking to you!"

After that I spoke to a man named Cleve. "Cleve has the best hair in LA," said his girlfriend, a woman named Clementine. Cleve told me he was working on a documentary about his hair, called THE WAVE. He planned on dedicating it to his daughter, who he hoped would grow up to have powerful hair like him. "I'm a DILF," he said. "A dad people wanna fuck." I said I knew what a DILF was, and that it must be hard work being a Dad. He said he only saw his daughter once a year, but he was still DILF material.

I bounced from group to group for the next two hours. People asked what I did. I said filmmaker. They got excited. Asked what kind of films I made. I told them. They left. Ari found me sitting on the edge of the jacuzzi, staring at my hands. "Come on. There's someone I want you to meet." She led me down a dark hallway, and that took us down a second dark hallway, then a third. Off the hallways were rooms, and in these rooms people chatted on chairs and rolled on long-haired white rugs. In one, an old woman painted a portrait of a young man flexing his muscles. The bunker was some sort of rabbit warren. On and on it went. Deeper and deeper. Had Rah-Rah dug his house into the core of the Hollywood Hills? After some time, we reached a long room with glass walls and low lighting. I looked through the walls, searching for signs of earth or maybe a tree, but saw only darkness. At a long table sat maybe ten or twenty men and women, Hollywood players all. They chatted about deals and credits and contracts. And all the powerful stuff that went to work on my frontal lobe like the best drugs you can sniff up your nose. Speaking of sniffing, the table was a spread of dishes from all corners of the world. We're talking sushi, soups, roast lamb, roast chicken, guacamole, sizzling fajitas, steaks, lentil curries, laksa, lobster thermidor, prawn dumplings, pork buns and san choy bow. At the head of the table sat a man with the look of a cat relaxing in the sun. His hair was silky grey, styled into an expensive mop. Save one gold incisor, his teeth were bright white, and when he smiled (which was often and easy) the gold incisor glowed. Unbuttoned to his diaphragm, he wore a white linen shirt tucked into perfectly faded 501s. These came to rest on white canvas tennis shoes that looked basic but cost more than your average family car. Ari told me who he was, but I already knew.

Rah-Rah.

A white suit-wearing Japanese woman whispered into his right ear, and he closed his eyes, so he did not see Ari shoo two men from the seats to his left. We sat in these seats. An old woman placed fresh dishes on the table – ribs and crab and loaves of bread, and what looked like a leek tart. The smells comingled, making me lightheaded. Behind her hand, Ari said:

"You have to pitch to him."

"The Untitled Original Series Set On Multiple Continents?"

"No, idiot, The Dream."

"Doesn't seem like a pitching format."

"I mean, if you're not up to it…"

I looked at Rah-Rah. He flashed me a smile, gold tooth twinkling. Goddamnit. I wanted to pitch that smug old dog into oblivion. I was feeling it. The juice. The anger. The swagger. Running in my veins like a million little rivers. All those people that snubbed me. That walked away, saw me as worthless. The bastards. I'd show them. I'd pitch and I'd sell.

"Fine," I said, squeezing her thigh so hard she twisted in her seat.

"Shit yes, daddy."

"So what's the big secret?" said Rah-Rah.

The Japanese woman was gone. As he spoke, he peeled the shell off a prawn. Dipped his fingers in a water bowl.

"This is Apollo," said Ari. "The hot-as-fuck director I told you about."

"Right. Right. Apollo."

Nothing he did was rushed. Every gesture relaxed. Every syllable slow. Like he had just come out of a hot stone massage. I gestured at the mountain of food in front of me.

"You mind if I…"

"Eat? My god, man, of course. If you want to make my mama happy, eat."

The old woman passed by. He reached out and rubbed her back. She nodded at me. Winked. I filled a plate with prawns, pork chops, mashed potato and moussaka. Approvingly, Mama Rah-Rah watched as I ate.

"It's delicious," I said. "Thank you so much."

Rah-Rah pointed a crab claw at Ari, but he spoke to me. "Now what lies has this little rascal told you about me."

"Only the most shameful ones," said Ari, tearing flesh from a chicken drumstick with her broken tooth.

"You know where she was when I found her?"

I shook my head.

"At the bus stop. All burned out. Used up. Ribs sticking out. Face all bruised. Ready to pack up the dream and go on home to goats-ville USA. But I have an eye for talent. She still had fire in her belly, I could see it. So I took her home, got her cleaned up and put her back on her feet. Not that she ever thanked me for it."

Ari dropped the chicken bone on her ceramic plate and burped. "Is that really what went down, Rah-Rah?"

"You got a different version, Ari? Then tell it."

Her cheeks flamed red, her nostrils flared. Her eyes had the same look as the day she screamed so loud she nearly ran us off the road. Last thing I needed was her screaming now, or causing a scene, and killing the pitch vibe.

"But listen, Rah-Rah, we have a show we want to talk to you about."

"Is that right? What's this show of yours about?"

Mama Rah-Rah turned to me. I felt the eyes of the table on me. All ears waiting for the pitch.

"It's about an influencer called The Dream, and she lives the dream life in LA, but then her life spins out of control and she ends up homeless on–"

"Listen, Apollo, I know you just got off the boat, so you don't know how this town works, but let me give you some free advice. One, you don't walk into a man's house uninvited, sit at his table, eat his Mama's food and fuck his best girl. Two, don't come at me while I'm enjoying my leisure time, and try to hustle me like some lowdown desperate maggot."

Episode Forty.

Sleep did not come. It stayed well clear of me, like I was poison. And I was poison. I rolled and thrashed, the disastrous pitch to Rah-Rah on repeat in my head. Over and over it played. I sunk deep into a shame spiral, soaking the threads of the sheets in sweat. But no matter how much liquid I lost – four litres, five litres – my system stayed toxic. Ari lay next to me. Her eyes closed. Mouth open a sliver. A small puddle of drool on the pillow next to her cheek. I leaned over, dipping the tip of my tongue in the drool puddle. Warm and sweet, it tasted like coconut water. I found that weird. But I also felt that coconut water tasted like watered down saliva. So maybe not so weird.

But that was just a distraction. I forgot about the coconut water-flavoured drool, and returned to the pitch to Rah-Rah. I saw the look in his eyes when he called me maggot. Heard the chuckles from the far end of the table. Tasted the prawn go sour in my mouth. It made me wretch, but, like a dog going back to lick up its vomit, I returned to the shame of the pitch time and time again. Yes I was punishing myself. Don't you do that too? When you stuff up the biggest opportunity of your life, don't you return to the scene of the crash and kick your corpse in its twisted spine? Because let's face it, I was cooked. The people at that table were the central nervous system of Hollywood. And they had seen me get immolated. The door had been opened a crack, then slammed shut in my face.

Ten minutes after the sun came up, Ari opened her eyes. She yawned, looked at the drool on her pillow, looked at me looking at the drool on her pillow, and smiled.

"Did you sleep at all?"

"Nope."

"Stressed about Rah-Rah?"

"I fucked it, didn't I. Like I properly fucked it."

"I don't know."

"I do."

"You know how many times I fucked it? He'll give you another shot. He just likes to humiliate people."

"He called me a maggot."

"He's a maggot."

She climbed out of bed and dug in her handbag. When she came back, she dangled a gold Rolex in front of my nose.

"From the maggot."

"He gave that to you?"

"I wouldn't say *gave*."

I took the watch and looked at it. The face was embedded with diamonds. I thought of Uncle Frank's jewellery box, with all his rings. Was my finger still in there? It'd be a bone by now. Dry and white. The flesh rotted away. Maybe he had fashioned the bone into a ring.

"We could get, like, ten grand for this," said Ari. "We can put that into The Dream."

I whistled. Handed her the watch back. She held it up, and watched the diamonds glitter in the morning light.

"What was that thing last night, between you two."

"What thing?"

"The bus stop story."

"Oh. That. Yeah. He's full of shit."

"How so?"

"Well, it's true that he found me at the bus stop, and it's true I was leaving LA for good. I was going home to my goats. But then Rah-Rah pulls up in his red Porsche. Starts talking 'bout how he saw something in me, then he offers me a spot on his new show. I was like, damn, just when you think you're all burned out, lady luck comes along and tongue kisses you on the mouth. So I got in his car, and we go back to his house in The Hills. I take a shower, eat a slice of his Mama's meatloaf, then he takes me into his room and forces his snout into my pussy."

"Jesus."

"He wasn't there."

"I'm so sorry you had to deal with that."

"That's his favourite sport. He cruises bus stops looking for burned out Hollywood boys and girls, promises them one last shot, then he takes them home and rapes them."

She twirled the gold watch on her finger. I wrapped my arms around her neck. "This is what you need to understand, Apollo. This town ain't give-take, it's take-take. You want something from someone like Rah-Rah, you better take it, because you give him half a sniff and he will sure as shit take from you."

Episode Forty-One.

Dawn the next day. Ari took the gold and diamond-encrusted Rolex to a twenty-four hour pawn shop. "Dawn is when you get the best deals," she said. "The staff are coming off a twelve hour graveyard shift, so they've lost the will to live, let along haggle." I stayed home to write fresh content for The Dream. It was rough. I worried she'd never take off. Doubt was seeping into my skin and setting up shop in my nerve endings. Right as I was working up a foamy lather of panic, Ari walked in with fifteen grand in cash. She told me to pack a bag, but not a big one. Enough clothes for three days, and swimwear too. Then she bundled me into the passenger seat of the neurotic black car, and slid behind the wheel with a jumbo iced coffee in hand.

"Where are we going?"

"Not telling."

To get to the coast, she took an intricate route comprised of back streets (apparently only LA newbies and the criminally insane took Sunset all the way to the ocean) then she took Pacific Coast Highway north. The clouds moved quick across the sky, creating dark patches on the ocean that looked like the shadows of monsters lurking in the deep.

"Are we going to San Francisco?"

"Not telling."

"Big Sur?"

"Not telling."

She turned off the coastal highway, cutting inland, through lush and green and bougie wine country. I saw people smiling at grapes they picked from vines. They reminded me of Anaru and Blow-arse, happy in their orchard. Also, I pulled up a map of California on my phone.

"Are we going to Monterey?"

"Not telling."

"King City?"

"Not telling."

"San Luis Obispo?"

"Not telling."

"Fresno?"

"Not telling."

"Capitan?"

"Not telling."

"Mussel Shoals?"

"Because I need you to shut the fuck up with the California placenames, I'll tell you. We're going to this dope-ass resort in Santa Barbara called Bacara. Oprah stays there. Motherfucking Oprah!"

"Can we afford it?"

"We just made fifteen grand. We deserve it. Besides, it's work. We stay a couple days and shoot a bunch of content for The Dream. Maybe she'll get off her ass and get some followers."

Bacara sat on a massive piece of prime coastal real estate, with multiple pools, golf holes, and lawns where you could ride a pony down the aisle to meet your botoxed bride. The buildings were what you'd expect to see at the Queen of Mexico's holiday compound. And when we walked into the lobby, we saw the type of people who get angry when told they aren't allowed to keep tigers as pets.

Our room had a balcony with marble pillars. I stood out there, staring at the pool as it glowed, orb-like, under a starless sky. Through the sliding doors I heard Ari scream. When I walked in, I found her sitting on the edge of the bed, pointing at the giant TV.

"Wanna watch Avatar?"

"You like that film?"

"I hate that film."

Turned out she had auditioned for a role as one of the blue aliens. It was her first big audition in Hollywood, and she got super close. Went through rounds and rounds of readings, met the producers and everything. And the closer she got, the more she believed she would get the role, that it would lead to bigger and better roles, and they would lead her up the stairs to the stage to collect the hallowed Best Actress Oscar. Obviously that never panned out. And she bore a deep resentment to the film, as well as the blue aliens in the film.

"I need you to fuck me while we're watching it, and then, right when the tree where all the aliens live gets blown up, and they lose their stupid spiritual village, I'm gonna need you to choke me until I pass out."

This was a damn funny idea. One I was more than happy to play a part in. The film got going, we got naked, and got into some heavy petting. But the climactic destruction scene was nearly three hours away, and I'd be out of gas by then. We skipped forward. Ari lay on her back, her head hanging off the side of the bed, watching the screen upside down. I was on top, watching the right way up. As I went to work, choppers fired rockets at the blue aliens, who shot back with bows and arrows. The army general guy was having a great old time. He stood in the main chopper, sipping from a mug of coffee as he ordered his men to blow the aliens to smithereens. The aliens died in great numbers. Each time one perished, Ari let out a moan of deep and genuine pleasure. She really hated those aliens. "FIRE!" yelled the general. The choppers shot their big boy rockets. This was the final attack. The rockets fizzed and sparked and smoked, whizzing for the trunk of the sacred tree. I pressed my thumbs into Ari's throat. She breathed out.

I felt her body tighten, then relax, then tighten, then relax. KABOOM! The rockets blasted the base of the tree, sending aliens screeching into the air. I squeezed tighter. Felt her neck tendons flex against my fingers. Fizzing and popping and screaming. Fireballs and explosions. She watched the aliens die on screen, her eyes watering, bulging in their sockets. Her face was scarlet. Burning hot. KA-WOOSH! The ancient tree burst into flames, began its slow crash through the forest foliage. The moment of truth was upon me. All I had to do was apply extra pressure, for ten more seconds, and she would pass out. Deep in her body an unspoken organ coiled in anticipation. CRASH! The tree hit the ground. Aliens wailed. Their spiritual home was gone. Ari pushed her throat into my palm, her red eyes pleading. But I couldn't do it. I couldn't finish the job.

We did not speak of my failure.
We watched the final act of the film.
We brushed our teeth.
We went to bed.
We woke–
–actually, I woke up alone. Ari's side of the bed was empty. Her bag was gone. On the bedside table sat a note:

> *Dear Apollo*
> *You made me feel so sad last night. So hopelessly ashamed. I'm sorry I wanted you to give what you could not give. I'm sorry I gave so much of myself. I always give too much. I think it's best if we don't see each other for a while.*
> *Love, Ari*

For seventeen minutes, I simmered with rage and shame. I made her feel so sad? That was a touch melodramatic. How did she think I felt after she walked out on me for not possessing the violence necessary to choke her out? And how much of herself did she give exactly? And what did she mean when she said we shouldn't see each other for a while? Were we over? Was The Dream over? We were not your average couple – we were also a dynamic creative partnership with a great big beating heart under construction. As quick as it came, my anger drifted out the sliding doors and down to the pool. Where I hoped it would take root in the hearts of the middle-aged adulterers cavorting in the clear blue water. I sat on the bed, staring at the note in my hand, and an episode descended on me. I was outside my body. A camera recording. From above my head, I filmed the note in my hand. I then filmed myself walk out the door, down to the lobby, and drive away in the neurotic black car.

I drove north. No destination in mind. All I saw were my hands on the wheel, and the white lines sliding under the black bonnet.

I found myself on a beach, walking on cold hard sand. Old couples walked past me, and I swear every single one of these couples had a golden retriever. The men wore sweaters tied around shoulders that had once been broad but now began to sag. And the women clutched at silk scarves they secured at their throats with gold brooches. The couples threw sticks into the water, and their golden retrievers bounded into the sea, splashing and smiling and poking their snouts under waves. Was there a factory up here that pumped out these golden retriever couples? A Republican convention nearby? Or was I walking up and down the beach for hours, passing the same couple walking the same dog, over and over.

The rocks were jagged and sharp under my feet. Waves crashed next to me, shooting white spray high in the air. Where were my shoes? Did I throw them in the ocean for a golden retriever to fetch? Why was I on the rocks? Maybe I wanted to walk to the next beach over. Maybe I needed a shot of myself in this cinematic landscape. Whatever. I found a cave in the base of a cliff. And when you find a cave, you have to go as far into the cave as you can. Those are the rules of the cave. It was cold and dark in the cave, with rock walls dripping salty-smelling slime from centuries ago. Deep into the cave I walked. And when it got too small to walk I crawled. Behind me, my cameraman-self urged me on. Scolding me for various weaknesses. My many failures. My inability to choke Ari. Deep in the heart of the cave

I found a soft patch of sand, and began to dig. My cameraman-self said I would find the jewellery box that contained my finger. I found no such box. But I did find a fishing line with a lure tied to the end. And I crawled then walked with it back to the mouth of the cave. Night had fallen. The tide was high. There was no way to make it back to the beach. I was stuck. For some reason I knew no harm would come to me on those rocks. Also, I had my fishing line. I walked to the edge and cast the lure into the choppy sea. I fished like that for hours. Watching shadowy clouds slip past the surface of the moon, the occasional flash on the horizon from lightning storms far out to sea. Coyotes howled from the cliffs behind me. They told me to swim back to whatever island I blew in from. And the ocean said it had no fish for me. The salty wind froze my ears and burned my lips. A crab bit my toe. I crawled to the back of the cave, where I slept on the soft patch of sand.

I woke up in the cave and walked out onto the rocks. The sun was high and the tide was low. I knew what I had to do. And so, barefoot and reeking of salty cave sweat, I drove back to LA.

I found a park in front of Ari's building. When I walked past Max and Deirdre's fountain, they stopped croaking. Like they knew all about the beef between me and the woman with the shaved head who sometimes fed them frozen yoghurt. I pressed the buzzer, and she let me in without a word. I found her lying on her bed in her underwear, staring at her phone.

"Get dressed."

She stared at the screen. "No."

"Get your ass off that bed and get dressed right now."

She looked up. "Or what?"

I picked up one of her Birkenstock sandals. "Or I'll whip your ass raw with this."

"You wouldn't dare."

I jumped onto the bed, pulled her onto my knee, yanked down her underwear and spanked her bare ass with the sole of the sandal. "Don't you ever" – SLAP! – "leave me" – SLAP! – "alone" – SLAP! – "in a fancy" – SLAP! – "resort" – SLAP! – "again" – SLAP!

With each slap, she moaned and cried and begged forgiveness. Her white cheeks turned a burning red. I slapped so hard the sting pulled me out of the cave and into the real world. I wasn't pretending. I wasn't watching myself, or filming myself, I was doing it for real. And I meant it. By god did I mean it. After fifty-odd slaps, I pulled her face to mine and kissed her. Our tongues went at each other like a couple of chained up fighting dogs off the leash. Our teeth clashed so hard I felt one chip, white ceramic powder sprinkling my gums. Were we trying to eat each other? We wanted to get as deep down the other's throat as possible. Our cheeks smudged, wet with hot tears. Usually I'd use a kiss like this to teleport to another dimension, but I stayed right there with her in her mouth. With her saliva strands and metal fillings, and the soft patch of flesh at the back of her tongue.

Episode Forty-Two.

I was asleep. And then I was not. I stared at shadows darting across the ceiling like apex predator fish. Ari lay next to me. Puddle of drool on her pillow. I didn't taste her drool this time. Over the last few days I had consumed such a colossal amount of her bodily fluids they had basically replaced my stomach lining, becoming a permanent part of me. Out the open window, people shouted on Main Street.

"Fuck you in my face for, motherfucker!"

"That's my hotdog!"

"The lord is my shepherd, he lays me down in green pastures!"

My brain did that thing where it sent me back to sleep, then for no good reason woke me up again an hour later. The drool puddle had doubled in size. I grabbed my phone from the bedside table, saw that it was 4am, and that I had ten missed calls from Anaru. Panic. When I leapt out of bed, a spoonful of bile lurched up my throat. I ran to the kitchen, spat in the sinkhole, and called him back.

He did not answer.

So I called him back.

He did not answer.

So I called him back.

He did not answer.

I sat in a chair near the window. From here I could see right down 6th Street. I watched two men kissing near the Starbucks. The night was still, and silent, and they looked sweet, kissing in a pool of light. Then a woman came round the corner and bottled one of them in the back of the head. My phone rang.

"Are you okay?"

"Dunno."

"Is it one of your episodes?"

"I can't–"

"Are you eating?"

"Well–"

"Where are you?"

"I'll tell you if you let me."

"Sorry. Worried."

"I can't sleep. I mean I can, but I don't want to. I mean I want to, I really want to. But. Uhh. Feels like I've slept, like, ten minutes in the last few days. Think I'm losing my mind. I've got tunnel vision and I keep hearing people calling my name. Whispering. And yeah, being outside in Saigon when you're like this, it's a for real psychotic episode, but–"

"Do you have any sleeping pills?"

"Well I've kind of been taking these speed pills, just to get through work."

"Oh speed pills, they're great for sleep."

"Don't be a dick."

"I just feel like if you want to sleep the last thing you take is speed pills."

"I need to work, bro. I'm taking Trammies to come down but now I'm all out of whack. And Blow-arse. I've been dreaming about… fighting in the stupid boxing ring they set up. In the dream I beat him to death. But I don't stop. I keep punching and kicking until his head is just a bloody pulp."

"Full on."

"Yeah, no shit. And it's fucking me up. I can't even breathe properly. So

I've been pulling twenty hour shifts, just cleaning the shit out of everything to avoid–"

"You want me to fly over?"

"What? Nah. I mean yes. I wanna see you. But you can't just dump everything and–"

"Just for a week maybe. To get you–"

"Nah. I can't. Wait. Hold on a sec? My guy's at the door. He's got the good Laotian pills."

Out my window, shit was escalating. Red and blue lights flashed the entire block. Sirens. Two paramedics wrapped bandages round the head of the man who got bottled, while the cops tried to restrain the woman who did the bottling. But she must have had super human strength, or been smoking super strength crack. When they tried to put her in the back of the squad car, she swung her legs up and pushed off the side with the soles of her feet, so her and the cops crashed to the ground in a pile of limbs. For the next hour I watched this farce. Spitting and cursing and falling back down in a fresh pile. LA's finest. I felt bad, but I was happy Anaru said no to my offer to fly out. I mean I would have gone. Obviously. But that would have thrown a spanner in the works with Ari. And The Dream. And the Untitled Original Series Set On Multiple Continents. Out on the street, the cops pulled out tasers.

Anaru called back. On Facetime. "Guess where I am," he said. His face filled the screen. Judging by the layer of sheen on his face, he had swallowed more than a few speed pills. Most people, when they take speed, get all jittery and annoying, and talk at length about their shit business ideas or their non-existent childhood trauma. But Anaru was built different. He seemed calm. Resolute. His voice was rock steady. His jaw didn't grind his gums to mulch. Yes, his pupils were like saucers, but that was the only outward sign of the high-grade amphetamines coursing through his central nervous system. Also, I didn't need to guess where he was, because I knew. He flipped his phone around, and I looked out at Saigon from the roof of the President Hotel. It was weird. In LA, the sun was just starting to think about rising. But in Saigon, it was sliding down the back of the city, bouncing its final rays off the slow brown surface of the river. It felt like it might disappear behind Saigon and pop up east of LA. "Anyway," he said, the slightest quiver in his jaw, "I haven't told anyone about what happened to Blow-arse, but I feel, like, if I don't get him outta my head these dreams will never stop."

And so, as the sun set in Saigon and rose in LA, he told me.

The daily boxing matches were gone, but no one bothered to take down the ring. The grass in the middle grew waist high, vines crept up the corner posts, and wound their way along the ropes. Anaru had to admit it: Blow-arse was smarter than he thought he was. He had orchestrated the fights to rid the ranch house of the rage of Justice, and it had worked. Justice now rose at dawn, meditated, ran ten kilometres, cooked an egg white omelette, reviewed the monthly figures, ordered fertilizer and other supplies online, and researched new and stronger hydroponic strains. But Blow-arse had also orchestrated the fights to prove himself to Justice. And it worked. It worked a treat. They were now BFFs. Together, they swam in the river, made kale smoothies, and set up a gym in the barn. This was next to the plants and the white hot lights, which Blow-arse sometimes used for tanning purposes.

Anaru tried not to let it show, but he felt left out.

And angry.

And alone.

And when he tended the crops in the barn, he had to wear headphones. To drown out the clank of weights, but also the endless grunting. When Justice and Blow-arse did squats, they grunted. When they kicked and punched the heavy bag, they grunted. When they guzzled creatine, they grunted, and when they slapped each other on the arse and said, 'nice form, bro', they grunted. The grunts were almost comically sexual. But comical or not, they planted all sorts of torturous images in Anaru's head. The images tied his stomach in knots, tightened his throat, and made him bristle with jealousy. But the grunting wasn't the worst of it, no, the worst of it was the whispering. From dawn 'til dusk, they plotted and schemed in conspiratorial tones. Just thinking of these plans made Anaru sicker and clammier than any image of Blow-arse in his cousin's arms, possibly in their secret pine needle spot upriver. Were they planning a new hydro set-up? Were they planning to get rid of the hydro set up to make way for a full scale meth cooking operation? Were they planning to import kilos from the Golden Triangle? Or were they just planning the world's most homo-erotic workout?

A Tuesday.

Anaru woke up alone.

He missed Blow-arse in his bed.

He missed picking fruit with him in the orchard.

He missed the way his skin smelled when they sat on the log feeding Kevin bacon.

He got dressed. In the living room, in front of smouldering fire, Mushy and Darryl played Grand Theft Auto. Spit slept on his face on the floor, and Kerry stared out the window. Empty beer cans covered the glass coffee table, and an ash tray spilled cigarette butts and roaches onto the once-white carpet.

"Any you guys seen Justice?"

Mushy gunned down an old lady on screen, and said: "Gone out. Him and Blow-arse."

"Any idea where?"

"Fuck knows."

In the kitchen, Anaru made coffee, fried two rashers of bacon, sliced them into squares and took them down to the river in a plastic container. He sat on the log that ran from bank to bank, looking over the large pond. The air was cold. Mist rose off the flat surface. He tossed a piece of bacon into the water. Grease swirled out from the meat, making paisley patterns on the surface. Swishing his tail, Kevin appeared from the deep. He glided to the log, pale blue eyes glancing up at Anaru. "Good morning," said Anaru. Kevin gulped the bacon down in one go. Anaru chucked him a second square. And a third. Sliding his hand into the water, he stroked the eel's slippery back, his ghostly white tummy. He scratched behind his shell-shaped fin. "Good boy. You like that don't you?" Kevin lunged, sinking his long hooked fangs into Anaru's right index finger. Anaru reeled back, yanking his finger from the water. But Kevin's fangs had punctured the fingernail, so he went too. For two horrifying seconds, Anaru stared at the fat eel hanging from his finger. Kevin bucked and wriggled, morning sun glistening on his gills and the sepia fin that ran the length of his spine. Then Anaru swung his arm, Kevin's fangs ripped free, and he sailed through the air, landing in the long grass. Immediately he tried to slither to the safety of the pond, but his bacon diet had made him slow. Anaru jumped off the log, skipped through the grass and pounced. With one hand, he gripped Kevin behind his head, pinning him to the ground. With his free hand, he punched and punched and punched. Like a veil, red mist fell over his eyes. The blows rained down. He lost all sense of his surroundings. When he came to, breathing hard, Kevin was no more than a bloody smear on the grass.

Anaru hated himself for what he had done.

He was worse than his cousin. Worse than Kerry and Darryl and Mushy and Spit.

At least they beat humans.

He beat a poor defenceless eel to death.

Well maybe not entirely defenceless. Those fangs were pretty good on defence, but still.

Also, Blow-arse loved Kevin. And while Anaru felt bad for killing him, he knew that news of his death would bring Blow-arse home. This made him feel good, which made him feel even worse than he felt about the killing. Yes, Blow-arse would call him a bloodthirsty murderer. He might hate him, and beat him the way Anaru beat Kevin. But at least this would be something. Far better than the nothing he'd been getting.

Holding back tears, he placed Kevin's remains in a plastic bag, and buried him in the back of the freezer. He then composed a message to Blow-arse. Writing and re-writing, he stayed up late, leaning into various tones and narrative structures. He said the farmer next-door had poisoned the pond, and Kevin had gone feral. It had been a mercy killing. He described an epic struggle between man and beast. A 'kill or be killed' type situation. In the end he scrapped the shit and told the truth. He had planned to send the message by midnight, but he slept on it. In the morning he made one or two minor tweaks, then hit send. Nothing. For the next three days, still nothing. "Any you guys heard from Justice or Blow-arse?" he asked the crew, whose lives had become one long, stoned game of Grand Theft Auto. "Nah," said Darryl. Kerry and Spit and Mushy were silent. But it was possible they had lost the power of speech, or their brains had stopped functioning entirely.

A week after Kevin's passing, Anaru removed his remains from the freezer, and buried him under the biggest orange tree in the orchard. The one that bore the most fruit. At the head of the grave, he placed a perfectly rounded rock he found in the river. Next to the rock, he placed a bird of paradise flower, plus a freshly fried and diced rasher of bacon. "One for the road. See you soon old mate." With his phone he shot photos of the grave, the rock, the flower and the bacon, and sent them to Blow-arse. No reply. His stomach lining twisted itself into a double knot. Something was wrong. Seriously wrong.

He got in his car and drove. He drove to Paihia, where he looked for Blow-arse in the pub and on the beach. He drove to Russell, where he also searched the pub, and the hill where Hone Heke axed the Union Jack. But he could not bring himself to drive past the house where his mother had died alone. For three days he drove the roads of the Bay of Islands, hunting in towns like Kawakawa, and Kaikohe, and Opua. He looked in over a dozen pubs, but all he found was the stale smell of booze-rotted carpets, and the vacant looks in the eyes of the daily drinkers hanging onto the plastic handles of their beer jugs. He looked in hospitals, he walked over paddocks, into the bush, and he sank up to his waist wading into a mangrove swamp. He rode a passenger ferry, and a car ferry, and he walked up and down wharves, searching the faces of the men who stared at the spots where their fishing lines entered the water. He did not find Blow-arse. Hell, he didn't even find anyone who'd heard the name. "Blow-arse? What did you call me, cunt?"

Where were Blow-arse's family? Did he have a family? At various times he had said his father was a tap-dancer, his mother a famous painter, and his great-great-grandfather one of the first European settlers to jump ship and live with a Maori tribe. His background was nothing more than a handful of fanciful tales.

Anaru drove home to Carolina Farms on empty. He found the crew where he left them, sinking into the couch like quicksand. The smell of bong water and fermented feet hung in the air.

"Justice is back," said Spit.

"Is Blow-arse with him?"

"Nah."

BOOM! A shotgun blast rang out from down by the river.

"Oh fuck," said Anaru.

"Yeah," said Kerry. "He's back on the pipe."

The sky was black when he found him. In the orchard. Darting from one tree to the next. Moonlight flashing on the barrel of his gun, the shiny leather of brand new riding boots. "Justice," whispered Anaru. Justice poked his head from behind a tree. Anaru saw the tweed cap, the tweed jacket, the white jodhpurs, the gun, and the eyes. Trembling with chemicals. Right at the back of his eyeballs, he looked to have some loose and sparking wires. They were empty too. Drained of life. "Where's Blow-arse?" Justice twitched, and then, clutching his shotgun to his chest, he bolted. Anaru ran after him. Down the row of trees and across the lawn. The veins in his cousin's legs pumped pure crack, and this made him fast, but Anaru was desperate, and he caught up to him by the river. Near the spot where he killed Kevin, they faced off, breathing hard. "Where the fuck is Blow-arse!!" Justice raised his gun, aimed the muzzle at his cousin's heart. Anaru froze. For ten long seconds they stood like this, water rushing over rocks nearby. "Just tell me where he is." Justice lowered his gun. His lips moved. And he ran. Faster than ever. As if pointing the gun at his cousin had recharged his batteries. He splashed into the river, bounded up the far bank, vanished in the long grass like a shadow.

In the barn, Anaru tended the crops. He dusted the hot white bulbs of the lights. He watered the plants, and fed them a fertilizer called blood and bone that was made from blood and bone, and smelled like rotting blood and bone. He hated the smell. But not as much as he hated the sweet chemical smell of the bluish purple buds that caused the whole mess in the first place. Next to the plants, he saw the bench press. Next to the bench press, he saw a giant tub of chocolate protein powder. For some reason, the tub spoke to him. He didn't even like chocolate. With some difficulty, he carried the tub into the house, then he rolled it down the hall to his room. Two days. Three days. Four. He stayed in his room, leaving only to use the toilet, and to fill the bottles of water he needed to make his chocolate protein shakes. Six shakes a day he drunk. Through the wall, he heard the crew, gunning people down on screen. Through the glass sliding door that opened onto the garden, he heard his cousin, gunning down rabbits and hedgehogs and mice. Maybe even insects. Dragonflies. The black and white and yellow-striped caterpillars that went into chrysalises, and came out black and orange monarch butterflies. Anaru knew there would be no such process for him. He would not emerge from his room radically transformed. He would stay locked up until Blow-arse returned, or his protein powder ran out, and he starved.

From deep in a dreamless sleep he sensed a presence. He opened his eyes, and saw the outline of a human form. Sitting in the dark on the edge of the bed.

"Blow-arse?"

"Nah."

Anaru sat up. It was Kerry.

"What's up?"

Kerry stared out the glass sliding door, at trees swaying in the night. "I know you two were a couple or whatever. We all knew. I know you think we cared. You reckon we're thugs, that we hate gays, but we don't. We didn't give a shit. We actually wanted you to be happy."

Anaru swallowed. Felt his throat closing.

"Anyway, your cousin will never tell you, but whatever, you need to know. It wasn't his fault but. Blow-arse was the one. You know how he was. He wanted to be a gangster so bad, but that was just another bullshit story to him. He should have stayed here with you. I told him, stay here man. This shit ain't for you. Nah but he wouldn't listen. Old Blow-arse, eh." Kerry lifted his chin to scratch at the stubble on his throat. Anaru tried not to show how hard he found it to breathe. "He set up some deal. They were gunna buy all the shit they needed for a lab, off some fulla named Rex. Reckoned they'd make millions cooking meth. And they probably would have too. Who knows. You know how it is, the gangs control that shit. And they weren't about to tolerate a couple yahoos coming in and setting up on their own. No way man. No fucking way. Anyway they set up the meet, and when Justice and Blow-arse got to the house, that dick Rex… who knows where he ended up. There were some heavy cunts there anyway. Fully patched dudes. High as fuck. Properly cooked. They gave our boys a bit of a hiding. Nothing too serious, just a few smacks with the old axe handle. They might've left it at that too, but you know Blow-arse, he never knew when to shut up. Said they couldn't stop him from doing shit. Dumb cunt thought all that boxing made him tough. Thought he was in GTA for real. So out come the guns. They said to Justice, you can either shoot your mouthy cunt of a mate here, or we're gonna kill you both. What was he gonna do? No point in both of them copping it. He took the gun and shot Blow-arse, and they made him bury him under the house."

In Anaru's chest, a volcano popped its top. A hot geyser of pain gushed up his esophagus. But it only made it to his wisdom teeth. It took all his strength, but he forced his throat to swallow. He reversed the geyser, burying it in a cave at the bottom of his large intestine.

In a trance, barely aware of what his hands were doing, he packed a bag. He was on autopilot. He started his car. At the end of the driveway, he unscrewed the *Carolina Farms* sign. In a ditch on the side of the road, with the help of some lighter fluid, he burned the sign. Then he drove all night, hitting Auckland in the morning. Rush hour. Bumper to bumper. Workers off to offices, applying make-up in fold-down mirrors. He ditched his car in the airport car park. As a plane flew overhead, he dropped the keys down a drain.

The first flight he saw went to Saigon.

He got on the plane.

He got off the plane.

He checked into The Spring Hotel.

Room 304.

The dread baby grew.

Episode Forty-Three.

A narrow river ran down the centre of the wide concrete basin. Dressed as The Dream, in her leather jacket, blonde bob wig and designer sneakers, Ari washed her black lace underwear in the river. The water was filthy. A mattress rotted on the bottom, with old boots and tires and shopping trolleys floating by, and used condoms snagged on sticks. This was the LA River. I stood behind a bush, filming Ari splash detergent on her underwear, pushing in on her hands as she scrubbed.

"Can you sing?" I asked.

"Sing? I'm washing my panties in the LA fucking river. Why would I sing?"

"Fair enough."

I moved around. Pulled wide. About a hundred metres behind her was an arched bridge, and I needed it in the shot. A plane flying overhead would really make it sing.

"Maybe you should cry?"

She stopped scrubbing, looked into the distance. Sure enough, the tears came. I zoomed in on the beads rolling down her cheeks.

Since her inception in Palm Springs, the plan had been to unravel The

Dream's dream life. For her to lose it all and wind up on the streets. But if her fall from grace was to go off like a social media atomic bomb, she needed fifty thousand followers at least. The Dream peaked at three thousand, and went backwards from there. Why? I'll tell you why. LA was overrun with wannabe influencers, all posting the same or similar content to The Dream – designer clothes, designer workouts, designer friends in designer clubs sipping from designer bottles of champagne that came to the table with sparks shooting out the top so everyone in the club knew who had the cash reserves for bottle service. Yuck. But yuck as it was, The Dream could not cut through, so we were forced to bring her downfall forward. Hence, the underwear washing scene at the LA River. That morning, bright and early, we parked our neurotic car at the top of a concrete bank a mile south of the Washington Boulevard Bridge. Here we set up a little camp, with a stove, washing line, milk crates for sitting, and sleeping bags in the backseat. There were trees and bushes nearby. And if you closed your eyes and listened to the birds tittering in the branches, and the water burbling by, and you were able to block out the constant hum of traffic, and the odd car backfiring (which may have been gunshots) you could convince yourself that you were in the countryside, and not in the bowels of a vast and cruel metropolis.

At 12:01pm, we posted the underwear-washing video to The Dream's Instagram. At 1:32pm, we posted shots of her cooking beans on her camping stove. And at 2:44pm, we posted four stories of her washing her frying pan in the river. The first post got 550 likes – 200 more likes than The Dream's most liked post. The beans-burning post attracted over a thousand likes, plus loads of comments, like: 'omg are you homeless', and, 'damn this girl in the streets for real.' Momentum was building. The third post pulled in a whopping 4678 likes, with 640 comments and a load of DMs. Some asking if she needed a place to stay, but most pleading for the salacious details on how she went from living the dream life to living in her car on the LA River. The schadenfreude was real. Finally, at around 8pm, as the sun set over the city, casting long apricot shadows down the concrete banks of the river, The Dream sat on the black bonnet of the car, and prepared to go live on Instagram. This was Ari's big moment. The performance of her lifetime. For years she had been working up to this – through all the rejection and the insults and the awful hunger – and she grabbed hold of it with both manicured hands.

7,850 people tuned into the livestream, and she gave them the most impassioned performance social media had ever seen, and is ever likely to see. With her made up face inches from the screen, she told them she had lost her soul in the pursuit of the dream life. She wept, admitting she had no friends, no family, that she had been cheated by her manager, assaulted by her agent, chewed up and spat out by a predatory industry. The tears she shed were real, creating multi-coloured rivers of make-up residue that ran down her cheeks and her throat. She climbed onto the roof of the car, where she sang songs that melted hearts and blew minds. She danced. She engaged with her fans' innermost feelings, answering questions from the heart, politely refusing offers of food and shelter. It's hard to put into words. I struggle to articulate the emotional force of her. But trust me when I say there was sorcery at play. Powerful magic. She was casting spells, performing a séance via social media. I saw it in her eyes. Her slightly pulsating pupils. The way her lips quivered when she spoke. The captivating shine on the bubbles of snot that popped from her perfectly formed nostrils. Vibrations rose off her skin, rippling the air like extreme heat. Needless to say I filmed the lot. But I knew this was no performance. I knew I was witnessing a person unload a lifetime of pain and trauma into a palm-sized screen.

The sky was black when the livestream ended. She climbed down from the car roof, handed me her phone, and went to sit by the river. She was spent. Emotionally exhausted. I cooked sausages, ate one sitting in the front seat, and checked The Dream's follower count:

Ten thousand.

An hour later: sixteen thousand.

By midnight she was up to seventy-seven thousand.

We slept in the back of the car, bodies huddled close in a sleeping blue bag. The first light of dawn pried open our eyes. Ari sat up and went for her phone.

"Oh."

"How many?"

"A hundred and thirty-seven thousand."

"You're kidding."

She showed me the screen. I stared at the beautiful number.

"We need more. We have to ride this wave."

Ari put her phone down, and pulled on her blonde wig.

The Dream documented her first full day of living on the LA River – posting select moments to social media. Using the wing mirror of the car, she gave a make-up tutorial. She spilled a can of tomato soup while heating it on the camping stove (great comedic content) and for an environmental message, she went live while fishing boots and bottles and plastic containers from the river. When the sun started to sink, turning the bottoms of the white clouds pink, we were nearly at two hundred thousand. I could hardly believe it. I wanted to celebrate with Ari, but The Dream had swallowed her whole. She refused to drop character. Answered only to The Dream. If I called her Ari, she looked around, asked who the hell I was talking to. And so, after a dinner of beans on toast, in search of "inspiration", The Dream went for a meandering walk along the river. I sat in the car on my computer, cutting the best of the day's footage into a sizzle reel. This is an arrow in the quiver of the branded social media content filmmaker. It's a montage of shots cut to music. And it's aim is to be so hot it sizzles, and hopefully sells the tone of your story idea. Once I was happy with the sizzle, I attached the reel to an email I wrote to Rah-Rah. This contained a short pitch for The Dream, her logline, and how her story arc worked for the first season of the Untitled Original Series Set On Multiple Continents.

When he called, I was sitting on a milk crate, staring at the soft halo of light that floated over the city. Ari – I mean The Dream – sat in the car, chatting to her new followers about contouring and yoga and life on the streets. She put him on speaker, and I stood near the open car door.

"What the fuck are you up to now, Ari?"

"Who's Ari?"

"What?"

"You're talking to The Dream."

"She's gone method," I said.

"Okay. Alright now. Love the commitment."

"What do you want?" she said. "I have fans that need me."

I tried to snatch the phone but she pulled it away and scowled at me.

"Well, Ari, I mean The Dream, the real question is, what do you want from me."

"We want you to produce our show," I said.

He was silent. Ari's phone buzzed with dozens of messages. Behind me, an animal, possibly a stray dog or possum, scratched around in the bush for food.

"I have to be honest, I like what you're doing, because it's fucked up. But I think it needs to be more fucked up. A lot more. If you ask me, you're only halfway there. You're safe right now. You're not in the jungle. Nowhere near the shit. There's zero risk. I want to see what happens when The Dream hits the skids for real, and I do mean for real."

"And if we do that you're in? You'll produce?"

"Well, Apollo, that all depends on what you mean by *do that*. Like I said, if you two can go balls deep on this thing, then you might get there. And if you strike gold, your old friend Rah-Rah will be in all the way."

The Dream returned her attention to her ever-growing army of followers, so I wandered down the river. Sitting on the bottom, half hidden by river slime, I saw the cover of an old porn DVD. The water had eroded most of the image, but I made out a woman with large natural breasts. She looked me dead in the eye and told me how to get Rah-Rah to finance the show. I called Barry.

"Apollo! My man!"

"How are you my friend?"

"Can't complain."

"I'm sorry about that job."

"No problemo."

"I have another one for you if you're interested."

"Fuckin' A, man."

"Not on a shoot, well, it is a shoot, but it's not as a soundie. But it does pay."

"I'm all ears, man."

Back at camp, I found the car headlights on. Ari/The Dream was back on Instagram live, dancing in the pools of light as her followers lit up her screen with likes and hearts and worship.

"Can you get off live please, I need to speak to Ari."

She spun and twirled, cooing at the screen. "I don't know who that is."

"Ari, please."

"My people need The Dream."

I grabbed the phone and turned it off.

"You naughty caveman." She reached out and touched my cheek. "Your skin is so dry. What cleanser do you use?"

"River slime."

"Such a barbarian."

"Can you please let Ari out?"

"I don't like that name, it's yucky. Like your face."

"Let her out for one minute, and you can go back to being The Dream."

"Sir, you need to stop harassing me. Would you like me to set my army on you? They're two hundred thousand stro–"

"Fine. Be whoever you want to be. But we're spending the night in Skid Row tomorrow night, okay? And we're going to film that content for Rah-Rah, you understand?"

"Is that supposed to scare me?"

"Dunno. Maybe."

The next day, at 2:03pm, we met Barry on the corner of Los Angeles and 7th Streets. He leaned on a lamppost, his face turned to the sun, absorbing warmth into his beard and the grimy lines on his face. He wore a green and black flannel shirt and his blue eyes shone. He wrapped me up in a hug that smelled of tobacco and tacos and dried leaves.

"Apollo, nice to see you man."

Ari shook his hand.

"I'm The Dream."

"The what?"

"The Dream."

Barry looked at me. "You sure you wanna do this, man? This place ain't for tourists."

"The Dream will be fine," said The Dream.

I scanned the block. People sat slumped in doorways, pushed shopping carts. They sung and prayed to the heavens. No one was watching us, so I slipped a wad of cash into Barry's shirt pocket.

"That's two grand. We'll give you another two when we leave."

"Appreciate it, man. Let's get moving. Need to cover some ground rules."

Down 7th Street he led us, deep into the chaotic heart of Skid Row. There were rows of tents in pink and blue and green, smashed TVs, mattresses stained black, shopping trolleys piled high with old clothes, mountains of trash that smelled like public urinals. Walking with her head held high, The Dream refused to take my hand. Residents shuffled past – muttering, singing, chatting. Most said hi to Barry. Some searched the gutters for cigarette butts, or scratched at sores or invisible bugs on their skin. A mother pushed a dummy-sucking baby in a stroller, children played with a three-legged dog, an old man with no teeth and pink lipstick read aloud from a bible. From across the street, at least three sets of eyes stared at The Dream.

"The Row is all about respect," said Barry, stepping over a toaster with dead daffodils sticking out of the slots, "you respect these folks and you'll be alright. Every one of these tents in somebody's home. Lotta folks been livin' in 'em for years, so don't go snoopin' around. Don't touch nobody. And don't touch nobody's stuff. If you do, say you're sorry, but say it quick, then move your ass on down the road. And do not, under any circumstances, give anyone money. If you get asked, just say you're broke too."

"Welcome to newbie street," said Barry. "This is where we set up shop." We were on a short and narrow street, sparsely populated. Maybe ten feet between each of the tents, and the people sitting in front of the tents looked as timid and confused as we were. Not a single soul smoked crack. And one of them, a man in his fifties, looked like a bank teller. Maybe three weeks ago we *was* a bank teller. We unrolled our tent – a purple two person number. Barry helped us pitch it, then he walked around the corner, and came back five minutes later with a lawn chair for Ari. He sat on a cardboard box flattened to the concrete, and I sat next to him. The Dream sat on her lawn chair like a throne. Surveying the street, she pulled the camping stove and a pack of sausages from her oversized handbag.

"Who's hungry?"

"That might not be such a good idea," said Barry. "Folks get a whiff of those links, you'll pull a pretty big crowd."

She put the sausages away and walked down the street. By the way she held her phone above her face, I could see she was livestreaming.

"What's she doing?" asked Barry.

"She's on Instagram live."

"What the fuck is that?"

"It's a social me–"

"You better tell her to cool it, man. That shit won't fly out here."

I walked down to where she spun in circles, blowing kisses to her fans. "Here we are," she said to the screen, "the final destination… Shangri La…" Three or four faces scowled at her from the flaps of tents.

"Ari."

She ignored me.

"The Dream!"

She spun around.

"You need to stop."

"Stop what?"

A woman pushing a shopping cart with a road cone in it pointed a crooked finger at Ari, and shrieked with laughter.

"What do you think?"

"We need content."

"And we'll get it, when everyone goes to sleep. But if you want to make it through the night, you need to cut the fucking livestream right fucking now."

She slid her phone into her pocket, stomped back to the tent, crawled in the door and zipped it up. I felt hidden eyes on me. Beads of sweat broke out on the bridge of my nose. My stomach felt like a prehistoric tar pit, belching up bubbles of pernicious gas. I sat down next to Barry.

"The Row is all about respect, I told you that. Your girl goes dancin' around with a thousand dollar phone in front of folks who got less than nuthin', that ain't respect, Apollo."

"I know. I'm sorry."

"You gotta get her under–"

The Dream burst out of the tent.

"Look at this glorious light!"

I hadn't noticed (due to the noxious bubbles slipping into my blood-stream) but the sun was setting, draping the block in a champagne gold haze. The Dream bounded up and down the street, snapping selfies, searching for the perfect angle. Barry looked at me, fear flooding his irises.

"Do something, man!"

I was already on my feet. But she skipped away from me, ducking my attempts to snatch the phone. I had to wrap her up in a hug and pry it from her fingers like a stubborn toddler.

"What about the light?"

"Fuck the light."

I shoved her in the tent. Rustling and muttering about content, she zipped it shut. I sat in the lawn chair. Barry stared at the oily patch of pavement between his feet.

"I'm really sorry, man."

He shook his head. I could see that he regretted our deal. That he wished he never met me. That we were putting him in as much or possibly more danger than our middle class vulture asses.

"Listen," he said, "I need to head out for a while." I must have looked alarmed, because he followed up with: "I'll be back. I promise. But your girl has ruffled some feathers, and I gotta make it right."

"Do you need more cash?"

"What I need is for you to keep her in the tent."

"I can do that."

He stood up and walked down the street. My torso felt like a concrete mixer, churning my organs and intestines, turning them into a pulpy meat smoothie. I crawled into the tent. Ari lay on a sleeping bag. Her eyes closed. The last light of the day poured through the purple walls, creating a surreal cave-like atmosphere.

"Are you okay?"

"I took a Xanax."

"Okay, good."

"You want one? There's one right here."

Her head rolled to the side, and her breath came soft and slow. In her outstretched palm I saw a tiny pink pill. It's hard to say how long I sat in that tent, my legs crossed, staring at the purple polyester wall. Outside the vibe was heating up. Weeping, shouting, cackling, slapping. Music blaring, bottles smashing. I heard a woman propose to a man, then take it back, then propose again. Fists on skin and bone. Fireworks or maybe gunfire. Sirens. Kissing. Flashing blue and red lights luminous. The hypnotic beat of helicopter blades, building to a deafening chant in the black sky above. The penetrating beam of its white searching light, strafing the street like the eye of an expert hunter. It hovered over our tent, bathing the lips and eyes and nose on Ari's face in white light, before swooping off to find a more thrilling chase. I looked at my hands, then my whole body shot up into the night sky. From such a height I saw Skid Row in all its complex glory. I saw shooters shooting, dealers dealing, smokers smoking. I saw mothers brushing hair, fathers kicking balls to laughing kids, babies bathing in makeshift tubs. People of all stripes, fucking and fighting and loving and swooning. I wanted to stay up there, to watch two men sparring, who then started waltzing, which escalated to a vicious form of grappling. We needed footage. I reached for my camera, saw the pink pill had vanished. I had swallowed it. But when? No matter. The content called to me. For The Dream. For Rah-Rah. For The Untitled Original Series Set On Multiple Continents. But my muscles were sagging, my eyelids drooping.

Ari woke up first.

She took my head in her hands and shook so hard she nearly popped it off. When I opened my eyes, I saw terror in hers. Were we inside the sun? A star in its death throes. My toes poked out the bottom of the flap, and they were melting. Orange flames licked the purple walls of the tent, smoke choked our lungs, the smell of burning flesh and plastic filled the air. My first thought was to hit record. We had nothing. No fucked up content for Rah-Rah. I grabbed my camera, popped the lens cap. "What the fuck!" yelled Ari/The Dream. "We're on fire!" I unzipped the flap, and a fist of heat punched me in the face, knocking us both on our backs. I pointed the camera out the door. On the screen on the back, I saw burning mattresses on their sides. They surrounded the tent like a fiery castle wall. This was an exquisite shot, even if it was a shot that wanted us dead. With my free hand I grabbed the back of Ari's head, and tucked it into my armpit. Pulling us free of the tent, I filmed the flames, the plumes of black smoke billowing into the sky. I tucked her tighter, panning left and right. The flames responded with a roar. They lashed my hands, my fingers and my forearms. The skin slid off my wrist like a glove. A bubble of fat dripped from my elbow and sizzled on the hot concrete. I kicked a mattress and it fell. An opening. We leapt through the hole, flames pleading, trying desperately to pull us back into the blazing circle.

Ari/The Dream bolted down the street, and I ran after her. But I turned to film our purple tent, zooming in to capture the moment it popped and sizzled, collapsing in a ball of flame.

Episode Forty-Four.

Both my arms were bandaged to the bicep. They were suspended in spongey loops that hung from the ceiling, so I lay in bed with my arms sticking out at forty-five degree angles. The bed was a hospital bed. The room was beige, and it smelled of bleach and singed hair. Tears bubbled up from my brain stem, and rolled down my cheeks to the corners of my mouth. They tasted of cheap medicinal chemicals.

"It's okay."

Ari sat in a chair next to the bed. She wore the blonde wig of The Dream, and a yellow leather jacket I had never seen. Her blue eyes shimmered.

"Are you Ari?"

"I keep telling you, I don't know who Ari is."

"What happened?"

"You got burned pretty bad. You had surgery. They took some skin from your butt and put it on your arms."

"Are you okay."

"The flames didn't touch me."

"What about Barry?"

"The homeless man? He came to see you. I told the nurse to send him away."

"Why?"

"He left us."

"Yeah, but–tell them to let him in if he comes back."

I moved my chin, and rivers of pain shot from my wrists to my shoulders.

"I have to go out soon. I have some meetings, okay?"

"It really hurts."

"I'll get the doctor."

She left the room. A minute later she came back with a young Black doctor with purple nails.

"What's your pain level from one to ten?" asked the doctor.

"It feels like a thousand wasps are stinging me. Scorpions too."

"So, about a ten?"

"Let's say nine-point-five."

She pulled out a syringe of pale liquid, and jabbed it into the drip attached to my arm. My eyelids felt like they were made of cement. Then I was out.

"Hey man, hey."

Barry sat next to the bed.

"Listen, man, I'm sorry about the fire. I didn't start that shit. You know I wouldn't do that to ya, buddy."

"I know."

"Good. That's good man. They treatin' you right? You getting the good shit?"

"Are you good?'

"I'm good. But look man, I don't feel right bringing this up, but we did have a deal, and–"

"I don't have it."

"Well, okay."

"I can get it. Just let me sleep and I'll get it, okay?"

When I next opened my eyes, the room was dark. Ari, I mean The Dream, sat on a chair to my right. Rah-Rah sat to my left. He wore faded blue jeans, lilac loafers, and a linen shirt with vertical blue and white stripes. He pushed his grey hair back on his head, and when he smiled, his gold tooth winked at me.

"Here he is."

"You're awake!" said The Dream.

The spongey loops were gone, and my bandaged arms lay at my sides. Rah-Rah leaned in. "A good friend of mine runs the cancer ward here–"

"I have cancer?"

"You're in the burn unit, but I pulled some strings and–"

"He got you a new room," said The Dream.

I turned my face to the left. A massive window behind Rah-Rah's salt and pepper coif. On the other side of the reflective glass, a chopper swooped over the shimmering city. My whole body bucked. My jaw clamped down so hard I bit my tongue. Tubes nearly popped out of my arm.

"Woah there," said Rah-Rah. "It's okay. You're okay."

The Dream took my hand in hers. "We have some big news."

"The Dream showed me your footage," said Rah-Rah. "What you shot was fucked up. Fucked up and insane and totally beautiful. Right up my alley."

"Rah-Rah wants to make the show! We're turning The Dream, ha-ha, me, into a series. Isn't that the coolest thing?"

A heavenly glow shone out from my gut, healing the pain in my arms. I sat up. I wanted to rip the bandages from my skin, and do one of those Cossack dances where you crouch down and kick your legs out. But when I moved, my brain wobbled and my vision went blurry.

"Steady on there, buddy," said Rah-Rah. "Hold your horses."

I lay my head back on the pillow and closed my eyes. Visions flashed in my brain like grains of gold dust: me on set on the first day of production. Giving direction. Owning it. Loving life.

"We're going to make this show," he said, "but the thing is, and look, I feel awful telling you this, but here's the deal – we need a big name director. A fucking gun. You feel me? We need the networks on board. Now I'm not saying you're not talented, because the evidence is clear. But to sell a show like this to a major network, we need credits, and I'm sorry, Apollo, but your social media content stuff just won't cut it, so what I–"

"Fuck off."

"I understand you're upset."

"This is my show. I own it."

"Actually it's mine," said Ari. "I'm The Dream. I came up with the idea–"

"We came up with it together!"

"Well, technically, I registered the Instagram account, and the show is an adaptation of the account, so yeah, technically, legally, I own her, I mean me."

I tried to leap off the bed. I wanted to strangle her. To choke them both until their tongues hung limp from their mouths and they had little crosses over their eyes. The rage was like an electrical storm inside my brain. Hundred mile winds blowing sand and grit and tiny lightning bolts through my pre-frontal cortex. The storm lifted me up, my burned arms outstretched. Ari jumped back from the bed. A flash of light behind my eyes, like a triple-scoop ice cream headache. The storm short-circuited me, blacking me out for a second or two. Long enough for Rah-Rah to push me back down on the bed, his hands on my shoulders. The pain nearly blacked me out again. It took all my strength to stay conscious. To breathe. To keep my heart beating. No reserves for words.

"You had surgery," said Rah-Rah. "Skin grafts. The whole deal. You've been in hospital for five days, and you don't have insurance. Know how much your bill is?" I looked into his blue eyes. "Over two hundred thousand. You got that kind of money? No? Didn't think so. And if you can't pay, they'll bankrupt you. They'll ruin you. No studio will touch you. But I got a deal for you. Give us The Dream, and I'll pick up your tab. It's a good deal. Two hundred grand. A lot more than most get for a show. And I don't even have to do it. Not legally. But I will, because I know Ari here cares so much for you. So what do you say? Let's do this. Let's make The Dream a reality."

I closed my eyes. He let me go.

"Pay Barry."

"The homeless man?" said Ari.

"Pay Barry. Pay my bill. And get the fuck out."

For two days I stared at the beige ceiling. Doctors checked the chart at the foot of my bed, nurses redressed my bandages. The treatment was top notch. Great meals. Ice cream. Raspberry jelly. I ate nothing. "If you don't eat," said a nurse, "we'll put the nutrients straight in your arm." Who cared? Not me. I didn't care if I starved. If my arms got infected and fell off and I bled out on the hospital floor.

On the bedside table, next to an untouched plate of peach slices, something buzzed. The buzzing was urgent. Desperate. I had no idea what it was. But I was in that weird space between awake and asleep, alive and dead, so I wasn't sure what anything was. Was it a fly? Were my organs failing? Was an alarm alerting a doctor and was the doctor sitting on the toilet scrolling Instagram? My phone. That's what it was. I reached out, saw the name on the screen, and nearly blubbered uncontrollably. But I held back, and in what must have been a strangled voice, I said:

"Anaru."

"What's wrong?"

"Nothing. I'm good."

"No you're not. Tell me."

Still holding back a dam-breaking measure of pain, I told him. It was a rambling jumble of words, and I sounded crazy coming out of my mouth, but I told him about Ari, and Rah-Rah, and the fire, and the skin graft surgery.

"You're coming back here."

"To Saigon?"

"You can stay with me. As long as you need."

"I can't afford the ticket."

"I'll sort that out–"

"But–"

"You can pay me back. Work it off. I don't care. I'm booking it now. Can you make it to the airport?"

"Thank you."
"All good, my friend. All good."

Episode Forty-Five.

In his black jeans and his tight white t-shirt, he stood under the fluorescent lights in the arrivals hall of Tan Son Nhat airport. His hair was slicked back, with sweat or some sort of grease. He looked like a younger and maybe better looking but definitely less snarly Elvis. Tourists pulled suitcases past him, mopping their soggy hairlines, avoiding aggressive sales pitches from possibly sketchy taxi drivers. When I hugged him, I think I blacked out. My face slumped against his right shoulder. He must have felt my body go limp, or my breath change, or drool leak onto the clean white fabric of his shirt.

"Are you alright?"

"My arms."

I came to on the back of Gloria. Beautiful old Gloria. With her scratches, her dents and her dings, and her spider-webbed wing mirrors, she was still a sight to behold. My cheek rested on his spine, my arms were wrapped around his middle, and he held them in place with his left hand and steered with his right. The sun sat high in the sky. Heat compressed my skull, restricting oxygen flow to my brain, limiting my cognitive abilities. Smells hit me from every angle. Herbs and petrol fumes and jasmine and fish sauce. Men pulling engines apart. Old women smearing pate on banh mi. And there were all manner of beeps – long beeps and sharp beeps and rude beeps and very cute excuse me coming through beeps. Scooters careered around us on all sides, hundreds of them, weaving and tilting and swerving. At first it felt chaotic. But then we seemed to all be part of one organism, like a giant creature with a thousand eyes, and scales made from red and pink and blue and light green painted metal.

"Are we going to the President Hotel?"

"I'm taking you to a doctor."

Her name was Dr. Lieu, and her red lipstick went well with her long grey hair. Anaru swore by her. Her office was spotless and minimal – a desk and a bed and a sink, and a bonsai tree on a table near a window that opened onto an overgrown garden. The heat and the noise of the city felt miles away – the perfect space to reveal your third degree and possibly infected burns. And she was the kind of doctor who softly told you the thing she was about to do, and then did that thing. She told me she was going to run my bandages under water, then lay me down, then remove my bandages. And she did exactly that. When she peeled the bandages back from the skin, a smell filled the air. Bleach and singed hair – the smell from the LA burn unit – mixed with sweat and musk from twenty-odd hours in planes and airports. Anaru gasped. I hoped more from the sight than the smell. From my elbows to my wrists, both arms were red and pink and boiled, and severely charred, with criss-cross patterns from the skin graft gauze. The fleshier, fattier areas of my arms were bubbled and shiny, like burned crackling on a spit-roasted pig. My little finger was still gone (I don't know why but I had this weird hope the surgeon might have given me a fake one, as a sort of bonus). All in all, my most outstanding bodily features had been reduced to a ghastly horror show. Dr. Lieu turned them over, then turned them over again and again. For every inch of charred flesh she inspected, she let out a sigh, like she was relieved for me. Like maybe when I walked in she had been ready to read me my last rights.

"No infection," said Dr. Lieu. "You are very lucky."

Back on Gloria, we wove through traffic. The sun was setting. Seven million people riding home from work, to cook and eat and talk and laugh and binge the latest show before bed. "Now are we going to the President Hotel?" He opened his mouth to tell me no, that I needed rest. But he changed his mind, and we slid down the congested lanes of Tran Hung Dao and into Cho Lon. We parked Gloria, paid the old man in the lawn chair at the entrance, and walked up the hole-ridden stairs. On the roof, the sun bounced off glass towers, and the surface of the river, and flooded our eyes with a million shards of orange light. It blinded me. Anaru led me to the edge. We sat down. I closed my eyes. Felt the weight of his arm as he lay it on my shoulder, and the light of the sun penetrate the pink interior of my eyelids.

That night, I slept in Anaru's bed.

In his arms.

I felt the soft skin of his cheek on mine, the warm life beating out from the ore of his being.

I slipped in and out of consciousness, but mostly I cried. I cried like a toddler who's lost their mother in a shopping mall. The dam broke. All the pain I held back on the phone came flooding out of me. My eyes and my mouth and my nose and my pores. The harder I shook, and sobbed, and caterwauled, the tighter he held me. For three nights I cried like this. Every night he pulled me closer, shushed me, told me I was safe, until the tears dried up. I was done purging my pain into his arms. He had taken it all from me. But I couldn't leave his bed. I needed to be near him. So we slept together every night. Skin touching, bodies pressing close, lungs working inches from kidneys. His dark hair falling over my flame-shortened eyelashes.

In the mornings, over coffee and fruit and fresh donuts from the bakery on the corner, he helped tend my wounds. We peeled the bandages off, washed the burns the way Dr. Lieu showed us, applied an antibiotic ointment, then redressed them. At ten, he went to work at the Karaoke Kingdom. Most days I went with him. I wanted to help out, to pay him back for flying me out, but my burned hands were not much use. The one thing I could do to any level of competency was dust, and so I took a purple feather duster to the rooms – the Louis Vuitton Room, the Versace Room, the

James Bond Room, the Olympus Room and the Cavalli Room. The thing is, my heart has always held a place for certain mundane tasks. Washing dishes, no. Ironing, yes. I need enough of a task for my brain to focus on, but not so much that I actually have to use my brain. Pushing the iron back and forth, the steam button, washing creases vanish as I mow them down. I love it. And dusting was no different. At Karaoke Kingdom, I walked into a room armed with my feather duster, and battled the first surface that dared step to me – gold couches, white satin pillows, monster TV screens. From here I worked over all the hidden corners and forsaken crannies, until every speck of dust had been vanquished. Each room presented its own unique challenge – some had sofas with ornate gilt frames, some glass coffee tables, some silver plinths. I had to focus on the dust, but I didn't have to focus on the dust. There was enough to hold my attention, and keep my brain from suckling on the loss of The Dream and the Untitled Original Series Set On Multiple Continents. And if, like nasty poison darts, images of Ari and Rah-Rah attacked my brain, I buried my snout in the dustiest corner I could find. It didn't always work. Some days I saw their faces on repeat. They came at me laughing, like a million gruesome wasps on meth. And when the rage spread from my burned arms to my heart, threatening to pop the thing clean out of my chest, I walked out the door and down the road to Tao Dan Park, where I studied the wide blades of tropical grass.

After two weeks of dusting, I moved onto spraying and wiping and sweeping. And after four weeks of spraying and wiping and sweeping, while dusting the dust that fell in those four weeks, my burns were well on the mend.

Holding and operating a camera was no problem, so I phoned Mai-Mai, and we met for coffee at L'usine on Le Loi. I was in luck. Her real estate business was booming, and she needed my content creation skills to lure expats into paying more for an apartment than any local would dream of. She put me to work the very next day. It was just like old times. I rose at seven, grabbed two coffees, and she picked me up on the street in front of

Anaru's building. We zipped around the city. We shot studio apartments
with views of rubbish strewn allies, and three bedroom apartments with
sweeping views of the city. At night, while Anaru worked on Swappy, his
scooter-sharing app, I cut the footage into 90 second clips.

On a searing hot day, we shot an underground cave of an apartment. No
windows. Tiny bathroom. A bug scuttling up the wall. It stirred up a greasy
ache in my heart. I longed for the island. I longed for Nhu.

I can't lie, I had been thinking about her since I touched down. And so
on a Saturday, when Anaru went record shopping, and the air con in his
apartment went down, I walked down Ly Tu Trong, and found myself at
the door to the old curved building on the corner of Dong Khoi. Rattling
and shaking, the iron cage elevator carried me to the third floor. At the end
of the dark hallway, I found the STATION sign still on the wall. I tried the
door and it opened. The space was empty, with fresh white paint on the
walls.

"Hello?"

From the back office, I heard chair legs shunt over wooden floorboards.
A second later she stood in front of me. She wore white sneakers, a flowing
black skirt that reached her ankles, a white t-shirt and a black ribbon in
her hair. The corner of her mouth lifted into what might have been a snarl
or a tiny smile.

"What happened to your arms?"

"I was in a fire."

"Show me."

As I walked towards her, I peeled the bandages from my arms. Scar tissue was taking over the wounds. Pink and twisted ropes snaked up and
down my arms. In some places they coiled, in others they curdled.

"Does it hurt?"

"It did."

"I want to touch."

I held my arms out to her, and she took them in her hands. I had forgotten how strong yet delicate her fingers were. She turned my arms over,

inspecting the ravaged landscape of skin and sunken muscle. Her nostrils flared, and when she looked at me, I saw her pupils dilate. She held my gaze. And then, bending her head, she kissed the scars on my left arm, and my right arm.

Episode Forty-Six.

Nhu held the wheel of a green Toyota Camry, and we gunned through a small Cambodian village. Roosters squawked, dogs and children scampered to the side of the road. I gripped the sides of the seat so hard my scars were on the verge of popping open. She fish-tailed round a corner, just about ploughed into the side of a sleepy-looking water buffalo. I swore the last thing I'd see would be the ring in its nose as it shattered the windshield.

Why were we in Cambodia? Let me back up a sec.

The Karaoke Kingdom was going through a surge in popularity (I liked to think it had something to do with the lack of dust) and Anaru was managing the joint around the clock, while also working on Swappy (he hired a UX design student as a waiter at the Kingdom, and they spent hours working on designs of wireframes or whatever they're called) so he was out of commission for eighteen hours a day. That was fine. Our friendship was like a cactus, in that it didn't need regular watering, and flourished in harsh conditions. As a result, I spent most of my time on the island with Nhu. We lay about on the bed in her tiny apartment off the underground car park, and ate noodles, and tubes of Pringles, and she smoked weed and

I watched her deliver loads of goods across Europe in her trucks. She told me to wash the dishes, and scrub the shower, and go down on her, and polish her boots, and brush her hair, and kiss her for no longer than thirty-nine seconds, and I liked being told to do these things and I did them with gusto.

Also, while driving a load of Turkish rugs down the autobahn outside Munich, she informed me of her career shift: "I'm no longer curating, I'm an artist now. This is the only way for me. I'm tired of showing work for other people, I want to show my own. But I need a big idea to launch me. And lucky me I have one. Want to know what it is?" I opened my mouth to speak, but she cut me off. "I'm filling the gallery with soil. With earth. Like two tons of earth. So it's maybe two feet deep in the whole of the gallery. I will bury a landmine in the earth. This mine will be active. It can explode. When people come to the show, they won't know where it is buried. Will they walk on the earth? Who knows. That is the show." I opened my mouth a second time. "Shush. I know what you ask. The landmine will come from this guy I know in Cambodia. Nemo. He's a rich guy. He's connected. He can get this for me. I'm driving there tomorrow. You are coming with me."

That was how we came to be in the green Toyota Camry, roaring through rainforest, flying past temples, hitting potholes so big they nearly ripped the wheels clean off the axles. When I asked her to slow down, she called me a little bitch and said I loved it. Which I sort of did. Still. The second she stopped the car, not far from a coastal town named Kep, my frazzled brain relaxed. Through the dirty, dead-bug-splattered windshield, I saw a modernist masterpiece villa poking out of the jungle. It was the kind of house people see on Instagram, look around their own cramped one bedroom apartment, and want to slash their wrists. Did I mention it was dusk? The sun sank low over the tops of the trees, and the complex jungle ecosystems clicked and buzzed.

As we stepped from the car – the engine ticking in pain – an old man in a long white linen muumuu stepped out of the shadows.

"Hello. I am Dara. Are you Nhu?"

"Yes, hello. This is Apollo, my boyfriend."

I looked at her but she refused to meet my gaze. Dara smiled at us. "Please come this way. Mr Nemo is resting near the pool."

Dara led us into the house. The interior was more impressive than the entrance – concrete and caramel timber, ceilings that reached the stratosphere, wide open spaces, and massive windows that acted as portals to the beating heart of the jungle. The furniture was purple and rust orange in colour, and looked like it came from a Seventies Italian film about existential dread. And the art was ugly and confronting in beautiful ways that spoke to me. We walked out to a dark blue pool surrounded by lights that looked smudged in the humid atmosphere. A tall man in lemon yellow shorts sat on the edge, dangling his long legs in the water. His hair was shaved close to his head, but the spikes were thick and black. On the drive down, I had asked Nhu what Nemo did for work, but she was cagey, muttering about business. To look at him you would think he was a wayward prince of indeterminate age. Dara bowed and returned to the house. We stood on the grass, watching Nemo watch his feet swish in the water.

"Nemo," said Nhu.

He looked at us, and I saw the stub of a joint in his mouth. His eyes were red and vacant, like he had been lying around in his chlorinated pool and smoking weed for weeks. Maybe he had.

"Nhu," she said.

He nodded.

"This is Apollo, my boyfriend."

He smiled at me, and then he went back to looking at his feet in the water. We slipped off our shoes and socks, and as we dipped them in the cool water, I swear steam rose off them.

"How are you?" asked Nhu.

Nemo puffed his joint. Dara walked out with a tray. He handed us tall glasses of iced tea, then went back into the house. We sipped the tea. Nhu said:

"Apollo makes films."

Nemo looked at me.

"Really bad ones," I said. "About apartments and houses. I can make one about your house if you like."

Nemo smiled, puffed his joint, looked at his feet in the water.

For the next four minutes, we sat in total silence. Sweat beads rolled down the backs of our necks. We sipped our tea, swished our feet in the water. Listened to the chattering life of the jungle.

"You remember why I came?" said Nhu.

Nemo looked at her.

"We spoke on the phone? About the landmine? For my show."

Nemo tossed his joint in the pool, stood up, padded across the grass, and slipped inside his villa.

Dara took us to our room. It had a king bed with mustard yellow sheets, an en suite, and a massive window looking over the jungle, which sent a thin mist into the violet night sky. I lay on the bed. Nhu sat on the edge and stared out the window. I reached out to her, but she shrugged me off.

"But I'm your boyfriend."

"Is that what you want?"

"Is that what you want?"

"I want a favour from Nemo, so he will want a favour from me. Better for me to come here with a boyfriend."

"Fake it 'til you make it."

She turned to look at me.

"Go in the bathroom."

"And do what?"

"Jerk off."

"What will you do."

"Not your business."

In the bathroom I shut the door behind me. The sink was made from sleek black slate, as were the floor tiles. The roof was basically one massive skylight, so the moon and the stars shone down on me as I sat on the toilet and did as I was told. But the image of Nemo's feet kept violating my mind.

To banish them, I knelt at the door and peeped through the key-hole. I saw Nhu lying on the bed with her hand down the front of her shorts. Her eyes were closed, head turned to the side. I pushed my eye closer, but my elbow banged the door. She stopped. Got up and opened the door. Saw me kneeling before her.

"You dirty little pervert. Sneaky little worm."

She kicked me in the chest and I fell back on the tiles. Then she stood on my burned right wrist.

"Does that hurt?"

"Yes."

"Do you like it?"

"It's okay."

She pressed her foot down hard, pinning my wrist to the floor. Pain shot up my arm. The scars felt like they might split open. But it made me hard.

"Go on. Disgusting boy."

After about thirty-seven seconds, I came all over the black tiles. She lifted her foot off my arm.

"Now clean it up."

The central puddle of cum was the size of a large coin. I bent over, stuck out my tongue, and wiggled the tip an inch from the opaque liquid. I looked up at Nhu. Then I licked up the cum, swished it around my mouth and swallowed the lot. Her eyes glowed hot. Never had I seen her so happy. Maybe we would make it as a real couple after all. Also, I had been drinking lots of fruit smoothies, so my cum tasted sweet. I'm not trying to brag here. I'm not saying my cum was some sort of delicacy, I'm just giving you the facts.

A ding woke me up. Nhu was asleep. Curled up in her usual caterpillar position. Looking cute. A far cry from the woman that stepped on my still-healing third degree burns. Out the window, shadows slipped between trees. I reached for my phone and saw the time: 3am. I also saw the source of the ding: an email from Ari. Or The Dream or whatever the hell.

Dear Apollo

I'm sorry. I'm so so so so so so so so so sorry. That's all I want to say for now. I hope you can find it in your heart to forgive me. But if you can't, that's fine too. I'm writing to you from up north. I moved up here to live in a commune, right near Big Sur. It's so beautiful here – with the ocean and the forests with giant trees. I live in a yurt! And I have a goat named Adrian! Things kind of went to shit between me and Rah-Rah. That was my own dumb fault. I got so deep into the character of The Dream that I lost my-self. You saw some of that I guess, but it got so much worse, Apollo. I had a full on breakdown. I'm better now I think. I'm getting help & starting to put the pieces back together. But it's hard! You proba-bly don't care, but I think about you a lot. I don't know where you are or if you're okay. I hope you're doing okay? I know I hurt you so bad and I'm super sorry for that. A part of my treatment is making amends to the people I hurt. I know how hard you worked on our series, how much it meant to you. So I think if you still want to make it then you should call Rah-Rah. He likes you. And since The Dream fell over, he's looking for new content. His number is below. Use it if you want. And write me back? Or not. Just to say you're okay. Or that you hate me.

Love you, Ari

FOR two hours I sat on the end of the bed, staring out at the dark jungle, while Nhu slept curled up behind me. I thought I saw a tiger, and a pan-golin, but my eyes were playing tricks on me. My brain was playing tricks too. It told me to call Rah-Rah. It whispered at me in the most seductive fashion, telling me he had the medicine. Saying he could revive the Unti-tled Original Series Set On Multiple Continents. That it wasn't dead. And even if it was dead, we could exhume its corpse and breathe fresh air into its rotting lungs. In the hour before dawn, the sky turned into a light pink dance of darting birds and ravenous insects. A light rain came down, pit-ter-pattering on the leaves of the trees, sounding like fresh whispers com-ing at me from the jungle, which, when combined with the voices in my head, reached a very loud volume indeed.

The smell of jasmine woke me up. It was Nhu. Actually the jasmine smell came from her hair, which she had just washed with what must have been a boutique and premium brand of shampoo. She sat on the chair near the bed, pulling on her sneakers.

"I have the mine."

"Where is it?"

"In the car. We need to go."

"Where's Nemo?"

"Where do you think. Smoking weed in his pool."

The landmine sat in a crate stuffed with straw. It was smaller than I had imagined. About the size of a blueberry muffin, but a whole lot nastier. We wrapped the crate in a leather jacket, then wrapped that in four towels. Then we strapped it into the backseat of the green Toyota Camry. As we pulled away from Nemo's jungle villa, the rain hissed down. Not ideal landmine transporting conditions. If we went over a single pot-hole at speed, the backs of our heads would get shredded. Our kidneys fragged. Needless to say, I was worried about Nhu's driving. But she ditched the half-blind rally driver, and became a sweet old lady on her way to her weekly bridge game. With a long line of cars and bikes and buses beeping behind us, we crept along the vast Cambodian highway. At the border, she scattered her dirty clothes across the mine, shot a jet of perfume at her neck, and brushed the arm of the border guard. He waved us through. No questions asked. After that, I relaxed. Over the next hour, I told her about Ari's email, and every-thing that happened in the months before the email, with Rah-Rah and The Dream and the Untitled Original Series Set On Multiple Continents.

"You need to call him."

"I don't trust him."

"If you don't I won't speak to you again."

I looked at her, but she looked at the road ahead.

"If you don't call him that makes you what? A pussycat?"

"A pussy?"

"I don't speak to pussycats."

The rain followed us all the way into Saigon. Great bucket-loads poured down on the pink and white and yellow polka-dotted raincoats of the scooter riders. Nhu drove us down the ramp and into the underground car park of the Saigon Pearl complex. We unbuckled the heavily wrapped landmine, carried it into her apartment and set it down on the island. She changed into jeans, a black singlet and a pair of army boots that made me want to clean up my mess again.

"The soil comes to the gallery in one hour," she said. "You stay here, learn about the mine. I will pick you up and take you to the gallery, then you will bury it."

"I will bury it?'

"Yes."

"It's your show."

"You must do it."

"Why don't we do it together?"

"Like boyfriend and girlfriend?"

She kissed any words I was about to speak back down my throat, and walked out the door. I sat on the bed and called Anaru. Told him what I was sitting next to, and what it was for. He said that flying me back from LA was one thing, but peeling my flesh from gallery walls and putting me back together was beyond his powers. He sounded distracted. I knew what it was. He was deep in a debugging mission of the latest version of the app, so I promised not to blow myself apart and let him go.

I opened up the crate and looked at the mine, sitting in the straw all sweet and innocent looking. There was a brochure in the straw, with the activation instructions written by what might have been a typewriter. This did not fill me with confidence. The mine itself was called an M14 blast mine, so I looked it up online. Turns out, the M14 was nicknamed the 'toe-popper.' No prizes for guessing why. The toe-popper weighed 108 grams, and contained 29 grams of explosive content, which was tetryl. This is a yellow crystalline powder, and it's detonated by friction, shock or spark. My sweet M14, she was 56mm in diameter and 40mm in height, and her operating pressure was 9 to 16kg. So yeah, she was light and lethal. The blast wouldn't kill you, but it would blow your foot apart. It you were barefoot or wearing sandals, it would destroy your leg up to the knee. Almost certainly, it would pop your toes clean off. She was a vicious little critter. But Nhu was smart. Her show was a commentary on military tourism, and the idea in the execution was that no one would dare set foot in the gallery. But if some hero did, and they stepped on the M14, it wouldn't kill them, or blow up the entire room.

After I read about the construction and deployment of the toe-popper, I studied the activation instructions:

Place the mine in a shallow hole in the ground, flush with the surface

Use the arming spanner to rotate the pressure plate from the safety position to the arming position

Pull on the attached cord to remove the U-shaped metal safety clip

The mine is now fully armed

It was dark when Nhu came back. We loaded the land mine into the back of the Camry, and drove up the ramp into the night. The rain had only just stopped. The streets were wet and shiny, the city eerily silent. Nhu parked on the sidewalk, and I carried the crate into the curved building on the corner. With the old iron elevator so shaky, we opted for the staircase. Never before had lifting my left foot and then my right foot had such high stakes. I was thinking so much about not tripping that I nearly tripped. But we made it to the top. Nhu opened the door and flicked on the lights, and I saw the layer of soil. It reached all four walls and into every corner. It came about halfway up my shin, and it smelled musty, and obviously earthy, but also biological. Also, the AC had crashed, so the air was moist and dense with spores. I got the feeling entire ecosystems were getting going in there.

She touched my forearm, and I felt her fingers quiver. Her eyes were wide too. I had never seen her anywhere close to scared. I ditched the team effort idea.

"Where do you want it?"

She pointed. "By the window."

"Okay, can you come with me?"

She shook her head.

"You don't have to touch it, but I need you to read the instructions. Okay?"

She took my phone from my pocket (I had written the activation instructions in the notes app) and we stepped onto the soil. Walking like there were mines underfoot already, we reached the spot where she wanted it, about four feet in from the window. I knelt down, placing the crate on the soil. With my hands, I dug a shallow hole. It was getting hotter by the second. Condensation, or some sort of earth juice, ran down the window-pane, leaving light brown trails on the glass. Sweat dripped from my forehead. Coated my palms. Why didn't I bring some sort of rag?

"Here," said Nhu.

She pulled off her black singlet and handed it to me. As I wiped the sweat from my hands, I stared at her purple bra.

"Forget my tits and get to work."

I pulled the lid off the crate, cleared away the straw, and stared at the toe-popper. She was made from army green metal. I lifted her out. And lowered her into the hole.

"Now read me those instructions."

"Use the arming spanner to rotate the pressure plate from the safety position to the arming position."

I executed the task. And look, I don't mean to brag, but you'd think that after all my hands had been through, they'd shake like crazy. Steady as rocks they were. They must have sensed the stakes. And they rose to the high pressure occasion. I couldn't have been prouder.

"Pull the cord to remove the U-shaped safety clip."

I pulled the cord. With a soft 'chink' sound, the safety clip came away. I picked up a handful of earth, and sprinkled it over the top.

"It's armed."

PLANTING the toe-popper juiced me to the gills. If I could do that, I could do anything. Right? Damn right. I was flooded with an overwhelming and quite possibly over-inflated sense of my own abilities. I pulled Nhu close, and kissed her in a way I knew as too intense. Way too damn eager. My needy and desperate lips sucked the spark from whatever it was we had. But I couldn't stop them. In that moment, I wanted Nhu as much as I wanted to make the Untitled Original Series Set On Multiple Continents. Well maybe not that much, but not far off. She pulled back and stared at me, and I knew we were toast.

"I'll go get us coffee," she said.

"I'll meet you downstairs. I'm going to make this call."

She nodded.

I watched her walk across the soil, pulling her black singlet over her purple bra. When she was gone, I sat on the warm earth, breathed in the explosive and destructive vibes from the landmine buried next to me, and called Rah-Rah.

Episode Forty-Seven.

Rah-Rah didn't answer. And that was good. If he did answer, and I said I wanted to pitch an idea, he might have asked me to pitch on the spot. And I would have stammered and stuttered and possibly fallen face-first on the landmine I had just buried in the dirt. Kaboom. Hello? Hello? Apollo, are you there?

He didn't have voicemail (no real boss does) and Nhu did not return with the coffees (no surprises there) so I said goodbye to the toe-popper, walked across the soil floor, out the door, down the stairs and into the damp night. On Dong Khoi, the bars were closing. Couples on scooters pulled lovingly away from curbs, a lonely plastic bag danced down the gutter. On the off chance that Rah-Rah phoned back, I needed to be ready. So as I walked the streets, taking in the smells of jasmine and fish sauce and sometimes sewage, I crafted the perfect pitch for the Untitled Original Series Set On Multiple Continents. After three hours and about eighteen thousand steps, and with six drafts rattling around my brain, I stood on a bridge, staring down at a fishing boat gliding along the inky surface of the usually brown river. My phone was in my hand. When it rang it nearly sprang out of my grasp and over the side.

"Who is this?"

"Apollo."

He was silent for a second, and then he said:

"Apollo, I owe you an apology."

"It's alright."

"No it's not alright. Listen. We took your idea, and it was a damn fine idea. Damn fine. I really believe The Dream was a winner. I've been trying to get out of the reality game for years, do something prestige, and The Dream was it. But Ari, well, she's been stealing from me for years. Watches, my mother's jewellery, you name it. Maybe I had it coming. Maybe I wanted to make it right between me and her, but I fucked you, Apollo. And then of course my old friend karma shows up. Ari goes crazy, I mean she really loses it, and now The Dream is dead."

"I got more where The Dream came from."

"Hit me."

"Well, that's the thing, Rah-Rah, you already took one show from me."

"I get it. You don't trust me."

"I want to."

"Listen, Rah-Rah is a man who pays his debts. And this is him doing that. I know a hundred creators who would give their left nut or their right tit to be on this call."

"I'm aware of the privilege."

"You want to give me your right nut? Put it on a plate and I'll take it."

I said nothing, so he said:

"There's maybe ten people in this town who can pick up the phone to the head of HBO or Netflix, and put the phone down with a deal in hand. And buddy, you're talking to one of them right now."

"I hear you."

"Go."

"You know I always only intended The Dream to be the first season in a big, sprawling series."

"No, but okay."

"It's an Untitled Original Series Set On Multiple Continents. It will run on TV, on social media, in cinemas, everywhere."

"Sounds expensive."

"Not if we work with a small crew. The production will be nimble. The characters will be colourful and crazy, the stories propulsive."

"Go on."

"Okay, well, the first season is about a gay guy who runs a drug-trafficking operation with his boyfriend. They get into a turf war with a psychotic gang, and the gang kills the main character's boyfriend. So it's a drug-fuelled gangster story but it's also a love story."

"I like the gay drug lord approach. Very fresh."

"And we can run sixty minute episodes on TV, and shorter episodes on social media. We can make it a whole interactive experience. No one is doing his shit. We'll be the first."

"What happens in season two?"

"At the end of season one the main character has to flee, and season two picks him up in South East Asia. He's broke, but he wants revenge on the gang, and the entire season is a heist story-cum-revenge story."

"I love a good heist story, but they're tough. They need to be authentic. We'll need consultants. Safe-crackers and the like."

"I have firsthand experience."

"Don't bullshit me, kid."

"How do you think I lost that finger."

"Shit, that's what I like about you, Apollo. You got no limits. No goddam boundaries."

"So I've been told."

"When can you put a treatment together?"

"When can you put a contract together?"

"Treatment first."

"Contract."

"Treat–motherfucker, listen! I'm giving you a golden egg type opportunity here. You don't dictate terms to Rah-Rah."

"And I want to co-produce."

"Hahaha, holy cow. The balls on this kid."

"I'm all in with this show, Rah-Rah. I've worked too long to–"

"Uh-huh. Okay. I hear you tough guy. But listen. Lotta corporate bull-shit to deal with when you're producing. Why don't you stick to the fun creative stuff."

"I can't go through the whole Dream saga again. I just can't. I need–"

"Okay, okay."

"And I want to shoot a pilot."

"I hate pilots. But if you want one you'll need to front some cash. I won't carry that load on my own."

"How much?"

"Let's see… development, casting, plus all the other production whatnot and union bullshit, you'll need about four hundred thousand. So if we're co-producing, that's two hundred each. You got that kinda cash?"

"Not on me."

"You'll need to get it. Quick. And I want that treatment on my desk by tomorrow, and it better be top drawer. I love your ideas, but I'm an impatient man. I got what you call professional ADHD. I lose interest fast."

On Pham Ngu Lao, when the Highlands Coffee opened at seven, I was waiting at the door. I ordered an extra-large six-shot latte, put my computer on a table in the courtyard, and went to work on the treatment for Rah-Rah. The morning sun fell on my neck like dragon's breath. Sweat oozed from my fingers and onto the keys, making the 'M' key freeze. I plotted the entire first season. Anaru and Blow-arse became ostentatious drug lords, entangled in a burning love affair, and locked in a feud with a rival gang that ate extreme violence on cereal for breakfast. It worked. It more than worked. The story came out like birdsong. And actually, there were birds singing in the tree next to me, and I chose to see them as cheerleaders. As the sun rose higher in the sky, the skin on the back of my neck felt like bubbling pork fat, and the story grew more dramatic. I typed in a manic fury. No control over the words. Like a raging river with its mind set on washing a village out to sea, they flowed from my fingertips. The keyboard became a splashy puddle. My scarred hands creaked and groaned, and I moaned and laughed and spoke the dialogue out loud, my fellow diners staring at me over coffees. I looked like a madman at work on a sacred screed, and

I was exactly that. I slurped down iced coffees, and peach jellies, and milk coffee, and water chestnut tea, and yet more coffee. My stomach swelled up, inflating like a large balloon. Odious bubbles of gas floated from my mouth and into the calm atmosphere. And the curious looks turned to stares of disgust. Would the cops come? Arrest me for polluting the sweet café aromas? Too late. The treatment was done. I proofread it, emailed it to Rah-Rah, then ran into the street to vomit a waterfall of pink and brown and black and green muck into the gutter.

After washing my mouth in the bathroom sink, I entered into one of my states. My hands buzzed, and it felt like I had three or four of left and right, each pair more scarred and burned than the last. My mind slipped out the top of my skull, and I filmed myself climb on the back of a motorbike taxi, and race down a wide avenue. The driver swerved between the blazing rays of sun that fell between the tops of tall trees and dappled the road. I felt like I was in a video game, collecting coins to recharge my energy bar, which was also my soul. I stepped off the bike at full strength. And I needed it, because I was at Uncle Frank's house.

He saw me before I saw him. He sat on the couch in the front room, the door open, feeding a tiny baby a bottle. With his head he motioned for me to enter. I slipped off my shoes and sat next to him on the couch.

"This is Hoa."

"Hello Hoa."

"It means flower."

"She's beautiful."

"You want to hold her?"

"Uhhh."

"She won't bite you."

"I'm scared I'll drop her."

He handed me the tiny human bundle. I tensed up at first. Then she made a snuffling sound, and I smelled her sweet and powdery baby smell. The smell activated a deep and dormant region of my brain. I touched her hair. Held her close. Tears rolled down my cheeks. One landed on her cheek, and she sneezed. Uncle Frank giggled. I had no idea he knew how to giggle.

"You have come for your finger."

"Oh," I said. "Um."

"It is upstairs, in my jewellery box. The bones. The flesh rotted. It smelled so bad my wife told me to throw it out, but I want it."

"It belongs here."

"Good. But you must want something. A man like you always wants something."

"Is Anhtheman here?"

"He went to work this morning early. He opens the tourists shop."

"And Thao?"

"Come, Apollo. Tell me why you come to my house. You think I will hurt you when you hold my baby in your arms?"

"I want to go back to the casino."

He smiled, took baby Hoa back, and put the bottle teat in her mouth. She drank with vigour.

"I've changed, Uncle Frank. I've handled bombs. I nearly died in a fire. I won't get scared. I won't stuff it up this time."

He looked at the burns on my hand. "Yes, I see you change a lot. How much money you need?"

"Two hundred thousand."

As she fed, Baby Hoa widened her eyes, as if reacting to the ridiculous figure.

"What for?" asked Uncle Frank.

"A big thing. In LA."

"You like the big thing."

"I need it."

"When Hoa was born," said Uncle Frank, stroking his daughter's black feathery hair, "I feel something deep inside myself. The... I don't know how to say it. I stopped drinking, I stopped chasing the women, I stopped cutting off fingers too, ha-ha-ha. I want to stay with her always. Play with her. Sing to her. If I do the heist with you, I will miss these things."

"What about Thao?"

"Thao is gone."

"Gone where?"

"In the winds."

"Maybe the winds will bring her back."

Hoa spat the bottle teat out. Uncle Frank picked her up, lay her on his shoulder, patted her back, and she burped in my face.

THAT night, I was desperate to take Anaru to our beef noodle stew spot on Tran Hung Dao, then to the roof of the President Hotel. He had to work. But I pestered him so bad (I think I sent fifteen begging texts) he snuck out to meet me for bun bo hue down the road from the Karaoke Kingdom. We ate our pork knuckle and our beef slices, all in a steaming broth with lemongrass and congealed blood. Anaru spoke with great animation about the roaring success he was certain Swappy would become. Their latest round of tests had returned zero bugs, and it worked without crashing or turning the user's phone into a ball of flame or whatever badly behaved apps did. And the prospect of launching his baby into the word filled him with such nervous excitement he often thought about shutting the whole thing down and moving to a houseboat on a river in Laos. "I'm joking," he said when I gave him a sad face look. I had never seen him smile so much. It nearly made me forget all about my treatment. We clinked Coke cans. Then I walked him back to work and ran back to his apartment to sit up refreshing my email, waiting for a reply from Rah-Rah.

The room was dark when I woke up. And in the dark I saw a glowing white square. It was Anaru, sitting on the end of the bed with my computer in his lap. The treatment I sent to Rah-Rah on the screen. I must have left it open and drifted off. My heart sank through the bed and all the floors of the building, and took its place in the flow of human excrement floating in the sewer.

"I'm sorry."

"I thought you were my friend."

"I am."

"You're not. You're a piece of shit."

"I know."

"Fuck you. I flew you back from LA when you were fucked. I took you into my bed and held you while you cried like a baby for three fucking nights! What was that? Was that all bullshit?"

"No, it was real."

"No. No it–fuck! Jesus Christ. How did I not see this. You know what, Apollo? You destroy everything. All the people in your life. Yourself. Fucking everything. And I don't reckon you'll ever stop, and I don't really give a fuck either."

Episode Forty-Eight.

The rain came down harder than any rain I had seen come down in Saigon. Maybe the world. Ever. In the whole of history. Going right back to the dinosaurs and even further back to when some sick bastard crawled out of the ooze and hooked us all up with consciousness. The drops were bigger than baseballs. Every intersection was its own lake. Scooter riders were stuck all over town, submerged up to their knees. I thought I saw a pod of dolphins swimming down the street, but it was just my brain having a laugh at my expense.

I had nowhere to go.

With my bag next to me, I sat on the curb and let the stormwater wash over my bare legs. My plan was to let it wash me down the drain and out to sea. People shouted at me. An old man tried pulling me to my feet, but I was a stubborn ox that would not be moved. My phone rang. The screen was cracked and soaked, but somehow it worked. I hoped it was Anaru, telling me to come back inside, that he forgave me for everything. But it was Rah-Rah. "Apollo. Listen. I read the treatment. I read the damn thing five times. And I gotta tell ya, I love it. You're one mentally insane son of a bitch. So let's do this thing. You and me. Rah-Rah feels it! You can direct, and we'll co-produce, like you wanted. All you gotta do is get the two hundred grand and we're rollin.'"

I hauled myself out of the gutter.

Anaru was right.

I was a destroyer.

I destroyed everyone and everything. And I would keep destroying.

My brain was fried. It felt like it was swelling against my skull from years of adrenal stress and constant fight or flight mode. But I had one tiny flicker of hope. This was it. The final test. I had been pushed this far for a reason, and it sounds corny but the reason was that I needed to get pushed right to the edge and beyond to make truly great entertainment that connected. To make the Untitled Original Series Set On Multiple Continents, I had to sacrifice everything, including myself. If I did that, I knew the world would sit on the edge of its seat and watch. And so, tired and numb and soaked to the bone, I trudged through pounding rain, bag in hand, to the tourist shop in Pham Ngu Lao. I pushed open the door, saw Thao and Anhtheman sitting at the desk, and pitched forward onto my face.

In my right temple, I felt a beating heart. The beat was strong and steady. Much stronger than my own. Inhumanly strong. Each beat resounding like a cymbal crash. I was on the back of a bike, my face resting on the back of the driver. The driver was Thao. We raced down a road that sliced open a rice paddy, and the pink beams of the setting sun bounced off the puddles in the paddy and burned holes in my retinas. I was wearing a suit. How did my body get into the suit? Thao wore the long gown made from blue sequins (the one Uncle Frank gave to her) and when you added the sequins to the pink light, they brought a whole other level of craziness to the refractions coming off the paddy water. Was this Cambodian paddy water? Or Vietnamese paddy water? On the road behind us, Anhtheman rode a bike of his own. He waved at me. How did we get here? We were heading for the casino, I knew that much. But how? What was the plan? Did we have a plan? I scanned my brain, but it was like a filing cabinet that had been picked up and emptied out on the floor. The information scattered all over...

Thao had seen my face in a dream.

She had come home.

She held her new baby sister. Hoa. She smelled my tear on her cheek. Uncle Frank told her I had come, that I wanted the heist. One more shot at the heist. He gave her and Anhtheman his blessing.

Anhtheman spoke to Sam. Remember Sam? The croupier with high cheekbones. Sam was our man.

Lunar New Year, Sam told Anhtheman. Tomorrow night. Big gamblers flying in on private jets. Whales. Billionaires. Wahoo.

In the Pham Ngu Lao tourist shop, Thao had taken my hands in hers. She stroked the scars. Ran her finger over the stump. Sparks of energy danced from her bone marrow into mine. I swear I watched one of my burns shrivel up and disappear. Going with her was the only way to heal me.

We left the pink light of the rice paddies, and rode into the dark embrace of the jungle. The air was moist and thick with microscopic insects that stabbed at my skin in search of blood. We popped out into light, then sunk back into darkness once more. The next time we emerged, I saw her. The casino. Like the highest points of an excavated city, it rose out of the jungle. The purple neon sign on the front blared: HA TIEN VEGAS! Spotlights searched the darkening sky. Fireworks popped and fizzed and banged. The dirt road that led to the front doors was dead straight, and lined with black and white limousines, Hummers, and long diplomatic corps looking Mercedes. The shanty town was gone. So too the stray dogs. Razed to make way for the whales.

Thao stopped near a white limousine. Sliding off her helmet, she shook out her hair. In the wing mirror, she painted her lips red and her eyelids green. Anhtheman pulled up next to us, but did not get off his bike.

"What's the plan?" I asked him.

"You don't remember the training? You trained so hard."

Thao turned around, her top lip unpainted.

"Thao is your wife," said Anhtheman. "You have been married yesterday. This is your honeymoon. The bosses will focus on the whales in the private rooms, not the happy couple at the blackjack table. Smile! I must speak to the dealers. I will see you in three hours. Good luck!"

He roared up the dirt road, kicking up a cloud of dust that clung to my suit. As I brushed it off, Thao took my hand and yanked me up the road to the glowing casino.

"I'm serious. I don't know what to do. I don't remember the training. There's something wrong with my brain. I think I have a tumour."

She touched my head. "No tumours. The plan is simple. Anhtheman knows the dealers. We go to these dealers. We play, we win a little. But we win a lot. We do this more, then take the money to the hut."

"The hut?"

"For the money. It's too much to carry. Okay? Now we kiss."

"Yeah?"

"We are married. The people must see this."

She took my head in her hands and kissed me. Her entire body radiated heat and light. Her kiss was the opposite of my failed kiss to Nhu. Hers was not a needy kiss, but a giving kiss. With her red lips, she gave me her strength and her flair and her supernatural talents. And I drunk in more than my fair share.

The main gambling hall was a rollicking sea of sweaty bodies. Waves of bobbing heads rolled out from one wall, crashed into gold pillars, and purple card tables, then rolled all the way to the opposite wall. Thao squeezed my hand, I pulled her close, and we pushed our way into the crowd. Peering over the surface, I saw big hair, laughing mouths, wild eyes, army medals, feather in hats and jewels on necks. Up on stage a band played brass instruments, wet shirts clinging tight to their chests. On another stage, a golden horse wore full Roman battle armour. Men and women lined up to take photos sitting on its back. The horse snorted and sweated out foam as it pawed the purple carpet, eyes rolling back in its head. Next to the horse, a round man in a shiny emerald suit with peroxide hair slicked back on his head grabbed a microphone, introduced himself as the casino CEO, and wished the crowd good luck and a happy Lunar New

Year. The air crackled with nervous hormones. Waiters moved through the crowd, bowties askew, trays of full champagne flutes above their heads. Hands reached out for the glasses, ferried them to the gaping mouths of fat politicians, lithe models, army officers, businesswomen, and a gang of flirty teens who I guessed were the latest boy band sensation.

With one last push we popped out of the crowd and found ourselves at the blackjack table. I recognised the high cheekbones. Sam. Sam the dealer. He gave us a swift nod. Thao bought in, and I scanned the table. Two beautiful young men hung off the ends of their cigarettes, and held up an ancient man who clutched a wad of cash.

I kissed Thao.

We played our hand.

And a second hand. And six more hands. Sam made it so we won the big hands. And when he was meant to pass us hundred dollar chips, he passed us thousand dollar chips. We left his table with twenty-eight thousand in chips.

At the next table, we were joined by a gaggle of army officers. They smoked cigars and swilled from brandy balloons. Light pinged off medal-adorned chests. Their martial authority killed my confidence. Thao read me with a touch of her hand, and we moved on. At the third table, we won sixteen thousand. At the table after that, an old woman with spiky hair and smudged pink lipstick made me kiss the potato-sized emerald on her finger, and we won thirty-two thousand.

The crowd rolled and roared. The band played. Chips clacked. Drinks were spilled on the purple carpet. The golden Roman horse took a shit on stage, and a waiter – who was clearly at his first rodeo when it came to cleaning up horse shit – tried to sweep it up with a broom. "We need to change this," said Thao. Her handbag was stuffed with chips – yellow and orange and pink and black. And purple. Always purple at Ha Tien Vegas. They spilled out onto the sticky carpet. Feeling I had been unchivalrous to my new wife, I took the bag from her. When I slung it over my shoulder, the strap cut a groove in my flesh. It must have weighed 10kg. How many tables had we been to? Four? Five? Six? How much had we won so far? A hundred thousand? Two hundred thousand? The correct answer was one hundred and thirty nine thousand US dollars.

The man at the change window (who had a mole on his chin that was cultivating hairs as long as a kitten's tail) pushed the stacks of cash through in his brass drawer. We stuffed the cash in Thao's bag, in my jacket pockets, and my pants pockets. "Now we go to the hut," said Thao. From a passing tray, I snatched two bottles of water, and we necked them as we strode through the eerily quiet and echoing foyer that still smelled of freshly cut marble. On the front steps, under the marble column, we saw a guard. He was freakishly tall, like, seven foot. His black uniform pants flapped above his ankles, revealing ice white sports socks. He glared at us, a slightly embarrassed look in his eyes. From the too short pants or being teased about his height all his life or both. Thao kissed me. I closed my eyes and focused every nerve ending on the touch between her lips and mine. When she pulled back, the guard was gone. We dashed down the steps and into the jungle. Right away Thao found the path, which led us about a hundred meters deep. Where the air was dark and cool and wet, we found the hut. Inside, Anhtheman had dug a pit, which he covered with a sheet of wood and a table. We pushed the table and the wood aside, and tossed our stacks of cash in the pit.

"Look," said Thao.

We were in the tree line. Peering out from the jungle, watching the lanky guard patrol the colonnade in his flappy-legged pants and white socks. Above him, the purple neon glow of HA TIEN VEGAS! The thrum of the crowd vibrated through the walls.

"Next when we come out, he cannot see us. We must wait for the next guard. Anhtheman says they change each hour."

Back in the main hall, we were greeted by mayhem. The air con had collapsed. The crowd was a sweaty soup of wild eyes, flailing limbs and gnashing teeth. People danced, clambered up on stage, crashed into card tables. On the ground they scrapped for chips. Spitting and screaming. I didn't see anyone swing from the chandeliers, but I did see people climbing walls. A woman pissed in a pot-plant, only to get clobbered by guards. And the horse, oh my god the poor Roman horse – it reared up on hind legs, and when a man reached for the reins, he got his skull caved in by a hoof. Blood splattered a wall. Thao stared in horror.

"We must go."

"Why?"

"I see bad things."

"Could be worse."

"Not here. For us. In the future."

"But this is what we want. Don't you see? Chaos is good for us."

I put my arm around her and pulled her into the crowd. A man lunged at her, and she socked him in the jaw with her handbag. Knocked him out cold. He may have gotten trampled, but we were carried to fast by the crowd to see. Anyway, that's what happens when you lunge. At least Thao was back in the swing of things, so to say. And I was right, the chaos worked in our favour. The staff and the guards had their hands full with people fighting dealers for chips, or jumping the bars to pinch bottles of whisky and gin. From table to table we went. Thao had stored the faces of the dealers in her tremendous memory. Most of them were mad at having to work in such a mess, so they basically threw thousand dollar chips in her bag. I felt like I was in a video game. Or my own epic film. Everything went into hyper mode. Time sped up, colours blurred, time slowed down, then sped up to warp speed. Like a set of stunning anamorphic lenses, my eyes took in millions of pixels of visual information. I was in my climactic scene. The scene where I clawed my way back from rock-bottom to triumph over adversity. The carnage of the room flowed into me. Bring on the maelstrom! It surged through my arteries like pure electricity, turning the synapses of my brain into neon tracer fire. Thao shovelled chips into a plastic bag she took from the lining of a trash can, and I face-timed Rah-Rah, panning the hall in a glorious 360 degree shot.

"Where in the hell are you?"

"In the final episode of our show!"

"What?"

"I'm heisting the casino!!"

"Jesus, you crazy mother–"

The line went dead. I was out of service. Or battery. Or both. No matter. We needed to change our chips and head to the cash hut. At the window, the vibe was jittery. The eyes of the long-haired mole man darted from side to side. As he counted out our three hundred and eighty seven thousand dollars, he tugged so hard at the hairs he nearly pulled the mole clean off his chin. He may have given us extra. It was hard to tell above the yelling, the horse neighing, and despite it all, the band still blowing their trumpets and saxophones and tubas. Which, to be honest, added serious cache to the meltdown at the end of the word vibe.

"Run!" yelled Thao.

The door was unmanned. The lanky guard had abandoned his post under the purple neon. We dashed down the steps, into the jungle, along the path that led to the hut. When we burst in, we saw the guard, his super long legs standing astride our money pit. Thao shouted a stream of invective at him. My body reacted before my brain had a chance to stop it. I charged him, but he fended me to the ground with an arm as long and stiff as an oar. Pop! Pop! Pop! I heard fireworks. But when I turned, I saw the casino CEO. He of the peroxide hair and emerald green suit. He was so close I could see that his cheeks were pocked with deep acne scars, and the golden pistol he pointed at my head had a pearl handle.

Episode Forty-Nine.

The emerald-suited CEO gave the lanky guard a swift nod, and he slapped my right ear so hard the birds in the trees above the hut flapped into the night sky in fright. The CEO's eyes twinkled. He gave the guard a second nod, and he slapped my left ear. Another nod. Another slap. The guard's hands were long and slender (and possibly more beautiful than mine pre burning and finger severing) but boy were they strong. With each slap, my eardrums teetered on the verge of rupture. On the tenth nod, he took a massive wind up, and slapped me so hard I toppled over, my face pounding the mud on the floor of the pit.

Out cold.

I came to with the guard's long fingers in my mouth. He had them hooked in the little gulley behind my top teeth, and was dragging me into the jungle. I could taste what he ate for dinner, and it tasted like steak and sushi pilfered from the buffet. Behind me, the CEO dragged Thao. Her nose dripped blood and her bottom lip was fat, but her eyes were clear and resolute. "They want the names of the dealers," she said. "If we tell them, they kill us. If we don't tell them, they kill us." She read the look on my face. "Yes. We will die in this jungle. I have seen it. Do not be afraid, Apollo. Death is no such thing."

After a while they stopped dragging us and made us walk. The lanky guard led the way, chopping at the undergrowth with hands like machete blades. Thao was in front of me, the blue sequins of her dress glinting in the moonlight. And the CEO brought up the rear, his pearl-handled gun pointed at my back. The air was dense, like breathing underwater, and sweat gushed from my pores at a rate of five drops per second. I smelled compost, then pollen, then spider eggs, then rotting bark on rotting logs, then what I was sure was tiger urine, even though I had never in my life smelled tiger urine so had no way of identifying the scent. I saw myself spinning round, grabbing the pearl-handled pistol, snapping the emerald-suited CEO's wrist, and shooting the lanky guard between the eyes. I saw Thao snap-kicking the guard in the spine, then darting into the jungle only to leap from a tree and ram a stake into the CEO's brain stem. But then we came to a clearing, and I saw four mounds of earth, all about the length of a body. From two of the mounds grew fresh green shoots, and saplings sprouted from the other two, racing to the canopy to meet their friends. When he saw me see the graves, the CEO chuckled. "These people steal from me also."

By the time the word 'steal' left his lips, twin rivers of warm liquid ran down my inner thighs. Yes, one was urine. Yes, the other might have been shit. I wished they weren't. I wished I were as brave as Thao, who as far as I could see had gracefully accepted her fate. But I also felt those rivers were perfectly reasonable responses from my body, given the circumstances. The CEO pushed Thao to her knees, and the guard grabbed two shovels that were leaning on a tree, and covered his nose as he put one in my quivering hands.

"Dig," said the CEO.

"Please. Please don't do this. I can–"

CLANG!

The guard whacked the back of my head with his shovel. My knees wobbled and I sank into the mud. The CEO pressed the golden muzzle of his gun to Thao's temple.

"Dig."

I slid out of my suit jacket and sliced open the soil. The earth was hot and damp and alive with aromas – from the worms to the dinosaur bones ground into dust over millions of years, to the magical plants that could disarm a murderous casino CEO, but were yet to evolve. The digging was hard work. Splinters pierced the fresh scar tissue on my burned hands, spraying blood on the moonlit mud. Ants crawled into my swollen ear canals and bit into sensitive machinery, families of mosquitoes feasted on my flesh like a ten course degustation, and a centipede as long and black as an asp crawled up my trouser leg in search of a warm bed. And then, as if from the silvery undersides of the leaves, a bewitching harmony fell upon our ears. It was Thao. Humming a lullaby that sounded like it sprung from the depths of her soul. The jungle creatures joined her – arachnids and aphids, frogs and birds, swingers and slitherers, furry mammals and scaly reptilians – clicking and howling and pining along to her enchanting song. I dug faster. My blade cut the earth in time to the chorus. The sounds swelled into a grand symphony, and the CEO grew nervous. He kicked Thao in the back, but this made her hum louder, which made the creatures purr and hoot and growl louder, which stirred an unknown entity lurking deep in the uncharted ravines of my being. I hacked at the earth. I ripped my shirt and my pants and all remaining fabric from my body. I smeared the blood from my wounds on my face and my chest. I screamed and cried and pissed and shat and puked and rolled around, mixing my fluids in with the sap and sweat that oozed from the pores of the soil. I ripped out my hair and scratched at my retinas. I punched at bones in my face, tore a chunk of lobe from an ear and tried to yank my once seductive fingers from their sockets.

I heard a shot.

The moon switched off and the world went dark.

"WAKE up. Apollo. Wake up."

"Am I dead?"

"No."

"Where are we?"

"We must go."

Thao stood over me, her blue sequin dress splattered with mud and blood. I lay naked on the ground, every inch of skin streaked with every type of fluid that comes from the body and the earth. I looked around for the CEO and the guard, but saw only jungle, which had stopped singing.

"Where are they?"

"Gone."

"Gone where? Did they kill us?"

She tossed my pants and shirt and jacket in my face. I guess I took too long getting dressed, because she walked into the jungle. I ran after her, but she walked fast. Pushing branches out of her face, hopping over logs with entire mini jungles on their backs.

"What happened back there?"

"You dishonour us."

"How?"

"You become a baby. You scream and kick and cry. I am so embarrassed. The boss tries to shoot you, but his bullets fire into the jungle and kills one animal. Now all the animals go really crazy. The boss thinks it is a curse. He thinks the animals will attack, so they leave. But you keep with your crying and shitting. I can't look at you."

"Sorry."

"Shut up."

"We're alive at least."

"Alive? Who cares about alive. Dying is nothing. When you die all else is still living, so who cares. Only you. Because you care only for your own stupid life."

We walked for hours. Serrated leaves whipped my neck and my face. Undiscovered insects bit the backs of my knees. The mud nearly sucked the skin off my bare feet, and I sweated out my lymphatic fluids, so my vital organs felt like old prunes. But I didn't care. I was alive. I was back in my life. If we made it out of the jungle, I would find a home. Or make a home. I had never had one. I would be the opposite of the person that stole from Anaru. I would stop being the destroyer. I gave a tree a friendly pat. A massive mosquito slid its purple proboscis into the soft skin on the underside of my forearm. "Drink, my friend, drink of me." As it pulled out, shards of dawn light filtered down through the tops of the trees. The sun climbed on top of us and sat on our chest. I bent to drink from a puddle, but Thao pulled me up by my hair.

The road took us by surprise. Long and dusty, it meandered along through tall trees. We walked. We sat. We walked and then we sat some more. I held my head in my hands. Closed my eyes. The ground rumbled. Thao pulled me to my feet. A bus. The pink neon lights of the cabin glowing in the clouds of dust the wheels kicked up. Thao pulled up her blue sequin dress, and I saw bundles of cash stashed in her bra and underwear. Peeling off some sticky notes, she stuffed them in my hand. "This bus will take you to the airport." I turned to see the bus lights flash. When I turned back to say goodbye, to hug her, to feel the jolts pass from her body into mine one last time, she was gone. Not a word. Not a click or a hum from the jungle. The brakes of the bus hissed as it stopped. The faces of tourists peered down at me, a lanky young man made of cuts and burns and gashes and bruises and scars, with one finger missing.

Acknowledgments

A very massive and heartfelt thank you to all these great people: Thuy Phan and Lynn Tran – for your help with the Vietnam sections of the book. Mark Pogodzinski – for all your work and for believing in this novel. Mackenzie Reynolds – for your empathetic edits and your great help with titles. Scott Camplin – for reading every draft and helping to make them all betterer. Kieran Ots – for your time and your smarts and for being excellent to talk to about structure and cool stuff like that. Imogen Taylor – for the amazing cover artwork. John-Henry Pajak – for designing the sickest cover ever. And to Biljana and Milica, for being a loving and wonderful family.

Made in the USA
Middletown, DE
18 June 2024

55590874R00176